VEILMARCH

HALLIE PURSEL

CARIAD PUBLISHING HOUSE

Copyright © 2025 by Hallie Pursel

All rights reserved.

No part of this publication may be reproduced, distributed, transmitted, stored in a retrieval system, or used in any form or by any means—electronic, mechanical, photocopying, recording, scanning, or otherwise—without the prior written permission of the publisher or author, except as permitted under U.S. copyright law, including fair use for brief quotations in reviews or scholarly works.

This book may not be used, reproduced, distributed, or otherwise exploited for the purpose of training, developing, or improving artificial intelligence systems, machine learning models, large language models, or similar technologies, whether commercial or non-commercial, without the express prior written consent of the author.

This is a work of fiction. Names, characters, places, institutions, and incidents are products of the author's imagination or are used fictitiously. Any resemblance to actual persons, living or dead, events, or locales is entirely coincidental.

Edited by Cassidy Wallace
Cover illustration and design by Duhan Tarhan

ISBN: 979-8-9999714-0-1

Published by Cariad Publishing House LLC
United States of America

Dedication

To my mother.
This is my bittersweet love letter to life, the one you began long ago while chasing fireflies in the dark.
I love you. You are magic.

AUTHORS NOTE

Content Warning: Suicidal ideation, extreme gore, implied sexual assault, and explicit consensual sexual content.

If you are a member of my family or a co-worker, be mindful that there is sauciness inside this novel. I was just as surprised as you were! I don't even know some of those words! I think they were supplemented with a ghostwriter or something. For legal reasons, this is a lie. Can't wait to look you in the eye the next time our paths cross!

Part I

The Book of the Veil

"Sealed in the first days, spoken in the last, unbroken until the end of all things."

I. The First Covenant

1. In the days of famine and plague, Hiram the Devout stood before Death.

2. And Death said: *"I do not strike, I only gather. Yet kings defy Me, priests write themselves outside My book, and the world groans beneath lives that will not end."*

3. And Hiram answered: *"Then take one set apart. Clothe them in shadow. Let them be Your hand in the world."*

4. And Death decreed: *"So it shall be. Year by year, one shall walk the roads of autumn and winter, striking down those who deny their fate. They shall have no kin, no children, no name but Mine. In return, your line and Annon shall endure."*

5. Thus was the covenant bound.

6. Thus was the Veilwalker made.

7. Vasha.

Chapter 1

Ninth Year in the Life of Ilys of the Veil

Ilys did not fear the knife in her hand.

She was too young to understand the permanence of sharp things—how they forged final moments, how they forced bodies still—but not too young to take a life. Such is the nature of a Veilwalker.

Chosen. Obedient. Cleansed by blood.

Birds trilled in the canopy above, the green of spring clawing over every hard surface, swallowing stone and bark alike.

"Above your head, shoulders back." Grim toed the nearest rock, flexing and unflexing his hands.

Ilys lifted her chin in regal defiance, her veil brushing against her cheek like a hand she trusted more than her own. It steadied her. Hid her. Reminded her she was not merely a girl, but sacred.

"On three, you'll push your will through the hilt. Guide it deep."

She nodded, eager to win Grim's approval. Eyes shut, she absorbed his counted cadence, driving the knife through the belly of the rabbit at his direction. Blood spattered her black veil, warm and quick, flecking her fingers like paint.

"Now, what do we say, Ilys?"

Wide-eyed, she turned to Grim, uncertain. She knew some of the words, but the orders eluded her.

"Ilys," he chided gently, kneeling before her. "Repeat after me," he instructed, tilting his veiled face toward the sky. His voice carried easily through the clearing, the words practiced and unwavering. "Thy thread is cut."

"Thy thread is cut," Ilys echoed, guileless and pliant.

"Thy name is lost."

"Thy name is lost," she followed.

"The Veil shall hold."

"The Veil shall hold." She took a breath, then sealed it with the last word of every prayer, her affirmation of faith. "Vasha."

The clearing held its breath, while the blood still steamed in the spring air.

Grim nodded. "Well done." He extended a hand, and she took it, his grip firm as he pulled her back to her feet. "Let's return you to the priestesses, shall we?"

Ilys hesitated, glancing at the rabbit's fur matted with blood, its stillness unnatural against the forest floor.

"What about that?" she asked.

Grim barely spared it a glance. "Nature will take care of the body."

Ilys frowned. "No. Can we take it back for dinner?"

"Rabbit is for the faithful," he reminded, amusement twitching at the corners of his mouth as he referenced the common worshippers of the Veil. "It is beneath us."

She tilted her head. "Let me take it to the faithful then."

"No."

"Why?"

"You know why. A Veilwalker does not serve the faithful, nor speak with them beyond what the rites demand." His tone caged her indignation, but at nine years, testing boundaries was a beloved sport.

"I seek to prevent waste."

Grim sighed, weary of the conversation. "You seek to circumvent Veil law."

Ilys crossed her arms, tone flat yet curious. "You seek to be an ass."

Grim's head turned toward her, veil concealing his expression, but she could feel the burden of his paternal attention.

"Don't test your tongue where it's not welcome."

"You've said much worse to Baron," she quipped.

Steely silence met her words.

"Waste is a sin," she tried again, juvenile in her stubbornness.

Grim expertly dodged. "Cleverness does not redeem disobedience."

The path twisted beneath the dense canopy, roots curling from the earth like skeletal fingers. Sunlight speckled through the leaves, gilding the edges of Grim's ebony veil. The trees were old here, their bark knotted like scarred skin. Somewhere in the distance, a brook sang over stone, its voice barely rising above the rustling of leaves.

Ilys fell into step beside him, matching his pace, sensing their verbal sparring had reached its denouement. Grim disliked it when she hurried. He disliked it when she lagged. Earning his favor felt impossible most days. And as she grew, his distance and irritation only deepened. She scolded herself for her immaturity, yet she still drove him away with her hunger for life and independence.

She bit the inside of her cheek, words escaping before judgment took its pass.

"You don't deny it," she began once more.

Grim exhaled, though whether in amusement or irritation, she could not tell.

"Deny what?"

"That Baron dares to speak to you so. *He* is one of the Faithful."

His delay in answering extended so long, Ilys was sure he should never speak again. The wind sighed through the branches and from the distant castle on the hill, temple bells rang softly, the sound of the inevitable.

At last, he responded, "He is allowed such liberties."

"By whom?"

Grim turned his veiled face toward her. "By me."

"Why?" The young girl cowed at yet another set of escapee words.

"So curious today. Like a thorn in the ear." He stepped over a fallen branch, boots sinking into the moss-softened earth, glancing back to ensure she was following.

Beyond the trees, the castle loomed in the distance, its spires swallowing the sky. The sigil of the Veil watched them from above in pale banners that clung to the stone. The Faithful would be gathering soon, whispering their prayers beneath candlelight, their voices winding through the corridors like mist.

"Shall we play Fox and Geese tomorrow evening?"

Ilys grinned. Grim never offered to play. "Why?"

"By the unbound, you chit. Do you want to play or not?"

"I should like to play. Thank you," she replied primly, proud of such politeness.

"Rest your tongue, and we shall."

The priestesses awaited.

They stood in a quiet line at the Sanctum's mouth, motionless statues carved to witness the passage of the divine.

Ilys stepped forward on her own.

Grim had already left. He could have stayed, could have followed her to the center of the room where they would have huddled in pious familiarity, but when the duty was hers, he often left.

Not from prohibition, but because it still felt strange to him. Grim was slow to learn how to be with Ilys. So much of what lay between them echoed a father and daughter, yet she belonged to no one. She only existed as a replacement, a successor. One day, all his duties would be her own.

Outside these walls, their relationship *would* be strange. Men commanded. Women obeyed. And for an unmarried man and girl to speak alone? Unthinkable. They certainly would not spar. Nor travel. Nor any number of the duties she and Grim did without question.

Ilys found Veilwalkers to be anomalies. Outsiders. Strangers to humanity.

The Sanctum yawned before her, its high ceilings lost to the shadows above. Stone pillars stretched toward the heavens, surfaces carved with the sacred script of *The Book of the Veil*, each passage a prayer, a command, a truth. A thousand candles wept light down the walls, their melted bodies hunched in devotion.

Ilys approached the altar, a slab of black stone worn smooth by centuries of bowed foreheads and whispered vows. She pressed her fingers to its cool surface, tracing the etchings beneath her touch. The sigil of the Veil. The barley laurel crest of the King. The carved silhouette of a Veilwalker.

Here stood Annon's past and present. The country's beliefs pressed into unyielding rock.

She knelt, cringing at the slate biting through her gown, pressing sharp and cold against bone. The prayer bell tolled, while she fought to get comfortable.

"The King is eternal," she intoned, voice small in the vast hollow of the chamber. Ignoring her ungainly positioning, her heart leapt to recite every word. She loved her King as a veil loves the wind: shaped and defined by it, never needing to see its source. She wished the King and Grim might trade places. How tenderly the King doted on her.

"His will is law," she continued, breath undeviating. "The Veil shall hold." She pressed her forehead to the altar in closing. "Vasha."

When she rose, the five priestesses stepped back in perfect unison, parting to allow her passage. They did not touch her. They did not speak. They led her through the corridors, each step muffled by the thick hush of the temple halls. The torches along the walls flickered as they passed, their glow dancing across polished stone, casting shadows that stretched and shivered.

Her chamber's warmth greeted her entrance. A fire crackled low in the hearth, its scent mingling with the ever-present aroma of temple oils and incense.

The priestesses moved with careful precision, their hands light as they unfastened the clasps of her outer robes. They guided her through each motion with wordless efficiency, lifting the heavy ceremonial layers and replacing them with softer linens, then pulling thick stockings over her feet so she would not feel the cold of the stone in the night. Their touch held neither warmth nor chill. Only detachment. After swathing Ilys in the nightdress, they faded from her reach.

A pause. A breath.

Then, in perfect unison, they turned and filed out of the room. The door closed softly behind them, leaving her alone.

Only then did Ilys reach up and remove her veil. She removed it tenderly, willfully. It was an old, familiar ritual, more intimate than the prayers, more sacred than the altar itself. Her veil had been stitched by the consecrated. Dipped in ashwater. Pressed with the sigil of the Veil before she could walk in it. The cloth slipped through her fingers like water, cool and silken. But beneath the softness, the grit of ash clung to the threads. Ilys folded the veil carefully, the way one might fold a shroud. The veil had always known better than she did. It carried her breath, caught her tears, held her silence. It spared her the burden of beauty. Of shame. Of being seen before she was ready to be judged.

When she wore it, she was no child.

She was important. She was divine.

She unsheathed her blade, peeking at her reflection in the glint of the metal: round hooded eyes, tawny skin, and gaunt cheeks.

"Hello face," she whispered, not unkindly.

She slid the blade away and abandoned her makeshift mirror. Ilys climbed into bed, the heavy blankets swallowing her small frame. Through the high window, the night sky stretched endless and dark, stars pulsing against the void like distant embers.

"Vasha," she hummed to herself, closing her eyes.

A tether. A truth. And then, she slept.

Grim ate like he always did, efficiently and without ceremony. He tore off a piece of bread with his teeth, chewing as he spoke. "I will leave in three weeks' time."

Ilys froze, melancholy dragging a pointed finger up her spine. Attachment, ugly and adolescent, crept where it didn't belong, and she knew better than to let it linger. She lifted her veil, scooping another bite of venison broth into her mouth and urging the warmth to smooth the unwelcome prickle at the base of her neck.

"We have three weeks to prepare," he continued. "Death has duties for you while I'm away this time."

Her spoon stilled against the bowl's rim. "What sort of duties?"

"Whatever duties he sees fit."

"What use is preparation if the duties remain unknown?"

Grim sighed, shaking his head. "I know the nature of them. They are the nature of all Veilwalkers."

"Can I not learn alongside you?" she offered. "Travel with you?"

She didn't hunger for the work, only the time between it, the quiet spans where he might see her, not overlook her.

Whatever might have been said withered before it reached the air. She bit back a sigh, staring at the bowl; the broth lay still and cooling.

Grim stood, his chair grating against the stone as he nodded to the meal in front of her. "Meet me in the yard when you finish."

Grim stood near the weapons rack, rolling his shoulders, testing the grip of a simple dagger. He trained with the real thing. No dulled edges. No blunted tips.

He tossed one to her.

She caught it, though barely.

"That grip will get you killed," he remarked, not brusquely. But not softly either.

"I caught it," she pointed out.

He ignored her. "Show me."

Ilys adjusted her stance, raising the blade into a semblance of readiness.

Grim studied her for a long moment, his fingers tapping absently against his thigh. He stepped forward, reaching for her wrist and she barely had time to react before he knocked the dagger from her hand, sending it skidding across the dirt.

"Stop holding it so tight," he demanded. "It makes you slow."

Ilys flexed her fingers, irritation pricking at the back of her throat. She retrieved the dagger, resetting her stance. Grim watched, waiting.

She lunged.

He caught her wrist. Too slow.

She tried again, twisting to strike from the side, but Grim deflected easily, guiding her own momentum off course until she staggered.

Her breath came faster. Her feet slipped in the ground.

She hated this. She hated the smallness that crept in. The way slowness felt like shame. The unreadiness felt like failure.

Grim stepped back, watching her carefully. "Again."

They fell into the rhythm. Strike. Parry. Misdirection. Counter.

Slower this time. More calculated. She feinted right, then shifted her weight, aiming lower. Grim sidestepped at the last moment, catching her by the arm.

She grit her teeth, cursing Grim's stringent routines and bare-boned demeanor. She wanted to swim. She wanted to play. She wanted Grim for once to be pleased and satisfied and to let her be.

"Again."

The pattern continued. Over and over.

Strike. Parry. Misdirection. Counter.

Her veil clung to her sticky skin. The hidden pins at her temple and neck tugging with every motion. She couldn't see well around its edge. The world narrowed to the blade in her palm, the rhythm of her own breath, the feeling of the ground beneath her boots. She could feel the ache settling into her limbs, the stiffness creeping into her fingers.

Finally and mercifully, Grim stepped back. "Enough."

He always stopped just before she broke. Never a second sooner.

Ilys rolled her sore shoulders, veil swaying and wetted with sweat. The morning air no longer felt cold.

Grim watched her, unreadable. Then, softer, he added, "Better."

Not praise. Not exactly. But coming from Grim, it felt close to a miracle.

Boots on stone broke the quiet.

Ilys turned as Baron, Captain of the Guard, strode into the courtyard. He wore plain dark leather with steel set at the shoulders, marking his role as a soldier. His sword hung easy at his hip, but tension still held his spine. He greeted her with a dim smile, then looked to Grim.

"Grim," Baron addressed, his grin teasing wider at the sight of him.

"Baron," Grim replied, wiping the sweat from his palms against his tunic. His body denied the enthusiasm that sparked in his eyes at the Captain's arrival.

Ilys adjusted her grip on the dagger. The fight had cooled in her muscles, but she still felt the training clinging to her skin, clammy and familiar.

Grim turned to her. "Go."

She hesitated. She liked when Baron came around. But Grim never missed a chance to ruin her fun and send her away.

"Ilys." His voice left no room for argument.

She bowed her head. Stepped away. Baron wiggled his eyebrows at her, mocking Grim's sour and dowdy tone.

At the threshold, she lingered, half-hidden behind the stone archway and desperate to hear. Grim and Baron spoke in low voices, their words hushed beneath the wind threading through the courtyard.

"You'll be leaving soon," Baron said, tucking the stray folds of Grim's tunic back under his belt.

"Three weeks."

Baron's gaze shifted, sorrow in his eyes, his fingers tapping once against the hilt of his sword. "It's not long."

A pause.

Ilys turned away before either man noticed her listening.

The temple gardens were a favorite escape of Ilys's. Vines curled against the stone walls, their leaves stretching toward the weak sunlight filtering through the lattice overhead.

She wandered without purpose, hands tucked behind her back, the ends of her sleeves damp where she had idly traced them along the well stones.

Near the western edge of the garden, by a patch of freshly turned soil, she spotted one of the priestesses' girls; Rowenna, Ilys had heard them call her. The girl knelt in the dirt, fingers sinking deep into the earth, coaxing stubborn roots free with slow, practiced care. Loose strands of flaxen hair clung to her forehead, darkened with sweat and soil.

Ilys stepped closer, heart racing. She felt sure of her place in this world and of the power she carried, yet her influence still felt new, her confidence tentative, and her presence beside others was a discipline she had not yet mastered.

"What are you doing?"

The girl startled, her eyes flicking up to Ilys's veil before dropping quickly to her hands and bowing her head.

"Vasha," Rowenna greeted.

Ilys ignored the reverence in her tone, stepping forward until her shadow stretched over the small patch of earth. "What are you doing?"

The girl swallowed before answering. "Gardening. The frost killed some of the plants."

Ilys crouched beside her, peering at the fragile green shoots pushing through the dirt. They were thin, weak-looking. Insignificant.

"They don't look like much," she observed.

"Not yet."

The girl pressed her fingers into the soil, careful, methodical. She uncovered the base of a small stem, brushing away the loose dirt that clung to it. Rowenna's fingers worked with a patience Ilys didn't understand. Her own hands were made for rituals and leather-bound hilts, not coaxing life from buried things.

Ilys tilted her head. "I killed a rabbit yesterday."

The girl stilled, fingers tightening around the trowel she had been using.

Ilys traced a pattern in the dirt beside her. "Do you enjoy the sinew of rabbit?"

The girl blinked, uncertain. "The... sinew?"

"I wanted to bring you a rabbit. I heard the Faithful love it," Ilys said, brushing soil from her fingertips. "But my father said no."

She cringed at the practiced fall of that paternal word. She knew he wasn't her father, but she'd taken a liking to using it. It made her just like all the others to say she had a father, and in many ways, Grim might as well have been.

The girl's lips parted, a response flickering and fading before it found a voice. She lowered her gaze. "I... think I like rabbit stew."

Ilys hummed, "I wouldn't know. I am not allowed to eat it."

The girl resumed her tending, sifting dirt through her fingers, and Ilys watched, drawn to the steady rhythm of her hands. So much care in a gesture so small. Nothing in her life ever allowed such softness.

A shadow stretched across the dirt.

"Ilys."

She turned to find Grim at the garden's edge, arms crossed, his veil cast in morning shadow. His stance said he'd been watching for some time.

"Come," he directed. "You have more training."

Ilys dithered. Her eyes flicked back to the girl, but she had already returned to her work, head bent over the soil, pretending the conversation had never happened.

Ilys stood and without another word, she followed Grim out of the garden. As they turned the corner toward the training grounds, Grim spoke.

"I am not your father, Ilys. You have none."

Chapter 2

Eleventh Year in the Life of Ilys of the Veil

The chamber reeked of tallow and parchment, incense smoke coiling like ghosts through the high rafters. Candles guttered along the long stone table where the priestesses sat, wax pooling in quiet surrender. Ilys, now eleven years of age, knelt before them, her knees pressed into cold flagstone, her bored hands resting atop a scroll whose ink shimmered black against the vellum's pallor.

"*The Book of the Veil* tells us of a woman's duty." Mother Inrith's voice flowed smooth and practiced, each syllable worn into shape by decades of ritual recitation. Her white eyes searched the air, yet her voice found what sight could not. "She is the keeper of order, the vessel of faith, the pillar upon which the King's will is upheld."

Ilys traced her finger along the delicate script, pausing at the curling lines of ink before reading aloud.

"A woman of Annon walks in service.

She does not question the thread, for it is already woven.

She does not crave power, for she cradles it in silence."

The words knelled uniform and adamantine. Ilys liked the structured way they fit together like the unmoving walls of the temple itself.

She sat back, eyes flicking to the next passage.

"A woman is a mother, a wife, a daughter."

Ilys frowned, the words catching strangely in her throat.

"I'm not any of those things." The realization arrived strangled and hushed.

Mother Inrith's hands remained folded neatly in her lap. "You are a daughter of faith."

“I have no mother. No father. To whom am I a daughter?”

Mother Inrith's voice ran ahead, calm and calculated. "That passage does not speak to your path."

Ilys tapped a finger against the parchment. "Then why do I have to learn it?"

"You are learning the ways of all women, not just yourself,” Mother Inrith explained, her voice dry as an old psalm. "You must understand the roles of others, even if you do not share them."

The Mother moved steadily through the scriptorium, white eyes unseeing, but her steps sure. Her gnarled fingers brushed over ritual implements with reverence: an ash-blown reliquary, a vial of yellowing marrow, a faded ribbon once tied to a martyr's throat.

The Book of the Veil spoke of women in sacred terms; keepers of order, bearers of life, and the gentle hands behind kings and sanctums alike. It spoke of hearth-tenders and cradle-rockers, of those who water gardens and whisper scripture to children with milk-sweet breath.

“The Book says a woman serves her household,” Ilys said at last, bewildered. “I have no household.”

Mother Inrith's hand stilled on a jar of ceremonial chalk. “You are no woman. You are the Veilwalker—a gift from Annon to Death, a blessed sacrifice.”

She must have sensed the grief moving through Ilys, piecing it together as she steered the conversation elsewhere.

“It's been some time since we visited the Bargain itself.” The Mother gestured to a priestess working beside her. The woman primly scoured the pages, selected one, and presented it to Ilys.

“And it is told that in the days of unnumbered dead, when pestilence blackened the lungs of children and famine hollowed the bones of kings, Death himself walked the roads of Annon. Cloaked in shadow, he gathered what was due. He did not hasten the end, nor strike the living down—Death only carried away those whose thread had unraveled. Still, the people wept, for his harvest was heavy, and the graves of Annon overflowed.

Then Hiram the Devout, first King of Annon, went out into the frost and met him upon the plain. The King said: “Why must you come at all? If you stayed your hand, let us endure, might we not carry the weight together? Might man not bear what you take from him?”

And Death answered: “The world cannot bear such weight. Grain withers when the field is overgrown. Rivers choke when they are dammed. So too does creation rot when no soul is gathered in its time. If I do not come, the burden breaks all."

Then the King raised his sword, gleaming in the starlight, and said: "Then let me resist you. Let me keep them still. Let me hold back the hour, though the world should strain beneath it."

And Death did not flinch, but said: "Raise your blade if you will. But know this: I am inevitable. I do not pass away. Should this body fall, another will take up the mantle. My form may change, my will or voice may alter, yet always there will be a Death walking among you. For though I am not eternal, I am constant."

Hiram's hand faltered, and at last he lowered the sword. He wept, and said: "Then if Death cannot be denied, make me this bargain. Spare my people the plagues that rip through kingdoms. Shield us from famine's devouring teeth. If I give you one hand among us, year after year, to do the striking you will not do—then come not for Annon before its appointed time."

And Death inclined his head, and answered: "It shall be as you say. Give me one who belongs not to man but to the Veil. Let them sever the threads of those who defy their end, who steal years not theirs to claim. And while their blade is lifted for me, my face shall turn aside from Annon."

So the covenant was bound: That the King should appoint a Veilwalker, sworn to the Veil and not to life. That the Veilwalker should have no house, no spouse, no child, for their blood belonged not to man but to Death. That they should strike those who clung past their hour, whether king or beggar, priest or thief. And though Death may change his mask, his harvest shall remain. And while the Bargain is kept, Annon shall endure."

Mother Inrith's gaze did not waver. "Be glad, Ilys, that you are no mere woman. You will be remembered. You are divine."

"But I am not truly a Veilwalker until Consecration," Ilys said. "Am I not a girl until then?"

They said a Veilwalker's true service began with Consecration, though no one spoke of it in detail. Only that it took place in the Hollow Hall, beneath blackstone arches, where Death would weigh the worth of her devotion.

The Mother's lips curved faintly. "You are like the seed within the fruit: formed, whole, and living, but not yet planted. You grow in a place between."

"When will my rites come?" Ilys asked.

"Only Death can answer that," the Mother replied.

Before she could ask another question, a knock at the door interrupted the lesson. One of the younger priestesses rose to unfasten the latch and

Grim stood in the doorway, haloed in the pale corridor light. His cloak carried a dusting of snowmelt, the scent of frost and pine following him like a whisper from a freer world.

Mother Inrith inclined her head. "Veilwalker."

"Mother," he greeted in turn.

Grim's attention swiveled to Ilys, voice materializing even, unburdened. "I'm leaving."

She straightened instinctively. "Five months," she reiterated from an early conversation. "No longer."

Grim tilted his head. "No longer."

She studied him carefully. "Last year you were three days late," she pointed out.

"The snow was heavy."

"Will that happen again?"

"Possibly."

She frowned. "Then should you leave sooner?"

Grim huffed a quiet breath that might have been amusement. "Would you like to walk the frozen expanse?"

She shook her head. "No."

"Then neither would I."

She nodded, satisfied with the logic but another thought took root. "If you do not return, will they send someone for you?"

Grim let go of a greedy breath. "No."

"Why not?"

"Because there is no need."

Ilys' frown returned for a second performance. "Then how will we know what happened to you?"

"You will not," Grim said, tone final and intonation pitchy.

She padded over to him, swallowing her pride as she wrapped her arms around him. He stiffened at the contact, but after a moment dropped his hand for a brief, awkward pat on her head, where it lingered before sliding to her fingers and squeezing. Once. Twice. Three times. Their code. Their language. It meant he would come back. Ilys liked to think it meant *I love you*.

"Ilys," the Mother called, beckoning her back to the lesson.

An itchy, desperate feeling twisted in the girl's stomach. She pressed her lips together, tasting the question she could not name.

The words of *The Book of the Veil* waited patiently before her.

When she turned back, the doorway glowered, empty. Grim gone.

Though just two weeks had passed since Grim's departure, the temple corridors grew ice cold, the stone leeching warmth through the soles of Ilys's slippers. She stayed near the wall, her breath stirring faint wisps of chilled air.

Rowenna ambled ahead, her arms full of firewood. A twig slipped free, skittering across the floor. She muttered under her breath as she bent to retrieve it. It was this clumsy movement that caught Ilys, more instinct than reason, and she followed before she could question it.

Another twig tumbled free. Rowenna straightened, frustrated.

"You'll lose the rest," Ilys called out, "if you don't tame them now."

Rowenna startled, spinning. "Oh—" She blinked fast, her eyes catching the Veil sigil on Ilys's chest. Her tone shifted. "Veilwalker." Rowenna adjusted the bundle, hugging it tighter. "I didn't hear you."

"I'm not meant to be heard." Ilys shrugged.

Rowenna gave a small, unsure laugh. "Right." She looked down the corridor, then back. "I should keep going."

"I could help."

Rowenna halted, looking on, confused.

"I could carry some. If it's heavy," Ilys explained further.

Rowenna stared at her for a beat too long, hands tightening around the bundle. "It's fine," she said. "But... thank you."

Rowenna turned to leave, but after a few steps, she paused and looked back, conflict brewing in her eyes.

"Are you coming?"

Ilys blinked. "What?"

"You followed me. Walk with me, if you're going to hover."

"I wasn't hovering," Ilys denied.

Rowenna gave an awkward shrug and not quite a smile. "Suit yourself."

Red-faced, Ilys shuffled faster, catching up to the girl. They moved through the dim passage like ghosts, footsteps fading into slate.

"Being quiet is good," Rowenna said, "but if a priestess passes, don't linger near me."

Ilys nodded, ever eager to please.

Far from the temple's ornate wings, the lesser hearth tucked into a soot-dark alcove. Rowenna knelt with practiced ease, stacking the kindling with quick, sure hands. Ilys stood off to the side, unsure what to do.

"You can sit," Rowenna ushered without looking up. "If you want."

Ilys lowered herself heavily, knees brushing ash. "Do you do this every night?"

"Most nights."

"Do you mind?"

"It's warm," Rowenna replied, adjusting the wood with practiced precision.

Ilys inclined her head, though she didn't feel the warmth yet. She looked down to her hands, trying to smooth her fingers flat.

"You're quieter these days," Rowenna remarked after a moment. "Last time we spoke, you were smaller and wouldn't stop talking about rabbits."

A small laugh of exasperation escaped Ilys, along with a flush of heat to her cheeks.

"In here you can make conversation." Rowenna raised an eyebrow. "The priestesses don't bother us here."

Ilys grappled for words, a newfound self consciousness strangling her vocal chords.

"Well." Rowenna reached for a pouch tied at her waist and tugged it open. "Then I guess I will make noise for both of us."

She held out two flat gray stones, fitting snugly in the center of Rowenna's palm.

"Toss marks," she said. "You know it?"

Ilys shook her head.

Rowenna pointed to a faint crack in the wall. "We aim for that. Closest wins. The winner gets to ask a question."

"What kind of question?"

"Any kind." Rowenna's left eyebrow arched once more, a thick brown caterpillar of a thing. Ilys welcomed the sight; she tucked the mannerism close, a souvenir of familiarity. "But I'll keep it fair. No Veilwalker secrets."

Ilys teetered, then bobbed her head avidly before urging her body not to give away just how pleased she was to make a friend.

Rowenna tossed first. The stone clicked against the wall. Close, but not perfect.

Ilys's stone missed wide. She winced.

"Try again," Rowenna directed.

The next few tosses were closer. Rowenna landed one just shy of the crack and grinned. "That one is mine."

Ilys managed half a smile. "What do you want to ask?"

Rowenna's mouth curved, theatrical in her delivery. "Who do you find the most pleasing to look at?"

Ilys stared into the fire, thinking hard. She was new to this sort of game and still learning the rules, uncertain what counted as an answer.

"Baron," she tried at last, tentative.

Rowenna looked up, disgusted. "The captain? He's a million years old."

Heat climbed into Ilys's cheeks. It wasn't his face that drew her. He treated her kindly, kinder than most. She sometimes wished he could be her father; on the loneliest nights, she even let herself believe it.

Rowenna's gaze softened, but her confident resolve remained. "Try again. Someone nearer your age."

Ilys sifted through the halls in her mind, uncertain, then found herself picturing the stablemaster's son, Jorrin, with hay in his dark hair and that unshakeable grin that always seemed to make room for her.

"Jorrin," she delivered.

Rowenna's smile returned, pleased and approving. "Now that, I understand."

No candles burned in the Study Wing chamber, but pale, grudging light teased from the narrow windows. The priestesses sat silently in their stiff rows, while Mother Inrith spoke.

"The Veilwalker walks with Death. You understand this?"

Ilys nodded, urging her mind to disengage from the muffled noise in hallways beyond. How she longed to leap from the chilly stone floor and join anything else. Swallowing the dry air, Ilys chided the child inside. *Focus*, she iterated. *Gods, Ilys.*

Mother Inrith continued, oblivious to the battle for attention. "From the first frost of autumn to the last thaw of winter, you will leave the city and cleanse Annon with Death at your side. You will seek those who have bound themselves against fate: Cursed kings. Priests who have written their names out of The Book of Endings. Warriors anchored to relics. You will strike them down so their souls may be taken. When you return to Annon, you will not rest—you will answer Death's summons here, carrying out executions the King himself cannot touch. This is your charge."

Ilys's fingers curled against her thighs. She had been chosen when she was so small she could barely stand, before she could remember what her own name had been. That name was gone now, lost somewhere she could not reach, and in its place was *Ilys the Veilwalker*, a name she would live and die under. One day it would be written in the great books read aloud to the Faithful, her life condensed into a line of service: *Ilys, Keeper of the Veil, Rider with Death, Executioner of the Faithless.*

The Mother's eyes stayed on her. "You will not marry. You will not bear children. You will not serve as the women of the temple do. You were born to the Bargain, not to the womb. That is all you are, and all you must be."

The words lodged in Ilys's chest. She tried to picture herself as the girl she might have been were it not for the robe, the blade, and the temple's walls closed around her. The image slipped away.

When the lesson ended, she did not return to her room. Her feet carried her past the cloisters, down the worn path to the garden behind the Sanctum, a place where the walls felt farther away. The garden behind the Sanctum had gone feral, untouched by shears and steeped in golden light. Here, the air felt lighter. Her spine uncoiled, her mind stilled, and the world seemed impossibly small and endlessly wide all at once.

She'd fashioned wings from two bent branches, a scrap of ribbon, and her veil. They sagged and scraped the ground, yet in her mind they floated, dignified, catching the wind.

Through the tall grasses she ran, scratchy stalks brushing her legs. She leapt from stone to stone, mud clinging to the hem of her skirt. A giggle escaped her, startling sparrows into the air, and oh, how she longed to follow—higher and higher, past the clouds, across the spacious, open sky.

She closed her eyes, pressing the feeling into herself like a fossil into amber.

In her mind, she was never alone. The King would watch her fondly from his dais, declaring, *Be careful, my beloved.* Grim and Baron follow behind, laughing at her mischief, pride unspoken but certain. *This one's mine,* they would think.

She climbed onto the cracked altar beneath the ash tree, wings trembling in the wind.

Ilys, the bird, was loved. Ilys, the bird, was safe. Ilys, the bird, could fly.

Chapter 3

That evening, Mother Inrith's measured voice rang through the hall. "Put her in ceremonial dress. The King will arrive shortly."

The priestesses bowed their heads in silent acknowledgment before rising to carry out her order.

Mother Inrith turned to Ilys. "You must be still," she enjoined. "The King values reverence."

Ilys fought to sit as the priestesses worked, but her body hummed with excitement.

The King! How she adored him.

Swift and practiced hands pulled layers of black muslin over her shoulders, fastening the silver clasps at her throat, pious in their grazing of skin.

"Your hands, Veilwalker," one ushered. She obeyed.

They slid the gloves over her fingers, their fabric black as night, embroidered in thread so fine it shimmered when it caught the light. The Veilwalker's hands must rarely be seen, The Book dictated. To look upon them is to look upon Death's judgment itself.

Beyond the temple walls, horns sounded signaling the King's arrival. She stayed still as they set the last piece, a silver circlet with a single obsidian drop, centered like a third eye.

Mother Inrith stepped forward, inspecting her.

"Rise," she said. Then, quieter, "Grim bears the mantle for now. But the weight will pass to you. And sooner than you think." Mother Inrith's eyes looked beyond her. "Show the Shepherd you will serve him well."

The great doors opened, and cold wind rushed in, carrying the scent of distant rain. Light poured through the cracks: pale, thin, and lifeless.

And then, he stepped inside.

Like the sun made human, the King glided into the room. His deep red robes, heavy with gold embroidery, swept the floor behind him languidly. His crown sat low on his brow, his beard neatly trimmed, and his presence filled the hall with an unspoken authority.

But his blue eyes softened when they fell upon her.

"Ilys," he breathed, tasting the word and she smiled.

He had always been good to her. He had given her to the Veil, yes, but he had not done so lightly. He visited when he could, persisting just long enough for her to see his affection, just long enough for her to feel like she was his, if only in a distant, untouchable way.

He stepped forward and took her hand, pressing the silk of her glove between his fingers like a precious artifact. Then, gradually, he knelt.

"My Veilwalker." His voice reverently balmed.

She studied his expression from beneath the veil. While young, she was no fool; he grieved for her in his way, yes, but he marveled at her, too.

She was his gift to Death. The one no one else could ever have.

"Today is a special day," he elucidated. "Today, you keep our kingdom safe. Today, you support Grim's heavy burden and learn what it means to serve the Veil." He continued in a whisper. "There are those who would tear it apart, if not for your sacrifice."

He released her hand but did not rise. Instead, he studied her, his crinkled eyes tracing every inch of her form, committing it to memory.

"You are nearly grown," he observed gently. "It happens too quickly."

She wanted to tell him she was still small, still learning, still young beneath the burden of the temple. But she did not. She simply watched him, waiting until he released a nostalgic breath and finally stood, shaking his head, clearing a thought from his mind.

"Come."

She followed. Silent. Obedient. She yearned for his praise like a flower stretching for sunlight.

He guided her to the King's carriage, gleaming with black-lacquered wood, inlaid with gold filigree. Its doors bore the sigil of the Divine Veil: a thorned circle broken by four piercing lines, like a celestial compass carved in barbs. It marked the boundary between life and death, fragile yet unbending.

Ilys stepped inside, settling onto the velvet seat across from the King. But they were not alone.

Lord Veylen lounged in the shadows, his black robes blending into the dim interior. He wore a silver ring etched with the sacred division between light and dark at his throat, the insignia of the Ebon Choir. It glinted like a warning. Those belonging to the Choir were both priest and inquisitor, men who thundered sermons in temples across Annon and bent the people toward obedience. In the city and castle, their council sat close to the King, whispering counsel and delivering judgment with equal authority. They were secretive men, unsettling to behold. To the faithful they were shepherds, and to the guilty, cold judgement.

"Hello, Veilwalker." His voice rasped against her skin, a sound more felt than heard. "Shall we walk through the ceremony?"

Ilys turned toward the window, silently peering out at the landscape beyond the dead stretch of land. He continued, feigning paired agreement, "Yes, I think we shall. When we arrive, you will not look at the crowd." Leaning in, his breath coaxed against the fine silk of her veil. "That is beneath a Veilwalker. You will move directly to the dais, demurely, reverently, head held high." The smoothness of his voice betrayed its artifice. Every word polished, every pause calculated. It needled under her skin. "Grim has shown you what comes next, yes?"

Ilys shrank behind the veil, stomach twisting. She did not like the way his beady eyes fell upon her.

Veylen's smirk sharpened. "Has someone not paid attention to their lessons?" His fingers tapped idly against the armrest before he resumed, "You will take the blade from the attendant, step to the center of the block, raise it above your head, and drive it into the heart of the naysayer."

The King's disappointed gaze flicked toward him.

Veylen's mouth curled at the edges. "Unbound," he corrected. "Yes, my apologies. Into the heart of the unbound, the faithless." His voice dipped to a wry, cutting note. "Our precious Saint Ilys, un-blighting tainted Veyth before our very eyes."

Veyth, life threads, were said to bind every living thing together. No one owned their own thread; each was part of a greater weave that held the world in balance. The children of the Sanctum were taught that when a person lived well, their thread strengthened the skein. When they died, that strength returned to the whole.

But sometimes, a thread could rot. A soul could twist, darken, threaten to unravel what it touched. When that happened, the thread had to be cut before the corruption spread. Better to lose one life than risk the entire weave. That was the mercy they were taught to see in the blade.

The King ignored him, turning his attention back to Ilys. He reached for her hand, his fingers settling over hers in a careful grip.

"You are my greatest treasure. My most hated sacrifice." His thumb swept the silk of her glove. "You will make Annon proud."

Unsure of a response, she merely nodded.

His head tilted, disapproval flashing. "Yes?"

"Yes, my shepherd."

He smiled, pleased. "Good girl." A gentle pat to her hand, and then he withdrew, returning his gaze to the window. The city square loomed ahead.

When the doors opened she clumsily stepped from the carriage, wind tearing at her veil, dragging fabric against her skin, while icy spray lashed against the black muslin of her gloves. Snowflakes clung to the heavy folds of her dress, melting against the warmth of her body.

Lord Veylen extended a hand to help her down. One she dared not refuse. His brief touch polluted the air between them, an unspoken trespass. No one but the King and the priestesses were meant to lay a hand on the Veilwalker.

The square stretched wide before her, but the gathered crowd pressed close, their forms hunched against the cold. Ilys fought the urge to look at them, to take them in. She had never been this close to the world beyond the temple walls. She could feel them. Their stares. Their unease. Their fascination.

They had not expected someone so young. So small.

But she held herself as she had been taught, poised and pious.

The dais loomed ahead, stark against the pale wash of the sky. She walked toward it with careful steps, her movements fighting against the wind. A body lay sprawled atop the polished black stone of the executioner's block, familiar as the obsidian altar she knelt before in prayer. His wrists and ankles were bound, his clothes threadbare. As she approached, the details sharpened. Dark eyes, weary and watchful. Cuts along his arms, wounds fresh and clumsy. Lines around his mouth, deepened by exhaustion. He was near Grim's age.

Probably a father, unlike Grim.

A thousand thoughts converged, tangled, and pulled at her mind. The rhythm of the ritual pressed against her. *Take the sword, Ilys. Look into his eyes, Ilys. Raise the blade, Ilys.* But another thought surfaced, quiet and disobedient, *what is his name?*

Her arm wavered. Only once. Beneath her veil, her eyes flicked to the King.

And the blade fell.

The world suspended.

He inhaled. She exhaled.

Steel met flesh, slipping through that fickle place between the ribs, where the blood lives. Where life lives. Where Ilys would now take it away.

A sharp gasp. A body stiffening. The crowd baying like wolves.

Quick and encompassing, akin to lightning her stomach roiled. She had forgotten the blessing.

No one would know. The veil hid her face. The crowd devoured her voice.

But she knew.

The black stone glistened, so much like the Sanctum altar she knew, but there were no prayers here. Only blood.

She turned, her movements prudent, her steps careful. The King's steady eyes met hers, warm in their depths. Banked low like a hearth fire, she saw his praise. The recognition was a sacred, secret joy she clung to, even as the blood on her gloves began to chill.

And yet, as she approached the waiting carriage, the blade protested in her hand. Lord Veylen stood at the open door, one hand resting against the frame.

"Good girl," he awarded with mock sincerity.

She stepped past him without a word, propelled by her palpable, indisputable divinity.

Ilys opened her eyes, face down in the water. The bath had cooled long ago, but she remained, forehead pressed against the porcelain lip, watching her breath ripple against the surface. The room lingered in half-light, lit only by the dying embers in the hearth, their glow too faint to warm the chill clinging to her skin.

Breaking the surface, she breathed in. Reflected on the breaths she had stolen. The ones that would never rise again.

Eyes were such telling features. She pondered on the fear she had glimpsed in the man's eyes. The crinkle of that wary gaze, realizing the path before him had ended unexpectedly, violently. Shamed tears threatened to fall as Ilys shoved the image from her mind.

Hush, she urged, *you are a Veilwalker. Act like one.*

The tub's deep, tepid waters lulled against the edges. Wisps of steam had long since abandoned it. The scent of lavender oil clung faintly to the surface, delicate and misplaced. Her arms were numb where they rested along the rim.

Death is cruel, she thought, *to ask this of me.*

When the water grew well and truly frigid, she moved, the slow creak of her limbs protesting in soft cracks and tremors. Droplets trailed down her skin as she rose, unsteady, and wrapped herself in a fresh robe. Her dark hair clung to her neck, heavy and dripping as she staggered toward the mattress.

She collapsed onto it, trembling. She could have rung the bell, could have called for a fire, but she stayed still. The cold pressed deep into her bones, and she welcomed it, letting it seep through every inch of her, as though ice might preserve what she could not bear to lose.

She thought of her gloves. The black silk that had hidden the blood.

She thought of Grim.

Grim, who was somewhere multiplying their efforts.

A knock at the door came steadily, a quiet insistence that left no room to be ignored.

Ilys suspended, hands loosely folded in her lap, and allowed the knock to come again before she stood, pulling her veil into place. When she opened the door, Baron stood in the dim light of the corridor, a folded parchment in his hand.

"This is for you," he said, holding it out to her.

Her fingers tightened on the doorframe as she glanced at the letter. "From Grim?"

He nodded, confirming.

Ilys' gaze lingered on the parchment as she reached for it, hesitant. "He doesn't write."

"He did this time," Baron replied, a smile in his voice.

Forgoing a response she turned to place the letter on her desk. She didn't open it, instead letting her hand rest on the wood before stepping back. Baron stood in the doorway, watching her patiently before stepping inside.

"Do you plan to read it?" he asked, his voice calm and without expectation.

"Later," she noted.

His eyes flicked to the small table by the window, where the pieces of a Fox and Geese board lay scattered, remnants of a previous game. "You've been keeping to yourself. Usually I see you more when Grim is away."

She shrugged, her hands brushing against the sleeves of her robe.

Baron walked over to the table, picking up one of the wooden game pieces. He turned it over in his hand, unhurried. "Not chess, then?"

"No."

"Why not?"

"Too slow," she explained. "And the rules are too... many."

His lips twitched. "And Fox and Geese?"

"The fox always wins, if it plays well," she instructed, her tone quiet but certain. "It is simpler. More fair."

"You are often the fox, I assume?"

She nodded, smirking.

Baron set the silver fox back down gingerly, his gaze moving from the board to her. "We could train tomorrow. Out in the courtyard."

Her gaze flicked to him, her expression veiled, both literally and figuratively. "Train?"

"You've worked with Grim," he voiced. "I could help you keep sharp."

She peered at her hands, fingers loosely clasped. "I see to that already."

"I know," he replied, his voice gentle. "But it may be nice to have additional guidance."

Ilys's eyes lingered on the letter where it sat unopened.

Baron turned back to her, his expression curious and voice self-conscious. "You do not have to decide now. About the training. But think on it."

He stepped toward the door, pausing as his hand brushed the frame. "Good night, Ilys. Be kind to yourself," he said in farewell, his tone summery.

"Good night," she replied, her eyes fixed on the desk.

Baron left discreetly, door closing with a soft click behind him.

Ilys hovered over the letter as she tenderly unfolded it, focus shifting to the familiar scrawl of messy handwriting on the parchment. She was used to receiving notes from him late at night, detailing their schedules for the day to come. Not receiving one while he tended to duties away from her.

She moved to the bed, running her fingers over the twine before unraveling it. The parchment cooled her fingertips as she freed it.

A blade is made for cutting, child,
Not pondering its weight,
The whetstone does not ask the knife
If it regrets its fate.

The fox is trained to track the geese,

And when the chase is through,
No prayer nor hymn will call it back,
It does what it must do.

The crow does not lament the feast,
Nor question why it caws,
The hangman does not braid the noose
To meditate the laws.

Yet here you sit, with steady hands,
And wonder at the deed,
As if the fruit might bloom again
Once severed from the seed.

The wheel turns, the blade falls, and the world remains unchanged. Waste no thought on what was never yours to keep.
-Grim

She marveled at his detachment, yet held the parchment close, yearning to smell where he resided. *Where was he now?*

It reeked of woodsmoke, of old leather, of the cold wind that clung to him like a second skin and creased where his hands had folded it. She imagined him somewhere far from her, boots cutting through frost, cloak drawn tight against the gales. Perhaps he sat by a dying fire, writing with bare fingers, wind-chapped and unfeeling.

She pressed the letter to her chest, imploring it to answer her. She wanted to hate him for it. She wanted to let the words slip from her hands, let them flutter to the cold floor beside her discarded veil. He thought she would take comfort in this, in knowing she had done what had been asked of her, and that her grief, or what small, strange thing remained of it, was irrelevant.

Day in and day out, Grim had pressed the truth into her, and the priestess had religiously reiterated the message. Ilys should be seasoned to agree.

And maybe tomorrow she would be.

She folded the letter carefully, setting it on the bedside table, smoothing its edges like a relic of something that had mattered. Then she turned onto her side, staring at the ceiling, counting her breaths.

One after another.

Like they would never run out.

Chapter 4

Fifteenth Year in the Life of Ilys of the Veil

Days blurred in a cycle of obedience.

Ilys attended lesson after lesson, her mind drifting as the priestesses droned on about duty and sacrifice. The ink of *The Book of the Veil* obscured before her eyes, pressing into her skull like old, raised scars. When her restless nature truly fattened, she sought out Rowenna, who, if time allowed, indulged her in idle conversation or let her sit in companionable silence. But more often than not, Rowenna belonged to chores, and Ilys was left with only the hollow ache of solitude.

She'd taken to drawing in Grim's absence, if only to keep from dying of sheer boredom. Initially she spent the long, hollow months of his Veilmarch pacing the castle like a caged animal, restless and irritated, snapping at Baron more often than usual. He had tolerated it, as he always did, before shoving a piece of charcoal into her hand and telling her to go busy herself before she took his head off.

Death called for three executions that winter. The first, the King himself presided over. The last two, however, he could not attend. Instead, Lord Veylen stood beside her, his smirks tarrying like oil on water. How she missed the King's presence.

Ilys ignored the flicker of darkness that quickened in her when the orders came. Finally, a purpose. Finally, a task to anchor her. Regret always followed the blade's fall, yet for one breath before it struck, she touched the edge of peace.

She was now five-and-ten years of age. And Grim was late.

Two days past due.

The first thaw of sun broke through the frost, softening the land but not the ache beneath her ribs. Ilys stood outside, feigning interest in Grim's old exercises, the movements automatic and her thoughts elsewhere. Then she heard it, the moored rhythm of hooves on melting ground and her breath caught.

She turned, raptly watching as the gate creaked open. Grim rode through, his broad figure draped in dust and winter's weariness yet she'd know his gait in sleep. A familial ache unfurled in her chest.

But behind him, cloaked in dusk-black and astride a shadow-dark steed, rode another figure. His presence hit her not like a blow, but like drowning, quiet and all-consuming. The air pressed tighter with every breath. He didn't need to move. He imbibed everywhere.

Death.

She tried not to flinch, not to step back. Her spine stayed straight, but her skin crawled, his gaze seeming to move not over her body but through it, sorting soul from sinew. Judging. Measuring.

She squared her shoulders, lifting her chin in defiance.

Look all you want. Do your best to intimidate me. You depend on me.

Grim dismounted.

"Big chit," he noted, voice dry but warm.

"I've grown two spans," Ilys offered.

"I can see that."

Her gaze flickered past him. "Has he ever followed before?" She nodded toward Death, yards behind him, still silent, still watching.

Grim did not turn, but merely muttered, "No. I imagine he wanted a glimpse of his incoming Veilwalker."

She hummed, unimpressed. "I imagine he's disappointed."

Grim chuckled, low and reluctant, turning back to his saddlebags.

"Shall I tell Baron you've arrived?"

"No need for that," he clipped, tone guarded. "Walk me to my room first. Let me shed this dust before you start your interrogation."

She nodded but could not help looking again toward Death's form, still as a specter carved from night. "May I speak to him?"

Grim tilted his head. "You aren't scared at all?"

"Why should I be scared? We are bound. I to him. He to me."

Grim turned toward her fully now, weary scrawled across his face. "Is that what they're teaching you?"

"It's true." She met his gaze, unflinching. "He claimed you as Veilwalker. And soon he will claim me."

Grim shifted his weight, glancing at the guards, lowering his voice. “He’s not one for words.”

She stared longer at Death, dogged in her attention.

“Ilys, come.” Grim’s voice cut through the air, firmer now.

She stared past him, still watching Death. Testing his gaze.

“Ilys,” Grim chided, louder now. Inflexible.

Even as she walked away, she could feel Death watching, like cold fingers tracing the curve of her spine.

Grim set his things down with the practiced efficiency of a man who had lived too long on the road. He unfastened the straps of his saddlebags, laying out his weapons and provisions one by one. His movements were slow but precise. Weary. Familiar. The scent of leather and steel clung to him, softened only slightly by wool and travel dirt.

Ilys hovered in the doorway, arms folded. Watching.

He didn’t look up. “I meant to spend this time alone.”

She stepped further into the room, ignoring his shared sentiment.

Six moons. That’s how long he’d been gone. Six moons of cold routine and colder purpose. Five more choked with commands and names that she longed to forget.

She stopped at the edge of the table, her gaze drifting to the blade he’d placed down. The handle worn thin and the leather wrap darkened from use. She used to wonder what it felt like resting in his palm, the burden, the power, the quiet knowledge of what it could take. Now she knew. Her hands twitched at her sides, calloused fingers brushing against the seam of her cloak. Not idle hands, not anymore.

But now that he was back would the blade pass back to him? What would be left for her in the months to come? This was what she had been made for.

“The executions in the city… they’ll be yours again.” Ilys spoke, statement teasing questioning.

Grim’s hand stilled on the last buckle.

“You’ve grown,” he observed, voice low. Grim spoke not of height.

He sat heavily on the edge of the bed, smoothing his veil and tucking it into his gauntlet. The lines around his eyes seemed deeper now. His shoulders more burdened than before.

"I'll take them again," he said finally. "For now."

"The Consecration Rites are near. Would it not be best if I prepare in any way possible?"

"I will take them, Ilys." He stood, turning away from her and returning to his work.

Relief entered her mind, reserved and unsure and Ilys turned to the door ready to ignore the thoughts rallying around inside her head.

Ilys itched to recount the day's events to her confidant. Rowenna pushed open the wooden door to her small chamber with her hip, stepping inside as Ilys followed, careful to close it behind them. The room smelled of thistle soap and a small fire crackled in the hearth, casting golden light over the simple but tidy space.

Rowenna set the basket down on the bed and immediately set to work, drawing out a sheet and shaking it with practiced ease. The fabric rippled like a billowing sail before she folded it over itself with sharp, crisp movements.

"Start from the beginning," she demanded, not bothering to look up.

Ilys leaned against the post of the bed, tracing the wood grain. "Grim arrived just after first light. I heard his horse before I saw him."

Rowenna's hands never stopped moving. "And Death?"

"He sat behind him," Ilys explained, watching as Rowenna smoothed the linen with deft fingers. "On a black steed."

Rowenna folded the sheet into a perfect square. "That's how they always describe him," she muttered. "I have the same chills that comes over me in anEbon Choir sermon." Rowenna pulled a smaller cloth from the basket, folding with quick, precise gestures. "Could you see his face?"

"No," Ilys admitted. "His hood was drawn. But I felt him."

"Felt him?" Rowenna paused, her hands hovering over the next piece of linen.

Before Ilys could reply, the sound of footsteps echoed down the corridor, the rustle of heavy robes following close behind. The priestesses.

Ilys froze.

"Rowenna." Came the familiar voice of Mother Inrith.

Without hesitation, Ilys dropped to her knees and ducked beneath the bed, her breath shallow as she pressed herself into the shadows.

The door creaked open. Rowenna remained composed, smoothing the last linen with unhurried precision.

Mother Inrith stood in the doorway, her presence filling the small room. Her dark robes, embroidered with the golden sigil of the Veil, pooled at her feet.

"Rowenna," she addressed, her tone clipped but not unkind. "You are to attend to the services. We will need you ministering."

"Yes, Mother," Rowenna replied, dipping her head in deference.

Ilys remained deathly still beneath the bed, watching the hem of the priestess's robes shift as she turned. The slow synchronized footsteps of the others, following the Mother's departure.

The door shut, their previous conversation stretching between the pair.

Rowenna's fingers traced over the fabric, smoothing out an invisible crease before finally resolving the quiet.

"Continue, Ilys," Rowenna said, her voice tinged with quiet amusement. "I believe you were just about to tell me how you've been *feeling* Death." She waggled her eyebrows at the innuendo.

Time slipped by with an unnatural ease now that Grim arrived home.

The days settled into a familiar rhythm of training in the warming air, meals taken side by side, and the occasional evening spent in the dim glow of the hall, where Baron sometimes joined them.

Grim reclaimed his duty over the execution orders after his return. The blade once again rested in his hands, but now, Ilys stood beside him.

Lord Veylen never attended when Grim carried out the King's justice. Neither did the King himself.

Spring had come, but the air still carried the bite of winter's gnawing breath. Now, in the swaying hush of the carriage, she turned to Grim, restless energy twisting beneath her skin. She needed a distraction, any small act to quiet the slow-building frustration of watching, waiting, existing held from purpose.

"Tell me about the Veilmarch again," she pried, shifting her balance as the carriage rocked gently over the uneven road.

Grim, veiled as always, barely inclined his head. "You are fixated on this," he mused. "You never ask to hear about the necromancers or the immortals."

"The necromancer makes me ill." Ilys made a face, tugging absently at the hem of her gloves. "They never teach me about the Veilmarch. It feels like rabbit."

Grim huffed, amusement curling at the edge of his voice. "Rabbit?"

"Yes." She folded her arms. "Something kept from me, so now I must have it."

"Do you understand the Veil?" he asked, sharp as a peck. "You must, before you can understand the March."

"I understand it," she said, though without conviction. In her defense, Mother Inrith had droned on endlessly.

He gave a low chuckle, half sigh, half amusement. "Then you know the Veil is what steadies the weave. Think of it as the cloth stretched between worlds. When a life is cut, the thread slips through the Veil and feeds back into the Skein. Without the Veil, the threads would tangle, the pattern would collapse. That's the balance it keeps: life on one side, death on the other. And if you meddle by trying to preserve what was meant to be lost or undo what's already been cut, you don't just endanger a single thread. You snarl the whole loom."

He went on, voice braced. "The Veyth, life threads, rest in the Veil until they can be carried back into the Skein. That is one of our charges, alongside Death."

"You spend months just... moving dead people?" Ilys asked, eyebrows raised, her whole notion of the March tilting sideways.

He cleared his throat and leaned back, making himself comfortable. "The true March—what you'd call 'moving the dead,' you little chit—comes only at the very end. The rest of those months we spend walking at Death's side, culling tainted threads."

Grim shifted, rolling his shoulders. Then he asked, "Do you know why Death needs us, Ilys?"

"To aid his hunger for souls," she answered, repeating a lesson.

She felt Grim's smile even if she could not see it. "Not quite."

He adjusted his gloves, the leather creaking in the quiet. "Death needs Veilwalkers because he is but a collector. He carries souls at the natural end of their life. When a being has unnaturally extended such life, he requires a Veilwalker to execute them so that he may collect."

Ilys grimaced at this truth, her fingers tightening over the folds of her cloak.

"Then once a cycle," Grim continued, "Death walks the souls he has gathered into the arms of the Fates. That is the true Veilmarch."

Ilys released a heavy breath. "And you go with him?"

"We go with him," Grim confirmed. "It is required of every Veilwalker."

Ilys opened her mouth to push further, another question forming on her lips, but Grim let out a slow sigh and leaned back against the seat.

"I'm tired, Ilys." His voice stretched softer, coaxed with finality. "Hush now."

She swallowed her next words and sat back, letting the clatter of hooves speak where she could not.

Ilys stepped down from the carriage, the veil heavy over her face, dimming the golden light of the midmorning sun. A breeze stirred the banners that hung above the scaffold, pale and stitched with the sigil of the Veil.

The snow had melted, leaving the streets thick with mud, the scent musky and sulfuric. Buds had begun to form on the skeletal branches of the trees and the river ran full with the thaw.

The capitol people formed a loose semicircle around the raised platform, watching, waiting. Some hummed prayers under their breath. Others spat onto the muddy ground as Grim passed. Their hatred made no sound, settled like a second skin.

Grim ignored them. He climbed the scaffold's worn steps with slow, steady movements. The prisoner stood at the center, bound at the wrists, their breath coming quick and shallow. Iron chains looped around their hands, and Ilys saw their fingers twitch. Whether in defiance or terror, she did not know.

Ilys stopped at the foot of the platform, watching. She saw more now. The way the people turned their faces away as Grim drew his blade. The way their shoulders tensed, their breaths hitched, bracing for a pain not their own.

She noticed Grim's flickering hesitation, the shift in his stance, the tightening of his grip before he forced himself forward.

The prisoner did not beg. Their lips moved in silent prayer, eyes closing as Grim raised the sword.

Grim's voice steadied as he spoke the words of the blessing, "Thy thread is cut."

Ilys inhaled, then echoed, her voice softer, "Thy thread is cut."

Grim did not waver as he continued, "Thy name is lost."

"Thy name is lost."

The blade came down.

A sharp intake of breath rippled through the crowd. A few hands lifted to mark the sign of the Veil, warding off the presence of Death.

Blood splattered the wooden planks, stark against the sun-bleached scaffold.

Then Grim spoke the final words, a low and measured decree, "The Veil shall hold."

"Vasha."

The body crumpled and the guards moved in to deal with what remained. The people turned away, shuffling back to their lives, some murmuring relief, others barely concealing their contempt.

Grim descended the stairs, bearing himself like a man twice burdened. Ilys studied him, seeing the way he carried regret, tucked into the quiet spaces of his being. She saw the way the people hated him. And she saw the way he welcomed it.

Without a word, she fell into step beside him, eager to return home and musing on why she had been desperate to leave.

Never had there been a more awkward dinner.

The table stretched between the small party, candlelight flickering along the dark wood. Ilys pushed her food in idle circles, the meal's warmth unable to chase the memory of blood from the wood.

Grim ate in measured bites, his movements slow and methodical. Neither of them had spoken much since returning. The heaviness of the day clung to them both, thick as wool.

Then Baron strolled in. He paused just inside the doorway, gaze flicking from Grim to Ilys. He crossed the threshold with ease, holding a bottle aloft like a peace offering. He rested his chin on the top of Grim's head, dotingly.

"Well," he said, voice lighter than the air deserved. "You will never guess what I got my hands on today."

Neither Grim nor Ilys responded. She blinked at him once and Grim didn't bother to look up.

Baron plunked the bottle down at the center of the table. "Port. Half-decent, too."

They offered no respite from the awkwardness.

He sighed and uncorked it himself, pouring three glasses without comment. The rich scent curled into the air, earthy and sweet, a small gesture of normalcy.

Baron slid a glass toward each of them. "Don't worry, I'll drink yours if it comes to it," he promised, lifting his own. Grim finally glanced up, exhaling.

Baron took a sip, then leaned back with theatrical satisfaction. "So. Jorrin. You remember Jorrin? Face like a terrified hare, barely knows which end of the sword cuts?"

Ilys tilted her head, curiosity stirring. A mention of Jorrin was a sure way to her attention.

Baron grinned. "Today I find him trying to saddle a beast that clearly wants him dead. The horse is foaming. The boy is whispering sweet nothings like he's wooing a blushing maiden instead of a demon whore with hooves."

Grim let out a breath, half amused, half warning.

Baron ignored it, grinning wider. "The horse kicks him clean into the wall. Poor bastard's ribs are broken."

A sharp laugh escaped Ilys before she could stop it.

Baron continued, offering smaller absurdities from the day. Complaints from the baker. A crow that shits daily on the western watch. Sluggishly, the room warmed. By the time the meal dwindled, Baron and Grim were speaking in lower tones, while Baron kneaded the muscles in Grim's hand and forearm. Ilys tuned them out, nudging crumbs on her plate.

She glanced up. "May I be excused?"

"Where?" Grim's reply arrived suspiciously.

She wavered, then shrugged, deciding not to play coy. "To see Rowenna."

At that, Grim turned his veiled face toward her.

Baron, sensing the unspoken tension in the room, leaned back in his chair and drained the last of his port. His eyes steadily met Grim's, communicating in their silent way. He mouthed, *let her.*

Grim's posture eased. He caught Baron's hand, pressed a small kiss against his knuckles, then studied her. His fingers tapped once against the table. His voice, when it came, sated with compromise, bid her be careful. Yet what she wanted—what she ached for—was to be anything other than careful. Anything other than the Veilwalker.

Chapter 5

The knock came just past dawn.

Three brisk raps, then the door creaked open on its own. Grim rarely waited for an answer.

Ilys groaned, dragging the blanket up over her head. The fire in the hearth had long since gone out, and the stone floor sucked what little warmth remained from the room.

"Ilys." Grim's voice nicked her rest, breaking like a snap of frost underfoot.

She refused to answer.

"You've five minutes to dress and meet me in the yard," he said. "If you're not there, I'll drag you out by the heels."

She poked her head out, hair a tangled mess.

"I'm not training today," she announced, pulling the blanket back over herself.

Grim stepped further into the room. His tunic soaked and veil hanging loose around his neck with a sword belt slung across his back.

"No?" he asked. "And why's that?"

She turned to face the wall. "We don't fight. The condemned are bound. The King doesn't ask me to swing like a butcher. It does not make sense to train as we do."

He paused then, he strode to the bed and yanked the blanket away in one sharp motion.

She shrieked and curled into herself as the cold bit down. "Grim!"

"Get up."

"You're cruel."

"They are not always bound, Ilys. When you embark on the Veilmarch you will cry in gratitude for my training." He turned his nose up. "You are too soft."

She sat up, shivering, glaring daggers at his back as he turned and made for the door.

Back to her, he strode from the room. "Ten minutes. Dress warm. It's a hard frost." The door shut behind him with a final, solid thud.

Ilys groaned at the sight of the training ground cloaked in cool, whitish mist. She found the timing too early, the setting too muggy, and Grim to be an utter ass. The aforementioned ass stood in the center of the ring, waiting. As she trudged forward, he only tossed her a sword with a short nod.

She caught it and let it drop against her side. "I'm here. You need not be so dower."

"Take your stance."

"No good morning?"

"I don't waste words."

She muttered a coarse insult under her breath but obeyed, stepping into place, shoulders tense.

He walked a slow circle around her, appraising her posture like a blacksmith eyeing a flawed blade.

"Too stiff."

"I'm cold."

"Then warm up faster."

She adjusted, scowling. Grim nudged her elbow, tapped her wrist, shifted her boot with the toe of his own.

"You swing like your sword's made of pudding."

"I swing like someone who believes her duty isn't savagery."

Grim's mouth twitched.

"I don't perform for bloodlust," she added. "The Veil is sacred. I end unnatural lives cleanly and quickly, as the First Shepherd would have me."

"The king knows nothing of what is required of you. He does not care for you, Ilys, despite your believing so."

She laughed. "You are jealous that he prides himself in me."

"You think his pride will cradle you when facing unnatural magic?"

She bristled, grip tightening on the hilt.

"Your duty seems reverent and quiet now," Grim said. "Even with blood pooling at your feet. But come your Consecration Rites, you'll get dirty, Ilys. Filthy in ways you can't wash off."

Ilys cringed at the sentiment, her gut pulling taut. Grim often led with vague, ominous threats and warnings. Yet he always failed to speak plainly.

Then tell me. Tell me what awaits then, she urged in her mind.

"You'll look in the mirror," he went on, lost in his own weaving, "and you'll see me." He stepped closer, voice low and cold. "And you will hate yourself for it."

"And when I don't see you in that mirror, Grim?"

"Then you'll see no one. Be no one. Because a little girl with only psalms is no use in the Bargain with Death. Trust this."

"Tell me," she barked. "Tell me what more awaits that is so horrible that the sun turns to night watching me flail at your hand day in and day out?"

"I am showing you, Ilys. In every exercise, I am telling you."

"Put it into words, you ass. What is so horrible?"

Grim stepped back, shaking his head. He gestured towards the sword. "Again."

She didn't move.

"Tell me!" she cried. "I am tired of your distance. I am scared. I am lonely. I am lost. Tell me what I am made for, if I do not know."

"Death, Ilys," Grim said. "That is what you were made for. The executions you've carried out, those are only a taste. Horrible, yes. But beyond them you will see so many shades of death that you will forget what living feels like. Out there, the ones we cut down are not monsters, they are men and women who want what we all want: more days, more love, more time. And we are the ones who take it from them, again and again. That is the Veilmarch. That is the burden."

He reached across the space between them, shaking her. "So steel yourself. Take up your sword. Because if you falter, it will be me they send to carry your body home."

The words landed like a slap. Ilys looked away, throat hoarse. She took the blade again, grip firmer this time.

"Better," he said simply.

Their swords met in the cold morning light, and for the first time that day, she did not falter.

Training stretched on as the sun climbed. Sweat soaked Ilys's collar as Grim drilled her through each motion with merciless precision. Baron leaned against the wall nearby, watching with an easy patience that contrasted Grim's rough commands. Every so often he stepped in to correct a stance or a swing, his voice gentler, more coaxing.

"That's my girl," he said when her blade finally struck clean.

Across the yard, Jorrin, the stablemaster's son, passed by. He offered a small smile, wincing a bit as his gait rattled his broken ribs. Even veiled, Ilys felt heat rise to her cheeks as she murmured, "Hello, Jorrin."

Baron caught the exchange. His tone shifted, heavier in the space of a breath. He clapped Grim on the shoulder. "Take a break before you grind her into dust." Then he turned toward Ilys. "Walk with me."

They reached the ivy-shaded wall. Baron stayed beside her, silent in a way that felt borrowed from Grim. Finally, his voice low, Baron spoke, "There's a story. Once, a Veilwalker stripped off his veil—not for ritual, not for prayer, but for love. He gave himself to another for one night of joy."

The pause that followed suspended, broken only by the crackle of cicadas in nearby trees.

"Come dawn, Death arrived. He stood at the foot of their bed, raised his hand, and the story ended, as ours always do."

Ilys stiffened, the fabric of her veil clinging muggy against her lips. Baron tilted his head toward her. Not a warning, not pity, but an apology trying to take shape.

"Because love makes cowards of gods. And Death cannot stand to be afraid."

Later, long past night's bell, Ilys stood outside Grim's chamber. Quiet as breath, she slipped inside. The room lay small, spartan with a fire burning low in the grate. Grim sat beside it, cloak draped across his shoulders, his veil discarded, jaw shadowed by stubble. He read with his head bowed, eyes sharp on the page.

The wrongness struck her at once. No crest on the spine, no seal of the Archive. Too worn. Too real.

"You're not meant to have that," she said.

Grim didn't look up. "No?" His tone carried the condescension of someone who already knew the answer.

"Where did you get it?"

"Darrant."

Her breath caught. "You brought it back. From the last march."

He said nothing.

"What is it?"

He turned a page.

"Grim."

He sighed, low and tired. "Something old. The sort they'd never let us keep."

She moved closer. "Why not?"

"Because it speaks plainly."

She knelt beside the chair, the hem of her nightrobe brushing the stone.

"Why does that matter?" she asked.

He closed the book. "They don't want people thinking beyond the bounds. Books make things louder. Questions. Doubt. Desire."

Ilys studied his face. "Is that what it gave you?"

Grim didn't look up. "No. I had all of those already."

She sat with that, then said, "The Veilmarch."

He hummed in acknowledgement. "What is it truly like? Why does it take so long?"

He turned the book once in his hand, slow and thoughtful. "I'm not always at Veilmarch when I'm gone. The march itself is but a single day, near the end of spring. It's the path to it that takes time."

She watched him. "And what lies along that path?"

He glanced at her, then let his gaze drift back to the fire. "Those who live beyond the Fates' reach. Necromancers. Seers who look past the veil and try to bend what lies beyond. We deal with them while we wait for the call."

Her brow furrowed. "Are there many?"

"Few," he said. "But strong. Clever. Dangerous. No one endeavors to give up life so easily."

"But Death is with you," she said. "Is he not?"

"Death does not intervene. That's why we exist."

She nodded, but her fingers knotted tight in her lap.

"And if I'm not ready," she said, voice smaller now, "when the time comes... "

"You will be."

"And if I'm not?"

He looked at her then. A long look. The firelight caught in his eyes.

"I'll go with you."

She blinked. "What?"

"Your first march. I'll ride with you. See it done," he hummed, turning back to his book. "I'll see to it."

She studied him, searching for a smile. But tenderness in Grim took the shape of certainty. There lived his love; unsensational and immovable.

Grim turned another page. When his voice came, it creaked like armor easing open.

"*The path that is not drawn may yet be taken, if the soul hopes and yearns for more.*" His dry cadence recited the record instead of weaving a tale. But the words were doughy, and soon he shifted without realizing, his tone smoothing, deepening, finding a rhythm that wrapped around her like an embrace. "*The boy, nameless and known by none, passed beneath the pale sky. The stars made no sound, yet he listened still, for even in silence there is song.*"

Her eyes fluttered. Grim read on, voice an invariable thread in the dark. Time slowed. The fire crackled. His cloak rustled faintly as he turned another page.

"*And the boy wept, not from sorrow, but from knowing he could not turn back.*"

She drifted, comforted by the familiar timbre of his voice and a story so unlike *The Book of the Veil*. The chair's wood pressed cool against her cheek, but she didn't mind. She could still hear him. Still feel the echo of his promise in the room. She barely stirred as he moved. The heavy wool of a blanket fell across her shoulders, smelling faintly of ash and cedar. Then the brush of fingers, just at her temple, tucking her veil.

A breath. A moment. A kiss, pressed light to her veiled forehead, so light she might have dreamed it. And though she didn't open her eyes, her lips curved the smallest bit.

Because she was safe.

Because he was there.

CHAPTER 6

EIGHTEENTH YEAR IN THE LIFE OF ILYS OF THE VEIL

"Hello, Jorrin."

Ilys let the words drip from her tongue, mimicking the sultry tone of a lady who had once visited the castle, a woman wrapped in silks and whispers, who had drawn men toward her like moths to a lantern. She stepped carefully over a fresh pile of muck in the stables, tilting her veiled head just so, as she had seen noblewomen do.

"Veilwalker," he greeted, dipping his head. No hesitation or awe in his tone.

She waved a hand dismissively, the gesture more hurried than she intended. "Enough of that," she said, her voice softening at the edges. "I tire of titles."

Once, the castle's inhabitants had treated her as something other, something divine. Now, many still treated her with quiet respect, but others, like Jorrin, had ceased to flinch. They had adjusted to her. It left her unsure of where she stood in their world, an eternal shadow, too distant to be understood but too near to be ignored.

She had grown up here, among them, living in a space between untouchable and inescapable. And in that close proximity, some had come to see the cracks in the divine image she was meant to uphold. The human parts of her. Her fallibility.

And youth. Above all, they gawked at her youth.

Jorrin had been one of those who had grown alongside her, had seen her at her smallest, her most uncertain, her most mortal. Perhaps that was why instead of fear there was only quiet amusement in his face now.

"Ilys." He said her name plainly, without hesitation, and she found she rather liked it.

He had grown into his adult body well, broad shoulders, solid frame. The softness of youth had receded, leaving sharp lines and a trace of boyish warmth that refused to vanish. He wasn't much older than her, yet he bore himself as if time had favored him first.

He studied her, tilting his head. "What age marks you now?"

Ilys paused. No one had asked her that in some time. "Eight and ten," she said, pleased that it sounded more mature than it felt.

Jorrin nodded, thoughtful.

She moved to sit demurely on a hay bale, aiming for effortless grace, but misjudged the length of her veil. The fabric caught beneath her, yanking her head back with an undignified jolt.

Jorrin coughed to mask his laugh.

Ilys straightened stiffly, smoothing imaginary wrinkles from her cloak. "All is well," she declared, "I merely wondered if you might like to dine together."

Jorrin took a slow breath, his gaze unreadable.

"Is that lawful?"

Ilys lifted her shoulders in a careless shrug, though she was hyper-aware of the way her own pulse had quickened. "I don't see Death around to forbid such acts." She chuckled, but the sound did not come out quite as she intended, too sharp, too unnatural. Flirtation, she realized, was an art she had not yet mastered.

Jorrin looked unsure, his lips pressing into a thoughtful line.

Emboldened, she leaned forward, sealing the deal. "Meet me in my chambers at the eighth bell."

Then, before Jorrin could reply, she turned on her heel and strode from the stable, boots crunching over the fresh snowfall outside.

And promptly ran straight into Rowenna.

"By the Unbound, Ilys," Rowenna breathed, clutching her chest.

"What?" Ilys frowned.

Rowenna shook her head, eyes alight with barely contained laughter. "Put a blade in me before I ever have to bear witness to such a tragedy again."

Ilys huffed. "Hush."

But Rowenna doubled over, laughter spilling from her lips. "Torturous," she gasped between giggles. "Absolutely torturous."

Ilys shoved her, sending her stumbling into a snowdrift. Rowenna shrieked, flailing as she tumbled into the powdery cold, her cloak billowing up around her.

Ilys smirked down at her. "Still tortured?"

Rowenna sat up, shaking snow from her hair, cheeks flushed from both cold and amusement. "Oh, without question."

She stood, dusting flakes from her skirts, before falling into step beside Ilys, their boots crunching over the frost-kissed ground.

"I do hope he shows up," Rowenna mused, glancing over her shoulder toward the stable, where Jorrin's silhouette still lingered in the dim light.

Ilys scoffed, adjusting the folds of her veil. "You're insufferable."

"Mm," Rowenna hummed, clearly pleased with herself. Then, her tone shifted. "Have you heard from Grim?"

Ilys shook her head. "Not since a moon ago."

Rowenna winced, knowing how Ilys loathed his absence. She drew in a long, dramatic breath. "I have news. You won't like it. In fact, I recommend you hold your breath for at least five seconds after I say it."

Ilys narrowed her eyes. "Why do I feel a trap is being laid?"

Rowenna smirked, devoid of humor. "Agree to my terms, Veilwalker."

Ilys studied her friend carefully, then nodded once, the lines around her eyes still tight.

Rowenna inhaled deeply. "Mother Inrith has found me a match."

Ilys felt the words strike her like a blow to the chest. "A match?" The question entered the world strangled, crying.

Rowenna squared her shoulders. "Yes, a match."

A million questions battered at Ilys, pressing against her skull, but she swatted them away, forcing herself to focus. Ilys pictured Rowenna in someone else's house, wearing someone else's name, her laughter caged behind unfamiliar walls.

"To whom?" Her voice rang pitchy to her ears. Heart pounding loudly in her chest.

Rowenna hesitated just enough for Ilys to see the crack in her resolve. That hesitation alone drained some of the heat from Ilys's anger, leaving only unease in its place.

"You have no idea." Ilys realized.

"Mother Inrith wants what is best for me," Rowenna said carefully. "I trust her."

Ilys snorted, sharp and bitter. "Mother Inrith cannot differentiate between a babe and a hobbled old man. The woman's mind is gone."

"Our courtship will last three years. I'll be able to discern for myself in that time."

"Three years?" Ilys spat. "That feels irregular."

Rowenna picked at the dry skin beneath her nail beds. "He needs the time to pay my bridal tithe."

"Gods," Ilys muttered with a grimace. "Fattening you up before the slaughter."

Rowenna's face darkened, her posture stiffening. "I won't have any better paths to walk, Ilys."

Ilys grimaced. "There are a million other paths, and you know it."

Rowenna let out a short, tired laugh. "I know you think yourself married and chained to a grim, horrible fate, Ilys. But there is freedom in your duty. You are owed respect and choice at so many crossroads I am not."

Rowenna's comment soured in Ilys's stomach, sitting heavy and unmoving.

Rowenna turned and stalked away, her dark cloak billowing behind her. At the last moment, she glanced back, expression ineligible.

"I hope you and Jorrin have a lovely evening," she said, voice light but strained at the edges. And with that, Rowenna strode away, leaving Ilys standing alone in the cold.

Ilys had never prepared for a guest before. Not in any real way. Grim did not count; his presence in her chambers had never required thought. And Rowenna was more prone to invading than visiting. But now, with Jorrin expected, she found herself staring at her own space, seeing it for the first time as a place meant to be presentable.

Modest by the castle's standards, the chamber still felt wholly her own. The hearth lit, the glow flickering against the stone walls, casting long shadows. She had tidied in an absent-minded sort of way, straightening the furs on the bench by the window, brushing off the small wooden table, adjusting the simple plates and cups that she had set for them. She had even taken the trouble of setting a pitcher of mulled wine beside the meal that had been brought to her. And yet, standing in the middle of it all, Ilys felt a sudden, absurd wave of panic.

What did people do at these sorts of events? Should she be charming? Did one play games over dinner? Should she have practiced being more... alluring? She had tried in the stables and had nearly throttled herself with her own veil.

Ilys paced the chamber, hands clenched at her sides, her mind a restless tide of second-guessing. She practiced opening lines. Discarded them. Tried again.

Everything sounded wrong. Too stiff. Too formal. Too casual.

Then the eighth bell tolled, and Jorrin was nowhere to be found.

She glared at the door, willing sheer force to summon him. All the rules. All the lessons. Veilwalkers were not meant for attachments. Jorrin would not come. Rowenna would leave. Grim would retire. She would be cursed to walk all her days with only Death as her companion.

She blew out a breath and collapsed onto the bed, her arms flung out as she stared at the ceiling, frustration curling in her chest.

Just as she had resigned herself to her fate, a knock kissed the door.

Ilys shot up. She smoothed her veil, straightened her shoulders, and strode to the door, opening it with as much indifference as she could muster.

"You're late," she noted, tilting her head.

Jorrin lingered in the doorway, shifting awkwardly. "I debated coming at all." His gaze darted over her veiled form before he sighed, running a hand through his hair. "I revisited Veil Law." He gestured vaguely to the room. "This... would be frowned upon."

He hesitated only a moment before crossing the threshold, the door clicking softly shut behind him. The table waited for two, a modest spread of food and a pitcher of wine waiting between them.

Jorrin's eyes flicked to the meal, then back to her.

Ilys crossed her arms. "Not another word of boring Veil Law. I am a Veilwalker. I, above all, know what Death dictates and what the Shepherd allows."

Jorrin exhaled, the tension in his shoulders easing ever so.

She gestured awkwardly to the meal. "You're here now. Let's enjoy this."

He eyed her for a long moment before stepping forward, pulling out a chair. She did the same, sitting opposite him, watching as he surveyed the food with wary amusement.

She rushed to fill the pause before it turned awkward. "Tell me about your day."

Jorrin blinked. "That eager to hear about the riveting life of an aspiring soldier?"

"Desperately." She grabbed the pitcher and poured him a glass of wine, pushing it toward him.

Jorrin took a sip of wine, rolling the cup between his fingers before giving her a knowing look. "I will be dragged across the yard for this."

Ilys arched a brow beneath her veil. "Dragged? That's dramatic. You'll get a mild scolding, at worst."

"By Grim?" Jorrin scoffed. "He does not deal in mild scoldings. He looks at one like he's already planning your funeral."

"That is just his face." She smirked, reaching for the bread, tearing off a piece.

Jorrin shook his head, grinning. "I swear he's caught me looking at you before."

Ilys stilled, fingers curling around the crust of the bread. "Looking at me?"

Jorrin oscillated, then leaned forward, resting an elbow on the table. "You are the most terrifying creature in the castle. That demands attention."

She let out a short laugh. "Flattery. You should be more careful. I might start thinking you enjoy my company."

Jorrin animatedly shook his head. "Well, I must, considering I ignored every piece of sense in my body and came here."

"You debated coming," she corrected, lifting her cup. "But curiosity won in the end."

Jorrin tilted his head, watching her. "And why invite me? What great curiosity drove you?"

Ilys stilled. For a breath, she considered the truth. The real, unvarnished, wholly terrible truth that she wanted him. His voice settled in her skin. When he smiled—honest and unguarded—divinity bloomed beneath her ribs, owing itself to him alone, not fate. His hands were calloused and sure, and she had imagined them on her. At her waist. In her hair. Between her thighs. She had never been kissed, not truly, but she'd dreamed of it in stolen moments; a soft and slow, teeth grazing, lips desperate kiss. She'd dreamed of him.

She wanted to be touched.

To be tasted.

To be known.

Now, as Jorrin watched her across the table, Baron's story pressed against her skin like cold sweat.

She loved her King. She did. She loved the shape of her duty, the architecture of obedience. She loved the quiet reverence of a world in order, the sacred path she had been born to walk. It had been poured into her like oil. She had been forged for it, bled for it, blessed for it.

But gods—*gods*—how she wanted this instead, wanted *him*. The solid line of his shoulders. The balanced calm in his gaze. The thought of him above her, breath caught, eyes full of need.

She had never prepared for this kind of hunger, and now it ached in her bones.

She didn't tell him the story of the Veilwalker who'd died with his hands tangled in love and the scent of another on his skin. Instead, she looked at Jorrin, and her voice came out softer than she meant, almost a plea. "I wanted to remember what it means to choose."

"Have you ever had a choice?" he queried.

"Not remember then—discover what it felt like to choose," Ilys corrected.

Jorrin reached across the table, sympathy crinkling his eyes as he grasped for her gloved hand. "How lucky am I to be your first choice?"

She told him about Grim's worst defeat at Fox and Geese and how he still denied its existence. They argued over the best pastries in the castle kitchens, and Jorrin gasped in exaggerated horror when she admitted she did not care for apple tarts. They shared secrets, and loves, and hates, and all the crumbs of humanity they had to give.

Then a sharp rap attacked the door.

Ilys frowned. She ignored it.

Another knock followed, more insistent. She let out a slow sigh, turning toward the door.

"I am busy," she called.

A pause.

Then Baron's voice, exasperated, sighed, "Ilys."

Followed by the unmistakable sound of the door latch turning.

Jorrin tensed just as Baron stepped inside, the flickering firelight casting sharp shadows across his face. He took in the scene, the two of them seated at the small table, the half-empty pitcher of wine between them, the unmistakable ease in their postures.

He simply stared. Jorrin opened his mouth, possibly to stammer some defense, but Baron only looked at Ilys, his usual humor faded into soberness.

She had almost let the story slip from her mind—until now. Until Baron's voice, the scrape of the latch, his solemn face. The same expression he'd worn years ago, when he told her of the Veilwalker who loved and found themself undone for the sin of it.

And behind him came Grim, veiled and breathless, shadowing Baron's step.

Death calls. Just like he did then. The warmth drained from the room. Ilys inhaled, setting down her cup.

Reality had returned.

Chapter 7

Grim reached for her wrist, afraid she might vanish if he let go. He made no mention of the scene he had witnessed between her and Jorrin. His grip tighter than usual and hot, almost fevered.

"Grim?" Ilys pulled against him, but his strength overpowered her own.

"It's time."

She stumbled to keep up, her veil slipping askew. "Time?"

But she knew. Beneath her ribs her breath coiled, small and frightened, curling in on itself.

No one ever knew when the Consecration Rites would come. The ritual's power lived in its surprise, its inevitability. *Death decides,* they said. *Not man. Not the King.*

They took the long corridor down into the belly of the Sanctum, through the iron doors that groaned like old beasts, and into the deep places carved long ago by hands that never left names.

"The Hollow Hall?" she whispered. Panic clawed its way up her throat.

Baron raised a hand to halt Grim. "Give her a moment."

He cupped her veiled face, his touch gentle, fatherly. "This is where I leave you. Breathe, darling. It will be no trouble at all." His smile trembled, and she saw the fight it took for him to turn away. Grim only shook his head, unwilling to indulge such softness.

The great arches of the Hollow Hall rose before her like broken ribs. The stone drank the light, black and sharp with cold while the chill bit at her teeth as she crossed the threshold.

They were waiting. The King stood at the far end of the chamber, cloaked in fur and crimson. The Ebon Choir lined the edges of the hall with their arms crossed over their chests. And at the center, unmovable and terrible, stood Death. He wore no crown, no armor. Only a simple dark robe, his hands bare, his expression unreadable. The torchlight did not touch him. His presence was its own eclipse.

"Ilys of the Veil," Death greeted, stonily. The cold timbre echoed through the hall.

A low grinding sound echoed as a hidden mechanism gave way. The gate on the far wall creaked open, and three men stepped through. They weren't monsters. Just men, all pale-skinned, sunken-eyed, and bare-chested beneath linen trousers. Shackles clanked around their ankles, though no guards followed them. One looked too young, another too old, and the last had a soldier's stance—thin but upright.

"Three condemned," The King announced, plainly. "Each stands in judgment. But if one of them ends you, his life is returned."

Ilys stared, unblinking. Her heart pounded in her chest.

"A trial," the King gently clarified, "to prove the one who bears the Veil will not falter beneath it." His lips curved in a warm, measured smile. "And I know you will not fail."

Grim's eyes lingered on her. He had always seen the veil, always understood what it meant, but now fractals of himself reflected back where once there had just been Ilys. Her image was not the child he'd helped raise, but the weapon she had been shaped into. A mirror of Grim's own making. His gaze slid toward the condemned men waiting ahead, but memories would not let him go: Ilys small enough to clutch his leg, stubborn enough to demand answers, soft enough to need reassurance. He remembered the warmth of her hand in his, the silent rhythm he had pressed into her skin. Once. Twice. Three times. *I will come back. I love you.*

Now, through the thin barrier of gloves, he found her hand again. The squeeze came steady, deliberate. Once. Twice. Three times. The code rushed through her like a pulse. Once, it meant safety, promise, return. Now, at the threshold of the Hollow Hall, it throbbed with another meaning: farewell.

Her breath snagged in her throat. Her heart pressed hard against her veil, aching to break free.

Then Grim's hand slipped away.

And Ilys moved into the dark alone.

Her hand slipped to the dagger at her hip. The leather hilt pressed against her palm as she drew it free. The blade slid from its sheath with a low scrape. She bowed to the King, low enough that the veil brushed the cold stone floor.

"My King," she said, voice clear in the hush. "I serve."

He solemnly took in her form.

She straightened cautiously, then turned her attention to Death. He stood as though carved from shadow and memory, still and absolute. The air bent inward. Light seemed reluctant to touch him. He was the absence of all else.

Death turned his head toward the King. "Begin it how you please," he directed.

The King straightened further, his dark, fur robes dragging over the stone like spilled ink. The gaudy gold and jewel toned accents were nowhere to be found in his dress. He raised a single hand, not grandly or theatrically, but with the slow precision of one who has done this many times before.

"The Veil is constant," he intoned, voice echoing through the Hollow Hall. "The flesh is temporary. By trial of will, blade, and blood, let a Veilwalker's worth be revealed."

The King lowered his hand.

And the men rushed her.

No trumpet. No count. No signal beyond the shift of muscle and the scrape of feet against stone. They moved like men emptied of fear, the cost already paid.

The youngest lunged first. Barefoot, fast, and reckless. He didn't aim for the dagger, but in a move that surprised her, he aimed to tackle her, to get her under him and break her before the others could reach her. Ilys twisted out of the way, just barely. His shoulder clipped her ribs and they both stumbled, but she stayed upright. He skidded across the stone, elbows scraping raw.

She didn't get time to breathe.

The older man ran at her, not fast but purposeful, arms out, fingers curled like hooks. His nails were broken and yellowed, one eye nearly swollen shut.

She stepped back, raised her dagger and—

He swung. Not a punch. A full, clumsy backhand that caught her across the cheek and sent her spinning. She hit the ground hard. The stone grated her palms, and the veil half tore from her head. Blood pooled in her mouth from where her teeth had cut her lip.

Footsteps. Behind her.

She rolled just in time to see the third man—the soldier—charging forward, aiming a kick straight at her side. She caught his shin with her elbow. It threw him off balance, and he staggered past, slamming into the wall with a grunt.

She jumped to her feet before he recovered.

The younger one stood again, wild-eyed now, his mouth foaming, screaming something incoherent. He dove for her legs.

She didn't dodge. She brought the dagger down. It hit his shoulder first—off-mark, shallow—but it was enough to make him cry out. She yanked it free, fast and cruel, and drove it again. This time, lower. The blade met resistance in his stomach, then sank. She felt the warmth burst over her hands, the wet stutter of his breath as he fell forward onto her, his body convulsing.

She shoved him away; he hit the ground, limbs jerking, fingers raking through empty space.

No time.

The old man approached behind her now, breathing hard, moving like every joint hurt. She waited until he stepped close enough to smell, then drove the heel of her hand into his nose, eliciting a fustian crunch. He staggered. Blood poured, but still he swung again, wild. Ilys ducked, but he caught her veil, yanked hard. Her head snapped back.

She stabbed behind her, blindly, and felt it sink into soft tissue.

A groan. Hot breath on her neck.

She twisted the blade.

He fell like wet meat.

She pulled back, trembling, panting, soaked now in blood that wasn't hers. Her fingers slipped on the hilt. Only the soldier remained. He watched her, a terrible hush settling through his body—waiting.

Because now she was tired. Now her grip was slick, her breath uneven, her body shaking. Now, he thought, he had the advantage.

He came in close. Fast. He grabbed her wrist. They struggled, elbow to elbow, shoulder to shoulder. He tried to turn the blade in her hand. Tried to force it back toward her. She bit the meaty flesh of his neck, hard. Deep.

He screamed. Let go.

She drove the blade into his thigh, pulled it out, and dug in again, this time into his gut. He dropped to his knees, trying to clutch at her—to beg, maybe—but she didn't stop. She stabbed until he didn't move.

Until her arm shook with the effort.

Until her veil soaked through.

Only her breath remained, thin, ragged, and the blood dripped off her hands onto the stone. Her lungs dragged in the air around her like she'd been drowning. A sob ripped loose, cut short by the cloth at her mouth. She couldn't stop panting in short, shallow gasps that scraped her throat raw. Her hands wouldn't unclench. Her body wouldn't listen. Her knees knocked beneath her, and the dagger slipped once, clattering against the stone before she snatched it up again with trembling fingers. Water fell from the ceiling, diluting the blood staining her hands.

No. Tears, she realized.

"Ilys of the Veil," Death called, his voice shuddering through the hall. "You have marked your place at my side."

Ilys swallowed, shakes wreaking havoc on her form. A frenzied energy inside rendered her unable to move of her own accord. She felt the eyes of the room upon her.

The King approached, robes dragging. He spared no glance to the mangled bodies around her, instead holding out a hand to help Ilys to her feet.

"How proud we are, daughter." The King beamed. Ilys welcomed the flare of content that rose at his praise. "I knew from the moment I saw you what you were made for."

Ilys took his hand, standing. She urged her body to cooperate.

You are a Veilwalker, she thought. *Stop shaking.*

A sudden retching noise from the wall ahead stole the attention of the room. A member of the Ebon Choir keeled over, vomiting relentlessly.

"Some are weaker than others." The King shared a smile with her.

The sound had awoken Ilys's gaze to the rest of the room. The King in front of her. Death holding court at the top of the hall. And Grim.

Grim's hands had curled into fists. She knew him well enough to read what lay inside the gesture, even through the veil. Tension. Relief. The fight to stay still. Her chest loosened at the sight of him, a single anchor in the storm.

The King bent to her ear. "Let us finish the rites, my dear. Only your vows wait."

The King's hand steadied her shoulders as he guided her forward. At the far end of the hall, Death rose from his seat. He moved like smoke given shape, descending the dais with each step more solid, until what stood before her was a man. Mortal, though not. His eyes fixed on her, cruelly calm. Hooded eyes, defined facial bones, and tousled midnight hair. *Yes, He looked just as Death should*, Ilys thought to herself. She had the unbidden thought that she would like to draw him.

"Ilys of the Veil," he greeted. His mortal voice entered scratchy and low.

A ceremonial dagger placed in his palm, he drew a jagged line across the meat of his hand, the blood dark and heavy. He extended the blade to her.

Her fingers trembled as she took it. She tried for strength, but when the edge bit into her skin she gasped, the pain sharper than she expected. Her blood welled, hot and red, and she pressed her palm to his. Flesh met flesh, mortal to immortal. The mingled warmth dripped between their joined hands and stained the stones.

"Veilwalker." The King's voice dripped with formality. "Speak your vow."

Her voice wavered, but she forced it steady. "I vow to walk the Veil in your shadow. To carry death where the Fates command it. To give my strength, my sword, and my soul until my body is ash."

The King's gaze flicked to Death.

Death's lips curved, as though the words amused him. His voice echoed, resonant enough to make the stone shiver.

"I vow to guard Annon from ruin. To keep plague at its borders, to hold back atrocities, to preserve what must endure, within my power." Death went on, quieter now, his gaze fixed on the King. "And I vow to preserve the breath of its crown until his time is rightly ended. So long as this Bargain holds, he shall not fall by my natural hand."

Blood ran from their wrists, soaking into the stone like ink scribing an ancient covenant. Death studied the mingled crimson in his palm, then raised it to his mouth. He pressed his lips to the wound, sucking it clean, before glancing at her sidelong, his curiosity prickling her skin like an incoming storm.

The King cut the moment short, lifting his arms wide.

"It is done. The Veilwalker is bound, and Annon shall endure."

The King cradled Ilys's face in his hands, congratulating her. "My darling, how proud you've made me." The words echoed Baron's warmth, yet where his pride had once anchored her, the King's eyes burned with hunger.

He led her away from the blood, the bodies, and the remaining shreds of her innocence laid bare on the floor.

Chapter 8

Ilys had been waking earlier, taking her meals slower, walking longer paths through the gardens just to feel the bite of cold against her cheeks. She laughed more at dinner. Reached for the wine more than once. Let her hand linger at Jorrin's arm when he passed her the bread.

It had been weeks, but the shadows of the Consecration Rites peered at her behind every corner. So, she found warmth wherever it would lend itself. Tonight, the fire in the east wing hearth had burned low. Only embers now, casting the room in soft rust. She sat with Rowenna on the low-set divan, legs tucked beneath her, sipping a dark and strong port that Baron had smuggled in weeks ago.

Rowenna held a letter. She hadn't read it aloud. Just skimmed it once, then folded it and left it on the floor beside her cup.

"He says the roads are poor," Rowenna offered. "Fewer wagons are making it through the forest villages. There's talk of raids."

Rowenna looked at her then. Direct, but not probing.

"You've been... different," she said.

"No. You are just preoccupied." Ilys offered a half-smile, nodding to the letter. Rowenna's shoulders relaxed a fraction.

"He warns me to be careful," Rowenna noted.

"I think Leif is afraid," she added after a while. "Not of rebellion, but of inconvenience. Of disruption. He talks like a man whose parcels might arrive late."

Ilys glanced at her. "And yet, you'll marry the curmudgeon."

Her friend shrugged. "It's already decided. My opinion would only sour the ceremony."

That earned a sarcastic breath from Ilys. She tilted her head back against the wall and closed her eyes. Her body ached faintly in places she didn't name. Bruises still bloomed under her robe where the old man had struck her ribs. Her hands, clean now, still curled instinctively when she dreamed. She swallowed more of her glass, urging the past away.

Rowenna arched a brow. "I'm worried about you."

"Rowe..." Ilys groaned, slumping further toward the floor. Her friend only narrowed her eyes, gaze sharp and expectant, silently demanding the truth. At last, Ilys released a breath. "I haven't been sleeping well," she admitted.

Rowenna smirked tartly. "I assumed you were sneaking off to Jorrin's loft."

"I have," Ilys said. She didn't bother denying it. There'd be no point. "But I don't sleep there either."

Rowenna lifted her cup, a sly little coo escaping. "Oh my."

Ilys hurled a pillow at her. "Not what you think. He sleeps, and I just lie there, wide awake beside him."

"Bastard."

Ilys laughed softly, then let her head tip against Rowenna's shoulder.

"I'm not what I was," she said, barely audible.

Rowenna didn't move. "No," she replied, "you're not."

They sat like that until the fire died, and the walls no longer held any heat.

The sound of fists on flesh echoed through the guard's training yard.

A crowd had gathered of soldiers, servants, and even a few robed acolytes pretending not to watch. Two men circled each other in the dust, blood already bright at one's temple. The other grinned through a cracked lip, eyes gleaming with violence, hungry to prove themselves with pain.

Ilys stood at the edge of the cloister, half-shadowed beneath an arch. She hadn't meant to stop. But her feet had paused on their own.

The first blow landed hard. Wet. A cheer went up. Someone laughed.

Her stomach twisted. The stone beneath her boots felt unsteady, as though the ground itself might tip sideways and spill her into the Hollow Hall again, into blood and breath and twitching limbs. She turned sharply—and ran into Jorrin.

He caught her by the shoulders before she stumbled. "Easy," he said, low and warm.

Flesh struck flesh in the yard below.

The men circled like dogs, fists raised, teeth bared. One laughed through bloodied lips, eager. The other swung wide, missed, and caught a blow to the ribs.

She looked up at Jorrin, tilting her head.

"I was looking for you," she said, pretending easy confidence. She pushed the memories down further. "Come."

His brows lifted slightly, but he followed. She guided him up the stairwell, her pace unhurried and her posture clean. When she opened the door to her chambers, she didn't wait. She stepped inside, turned to face him, and pressed her mouth to his through the veil before he had time to speak. His hands rose instinctively, catching her hips. She pushed him backward until his legs met the edge of the bed.

"I've thought about this all day," she said into the linen between them, her breath warming his lips. "You?"

He nodded. Breathless.

Her fingers lingered at the edge of her veil. For a heartbeat, she faltered, then slipped it back, letting the cloth fall loose.

When she kissed him again, skin to skin, it grew fiercer. He reached for her like he couldn't help himself; his palms traced over her sides, her ribs, the dip of her spine. She guided him to sit, then climbed into his lap. She kissed him like she had something to prove. No tremble in her hands. No falter in her grip. She unfastened his belt with deft fingers, her touch bold and smooth.

When she eased herself onto him, her body resisted—a flash of tight, new pain. She masked it with a slow exhale and pushed down harder, refusing to waver. He shifted under her, trying to help her find a rhythm and she copied the movement, rigid at first, then smoother once her body found its place. Jorrin's eyes fluttered shut and his hands gripped her thighs, whispering her name with the inflection of the sacred.

But Ilys didn't close her eyes. She rode him with a kind of devotion utterly removed from love. He watched her with awe. She watched the shadows instead of his face until a sudden, unmistakably new ache pulled her back into her body.

This is mine, she thought. *This, at least, is mine.*

The memory came suddenly and sharp—

Bodies crumpled on the ground.

She ground down harder, silencing it.

Jorrin kissed her chest. Her neck. She let him.

Keep going. Keep going. Don't stop. Don't think.

She gripped the back of his hair. Pulled his mouth to hers. Bit his lower lip just enough to make him feel it.

He came with a groan, spine arching, hands desperate at her waist.

And she didn't make a sound.

"You are so beautiful," he whispered into her hair. "So perfect." He planted kisses down her body while his chest rose and fell against hers, damp with sweat.

Jorrin's hands were gentle, tracing lazy shapes across her spine, smoothing down her sides. She let them. He curled his arms around her, pulling her close, as though she might slip through him otherwise. His fingers threaded into her hair.

She let him hold her. Let him speak.

Let him love her like she hadn't buried men with her hands.

By the moon's late hours she slipped to the kitchen and found a butcher's knife sunk into half a wheel of salted cheese. Ilys helped herself to both. She tore bread from the crusted edge of a morning loaf, wedged a bruised pear into the crook of her elbow, and stole a pat of honey-wrapped butter. Past the painted corridors, down the half-forgotten stairwell where the plaster peeled like sunburned skin, she found the rear cloister doors still cracked for the washmaids to hang linens. She stepped through them quietly, the stone flagging slick beneath her boots.

Outside, the garden waited. Winter had quieted it. The hedges were skeletal, their spines bent in on themselves. Frost clung to the brittle leaves. Grass folded low to the earth. A false spring sun hung in a dull sky, warming the stone walls.

She picked her way past the broken path, boots sinking into the thawing dirt. The altar peeked beneath the ash tree, hunched and overgrown, its surface slick with lichen. She sat cross-legged on it, dropped the food beside her, and bit into the pear. Juice ran down her wrist. She didn't bother to wipe it.

The old ache in her ribs hummed beneath the surface, a ghost of the boots and fists and rage. She ignored it.

A sparrow hopped near, beady eyes fixed on her crust of bread.

"Greedy creature," she said to it dryly, tossing a corner its way.

It dove. She watched it tear the crust.

Only when the sun had dipped lower, painting the dead hedgerows in a rusted sort of gold, did she stir. She stood gingerly, her knees protesting the cold, the bruises. She dusted her hands and turned toward the path home.

A shape darted from the brush—something small, silent, low to the ground.

A rabbit.

It paused near the altar, nose twitching, ears flicking. Soft gray-brown fur caught the light, the left hind leg tipped in white just like the hare from that winter morning when she was nine and hadn't yet killed a man. The one she'd pinned with a trembling hand while Grim's voice droned instructions she barely heard.

It sniffed the air.

The sparrow's crust lay torn near her footprint. The rabbit edged closer and began to nibble.

She watched it long and hard.

The light had shifted. Everything looked a little unreal, caught between seasons, caught between past and present. The rabbit didn't startle, didn't run. It simply ate, soft jaws moving, body still.

Her throat tightened.

"I'm sorry," she offered quietly.

The rabbit's ears twitched. It didn't lift its head.

She lowered herself back onto the altar stone, resting her weight on her heels.

"I am what I was made to be," she defended.

The rabbit finished its crust. It gave no judgment. It simply turned and disappeared into the dry grass, vanishing the way small things do. without sound nor fuss.

Ilys stared after it a while longer until the sun set overhead.

Then she rose again, slower this time.

And walked toward the garden gate, where a polished carriage waited like a closed hand.

Chapter 9

The carriage had not been for the King.

Instead, Lord Veylen stood in his place, a spider poised at the center of its web. Torchlight danced along the stone, carving shadows across the sharp planes of his face.

Ilys halted in the doorway. "Such a late hour." She noted, keeping her voice even.

Lord Veylen smiled, all teeth, the glint of his Ebon Choir ring catching in the dim glow.

"Sometimes Death needs a message delivered rather quickly."

The words slithered between them, smooth and unhurried. Ilys did not answer. Instead, she merely inclined her head and followed him from the Sanctum, her steps quiet against the stone. She had walked these halls a thousand times before, but under Lord Veylen's watch, they felt narrower. More suffocating.

When they stepped outside, the cold air bit at her through the folds of her cloak. A waiting driver pulled the door open and Lord Veylen gestured her forward, his ring catching the light once more.

"After you."

He followed, settling across from her with the ease of a man who had never been denied a single thing in his life.

The carriage jerked forward.

Lord Veylen, of course, could not abide stillness. "You seemed disappointed that it was me who had come for you."

She kept her gaze fixed on the long, dark road, the torches lining the streets casting flickering shadows along the path.

"Perhaps you miss the King's attention," he mused.

Still, she did not speak.

Veylen, undeterred, let his silk voice unravel. "He's a very busy man, or else I am sure he would attend to you more often. You are such a darling of his."

Ilys finally turned, meeting his gaze through the dim carriage light. Her eyes glinted sharp and as cool as a cat's. "I find your common conversation beneath my office, Lord Veylen," she said smoothly. "Perhaps entertain yourself by some other means."

Veylen's lips thinned, the amusement in his expression curdling. His fingers twitched where they rested on his knee, before rising to absently toy with his Ebon Choir ring, twisting it against his skin. Then, almost idly, he caught at her skirts, rubbing the fabric between his fingers.

"So grown," he inveighed. "So sure."

Her pulse hammered. Heat rose sharp and indignant in her chest, but her body betrayed her; still and rigid, Ilys found herself unable to drive his hand away.

The carriage lurched, jostling him back and breaking the nearness. He didn't reach for her again.

As they neared the square, the air shifted. First came the smoke, curling under the carriage door. Then the acrid stench, layered with pitch and rot. And finally, orange light bled across the rooftops like an open wound. Ilys straightened, brow knitting as she caught the first flicker of orange light dancing beyond the rooftops.

Then came the noise.

Screaming.

Shouting.

The wailing of children as they clung to their mothers, pulled along by frantic hands. Men moved through the streets in clusters, some fleeing, others pressing forward. Shadows writhed in the firelight, some with torches, others with weapons. Chants echoed through the square, fractured and discordant, their meaning lost in the chaos.

She turned to Lord Veylen, curiosity winning out over disdain. "What is happening?"

He smiled. A slow, predatory leer. "Death is not pleased, Veilwalker."

She did not move, but her gut coiled tight.

Veylen leaned back into his seat, watching her with quiet amusement as the carriage rattled closer to the square.

"Thank the Fates," he congratulated, tilting his head, "that he sent you to unravel this untidy mess." His smile widened, flashing white in the firelight. "I would share more," he added, a mocking lilt to his voice, "but I find it would be beneath you."

The carriage lurched to a stop.

Outside, the Caer Amon burned. The city of executions—the place she'd walked to countless times, her narrow glimpse of the world beyond—now writhed in flame, consumed by its own undoing.

The carriage door swung open, and heat poured in. Smoke curled in the air, abundant and noxious, stinging Ilys's eyes even beneath her veil. Lord Veylen wrapped his fingers around her arm, pulling her to the street.

"By all means, don't hesitate now," he condescended, his grip bruising.

The square ablaze with torchlight, cowed while flames licking hungrily at the edges of buildings. The air roared with voices, a frenzied mix of rage and fear, the sound crashing in waves against the stone walls.

At the center of it all were six men.

They knelt on the scaffold, wrists bound in heavy iron chains, their clothes torn, dirt and blood smeared across their faces. They had been dragged here, beaten before they ever reached this place of execution. Guards stood in a dense line around them, shields locked, spears braced, but even they looked uneasy.

The crowd pressed close, their eyes gleaming in the firelight, pressing forward toward the men and chanting.

"*Tear the Veil, break it wide,*
It steals our sons, it steals our lives!
Tear the Veil, break it wide,
It steals our sons, it steals our lives!"

Ilys stepped forward, her boots meeting the wood with a dull thud. She scanned the prisoners. Some trembled. Some spat at her feet. One, a man with a shattered nose and blood crusted at his temple, met her gaze through the veil. His lips curled back.

"You are no servant of Death," he sneered. "Only the King's dog."

Shouts, clashes of steel, the distant splintering of wood. The fire crept ever closer.

She exhaled laggardly and unsheathed her sword, the edge gleaming even in the smoke-drenched air. The prayers had to be spoken. The rites had to be done.

She stepped before the first man. He did not plead, did not flinch. His eyes met hers through the veil, unblinking, unafraid.

She lifted her blade. "Thy thread is cut."

Steel met flesh. Blood surged over her hands like spilled wine from a broken altar. She drove the blade deep into his heart, twisting. His body convulsed, then stilled.

"Vasha."

The second bowed his head, lips moving in silent prayer, his shoulders trembling.

"Thy name is lost." The blade found its mark, piercing through ribs, tearing into his heart. A gasp breaking. "Vasha."

The third snarled, rage burning bright in his eyes.

"The Veil shall hold." She severed his fury with a single, brutal thrust. Blood gurgled in his throat as life drained from his body. "Vasha."

The fourth sobbed, shuddering as he collapsed forward. She plunged the sword into his chest, swift and merciful, uttering the sacred words.

The fifth looked skyward, searching for a sight unseen.

"Thy name is lost." This time, she drove between his ribs. He choked once, breath catching, then gone. "Vasha."

His body still jerked as she stepped toward the next. The mob roared around her, a wall of sound and flame, smoke clawing at the sky.

She hesitated.

The final man's chest rose and fell in ragged gasps, his eyes wide. She pressed the tip of the blade to his sternum.

"The Veil shall hold." She muscled the hilt home. "Vasha."

His body sagged, another thread severed, another soul claimed.

The people had not come to witness justice. They had come to see blood, to stoke their own rage. Ilys barely had time to sheathe her blade before she heard a woman's voice, sharp and filled with loathing. "Fucking bitch."

Spit, stocky and hot, slid down the fabric that separated her from the world.

A heartbeat later, someone rushed the scaffold.

The first blow knocked her off balance. The second drove her to her knees.

Hands tore at her cloak, wrenching her backward with such force that the fabric choked at her throat. Fingers clawed at her arms, ripping at the seams of her sleeves, nails raking over her skin like talons. Her head snapped to the side from a fist cracking against her jaw, the impact ringing through her skull. A boot slammed into her ribs. Pain exploded through her chest, white-hot, and her breath ripped from her lungs. Another blow, then another. Her knees buckled.

She lashed out—an elbow catching someone's nose, a vicious kick sending another staggering back—but it felt like striking a wall.

The mob surged.

A hand wrenched her veil, twisting it tight, yanking her down. Her skull cracked against the stone. Stars burst in her vision. A knee drove into her back. A boot smashed into her thigh. She twisted, gasping, her fingers scrabbling against the blood-slicked ground as fists pummeled her sides. A hand wrapped around her wrist, twisting savagely, forcing her arm back at an unnatural angle.

The veil meant to sanctify her now choked her, reeking of blood and spit.

A heel ground into her ribs as the guards shouted, but they may as well have been miles away. The mob had her. The city had her.

Then the flames whimpered, swallowed up in a second. A wind swept through the square. The air froze in her lungs and a shadow darker than smoke drew itself from the scaffold's edge, vast and endless, curling into the outline of a man.

Death stood before her, pressing a palm to her face.

Ilys surrendered to the darkness.

The world suffocated in as she came to: heat, cloth, breath. Her veil strangled her, each inhale a ragged negotiation. Blood, sweat, and predatory smoke clogged her senses. Pain lacerated her body, sharp and jagged, blooming in her ribs, her arms, her legs. Every inch of her throbbed, the echoes of fists and boots still reverberating like a war drum through her bones. She tried to move, but her limbs felt distant and unresponsive, a puppet with her strings cut.

A swollen eye cracked open.

Blurry figures swayed in her vision. No one touched her now, but they circled like scavengers, their voices a muddled hum.

A hand—not warm, not living—slipped between the veil and her lips. Fingers cold as river stone lifted the fabric just enough that air rushed in, sharp and biting, filling her starving lungs. She gasped, trembling, every breath a wound.

"Mine," a voice claimed, close enough to shake her bones. A voice no man could carry.

His grip steadied her chin, forcing her gaze upward. "Not yet," he said, quiet enough for only her to hear. His thumb brushed her throat where her pulse stuttered. "Breathe."

The world gave way again to the cold press of his palm against her cheek, the faintest mockery of comfort.

And the echo of his claim, ringing through her chest like a vow.

Mine.

Ilys woke once more to a world tilted in blurry shapes, flickering candlelight, and the distant crackling of fire. Pain roared through her body, every limb heavy, every breath raw and strained. Her ribs ached in a deep, bruising throb beneath the layers of linen bandages wrapped around her. The fabric of her veil had been loosened, fresh air cooled her sweat-slickened skin.

A gentle touch ghosted over her forehead, smoothing away wet strands of hair.

"Ilys." The voice was soft, familiar.

Rowenna.

Ilys blinked hard, dragging the room into focus. Rowenna knelt beside her, face pale with worry offering precise, clinical attention. As if she had decided Ilys would live, and made it true.

"You're awake." Rowenna breathed, relief softening her voice.

Ilys tried to speak, but her throat felt scraped raw. The words lodged, hefty and unformed.

Before she could try again, footsteps echoed outside the chamber.

The door creaked open as Lord Veylen stepped inside, his presence staining the space like ink spilled over parchment. His gaze swept over Ilys first, his expression callous, but then, maliciously, his eyes slid to Rowenna. Ilys did not like the way they lingered. Even in pain, she noticed. The tilt of his chin. The claws in his gaze. The gleam of hunger behind his civility.

He smiled. "Ah," he said, stepping closer, his boots clicking softly against the stone. "The Veilwalker wakes."

Rowenna stiffened beside her, her hands stilling against the wetted cloth.

"I was so worried when I could not reach you. What a shame it would've been to lose you to that chaos. A terror, truly." He savored her discomfort like a delicacy, before tilting his head. "The King will want to see you soon. Rest while you can."

Without waiting for a response, he turned on his heel and strolled toward the door, but he paused at the threshold. His gaze slid to Rowenna, measured, amused, and creeping too long, before he turned to leave.

"Ilys. Ilys. Ilys."

She must have drifted again. A hand pressed to her shoulder, insistent, coaxing her back from the depths.

Her eyes fluttered open. The world swam in strange tones that were soft and muted. As the haze lifted, she saw him, Grim, veiled and broad-shouldered, leaning over her.

He exhaled, relief evident even through the fabric obscuring his face.

"My girl," he crooned, voice low, rough with emotion. His gloved hand lifted, his thumb brushing across her veil-covered brow in a doting motion, assuring himself of her presence. Ilys blinked up at him, her body sluggish, pain still thrumming through every bone.

"Is it spring already?" she rasped, her voice scratchy and thin.

Grim stilled. His shoulders sank, not much, but enough. The air around him quieted.

"No, chit."

Realization dawned like ice water pouring over her. "What are you doing here?" The question came out hoarse, edged with disbelief.

Grim's jaw tensed. He lowered his head, his voice raw and strained. "Death felt it, Ilys. The moment your soul wavered. He was nearly at the threshold."

"I'm fine," she whispered. "Truly." But even she winced at the thin sound of her voice, trembling and too hollow.

Grim shook his head, exhaling through his nose, a sound full of exhaustion and something dangerously close to grief. He knelt beside her, lowering himself until his forehead rested lightly against her hand.

"You are going to rest," he demanded, his voice resolute. "And when you wake, I will hear everything. Every detail. Each soul will answer. We will bear down and drive them to the Veil."

Ilys frowned, exhaustion and confusion still muddling her thoughts.

His head lifted, and though she could not see his face beneath the veil, she felt the intensity of his stare.

"Rest, Ilys," he ordered gently. "I needed to hear your voice, but now it is time to sleep."

Ilys sat upright, rolling her shoulders as she tested the strength returning to her limbs. Two weeks had passed, and the stiffness in her ribs had lessened. The bruises were dark but no longer tender to the touch.

Grim hunched beside her at the table, idly shifting carved Fox and Geese pieces. He wasn't paying much attention to the game, but then, neither was she. More ritual than anything, a quiet way to fill the space between them.

Ilys nudged one of her pieces forward. "You're losing," she observed.

Grim snorted, "I'm humoring you."

She smirked, prepared to counter, but the door creaked open.

The moment Lord Veylen stepped inside, Grim stilled. The warmth vanished. The ease between them broke like thin glass and in its place came tension, sharp and sudden.

Grim sprung to his feet, the chair scraping violently against the stone as he strode forward, hand shooting out to seize Veylen by the front of his tunic. The force sent Veylen stumbling back, crashing into the wall with a dull thud. Before he could recover, Grim's dagger danced at his throat, the sharp edge pressing against his pale flesh.

Veylen froze.

Grim's voice hissed through his lips. "You sent her there knowing those people." His breath came hot through the veil. "Knowing their hearts. Knowing that if they had the chance they would not hesitate to send a message to the King."

Veylen tensed, but Grim did not give him room to speak.

"You sent her with little guard. No preparation." His grip tightened, the blade biting deeper. "And if she had died—" he let out a breath, sharp and lethal, tilting his head—"I would have dragged you to the Veil myself, and delighted in how your soul unspooled like thread."

Veylen swallowed carefully, his throat pressing against the unforgiving edge of the dagger. His usual smirk transformed, replaced with dark calculation.

Grim pressed in closer, his voice a low snarl. "She is necessary for this Bargain, Yannik," Grim spat, stripping the title from his voice. "You are not."

Veylen's hands curled into fists at his sides, but he did not fight back.

"When you play with her life," Grim continued, his tone digging an unmarked grave, "you play with all of ours." The dagger tilted, pressing just enough for a bead of blood to rise against the pale skin of Veylen's throat. Grim leaned in. His voice like a blade drawn in close. "Particularly your own."

Veylen, to his credit, did not flail or plead. Instead, after a long pause, his lips curled ever so, his voice calm despite the blade at his throat. "Are you going to slit my throat here in the Veilwalker's chambers?"

Grim let the following silence stretch, holding him there a beat longer before stepping back. Veylen's breath left him as he adjusted his tunic, and rolled his shoulders, shaking off the threat. His fingers brushed the shallow cut at his neck, feeling the blood there, his expression unreadable. He then turned his gaze to Ilys, eyes flicking over her, assessing.

"Your recovery seems to be going well," he noted, as though Grim had not just nearly gutted him. "The King will be pleased." With a polite bow of his head, he turned away. The door shut behind him.

Ilys sighed, rolling her head back against the pillow, allowing the moment to settle. Then, she gestured lazily toward the Fox and Geese board.

"Well," she drawled. "You fold faster than a temple novice."

He reached for the chair, and missed. "I let you win," he claimed.

Ilys smirked beneath her veil. "That is what a sore loser would say."

Grim huffed, but no real fire sparked behind it. He set the piece back onto the board, his fingers pausing, his mind clearly elsewhere.

She studied him before asking, "Does Death still wait outside?"

His fingers twitched, but he nodded, careful not to meet her eyes.

"You need to finish the season, yes?" she pressed.

"In time," he promised, adjusting her pillow with unnecessary precision. "You are still healing."

"I am nearly healed, Grim." He sighed and she continued, "And I worry of the consequences of your dawdling, as much as I like you near."

"Someone needs to bat Jorrin away."

"I do not kid, Grim." Ilys stared at his weary form.

"Neither do I. You are careless with Jorrin. If anyone knew... " His voice urged.

Ilys frowned, watching him carefully. "Do not change the subject."

After a pause, Grim lifted his head, his veiled gaze finally meeting hers. "Death is invested in your life," he said, voice low. "In your health, just as much as I."

A strange, slow chill curled through her at his words.

Grim considered her longer before leaning back, the tension in his posture painfully blatant.

"But I will bear what you've said in mind."

Chapter 10

Twenty-first year in the life of Ilys of the Veil

The gardens were bathed in a soft silvery glow, the moonlight cascading over the cobblestones. Ilys stood by the hedges, her figure shrouded in the black garment and veil that clung to her like a second skin. The fabric caught the faint breeze, shifting just enough to suggest the sharp, elegant angles of her face beneath.

She heard the familiar cadence of boots against stone before she saw him. Stepping out from the shadowed path, Jorrin's dark jacket was tailored to his broad frame and his crisp white shirt caught the glow of the lanterns. His high cheekbones were now more defined, carved by years of discipline and duty in the guard, though the boyish charm that once softened his expression still lingered faintly at the corners of his mouth. He'd combed his chocolate hair into neat order, but the wind caught at the strands near his temple.

"You always pick the loneliest corners," he said, gently teasing, though his gaze lingered on her as though she might disappear into the shadows.

Ilys turned her head toward him, though her veil concealed her expression. "Perhaps I like the company of my own thoughts."

"Your thoughts," Jorrin said lightly, stepping closer, "are weighty, homely little things. Let me send them away." He stopped a short distance from her, his eyes searching the dark fabric obscuring her face.

"Decades of Veilmarches," Ilys relayed, her voice light but edged with the memory of seemingly endless winters. "Yet I never quite learn how to fill the silence."

"Grim will be home soon enough," Jorrin assured. He moved closer until he stood within arm's reach. The veil swayed, teasing at the mystery it concealed. Jorrin's dark eyes lingered there.

Another breeze caught the veil, lifting it ever so before it resettled. Jorrin's hand twitched at his side. Finally, he spoke, his voice softer now. "May I?"

After a long moment, she inclined her head just enough to grant him permission. Jorrin's fingers climbed unperturbed as they brushed the edge of the veil, the fabric yielding under his touch. He lifted the veil inch by inch, until her face lay bare before him. The lantern light danced across her sharp features, casting delicate shadows that accentuated the angles of her cheekbones and the curve of her lips. Her eyes, dark and expressive, met his without flinching. The scars etched across her left cheekbone and jaw caught the lantern light, faint but unmistakable.

Jorrin stepped forward, his expression shifting. Not pity, not fear, but awe. He reached out, fingers grazing the ragged edges of her scar, mapping its path like a devoted cartographer. His touch grounded, his calloused fingers gentle against the rough texture.

"Three years," he whispered, his voice soft. "Still your skin clings to the memory."

Ilys's breath hitched, her eyes flickering with emotion that felt too raw to name. He cupped her face then, his thumb brushing lightly against her unmarred cheek, his touch grounding her in the moment. His lips met hers in a fierce yet fragile kiss.

When they parted, Ilys remained still, her veil resting forgotten in Jorrin's hand. "You are dangerous," she chided.

Jorrin's lips curved into a faint, knowing smile. "Only because you let me be." His forehead rested lightly against Ilys's, their breaths mingling in the cool night air. The veil, still held loosely in his hand, a symbol of boundaries briefly cast aside.

"Tomorrow will be difficult, yes?" He pressed light kisses across her brow. "You hate him, don't you?" he said into her skin, his lips brushing against hers.

Ilys let out a breathy laugh, though it held no humor. "The man Rowenna is to marry? I despise him."

"You've never met him," Jorrin accused, amusement coloring his tone as he pressed another kiss to the corner of her mouth.

"I do not need to," she replied, her voice low against his lips. "Anyone chosen by Mother Inrith for a match is bound to be insufferable."

Jorrin chuckled, the sound rumbling softly between them. "You are insufferable, as well."

"And yet," she whispered, pulling back just enough to meet his eyes, her own glittering with a sharp edge. "You're here."

He didn't answer, only kissed her again, deeper this time, his hands coming to rest at her waist.

Tomorrow's wedding loomed in the distance. Rowenna had insisted it be held in the Sanctum so that Ilys could attend, though the idea of standing amidst the ritual and revelry felt more like an ordeal than a celebration.

"So beautiful," he teased, pressing her close. "Even when you're sad. Don't be sad. Don't waste what little we have." His plea rolled in raw, threaded with urgency. Since Jorrin had taken up the guard's colors, their hours came in fragments, stolen from the jaws of duty.

Ilys pressed her forehead against his neck, forcing the dread of tomorrow away, clinging to this fragile present. "I won't waste a second."

And she tried. She really did.

The chamber smelled of sage, the air warm with candlelight and incense. Silken silver pooled across the floor like spilled moonlight.

Rowenna stood still in the center of it all, arms lifted as seamstresses adjusted the draping sleeves of the bridal garment. Her blonde hair had been braided and wrapped into a low coil, the silver veil not yet lowered. She looked mythic, like a story come to life, though her eyes flicked anxiously between the women fluttering around her like moths.

The bridal garment shimmered in the lamplight, woven with silver-threaded flax, dyed the pale gray of a storm-washed sky, in the tradition of Annon. Silver to reflect purity of heart and intention, to mirror the Veil itself: thin, delicate, radiant, and near invisible unless one knew how to look.

Ilys paused at the threshold, her own black robes stark against the soft brilliance of the room. Boots quiet against the stone floor, she stepped inside, and the seamstresses turned, bowing their heads.

"Leave us," Ilys said simply. "A Veilwalker's blessing must be given in private." They filed out without a word.

Rowenna's brows shot up. "What is a Veilwalker's blessing?"

Ilys didn't look at her until the door closed behind the last seamstress. Only then, she turned, letting her eyes settle on Rowenna's face.

She gave a dry, tired smile. "It's when I'm full of shit, but formal enough to be obeyed."

Rowenna snorted. "I must be immune."

Ilys tilted her head, stepping closer. "Yes, well. The wedding garb would indicate that."

That earned a breathy laugh, and the tension in Rowenna's shoulders seemed to ease. She stared down at the sleeves of her gown, brushing her palms against the embroidered fabric.

"I feel like a child playing pretend," she confessed.

Ilys reached out and adjusted a loose strand of hair that had fallen from the braid. "A beautiful ghost."

Rowenna met her gaze. Her eyes, always wide and dark, were teary at the corners. "I am terrified."

"I know."

"I have never even... kissed anyone," she whispered.

Ilys's smile faded into earnest empathy. "I know."

"But I'm getting married."

"Yes."

Rowenna's fingers twisted in the edge of her veil. "What if I don't know what to do? What if I can't pretend to like it?"

Ilys reached out to adjust the silver drape over Rowenna's shoulder. "You do not have to pretend. Not for me, not for the King, not for the gods." Her voice dropped to a careful rhythm. "Especially not tonight."

Rowenna looked at her. Really looked. "What would you know of it?"

"Nothing," Ilys said quietly. "But I know what fear feels like when it wears the mask of duty."

Rowenna blinked fast, her lips pressing into a thin line. "Is it wrong that I want to run?"

"No," Ilys confirmed, smoothing the silver fabric at her shoulder. "But it is brave that you won't."

She did not say what followed in her heart. She did not tell her to flee. She longed to give voice to Rowenna's doubt, to feed it like kindling and let it burn bright.

Run, her thoughts whispered silently. *Let us both abandon these cloaks of obedience. Let us play at being men, loud, sure, untouchable. Let us ravage the world and call it ambition. Let our desire be a shield, wrapping us like a woolen quilt against cold expectations. Let us make our own names feared so none may speak over us, none may say what we are or what we must become.*

But she said none of it.

Instead, she touched Rowenna's hand with familial emotion, and smoothed the veil over Rowenna's face. "You look beautiful," she said.

The candles flickered. Somewhere beyond the stone walls, a bell tolled to mark the hour.

"I wish," Rowenna said, her voice cracking, "that I had known you in a different time and place. As just girls. Before veils and blades and wedding cloth."

"You'd have found some other way to grow tired of me," Ilys dictated. "I would bore you in every lifetime."

Rowenna gave a shaky huff, half-sob, half-laugh, before lifting both hands to frame Ilys' face. Her thumbs brushed lightly over her cheekbones. Veil to veil, she faced her juxtaposed likeness; oh, how Ilys loved the reflection it offered her.

"You are everything," Rowenna said, fierce in her softness. "You are not something to tire of."

Tears slipped from Ilys's eyes, dancing for no one to see. The room felt small. Her clothes too tight. Why had she leapt towards adulthood, only to find loneliness waiting, patient, on the other side.

Rowenna drew a shaky breath.

Ilys leaned close, pressing their foreheads together, veils brushing like wings in the air between them.

"No matter how strange it feels," Ilys whispered, "you are not alone in it."

They stayed like that a moment longer, two girls who had grown too fast, still searching for softness in a world that had carved them into shapes they never asked for.

Then Ilys stepped back. "I'll be in the second row," she said, voice light. "I have all my daggers with me."

"Naturally."

"If you pull your veil three times I will know you find him ugly and I will dispose of him," Ilys promised, half in jest.

Rowenna let out a watery laugh. "Of course you will."

And when Ilys slipped from the room, back into the shadows of the hall, the scent of sage and silvery light already followed her like a memory.

The Sanctum shimmered, fractured beams streaming through high-arched windows and pooling across the stone floor. Incense hung saccharine in the air, sweet and cloying to the room. The congregation gathered, their dark robes blending into the shadows of the towering chamber walls. All eyes faced the altar, where Rowenna knelt beside her groom, bathed in the watchful gaze of the Ebon Choir.

The officiant stood behind them cloaked in black robes stitched with violet thread. At his throat, the Choir's insignia gleamed, catching the light like a sliver of moon. He stood motionless, hands resting lightly on the ceremonial blade before him, its hilt wrapped in ebony and its metal inlaid with ancient sigils that shimmered faintly in the glow.

"Sealed in the first days," Lord Hastell began, his voice deep and resonant. "Spoken in the last. Unbroken until the end of all things."

The congregation echoed him in low unison. The sound rolled through the chamber like thunder on distant hills.

Rowenna and her betrothed knelt before the altar as the Ebon Choir member lifted the blade high above them.

"The Veil did stir, and from its depths came the shadow. And the shadow did speak."

Even hidden, Rowenna stood tall, tension flickering in the line of her shoulders. Her plain groom knelt beside her, rigid and unreadable. Perfect. Lifeless.

"Bound upon flesh and soul, sealed in shadow and breath" intoned the officiant, his voice serene. "Through this union, you will stand together, not as one soul, but as two, tethered by the threads of the Fates."

Rowenna's voice lightened the room. "Before the Veil, I name you. Before the Fates, I claim you."

Her groom repeated the words, "Before the Veil, I name you. Before the Fates, I claim you."

Rowenna's words harbored an intensity that her groom's delivery lacked. "Through shadow and breath, I bind you," Rowenna promised.

"Through shadow and breath, I bind you," echoed her groom, the words falling flat.

"Through death and beyond, I keep you," they spoke in unison, their voices merging as the blade dipped to rest between their clasped hands.

The Choir member pressed the blade down gently, his tone low and reverent as he concluded, "And the Veil bears witness." A ripple of murmured approval moved through the congregation.

Ilys watched as Rowenna rose, the silver veil shimmering as it caught the lamplight. To the world: a union. To Ilys: a performance scripted in someone else's hand.

Ilys's gaze drifted across the room, seeking him. Jorrin stood near one of the arched windows, his face partially illuminated by the pale light streaming in from outside. Ilys's chest tightened at the concealed profile.

The vows, the finality of the blade's touch, the veiled promises of a future Rowenna would now claim, it all pressed against her like an immovable force. She could not tear her eyes away from Jorrin, even as the murmurs of congratulations rose around them.

He would never kneel before an altar with her. He would never speak vows in her name. And she, in turn, would never step into the light of such a union. Her path had been set long ago, her place carved out of duty and shadow. If they were ever to meet at the altar, it would not be for vows but for judgment, with a blade in Ilys's hand.

A clarity struck, cold and merciless. What was she doing? There was no happy end, no future to build. She was a Veilwalker. Her brief, fragile mortality had fooled her into weakness and into grasping at human thoughts that had no place in her. She mourned Rowenna's presence already; now, in this moment, she began to mourn Jorrin as well.

At that moment, his attention found her. But Ilys turned away.

Chapter 11

She had avoided Jorrin for as long as she could. She slipped past him in corridors and pretended her gaze fixed anywhere but on his. But elusion would not hold forever. Any lie would do, so long as it cut deep enough to stop him from fighting for them.

That evening, she forced the words out. They were cold, merciless animals meant to wound.

She no longer loved him. They could never be together.

If she did not close the door now, and close it hard, her resolve might fracture.

His reply was no reply at all; only a long look with those soulful eyes, too gentle, too knowing, as though he saw through every piece of distance she had tried to put between them. But he relented, pressing his lips to her veiled forehead in goodbye.

Later, the fire in the common room had burned low. The hour grew late enough that the Sanctum lay quiet, save for the wind sighing through the arches. Ilys slipped inside expecting solitude. Instead, Baron sat sprawled on one of the long benches with her sketchbook balanced carelessly in his hands. His boots rested on the table, his posture infuriatingly at ease. Breathing through her nose, she moved to nudge at his legs until he relented with a grin, dropping them to the floor. Still, he did not look at her, only flipped through the pages, his brow creased, weighing every line.

The faces stared back at them. Baron and Grim, Rowenna, and Jorrin. And beyond them, the others—the condemned and the lost, the faces of the Veil's quiet harvest. Baron dragged a finger along one face, tracing the ink, memorizing its shape.

"You both hold it too closely," he remarked. At last he glanced up, his expression cutting. "The guilt. The self-hatred. It's suffocating."

Ilys lowered herself beside him, her eyes on the sketch. She remembered that boy's eyes, pleading yet resigned. She had thought Death cruel for ordering it. Thought herself worse for obeying.

"I've broken it off with Jorrin," she confessed quietly.

Baron absorbed this without surprise, studying her instead of the book. Then he reached out, caught her chin between his fingers, and guided her away from the sketches. His touch firm but not unkind. It grounded her.

"Duty is not identity, Ilys," Baron said, his tone neither cruel nor indulgent.. His gaze cut through her resistance, adamant, willing her to believe him. "Everyone bears duty, and everyone must decide how much of themselves they will let it consume. You—" he faltered, the next words paining him—"you have let it take everything. You have bled for it. Killed for it. Let it dictate every step of your life as if you were born for nothing else."

She turned her face away, but he did not let her escape so easily. His fingers tilted her chin back toward him, forcing her to meet his gaze.

"You are lovely and kind," he continued, low and insistent. "The Fates have no say in how you spend the time that is yours."

Her chest tightened. She wanted to believe him, yet her gaze slipped to the book again and to the faces she had tried to preserve, to understand. It would never be enough.

"You make it sound simple," she bit back after a moment. "Separating the two."

"It is not simple," Baron replied, brushing a knuckle along her cheek. "I will not lie and say I am not relieved by your choice. The story I told you of the Veilwalker was no silly fable. My father lived when it happened. If the King were ever to suspect you and Jorrin... or Grim and I... " His jaw tightened, words hard to force out. "Someone would pay for the distraction. The throne does not forgive divided loyalties. It is a messy, terrifying truth."

Ilys thought of Jorrin—his warmth, his gentleness, the life still waiting for him—and felt the gravity of her choice settle more firmly.

"Let us speak of it no longer," she begged.

Sensing her resolve, Baron turned the page with exaggerated care. He studied the drawing, then snorted. "You were not kind to my midsection here, you little bitch."

Ilys barked out a laugh, sudden and sharp, and pressed closer beside him. Grateful for his ever present affinity for levity.

"You look strong," she shot back, patting his stomach. "Formidable, even. That's all muscle, obviously."

Baron's body shook with laughter as he dropped a paternal kiss to the top of her head. "Mm. Right."

The hills lay bare in winter, stretched beneath a pale sky the color of bone. Frost clung to the grasses in white lace, and the breath from Ilys's mouth curled into the air like incense smoke. She walked alone, wrapped in her black woolen cloak, her boots pressing silent paths into the frozen earth. She passed through the familiar stretch of pine and barren alder, following the narrow deer trail that led beyond the outer walls of the Sanctum.

And there, down the gentle slope, where the rocks bowed inwards and the earth cupped itself into a shallow hollow, lay the winter pool. A spring still fed it, so it did not freeze entirely. The surface rippled faintly, steam lifting where warmth clashed with cold.

She stepped close, boots crunching softly, her gloved hand drifting to the clasp at her collar. Breath slow, she slipped the cloak from her shoulders. Then her gloves. Her tunic. Her underthings. Each layer peeled away like bark from a tree, until she stood naked in the winter air, body pale against the dark trees, scars like pale river-etchings across her skin. The cold bit into her all at once, sharp and merciless. She did not resist the shudder that took her.

She needed to feel it, this proof of flesh. Proof of life. Proof of reality.

A quiet laugh escaped her, breathless and sharp, and she stepped into the pool. The shock of it stole her voice. She ducked under quickly, knowing hesitating would make it worse, and surfaced with a gasp, arms curling around her chest. It hurt and the ache burned through her, bright and cleansing. She drifted through the water in dawdling strokes, her hair streaming behind her like ink. Steam curled up around her, blurring the edges of the world. She floated on her back, lips tinged blue, but eyes open to the sky. Above her the clouds drifted, swollen with the snow that had yet to fall.

"I am here," she whispered, to no one.

To the wind.

To Grim, if he could hear her.

To Rowenna, wrapped in silver, tucked into a new life she did not choose.

To the little girl who had once yearned to fly.

Her teeth chattered as she emerged, pulling herself back onto the frost-bit stone. Her bare skin steamed against the cold, hair sticking to her back in frozen ropes. She did not rush to dress. She stood there instead, looking out over the glade, her arms loose at her sides. She had imagined this kind of solitude so often. A life where no one waited to command her, no hand reached for her blade, no Fate whispered at her heel.

Was it a virtue to sacrifice, or simply a transgression dressed in duty?

She pulled her cloak back over her body, fingers fumbling with the cold, and tied it tightly at her throat.

The frost crunched beneath her bare feet as she walked the winding trail back toward the Sanctum. Her clothes were bundled beneath one arm, wrinkled, and speckled with pine needles. Only her heavy cloak and black veil shielded her from the cold, and even then, the wind slipped through the gaps, teasing her skin with icy fingers. Her hair hung in wet ribbons down her back, strands catching the wind like dark ribbons.

She felt flushed, alive. The kind of warmth that followed a plunge into freezing water came over her, a breathless clarity pulsing through her limbs. Her cheeks burned, and her body hummed from the inside out.

As the forest thinned, the long stone wall of the Sanctum came into view, rising gray and silent against the sky. At the edge of the road, a black carriage waited, wheels dusted with frost, the emblem of the Ebon Choir etched in gleaming silver on its door. An attendant waited beside it, tall and thin in the black cassock of the inner order. His pallid face betrayed no emotion, and he held his hands clasped with careful precision behind his back.

"Veilwalker," he said crisply, giving her a shallow bow. "There is an execution scheduled at dusk. Death has called you to attend."

Ilys stopped a few paces from him, shifting the bundle of clothes beneath her arm. "Not yet," she said, voice mild.

He blinked, his brow tightening. "The order comes from Lord Veylen's seat. It is expected."

She tilted her head, the veil shadowing her expression. "I said, not yet."

He paused, measuring how far he dared to press. "Veilwalker... with all reverence, I must insist."

A grin ghosted across her lips beneath the veil.

In one swift motion, she opened her cloak. The wool parted to reveal bare, flushed skin beneath, still damp from the spring, still touched by winter's bite. Her scars glinted like pale ink across her ribs and hips.

The attendant's breath caught audibly. He recoiled as if struck, turning his face with a sharp, sputtering sound.

Ilys barked out a laugh, low and full in her chest, wild and wicked. "You insisted," she said.

She wrapped the cloak around herself again, tying it loosely at her throat, amusement curling a smile across her mouth. The attendant stammered indistinctly and stepped hurriedly toward the carriage, suddenly fascinated with the buckles on the side door.

She started walking again, back toward the Sanctum gates, her bare feet slapping softly against the snow-kissed path. Behind her, the attendant stood rigid and dismayed, likely reconsidering every life choice that had brought him to this unfortunate morning.

Ilys only laughed to herself, dry and brittle, a sound shaped by years and tempered by loss. Age had mottled her reverence, made her bold and unwieldy. No longer the solemn girl they once dressed in ink and blood, she had grown older, one-and-twenty now, and stranger too—looser in the bone, quicker to bite.

And cheekier, when the mood took her.

She looked back once over her shoulder, her dark veil fluttering with the motion.

"Tell them I'll be there before the blade dulls," she called.

And then she disappeared into the gates, humming softly, leaving behind a trail of melting footprints.

The city had grown heavier of late. Too many guards lined the streets. The rebellion that had flared in the villages had not been quenched. It was festering, smoldering. Refugees trickled through the gates with hollow eyes and bones pressing sharp against their skin, while those already within the walls fought over scraps of bread. Hunger haunted every alley. Sickness carried on the wind.

Ilys observed the crowd pressing in, their faces gray and drawn. She knew that look. Not devotion. Not reverence. A quiet, rotting hatred.

Why? The thought gnawed at her as it had for months. *Why had the Bargain not held? Why, after centuries of sacrifice, did famine still rot the harvest and plague still crawl through the streets? She had bled for the Veil, killed for it, and given her hands, her heart, her very name. And yet the kingdom starved. And yet the children died coughing blood into their mother's arms.*

Ilys waited at the foot of the dais, as she had done countless times before. Snowmelt clung to her veil, and mud and slush bled into the hem of her robes.

A ripple of voices carried through the square, a low murmur of agreement that pricked at her skin. Ilys's mind flashed back to the riot, to her body curled beneath fists and boots, breath crushed from her lungs. She saw that same fury in their eyes now, as clearly as she saw the guards shifting, knuckles white on their spears.

They no longer believed. Not in the King. Not in the Veil. Not in her.

"Traitor," Lord Veylen announced behind her, his voice carrying over the stonework. "Spy. Poisoner of Faith. Desecrator of the Veil."

The prisoner twisted, bloodied lips curled in contempt. "Your Veil is rot," he rasped.

Ilys paused, just a step below the prisoner. Her fingers tightened on the hilt.

"I know what you are," he said, eyes locking with hers through the veil. "Beneath your mask, beneath your names and prayers. I know what you really are."

She fought the fallible sentiment threatening her resolve. Raised the blade.

The prisoner screamed before the knife touched him. Fear marked many, but fury set him apart: a raw, howling defiance that filled the execution square and set the onlookers shifting, uneasy in their boots. The sound carried through the Capitol like a crack in the stone.

He lunged.

It happened too fast, the bonds snapping, the guards shouting, her body reacting before thought could catch up. He threw himself at her with desperation and ruined pride. The blade caught him low, too low, not in the heart. Blood erupted across her front, warm and immediate. It splattered the veil, painted the temple's holy sigil across her chest in arterial red. He crashed into her and they both went down. She hit the stone hard, air knocked from her lungs. He writhed on top of her, choking, clawing at her arms, his mouth a gory snarl.

She screamed.

Not in pain. Not in fear.

In rage.

The blade came down again, into his neck this time. Again. Again. It caught between bone. She twisted. She felt something snap.

He convulsed. Shuddered.

Stopped.

The square mourned and when she rose, her robes clung to her like a second skin, soaked through in crimson. Her veil drooped, half-torn, exposing one hollow eye. Her gloves had split at the seams from gripping the blade so tightly, and blood ran in thin rivulets down the inside of her wrists, warm and indistinguishable from the man's.

A woman's voice cracked out, "Murderer!" before being drowned by the hiss of others trying to hush her. The guards shifted nervously, shields raised, eyes sweeping the crowd, expecting a riot to break at any second. Ilys felt their stares sear through her veil: hungry, accusatory, unblinking.

Veylen approached at last. "Well done," he said, his smile crooked. "So thorough. So... zealous."

She didn't look at him.

She looked down.

At the ruin she had made.

Chapter 12

Twenty-second year in the life of Ilys of the Veil

"You're back."

Ilys ran to Grim. When she reached him, her arms wrapped around his neck, holding tight, anchoring herself to solidity after too long at sea.

Grim stiffened but after a breath's pause, his arms folded around her.

Near her ear, his voice came low, rough from travel. "There's a name-gift in the saddlebag."

Ilys swallowed, pressing her forehead briefly against his shoulder, allowing the warmth of his presence to settle over her before pulling back. "You remembered."

Grim exhaled through his nose, which could have meant "of course" or "don't make a fuss of it."

She didn't. Instead, she let her fingers linger before stepping away, her gaze flicking past him. Beyond the gate, Death waited. Black smoke curled from his form, trailing from his broad shoulders as his steed shifted beneath him with a slow exhale. His presence thickened the air, pressing against her skin like a coming storm.

Grim rolled his shoulders, already moving toward the kitchens. "Come," he muttered. "I'm starving."

Ilys stood still. "I'll be there in a moment."

Grim stopped, glancing back at her. His posture did not shift, but she could feel his scrutiny even from a distance.

"Two-and-twenty," he noted, not unkindly. "And now you think yourself above listening to me."

"I'll be but a moment," Ilys promised. The words were quiet, measured.

He watched her longer before turning, his footsteps fading into the courtyard. She waited until he disappeared. Only then did she turn.

Death lingered where he'd been, his shape merging with the beast beneath him, an absence of light rather than a presence. Ilys approached him with careful steps, like one might approach a wild creature, not out of fear, but to keep from sending it away.

No fear stirred in her chest, only excitement.

And she did not want excitement to be the thing that drove him from her.

"Will you speak to me, Death?" she asked, her voice hushed, carried by the cold night air. "Grim says you do not speak."

He met her with such characterization.

She lifted her chin. "The King says you are my father. Should you not speak to a daughter?"

A shift. A slow tilting of his head.

You are no daughter of mine.

The voice did not come as a sound, but words she felt, words that pressed against her ribs and curled into her lungs. Hard. Silvery. Weightless and sharp, like the cut of moonlight through frostbitten branches.

You are his lamb for slaughter.

Ilys held her ground, her breath shallow against the sentiment.

"Whose daughter am I then?" she asked, softer now. "What was I born of?"

A pause.

Do I look like a soothsayer? A fortune-teller? His voice cut through her, cold and edged. *I am the frost, the night, and the eternities.*

Ilys inhaled, slow and deep. The air between them felt thinner now. Standing too close to him unraveled the threads that tethered her to the world.

"Go on then," she challenged. "Leave. Bring the world to its knees and cease the happiness of another hundred mortal souls."

Death did not answer. His steed moved, hooves pressing into the earth without sound as he rode away from her, his cloak unfurling like smoke against the wind.

Dissatisfaction clawed at her ribs, whispering its mockery. Answers would never come, nor peace, nor clarity. She'd had her fill of half-truths, of Death's endless riddles, of the duty that chained her to him.

Ilys found Grim in the kitchen, where Baron had already joined him.

Heat rolled through the air, paunchy with the scent of roasted meat and fresh bread. Grim sat at the worn wooden table, leaning back in his chair, his veil shadowing his face, but his presence relaxed, settled. Baron's gaze flickered to him, watchful, assessing, and his expression softened at every movement Grim made, every tilt of his head, every shift of his fingers.

Grim regaled them with the stories of his time away, some with detail, others noticeably skimmed over. He spoke of roads he had traveled and people he had met, but Ilys could hear the gaps, the places where truth had been pared down into more palatable fables. She did not press him. Not yet.

One day, she would hear them all.

One day, she would find her fingerprints over countless lives, ones she had changed, ones she had ended.

For now, she already saw the shape of her impact, standing in the space Grim had left behind, carrying out Death's orders in his absence.

Baron reached into his pocket, pulling out a folded parchment. "Ah. I almost forgot." He tapped the seal. "Ilys, you have a letter."

Ilys turned the parchment in her hands, breaking the wax seal. Neat, careful strokes curved across the page in Rowenna's unmistakable hand. She skimmed over the first few lines, her quiet home, the longing threaded between words, the space left behind where Ilys should have been. Then, her stomach dropped.

She read the line twice. Then a third time, as if the ink might shift beneath her stare, as if Rowenna's words would rearrange themselves into something else. But the letters did not move.

Baron, ever watchful, caught the shift in her expression. "What?"

Ilys groaned, dragging a hand down her face. "The fat sod got her pregnant."

Baron choked on a laugh, leaning back in his chair, amused despite himself. Grim huffed, shaking his head with a low chuckle.

"You will be an auntie," Grim mused.

Ilys hummed, feigning deep contemplation. "I will swaddle him in my veils."

Baron made a noise of protest. "That feels sacrilegious."

"You know nothing," Ilys shot back.

Grim smirked, though his fingers still toyed absentmindedly with a piece of twine.

Ilys traced the edges of the parchment, her gaze skimming over the words again, even though she already knew what they said.

"Perhaps I will travel to her," she suggested, keeping her voice casual, light. "Meet the babe."

She did not miss the way the room shifted. Baron's amusement dimmed, his jaw tightening. Grim's hands stilled over the board, his knuckles flexing. They did not need to say it. She already knew their answer.

Ilys smirked, though it did not quite reach her voice. "Yes, well. I knew that, didn't I?"

Grim spoke first. "Ilys."

She shook her head. "Hush." Her fingers curled around the parchment, pressing the creases deeper into the page. "I'm fine," she said smoothly, her gut twisting at the lie. "So much excitement today. Makes one weary."

Neither of the men looked convinced, but she did not give them room to protest.

She pushed up from the table, forcing a smirk on her lips. "You two prattle on. Perhaps we'll find time for a game or a reading later."

She wiggled her fingers in mock farewell, turning before they could see the way her expression faltered, the way her throat tightened. The emotions curled in her stomach, combative and restless, but she swallowed them down, pressing them deep beneath the surface.

"Ilys."

A hand shook her awake, firm but gentle.

She groaned, blinking bleary eyes open to find Grim kneeling beside her bed, his face shadowed in the dim candlelight.

"Ilys," he called again, low and urgent. "There is a beast in the castle. We must run."

A mass landed on her waist, small but solid.

Still half-dazed with sleep, she frowned. "Grim, my veil," she requested, reaching groggily for it.

But then she sat up, properly taking in the supposed beast pressing its paws into her stomach.

A pup.

Perched on her bed, dark-furred and scruffy, and looking up at her with bright, young eyes, its tail thumping lazily against her blanket.

Ilys stared. "This," she deadpanned, "is the beast?"

From the corner, Baron erupted into laughter, his cackling loud enough to shake the walls. Grim spoke through the amused confession of his smile.

Ilys let out a measured breath, willing her heart to quiet. Then, remembering her poise, she pushed a hand through her dark curls and reached for her veil.

She cleared her throat, eyeing the pup with suspicion. "Why do you interrupt my sleep with a monster?"

"This monster," Grim quipped, his voice laced with humor, "is your own little babe."

Baron folded his arms, leaning against the post of her bed. "We know it's been hard without... "

"Attachments," Grim finished.

Ilys's fingers curled over the blanket.

Baron sighed. "We wanted you to have one of your own. A creature to love. As best as a Veilwalker can."

A warm, wet sensation bloomed against her calf. She inhaled sharply.

"Your attachment," she muttered dryly, "has just pissed on my leg."

"The duality of love," Baron offered, utterly unrepentant.

Grim shook his head, barely restraining a laugh as Ilys scowled down at the pup. Despite herself, she reached forward, brushing her fingers over his fur. Dark, coarse, unruly. The pup blinked up at her, oblivious to her scrutiny.

She hummed, thoughtful. "You are Morrigan."

"That's an awful name for a dog." Baron grimaced.

Ilys's eyes narrowed. "There was a priestess once. She looked just like him. If you saw her, you'd know it suits him."

"I've seen her." Grim chuckled under his breath. "It does."

Ilys ignored him, shifting forward. "Come here, Mors," she called, testing the name.

The pup wagged his tail.

Her scowl deepened. "He's just pissed again."

In the evening, the sound of clashing filled the training yard, a tempo carved from repetition as Ilys and Grim sparred. She moved quickly, her strikes precise, her footing light. Grim met her at every turn, his counters fluid, but she could see it now, the drag in his steps, the fraction of a second delay in his movement. His strength had not faded, not yet, but time had begun to sink into him, pressing at the edges of his endurance.

A year ago, she wouldn't have landed a hit on him. Today, she did.

She dropped low, pivoted sharply, and swept his legs from beneath him. Grim hit the ground with a solid thud, his sword skidding from his grasp as dust curled into the air.

Ilys straightened, waiting for his usual grumble, his usual quip about luck. But he didn't speak. He stayed there, his breath steady, but more sluggish than it once would have been. When he finally pushed himself up, elbows braced against his knees, his voice came quiet.

"This Veilmarch," he announced, "will be my last."

Ilys froze.

She gripped her sword tighter. "You don't mean that."

Grim's veiled gaze lifted to hers. "I do."

She could hear it in his tone. The finality.

"I've spent half my life walking with Death," he continued, voice even. "And the truth is, there is beauty in the Veilmarch. Beauty I'm excited for you to experience."

She frowned, uneasiness curling in her chest.

"Less pomp. Less ritual," he mused. "No priests, no processions, no empty prayers from those who don't understand what we do." He sighed, stretching one leg out. "Just us. Just the work. New sights, new drinks, new people. You'll see," he said, tilting his head, watching her. "When it's yours to take."

"Grim?" Ilys called earnestly, as he turned from her. "Tell me. Tell me everything."

"Tell you what, chit?"

"You are holding back. I can tell. You always have been. There is something you are not telling me." A battle flickered behind his eyes. He opened his mouth, shut it again.

"What I have to say helps nothing."

"You cannot possibly know that."

"It has not helped me," he admitted, voice low. "I cannot."

He pushed to his feet, brushing the dust from his tunic.

"Come. You need to eat."

Ilys did not move, her grip still firm on her sword.

"Forget it. You aren't needed yet," he said again, softer now. "You still have time. Breathe." The words carried a strange gentleness, borrowed almost, as though he were reaching for Baron's tone and falling short.

Not much time. But she didn't say that.

Instead, she let her blade fall to her side and followed.

After sup, the door creaked, a draft of winter air slipping in as Elspeth, Grim's attendant, entered with a tray balanced on her palms. Baron reached first, naturally. He plucked up a cup before Grim had even extended a hand, swirling it lazily.

"Elspeth, you're a jewel," he said, flashing her one of his unrepentant grins.

"Mm," she replied, unimpressed, though the corner of her mouth twitched as she retreated a step. Elspeth moved with the steadiness of the oak beams above, her frame solid, her braid of iron-grey hair coiled like rope at her crown.

Grim lounged at the worn wooden table, his broad form draped in dark layers, his ever-present veil casting his face in shadow. His hands, scarred, calloused from years of wielding a blade, idly shifted Fox and Geese pieces across the board, his fingers moving with slow deliberation.

Baron sprawled in the chair opposite him, a sharp contrast to Grim's constant tension. Where Baron, all ease, with one leg slung over the armrest overshadowed Grim's stoicism, a dowdy book balanced against his stomach. His auburn hair protested order, mussed from running his hands through it too many times while the candlelight caught in the gold flecks of his hazel eyes, making them glint with mischief.

Morrigan lay beneath the table, his dark, scruffy fur a tangled mess, his paws twitching in his sleep. One ear flopped lazily while the other remained at attention, listening to some far-off sound beyond the walls. His chest rose and fell steadily, blissfully unaware of the world around him.

Cross-legged on the floor, Ilys sat with parchment scattered in her lap, her fingers smudged black with charcoal. Strands of dark hair had slipped loose from the braid at her nape, curling at the edges of her veil where she had brushed against them. The veil itself shone lighter than the Tartarean ceremonial ones she wore for public duties, but it still framed her face in shadow.

Her charcoal glided over the page, shaping the familiar angles of Grim's shoulders, the way his fingers toyed absentmindedly with the board, the way his posture, always braced, always quiet, made him look as though he were still waiting for danger, even in rest.

Baron, of course, noticed her study first.

"Are you drawing me again?" His voice broke through the quiet, dry and accusatory.

Ilys hummed, "You have a good face for it."

"I do," he agreed at once, tilting his head toward her with mock solemnity. "Are you sketching Grim, too?"

She nodded, demure.

"Grim," Baron called, a grin tugging at his mouth. "Pose for her."

Grim exhaled, long-suffering. "I do not care."

Baron smirked. "Even better. You will be captured in all your veiled, brooding glory."

"I am not brooding," Grim muttered, moving another piece on the board.

"You are always brooding." Baron countered, flipping a page in his book without looking at it.

Ilys smirked, tilting her head as she examined Grim's portrait. "Brooding suits you."

Grim grumbled beneath his breath but didn't argue.

Baron, pleased, leaned forward to get a better look at the parchment. "And the dog? What role does he play in this grand artistic vision?"

Ilys cast a glance down at Morrigan, still sprawled between them, his breathing slow, tail flicking in his sleep.

"I've captured him in all his finest qualities," she said solemnly, turning the paper to reveal the sketch of him mid shit onto Grim.

Baron howled with laughter. Grim sighed, rubbing a hand down his face.

"Very dignified," Grim offered dryly. "Exactly what one expects of a woman of two-and-twenty."

Ilys grinned, folding the parchment and setting it aside. It was an absurd kind of bliss, one forged in exhaustion, in stubborn companionship, in lives built around blood but softened in stolen moments like these.

It was not meant to last.

None of it ever was.

Chapter 13

Ilys dreamed. Great, terrible dreams.

Darkness pressed around her, ardent and endless. She clawed for someone, anyone—Grim, Baron, Rowenna—but always woke alone. Death's words lingered in her skull, etched deep.

You are his lamb sent for slaughter.

Her breath came sharp and shallow until Mor pushed his nose against her jaw and curled close. His presence steadied her pulse, though the unease never truly left.

At first light she slipped outside. Frost clung to the stones beneath her feet, and the air stung her throat with every inhale. She settled near the temple wall, parchment spread across her lap, and set her charcoal to the page. Lines took shape beneath her hand, sharp and urgent, as though drawing might bind the dreams and keep them still.

So when Grim's voice broke the quiet, she startled.

"Do you remember when you were eight, and the King invited us to that..." He stalled. "That dinner?"

Ilys didn't turn, still shading the edge of a figure she hadn't yet named. "Vaguely," she answered. "Why?"

Grim's veil tickled against the doorway as he lingered, shifting. "We've been called to another. This evening."

She paused, finally looking up.

"I've told Mother Inrith. She'll help you ready yourself, but I just wanted to... " He stopped, his fingers tightening over the edge of the doorframe as he mulled over his words.

Ilys narrowed her gaze. "What?"

The veil dulled his voice, but not the strain in it. "These dinners are strange, Ilys."

She waited.

"You think we have power—" He met her gaze—"and we do," he relented. "But there are elements we wield no power over."

Cold crept up her spine. "I haven't the faintest sense of what you're trying to say."

Grim grunted, adjusting his footing, the floor creaking beneath the shift. "Be careful tonight," he said simply. "Be polite. Above all, be quiet."

Ilys frowned. Grim, never characterized as timid, faced her, braced in the doorway, seeming so small. He stood vulnerable in a way she had never seen before.

She appraised him, then gave a slow nod. "Of course."

"Good. Good." He stepped back. "I'll see you this evening." Then he left, and his warning echoed in her mind.

"Put her in the midnight veil. It suits the occasion more. And adorn her with the silver thorned circlet." Mother Inrith's voice cut through the low murmurs of the Sanctum, her tone carrying the same authority it always had, though age had softened its edges. The priestesses obeyed, their hands moving with practiced efficiency as they dressed Ilys for the evening ahead.

Ilys had seen many priestesses come and go over the years. Some stayed long enough to gray, while others disappeared like footprints in the snow, their names lost to time.

Years ago, Ilys witnessed two trees who had merged into one. Two branches, mangled, reached towards one another, binding in the middle and creating an entirely new entity, reaching now towards the sky. Mother Inrith and the sanctum mirrored that twisted tree. One had a hard time separating the two. Interdependent and metonymous. The years had settled into her bones, carving lines into her face and slowing her steps, but they had not dimmed her formidable spirit. She still hobbled through the Sanctum with sharp, unrelenting purpose, swatting away offered hands when she stumbled, treating every mundane duty as though its neglect might unravel the world. Her memory often slipped, her words muddled, yet her will forged on, iron and unbending. Ilys had grown to admire that.

"This will do," Mother Inrith announced, stepping back to examine her.

Her veil hung heavier than her usual one, its fine embroidery shimmering under the candlelight. Silver filigree edged its hem, subtle and intricate, meant to signify authority without excess. The circlet sat atop her head, delicate but barbed, the thorns pressing lightly against her scalp. Beneath the veil, she wore robes of deep indigo, layered and formal, the high collar stiff against her throat, the sleeves heavy with embroidery. She looked every bit the Veilwalker, save for the absence of blood on her hands.

A knock hit at the chamber door and Grim entered, dipping his head.

"It's time." His voice sounded formal and distant. He turned his attention to the elderly woman beside her, bowing his head in deference. "Mother."

Mother Inrith inclined her head in approval before shooing the priestesses away with a sharp flick of her wrist. Ilys moved after Grim, her stride composed, her pulse anything but.

Outside, the carriage waited, the horses shifting restlessly in the cold. Baron leaned casually against its side, his usual smirk in place.

"What are you doing here?" Ilys queried as she approached.

Baron smiled, straightening. "You are looking at one of the attendees of honor."

Grim silently climbed into the carriage, his posture stiff as a board.

Ilys lifted a brow. "Did you finally break the record for most pork legs devoured in one sitting?"

Baron let out a bark of laughter. "Ha ha, you chit."

"Veilwalker." Grim's voice sliced through the air.

The amusement drained from Baron's face.

Grim's thrust an inelastic gaze towards the pair. "From here to the castle and back, you will call her Veilwalker."

Baron's jaw tightened. A slow flush crept up his neck, his usual lighthearted demeanor rattled. Ilys felt the tension shift like a snapped thread.

Baron dallied, breathing through his nose. "I've been asked to bear the sigil."

An award of valor, the Sigil was given only to those who had proven loyalty in service. It was a mark worn by few, meant to set its bearer apart from the ranks.

After a long beat, he addressed her, "Veilwalker."

The door shut. Through the stifled travel, Ilys barely noticed the streets sliding past. The city blurred, and in her mind's eye, the black swirls from her dream began to curl and twist again.

The carriage slowed, the wheels crunching against the gravel of the grand courtyard. Outside, the castle loomed, its towering spires piercing the night sky. Banners of red and silver hung heavy at the gates, the sigil of the Veil gleaming at their heart.

A servant in white and blue robes stepped forward, bowing deeply. "Veilwalkers." His hands folded in reverence. "Welcome."

Grim stepped down beside her, silent, veil drawn tight. Baron followed, stiff as iron at her side, his usual smirk absent.

The servant straightened. "The King awaits. Please, follow me." He turned, gliding through the towering doors of the castle.

He guided them toward the dining hall, pausing only when they passed a group of nobles. One by one, he introduced them; their names and titles Ilys had no interest in remembering, and their faces she had no intention of keeping.

The chamber opened wide, its walls hung with banners and gilded frames. One painting in particular caught her eye, a portrait of the royal family. The King sat forward, steady-eyed; the Queen's hand rested protectively on the shoulder of a boy scarcely ten. Ilys realized with a start she had never seen them in public. She found herself admiring the King for it, for shielding them from the ceaseless games and ruthless machinations of court.

Conversation swelled as they entered, overlapping voices pulling at her attention.

"Enough coin has gone to war," one minister said, pitched loud enough for others to hear. "Plague relief must take priority. And trade—without it, famine will finish what the sickness began."

Another, older and sharper, cut in, "And still, the treasury is emptied into campaigns we cannot win."

Assent rippled through the room, soft from some, defiant from others. Politeness cloaked it all, thin as gauze over a wound.

A lady in pale green leaned toward her companion, voice low but urgent. "Did you hear? The eastern ports have closed. No grain from the Lowlands in three weeks."

Her companion, a young noble with ink-stained cuffs, snorted softly. "Closed, or seized? The sea's been crawling with rebels and thieves both. Perhaps the Veilwalkers should turn their knives toward that."

The jest drew a few nervous laughs. Ilys felt their eyes brush her veil like moths against glass. She tried to look past them, past the gleam of the silver plates and the too-bright chandeliers. A musician plucked at a lute in the corner, his song thin and mournful. Ilys's gaze snagged on the far wall, where a draft stirred one of the banners. Beneath its folds, she glimpsed the edge of another painting—a battlefield this time, horses rearing, the King astride his steed with sword aloft. She had seen the same image in a hundred chapels, but here, the paint had darkened. The sky behind him was the color of ash, and the faces of the dying had been rendered with too much detail.

At the far end, Lord Veylen stood near the throne, leaning so close his lips were brushing the King's ear. The King did not move, only nodded once, gesturing to a herald.

The bell struck three times.

"Please," the herald announced, gesturing toward the elongated table. "Be seated."

Ilys sat near the King, Grim beside her, Baron across. The King lifted his goblet, smiling faintly. "To the Veilwalkers, who keep faith with us."

A chorus of,"to the Veilwalkers," echoed, though not all voices met the toast with conviction. Crystal clinked like distant bells. Servants emerged from the shadows, bearing silver dishes that steamed in the candlelight. The smell of roasted pheasant mingled with sweet cloves and the faint iron tang of wine. Platters of honeyed carrots and dark bread passed from hand to hand while golden sauces gleamed like liquid fire beneath the chandeliers. Ilys reached for none of it. The smell turned her stomach. She kept her hands folded in her lap, veil falling like a curtain between her and the others.

Across the hall, laughter broke from another table, thin and rehearsed. The King's counselors leaned toward one another, voices low and serpentine. Ilys caught the name *Westmarch,* followed by *accusations*, and the sound of a chair scraping roughly against the stone. She focused instead on her plate, untouched. The silver caught her reflection, a ghostly shape mocking her.

"Eat," Grim directed without looking at her. "It's expected."

She obeyed, taking a bite of the bread. As she chewed, her gaze drifted down the table. Jewels flickered in candlelight like tiny suns. Laughter rose and fell, but the current sounded much too rehearsed. They glanced, they assessed, they performed. Ilys had once thought she might envy this, the crowded rooms, voices overlapping, a hundred souls pressed close enough to feel human again. But here, among them, she saw only performance and restraint. These were not free people. They were bound by silk and custom, shackled by politeness and fear.

It struck her then how different this was from her own small world. The long evenings in the Sanctum when Grim and Baron would argue over the placement of a blade on the game board, Rowenna humming while she mended the same torn hem for the third time. Those moments had felt ordinary then, almost dull. Now, they seemed impossibly rich. Honest.

And then the King rose.

At first, no one noticed his rise. The courteous scrape of his chair was the kind of sound that would normally go unheard beneath the clatter of plates. But one by one, voices faltered. A servant froze mid-pour. The low hum of the hall collapsed into stillness.

The King stood at the head of the table, his goblet still in hand, the candles glinting off the silver embroidery of his robe. He looked from face to face—ministers, nobles, the Veilwalkers—until the silence grew taut, expectant.

The King's voice filled the hall, low and steady, more priest than monarch. "It is written that no man may serve two masters, for a heart divided is a heart already lost. Where loyalty strays, rot follows. From one unfaithful oath, a kingdom may fall."

A murmur moved through the hall but he did not pause. His gaze swept over them, unhurried, almost tender.

"I have learned," he continued, "that the truest test of faith is not in abundance, but in adversity. A man may stand firm when praised, yet crumble when tried." He let the phrase hang, the echo of scripture heavy in the air.

He paced a step, the train of his robe whispering against the marble. "There are those among us who believed they could divide their hearts and offer one half to the crown. The other to rebellion. But the Veil does not divide. The Veil is whole, or it is nothing."

Silence deepened. Someone at the far end coughed, and the sound seemed almost profane. The firelight wavered across his face, golden and cold.

"These men have been weighed," he said, and his voice grew firmer. "Their allegiance was not whole. They pledged their faith to crown and cause, to obedience and rebellion. A choice divided is no choice at all. And so, though my soul recoils, I must speak the names that Death himself has weighed."

He stopped speaking. The silence that followed was total. Slowly, deliberately, his eyes moved from one end of the table to the other through the ranks of ministers, the soldiers, the servants pressed to the wall, until they came to rest upon the Veilwalkers.

"Lord Cestel of Westmarch," he said at last, the name falling like a bell-tone.

Voices shouted, chairs scraped. One man surged half to his feet, only to be shoved down by a guard's mailed hand.

"Minister Deyrin of the Treasury." A woman wailed, cut short when a hand clamped over her mouth.

"And—" His voice faltered, just for a heartbeat. His gaze flicked briefly toward Baron, whose expression had gone perfectly still.

"Baron Madog of the Guard."

The ministers clamored over each other in outrage, but the King lifted his hand, and his guards pressed the crowd back into order with spears.

Ilys did not move. She could not. The sound of Baron's name rang through her skull like a hollow bell. She remembered—absurdly—the way Lord Veylen had once toyed with her skirts, how she had gone rigid, unable to breathe, unable to think. And now that same paralysis gripped her, holding her fast in the hall while time unraveled around her.

How strange, she thought over and over. *How strange.*

Grim erupted from his seat, hands clamping to the table so fiercely the wood groaned and splintered beneath his grip. His veil hung askew, his breath sharp and ragged, his voice breaking as he fought against the guards who swarmed him. The entire demonstration raw, unrestrained, and alien from the man she knew.

Ilys stared, frozen, as if the ground itself had tilted. She had never seen him so undone.

Then the King's hand closed over hers, importunate, pulling her attention away.

"My daughter," he said, stepping close, his voice dropping low, intimate, as though there were only the two of them. He took her hands, warm and heavy, into his own. "Think not that I wish this. Would that I could turn Death's face aside, yet the Bargain binds us. The Veil demands it."

His eyes shone as he pleaded, soft enough for only her to hear. "Think of the children who cough themselves to dust in the alleys. Think of the mothers with nothing left to feed their babes. Famine waits. Plague devours. If we do not hold to the covenant, if we do not pay the price, what hope remains?" He leaned closer, his voice urgent, trembling. "It is you and me, my daughter. Only you and me, upholding what must be. Help me bear it. Help me make them understand."

The room still battled in disarray. Protests swimming across the table. Guards forcing order into the chaos.

Then Lord Veylen's voice cut through. "This is a moment to show loyalty to the Veil," he declared, sharp and unrelenting. "Be careful, lest Death catch your name in his mouth."

Obedience rippled outward. Heads bent. Backs straightened. Fear sealed every tongue.

The King turned to her, his voice gentle, coaxing. "Go on, my girl. Let us carry this together."

Her breath faltered, but her feet moved, slow and heavy, carrying her down the length of the hall. Every eye followed as she approached the three kneeling figures at the dais, their hands bound, shoulders braced for what waited ahead.

The first man—Lord Cestel of Westmarch—trembled as she drew near. She spoke the blessing with a voice that shook as she raised the blade. The sound of the strike echoed against the dining hall. His body folded, lifeless.

She lingered there, trembling, her throat raw, until the King's voice urged her softly again. Only then did she force herself onward.

Minister Deyrin met her eyes only briefly, a flicker of defiance quickly crushed beneath the guards' grip. Her own gaze blurred as she spoke the words. She swung once more. Blood spilled.

But when she reached the third, her steps faltered.

Baron.

He knelt as though in quiet repose, the same man who had once sprawled in her chair with a book in hand, laughing at his own irreverence. Strands of auburn fell loose across his brow, his hazel eyes on her.

"Ilys, no!" Grim's voice ripped through the chamber, ragged and wild. Guards strained against his thrashing, dragging him back, his veil hanging loose, his face bare and undone. "Do not touch him! Ilys!" His voice cracked with desperation. He bucked and shoved, splintering more wood beneath his heels as he fought. "*Baron*!"

The guards forced him through the doors, his cries echoing until they faded with distance.

The King's hand settled light against her shoulder, his voice low in her ear.

"The hardest trials always come to the most faithful," he said. "I have learned by experience that the greatest good is born from the deepest suffering. Our people will thank us, though they have no idea how cruel the god is we must tithe to. You are strong, Ilys."

She shuddered, throat closing. Stepped away from the King, towards Baron.

Baron lifted his head, his smile faint but consoling. His voice came hoarse, but warm—always warm. "It's okay, Ilys. It's no trouble at all."

Tears streaked her cheeks. She shook her head violently.

"My little darling," Baron whispered, eyes never leaving hers. "I love you."

Her sobs broke loose, her chest heaving as the world around her faded into blur. But his gaze held her, calm, heartening, and unafraid. His eyes—those eyes she had grown up with, the ones she had sketched a thousand times in a thousand expressions—were dull now, half-lidded with exhaustion. His voice, strangled with emotion, still reached her.

"It's okay, Ilys. It's okay."

Her throat locked. She could not.

"You have to," Baron urged, reading her mind. "Say the blessing. Nice and slow. I love the way you say it. One could fall asleep."

Her vision blurred with tears. She shook her head harder, with the humility and denial of a young child.

A ghost of a smile touched his lips, muted but moored. "Please, Ilys."

She gasped, sobbed, tried to breathe.

His words guided her, soft, reverent even now. "Thy thread is cut." He watched her flounder, waited for her to follow. "Come now."

Her lips trembled. The words were coals on her tongue, but still, she followed, "Thy thread is cut."

His head tilted faintly, urging her on. "Thy name is lost."

Her throat seized, but his gaze held her fast. She choked the words out, "Thy name is lost."

He inhaled, shallow but calm, and still he smiled.

"The Veil shall hold."

Her body shook. "The Veil shall hold."

His eyes flickered, faint as a candle flame guttering low. When she didn't move, his bound hands rose until his fingers found hers on the hilt. The guards shifted but did not stop him. His grip closed over hers, riveted and instructive.

"Together, then," he steered.

Her breath hitched. He guided her hand forward, guiding the blade toward his heart, their knuckles pressed close. She could feel his pulse beneath her fingers—fast, alive, terrified—and still, he smiled.

"Vasha," he whispered, one last time.

The sword slid in.

His breath left him in a single, broken sigh, his body folded to the stone. Blood spilled slow and red, baptizing the ground.

The hall had gone deathly still. No cries, no protests, only the shuffle of guards and the distant flicker of candlelight. Grim's voice faded down the corridor with his struggle, yet its echo still clawed at her ears.

Slowly, she turned her gaze to the King. His hands settled firm on her trembling shoulders. He turned her gently, guiding her away from the kneeling dead.

"Oh, my dear," he consoled paternally. "Well done."

She could not look back.

He steered her from the place of death, his hand anchoring her as the chamber remained bowed, and she let herself be carried, numb, away from what she had left behind.

Chapter 14

Ilys woke with a start, her breath catching against the pillow as though the sobs of the night before still pressed on her chest. Gray light pressed against the curtains. She sat up, veil caught at her throat, fingers cramped from the hold she'd kept on the blankets.

Baron's voice lingered in her ears—*It's no trouble, my girl*—and she nearly choked on the memory. She pressed her palm hard against her sternum, as though she could force the image down, bury it deep enough to breathe again.

She tried, uselessly, to piece the night together. She remembered Grim's struggle, the way he fought like a madman to reach Baron as guards were dragging him back, his voice raw as he shouted her name. She remembered, too, the King's hands upon her shoulders, his low murmur in her ear, *oh, my dear. Well done.* And then everything blurred. The throne hall dissolved into shadows, her grief a tide pulling her under. She had been guided away by the King, who placed her into the carriage as though she were a child.

Elspeth had been waiting back at the Sanctum, her eyes wide but demeanor collected. She had pressed a cup to Ilys's lips, a sleeping draft that tasted faintly of bitter herbs and honey. After that, darkness.

And now she awoke to a world without Baron.

She rose, her feet rickety, and drifted through the quiet halls. Her steps carried her toward Grim's quarters without thought, a child's instinct seeking the only tether she had left.

She rapped once and entered. The bed was stripped, the hearth gone cold, the game board cleared of its pieces. Only a single veil hung there still, black and frayed, swaying from its hook beside the bed.

Her throat closed. She reached for it without thought, fingers curling tight around the familiar cloth. It smelled faintly of smoke, sweat, and cedar. She pressed it once against her chest, then folded it and tucked it beneath her arm before leaving the chamber behind.

She found Mother Inrith in the antechamber of the temple, robes gathered neatly around her, her dark eyes lifting from a ledger as Ilys entered.

"Where is he?" Ilys's voice cracked against the stone. "Where is Grim?"

Mother Inrith regarded her with measured calm. "He has been released from service. His vows fulfilled, his burden complete. He has retired, as he has long prepared to do."

The words sliced cleanly, too easily. Ilys clenched the veil tighter beneath her arm.

"Released? Without farewell?"

"He is one of the faithful now," Mother Inrith said, closing the ledger with care. "His silence is part of his devotion. He may not speak with you. Nor you with him."

Ilys shook her head. "No," she denied. "No, I cannot allow that to happen."

"You presume much, child."

"I presume nothing," Ilys countered, forcing her voice even. She stood straighter, folding her grief into the posture they had drilled into her since girlhood. "If I am to stand where he stood, if I am to take up the rites and bear their weight, I must be prepared. You say Grim's silence serves the Veil, but my ignorance serves no one."

Mother Inrith's eyes narrowed. "You are not ignorant. You have been trained."

"Not wholly." Ilys's tone sharpened. "I need not speak to him socially. I seek no comfort. Only answers. If you would see me fail, deny me. If not—" she held the Mother's gaze—"then grant me what I ask."

At last, Mother Inrith inclined her head, long in the tooth. "I will inquire whether such a meeting can be permitted. But you would do well to remember, Ilys, that Grim is not yours. He is not even himself. He belongs wholly to the Veil now."

Ilys's jaw tightened. She forced a shallow bow, her fingers burning where they pressed Grim's veil against her ribs.

"Then let the Veil answer me through him," she said.

The answer came days later, while Elspeth led Ilys to the stables. She introduced her to a striking white horse; a proud, elegant creature that Morrigan immediately tried, and failed, to herd.

Grim had taught her to ride, though she had never owned a horse herself. She had never needed one. But now she was *the* Veilwalker. She would see the world at Death's side, and a horse was no longer a luxury but a necessity.

Ilys mounted awkwardly, cringing at the unfamiliar ache in her hips. Leaning forward, she patted the horse's neck.

"I shall call you Spire."

Elspeth tilted her head. "What an unusual name."

"It's descriptive," Ilys said dryly. "Mounting him feels like I've got one up my arse."

Elspeth blanched. Ilys held her stare.

"You are used to Grim. I imagine you'll dislike attending me."

"I am merely happy to serve," Elspeth said quickly.

To serve. Those fickle words.

A voice cut through the air behind them. Both women startled.

Mother Inrith stood in the stable doors, her shadow stretching long. "I have your answer, Veilwalker."

Ilys straightened in the saddle.

"He will not see you," Mother Inrith said flatly. "You must find other ways to supplement your... lacking knowledge."

Ilys's jaw clenched. She thought of Grim, gone without a goodbye, and of Baron, stolen in a single breath. How a day could strip a life away, burn it down, and leave nothing but ash.

Grief hollowed Ilys. She drifted like a wraith through the Sanctum, her body frail, her gaze empty, her days measured only by hunger. She carried Baron's sketches to the places she had drawn him, pressing charcoal ghosts against the stone as though the past might breathe again.

He was here. Now he was not. Over and over she practiced the exercise. Her mind could not reconcile the two.

She cursed Grim. She missed him. She needed him. And yet, deep down, she knew why he had gone. He could never forgive her for what she had done. Not Baron. Not like that.

At night, in dreams, she saw only their departures. Every face she loved turning away from her, and always, Death stood behind them, silent and watchful.

You are no one's daughter.

She despised him. What did Death know of loyalty, humor, or tenderness? He had not known Baron's softness, nor his wit. No divine will had demanded this, only Death's cruelty.

Her thoughts circled the Bargain. She replayed it again and again: the King raising his sword, Death's voice answering like stone.

One will always take my place. I am constant, though my will and voice may change.

And she understood. Death was no single god at all. It was but a role. Each Death bore his own will, his own cruelties, his own voice, and when one fell, another rose to carry the Bargain forward. The world did not end. It endured, bound to the pact.

The knowledge burned through her veins. So he could fall. *He could fall.*

And this Death, with his faulted, wicked agenda, expected her to kneel beside him? To play the puppet at his side?

Her grief curdled into fury. The one who ruined her, who spoiled her, who murdered Baron for daring to love—he was not eternal. He was replaceable.

She would inherit Grim's march, yes. She would walk beside this hollow tyrant, veil to veil. But not as his puppet.

As his undoing.

Her mind settled, cold and certain. She would put a blade through Death. Through the creature who thought himself inevitable.

She would find a way to kill him.

Part II

The Book of the Veil – Part II

"Sealed in the first days, spoken in the last, unbroken until the end of all things."

V. The Succession of the Veilwalker (Hiram 2:1-17)

1. And in those days, when the chosen had fulfilled their purpose and the weight of their duty had come to its end, the King did stand before the people and say:

2. "The blade must not dull. The burden must not falter. The covenant must not break."

3. And Death did answer him, saying:

4. "The path cannot be empty. One must follow where the other has gone, lest the balance slip from our grasp and the Veil be torn."

5. And so it was written that no Veilwalker would pass from the world without a successor to bear the weight, lest the kingdom stand unguarded and the debt go unpaid.

6. Thus, when the time came, the chosen one would be called before the King, and they would kneel, and the King, keeper of the

covenant, would take the sacred blade and say:

7. "You are given, not taken. You are chosen, not lost. You are bound, not forsaken."

8. And the faithful would answer:

9. "The Veil shall hold."

10. For the King is the shield of the people, and the Veilwalker is his blade. One cannot stand without the other. One cannot falter while the other remains.

11. And should the Veilwalker turn from their duty, should they forsake what has been given, then the burden shall fall to another, and the blade shall be lifted by one who will not break.

12. Thus was the law sealed, and thus shall it remain.

13. For the King speaks with the authority of the Fates, and the Veilwalker moves by his word alone.

14. And the faithful shall not question, nor shall they waver, for as the King stands, so does the covenant.

15. As the King rules, so does the Veil hold.

16. Vasha.

CHAPTER 15

Rowenna's letter arrived at the tail end of summer, when the sun clung to the horizon like a child refusing sleep. Ilys tore into it like a woman starved, for words, for affection, for the kind of company that didn't measure her by obedience. Gods, how she missed her.

My dearest Ilys,

The sky here is orange more often than not, and the pears bruise if you so much as think at them harshly. Which means, I suppose, it's nearly time for me to split open like a ripe fig and introduce the world to a very small, very loud person.

Would you like to see a child exit my body?

Directions (for your amusement and mild frustration): take the north road past the weeping alder. Follow the hill until the path becomes indecent. My cottage is tucked behind the blackberry thorns. Knock twice, then once, then shout something rude and possibly blasphemous.

There's a bed here. And tea. And me, terrified, yes, but oddly calm when I imagine your boots on my doorstep. Come if you will. I won't pretend it will make things easier, but it would make them lovelier.

Fat and desperate,
Rowenna

Ilys read it twice, then a third time, slower. Her hands trembled as she folded it again, her thumb pressed to the seam like a seal.

Could she leave?

Veil Law did not dictate where she went as long as she fulfilled her duty; though it did forbid the attachment that drew her away. What was the alternative? Staying, grieving, rotting until Death arrived for the march? She had lost so much. With her life given to the Bargain, could she not steal away for just a moment? Claim a shred of life as her own?

Baron had begged for her blade. Grim had left her in the hands of a fickle god. Death... Death held her like a vise for his amusement.

But Rowenna? Rowenna asked for only her presence. Even now, belly heavy with a new life and fear curled under her ribs, Rowenna had not summoned the Veilwalker or the executioner. She had called for Ilys. Simply Ilys.

Later, she could not sleep.

The Veilwalker lay curled beneath her thin covers, eyes open to the dark, tracing and retracing each step she would take from the Sanctum to the road, thoughts darting like minnows. Every sound in the stillness, creaking floorboards, the low sigh of wind through the shutters, seemed louder than it should be. Still, she waited. When she moved, she dropped low and fluid, like water slipping between cracks. She dressed in shadow, donning her cloak and lifting the satchel she had packed hours before. At the stables, the scent of hay and horse sweat greeted her. Her mare, Spire, lifted her head as Ilys approached, nostrils flaring, hooves shifting with impatience. Ilys reached out and brushed the forelock from Spire's eyes, fingers gentle, reverent.

"I will spoil you," she whispered, "if you do right by me now."

Spire snorted in cheeky approval.

Ilys led her out past the paddock, beyond the sleeping watchhouse, and into the pale wash of pre-dawn light. Ahead, Annon stretched wide and quiet.

She mounted in one smooth motion, the leather creaking beneath her. Then, with a breath she hadn't realized she'd been holding, Ilys pressed her heels to Spire's sides and began the ride.

Rowenna's cottage looked half-swallowed by the bramble thicket, just as promised, with blackberry canes like reaching arms, their last fruits gone soft with age. Ilys dismounted, her legs stiff, her cloak clinging with mist and travel's grit. Her heart thudded, eager and foolishly tender.

She knocked twice, then once, then shouted, "You still alive in there, you stubborn cow?"

The door opened at once. Rowenna stood barefoot in the threshold, face flushed, belly enormous beneath her linen dress. Her hair frizzed in a riot of waves, pulled back with a single ribbon that had given up hours ago. She looked tired and radiant and utterly unsurprised.

"You actually came," Rowenna noted, with unabashed sentiment.

Ilys stared for a beat too long before replying, "Gods, you're massive."

Rowenna barked a laugh. "I told you! Mother Inrith and the lot could move in."

"You're—" Ilys stepped inside, cloak slipping from her shoulders—"you're fat, Rowe."

"I am!" Rowenna grinned, arms open. "Now come say hello properly."

They embraced in the narrow cottage doorway, laughter muffled in the folds of each other's shoulders. Ilys held her tight, heart thudding beneath layers of wool and sweat and softness. When they finally pulled apart, Ilys dropped to her knees like a pilgrim and placed both hands on Rowenna's belly.

"I'm naming it," Ilys announced, palms warm against the wide curve of her unborn child.

"Oh?" Rowenna didn't open her eyes, her head resting against the crook of the doorframe, crown tilted.

"Woolf."

Now her eyes opened, one brow lifting just enough to register disapproval. "Woolf?"

"Two O's. Proper menace. Definitely the type to bite."

Rowenna snorted softly. "You're not naming a child, you're naming a mythic monster."

"Exactly," Ilys said, satisfied. "It fits. I can feel them plotting already."

Ilys shed her cloak and began tending to the hearth while Rowenna lowered herself carefully into a worn chair by the window, the kind that had once been stuffed properly but now sighed, thinning and mourning earlier days.

"Sit if you like," Rowenna said, eyes on the fire. "Or sweep the soot. I've no pride left, only dust and a list of things I can no longer reach."

Ilys took up the broom without a word, brushing the ashes into a waiting pan. They moved about the cottage in the easy hush of old familiarity, elbows brushing, breath syncing. They ate simply: stewed carrots, barley, and rough slices of bread. The kind of food that sticks to your ribs. Later, with her feet tucked beneath her and one hand resting idly on the rise of her belly, Rowenna spoke without turning her head.

"Leif's on the southern route again. Trade's thick this time of year. He'll miss the birth."

Ilys glanced up. "Does that trouble you?"

"No." Rowenna rubbed a reassuring circle against her side, where the child shifted restlessly. "He's dutiful. Good with coin. Quick with tools. Listens when I speak. That's more than I ever thought I'd bargain for."

She paused, then added with a faint glint in her eye, "And when it comes to intimacy, he's... teachable."

Ilys arched her brow, chiding frivolously, "Rowe."

"I'm only saying," Rowenna said with a faint laugh. "If one must lie with a man, it's a comfort when he's willing to be taught what's worth the trouble."

She turned her head at last, meeting Ilys's eyes with a look both wry and soft. "I don't feel wildly for him. I don't lie awake aching for his return. But I do not dread him. I admire his steadiness. His willingness to leave me be."

"That's love, then?" Ilys asked quietly.

"Perhaps." Rowenna leaned back, one hand trailing across her own collarbone. "Or it's the closest thing I've had that doesn't cut."

Night gathered in the corners of the cottage. The candles burned low, their wax puddling like pale petals across the table. Rain had begun to patter at the windows, plodding and uncertain.

"I don't know what sort of mold I'm meant to follow," Rowenna confessed, voice low. "I don't want to become her by accident. And I don't want to shape myself to be too brittle, too polished, too good. I just... I want to do this right. But I haven't the faintest idea what that looks like."

She spoke then of her mother, an unruly specter. A priestess who had made a mockery of her vows, abandoned Rowenna and then vanished without warning. Her mother's absence had taught her more than her presence ever had.

Ilys tightened her grip on Rowenna's hand.

"Then don't follow any mold," Ilys offered softly. "Make something new. Make you."

Rowenna's gaze didn't lift. "What if it's not enough?"

"It will be," Ilys said. "You're careful with the things you love, Rowe. You may not know the shape of this yet, but you'll hold it gently." She smiled, but it caught in her throat, tight and aching. Because she could see it now, the shape of the world bending. A child would arrive, loud and warm and needful, and Rowenna would pivot toward it as sunflowers follow the sun. It was natural. Ilys would not fault her.

But the grief was no less sharp for that reason.

This is how it ends, she thought.

She marveled at her own bitterness, the strange little ache blooming behind her ribs. What a strange, shameful thing, to envy a creature so small and soft and unborn. And yet, there it was.

Just once, she thought, *let someone choose me above all else*.

When Rowenna dozed at last, curled sideways on her narrow bed with her arm draped protectively over her belly, Ilys laid out her blanket near the hearth. The fire had died down to embers, glowing dim and red in the sooty stone.

She lay on her side, hands tucked to her chest, staring into the dark above. The sound of Rowenna's breathing, deep and uniform, filled the quiet.

And Ilys tried, as she always had, to untangle herself from her own longing.

Days later, Ilys awoke to Rowenna's hand on her shoulder. Ilys battled the sleep from her eyes and shifted beneath the heavy quilt.

Rowenna spoke through strain, her voice scraped clean of tenderness, "I waited as long as I could. It's time."

Ilys sat up, breath catching in her throat. Her eyes adjusted quickly to the dim light. Rowenna stood hunched beside the bed, one hand clamped around the bedpost, the other cradling the swell of her belly. Her nightdress clung to her thighs, soaked through at the hem. Her face, normally so composed, was drawn tight, jaw clenched, sweat already collecting at her brow.

Ilys didn't waste words. She threw on her cloak, bound her hair in a quick twist beneath the veil, and slipped out into the cold. Rowenna had told her what to do. Days ago, calmly, as they shelled peas or hung linens to dry, as though discussing anything else.

"When it starts," she'd began, "go to the edge of the village. Knock on the door with the cracked lintel. Rutha is her name."

The frost had crept in overnight, painting the earth silver. Ilys pulled her hood low and kept her head down. The village still slept, though a few lamps burned behind thick curtains. She found the door by memory, skewed on its hinges, swollen from rain.

She knocked three times, hard.

A rustling. A creak. Then Rutha stood there, wrapped in a shawl, braid already tight down her back.

"She's started?" the midwife asked, voice low and rough from sleep.

Ilys nodded. "She's upright. But close."

Rutha ducked inside, came back with her satchel. "Good. Better early than late."

Ilys was glad the rest of the world had yet to wake. She did not long for any eyes to peruse the strange sight: a Veilwalker and the midwife carrying on in familiar companionship. The black sky had begun to thin at the edges, a blade of pale light pressing against the horizon. By the time they returned, Rowenna had stripped the bed and lit two lamps. She sat in the armchair by the hearth, knees wide, hands braced on her thighs, rocking with each wave.

The moment Rutha entered, she took command.

Bag on the floor. Palms on Rowenna's belly. Fingers to her pulse.

"We've got time," Rutha said. "But not much."

She issued orders in short, clipped phrases.

"Boil water."

"Blankets, clean if you have them."

"Lay a cloth beneath her."

"Keep her upright as long as she can stand it."

Ilys moved quickly. She fed the fire until it roared, set the kettle on, soaked and wrung out cloths, and rolled up her sleeves. Her hands stayed rooted, even as the room filled with the scent of blood and iron, primal and vinous.

The labor dragged on. Hours. The light outside shifted from silver to gray, then gray to pale. The frost melted off the windows. The floor darkened with splashes of water. There were groans and cries, then guttural things torn from Rowenna's throat. Her face slickened with sweat, her hair plastered to her temples. Her thighs trembled, her grip bruising.

At one point she vomited into a bucket, breath heaving like a bellows, and groaned, "I can't," over and over again.

"You can," Rutha said flatly. "And you will."

Ilys knelt by the bed, wiping sweat from her forehead, offering her hand when asked, withdrawing when it was struck aside. She fetched, poured, cleaned. She stayed.

When the baby crowned, Rowenna's scream tore free. The cry of a woman breaking herself open, bone and skin and spirit. Her thighs shook. Her fingernails split. And then, one final, wrenching push, guided by a sound like tearing.

Ever punctual, Rutha caught the child in her hands, slick and red and loud. A wail rang out, peart yet overtired.

"It's a boy," she announced, voice softened. "Full head of hair on him."

Rowenna collapsed back against the pillows, mouth open, chest heaving. She looked spent, hollowed out. But when Rutha placed the child against her chest, Rowenna curled around him instinctively, arms trembling.

She didn't cry. She didn't smile. She just looked, really looked, at her son, as though already memorizing the shape of him. His tiny fists. His wet curls. His furious little face.

Ilys sat on the edge of the bed, reaching for a clean cloth to swaddle him. Her fingers brushed Rowenna's as she helped. The kettle hissed, boiling over and Rutha moved to tend it, wordless, already cleaning tools and bloody linens with practiced ease. Ilys stayed, knees stained, arms sore, hair sticking to her neck. She watched the two of them in this new shape they'd become. No celebration arrived. No sweeping music or miracle. Just breath. Sweat. Blood. The work of birth.

And Ilys, who had ushered so many into the dark, now bore witness to something else: a beginning.

CHAPTER 16

The cottage felt strangely quiet in the days after Woolf arrived, as if the whole place were holding its breath. Ilys felt time slipping away; worry of her absence at the Sanctum pricked her. Yet Rowenna lay pale and hollowed, her limbs loose with fatigue, curls clinging damp to her temples.

She slept more than she spoke, breath rasping low as her body remembered itself. Sometimes she stirred and whispered nonsense. Sometimes she reached blindly and whispered, "Are they all right?" before sinking again.

Ilys had never felt more ill-equipped and displaced.

The child—Woolf, as the name had somehow clung—seemed impossibly small. His fists curled like little seeds. His mouth opened and closed in wordless complaint. His eyes, when they opened, were dark and fathomless, like rain water pooled in a hollow stone.

Ilys held him like she might break him by thinking too loudly. Her hands, made for sword-hilts and saddles, were all wrong for this kind of softness. She hovered when he cried. She flinched when he rooted. She cleaned him like one might disarm a trap.

"You are a damp, shrieking mystery," she whispered once, eyes narrowed as she changed a nappy with the delicacy of a mutt braiding hair.

But Rowenna needed rest. And no one else was coming.

So, Ilys fed Woolf awkwardly, with one arm and half a prayer, rocked him in the creaky old chair by the hearth, and sang nonsense songs in a voice she hadn't used since she was a girl. She burned the porridge twice. She kept the fire going. She learned, slowly, the difference between a hunger cry and a tired one.

And Woolf, for his part, tolerated her.

Somewhere in the second night, after feeding and tending to Spire, Ilys sat curled with the child in her lap, half asleep. Woolf had stopped crying some time ago and now blinked at her with unnerving calm, studying her veil to find the face beneath.

"You don't know who I am," Ilys remarked. "And I don't know what I'm doing."

Woolf made a soft snuffling sound and smacked his lips in approval, apparently unbothered.

Ilys touched his brow with one calloused thumb. "But you're not so awful. For an animal that came screaming into the world." Her voice, roughened to a hush, barely reached the air. "You're not what I expected," she admitted. "And yet... here you are. Stealing hours from me like it's your right."

She didn't realize she'd begun to sway, back and forth in the chair, a rhythm older than memory.

By morning, when Rowenna finally woke, bleary, sore, and blinking against the gray light, Ilys dowsed in the chair, Woolf curled against her chest, fast asleep.

And Ilys, though she never quite said it aloud, had already begun to fall in love with the little thief who now slept like he had always belonged in the crook of her arm.

The days grew longer, and Rowenna began to rise.

She moved with caution at first, hand catching on every surface, breath hitching at each turn, each step. But strength returned to her by degrees, like sunlight returning to a frost-hardened field. She no longer slept through Woolf's cries. She hummed as she swept, stopped to pick dried herbs from the rafters, lifted her son with a surety that spoke of blood-knowledge.

Ilys watched from the table, elbow-deep in laundry, and felt a mystified emotion bloom and twist inside her.

She told herself it was pride. Relief. Maybe it was.

But there was a sting to it too.

Rowenna had her arms back now. Her voice, her footing. She didn't need Ilys for every small thing anymore.

So when Rowenna paused near the hearth one evening, babe in arms and cheeks flushed from movement, Ilys crossed the room and held out her hands.

"Give me my Woolf."

Rowenna turned, amused. "You know we'll have to call him another name eventually." She sighed, pressing her lips to the child's forehead. "Leif wants to name him after his father, Beck." Rowenna furrowed her brow and looked down at the boy in her arms. "I think it fits him. Sturdy little thing."

Ilys took him carefully, holding him close against her chest. "Look at this head of hair," she grumbled. "He's got more than most grown men. Wild as brambles. He's my Woolf."

Rowenna lethargic smile manifested dotingly. "Then he'll be both."

She brushed her knuckles gently across his cheek, then looked up at Ilys, fondness and knowing in her gaze. "You are Ilys," she said, "and Veilwalker. My boy is Beck... and Woolf."

Outside, the wind stirred the trees, whispering its own old names. Inside, the world felt small, and safe, and real. Ilys looked down at the boy, Beck-Woolf, with his unruly hair and tiny, clutching fingers. He blinked up at her, solemn and strange.

"Both, then," she dictated. "Lucky thing."

The child yawned, soft and sudden, and the room seemed to still, as if even the world had paused to witness this very small, very loud person begin to stretch into his many names.

The hooves were too fast.

Rowenna looked up from the cradle near the hearth, her brow creasing. "Is someone—?"

Ilys bounded to the door.

She opened it just as Lord Veylen dismounted, his cloak a wet, angry flare in the mist. The horse frothed at the mouth, flanks heaving. The man hadn't ridden, he had hunted.

Veylen crossed the yard in four long strides and struck Ilys full across the face. The crack of it echoed through the still morning like a snapped branch.

She didn't fall. Her head jerked sideways, blood blooming along her lip, but she held her stance. Inside the cottage, Rowenna stood frozen, clutching Woolf close to her chest.

"Did you think," Veylen hissed, voice low and furious, "that there was anywhere in this kingdom you could go where I wouldn't find you?"

Ilys didn't answer.

He stepped closer, breath hot with cold fury. "You, who wear Death's mark, you think that earns you privilege? That it gives you rights?" His gloved hand reached for her cloak, bunching the fabric near her collar. "You forget yourself. And if you think I won't teach you the cost of your disobedience by turning this cottage to ash, you haven't been listening."

Ilys's hand twitched at her side, but she did not reach for a blade. Not with Rowenna behind her. Not with the child.

Instead, her voice came low and even. "Surrender your threats."

Veylen stilled.

"I will come," she said. "I'll gather my things."

He stared at her for a long, hateful moment. Then he released her cloak with a sharp flick, straightening his spine.

"Good," he said. "Obedient, at last. The King will be pleased."

He turned, already striding back through the fog toward his mount. "Dusk," he called over his shoulder. "If you make me wait, I'll make you regret it."

The horse reared once as the odious man mounted, then vanished into the mist.

Ilys stood in the doorway, the taste of blood in her mouth. Behind her, the cottage lounged still and warm and small, the last place she had ever known peace.

Guilt curled in her chest, nestling in its favorite crevice. She cursed the weak naivete that had brought her here and made her think she deserved such. She forced her feet forward, already grieving the last of her love she had to give.

You are too soft. She heard Grim's voice in her head.

And it had almost cost her everything once more.

Chapter 17

Months later, Ilys stood with her arms folded, watching as Morrigan darted after a bundle of cloth Elspeth had tossed into the air. The dog leapt, catching it between his teeth with a sharp snap before landing in a flurry of paws and dirt. His tail wagged fiercely, his dark, scruffy fur shaking as he trotted back to Elspeth, dropping the cloth at her feet, expecting a grand reward.

"You see," Ilys observed. "He prefers a proper chase. If you throw it too lightly, he won't bother."

Elspeth nodded, her graying hair slipping from the loose knot at the nape of her neck. She picked up the cloth and tossed it again, higher, faster. Morrigan barked once, then took off after it, his legs a blur.

"He's always so lively," Elspeth said, grinning as she watched him tumble into a pile of leaves, shake himself free, and bound back toward them.

"He'll need the exercise while I'm gone," Ilys reminded her. "Twice a day if you can manage, or he'll tear the laundry apart just to entertain himself."

Elspeth laughed. "Understood."

Morrigan returned, dropping the cloth with a huff before flopping onto the ground, rolling onto his back, paws twitching lazily in the air. His tail thumped once, then again, waiting for another game, another chase. But Ilys didn't move to throw the cloth this time. Instead, she crouched beside him, running her fingers along his ribs.

He was strong now, though still lean. His fur had grown coarser since his pup days, and beneath it, she felt the orderly pattern of his breath, the solid warmth of his body pressed against her leg. He rolled upon the fabric tendrils of the veil that tickled the ground, grounding his scent into the dark cloth. Ilys wore Grim's veil now. The one she had plucked from his room after finding him gone. After so many weeks of wear, his scent had begun to fade. She supposed that was for the best. She told herself not to be so childish.

Mor huffed dramatically as she scratched behind his ears, stretching out further to demand more. The darling mutt so often whored for attention.

Then time slowed, stretching its incorporeal arms to cover the garden in a sheet of lethargy. The air around them thickened, a weariness pressing down over the courtyard like a held breath. The sky, once bright with the crispness of autumn, darkened as clouds rolled in unnaturally fast, their edges tinged in shades of gray and deep violet. The lilies at the garden's edge, vibrant just days before, wilted in an instant, their petals curling inward and their stems bending. The cool wind stilled entirely. Even Morrigan, who had been so full of life just moments ago, tensed beneath her touch, his ears flattening as his body pressed closer to the ground.

Ilys scowled at the sky and held Mor close.

"My boy," she resigned, pressing her nose to his, feeling the soft warmth of his breath against her veil. "I'll be leaving now."

Morrigan nuzzled against her, but an indulgent unease shifted through his disposition.

She forced a smile, running a hand over his head, smoothing back the fur at his ears. "Be handsome. No mischief, yes?"

Morrigan, in response, licked the side of her face with exaggerated enthusiasm.

Ilys sighed, pushing him away lightly before rising to her feet. She dusted off her robes, her fingers curling into the fabric, grounding herself.

"The satchel, Elspeth."

The attendant stood a few steps away, silent, watching.

Ilys turned, tilting her veiled face at her. "The satchel?"

Elspeth blinked, startled, caught in some distant thought. "Yes. I'm so sorry. I'll bring it now."

Morrigan whined, rolling onto his side, his eyes flicking between them as if he, too, knew what lingered just beyond sight.

She did not look back as Elspeth hurried away. She didn't need to.

She already knew Death had arrived.

Veilmarch had begun.

With satchel in hand, Ilys readied Spire for departure. The mare's restless breath misted in the evening air, hooves shifting against the dirt. In contrast, Death's mount stood unnaturally still, its black form nearly indistinguishable from the shifting tendrils of shadow curling around its legs. Its rider bore a similar smoky shape. The form of a man made up of plumes of ash. Whether out of cowardice or defiance, her gaze avoided his personage.

Ilys swung into the saddle without hesitation. Death did not gesture for her to follow. He did not need to. She clicked her heels, and her horse obeyed, falling into stride beside him. *How obedient and devoted he must find her.* She thought. How disappointed he will be.

The road stretched long before them, winding through the hills, disappearing into the deep gray of the horizon. If she had been expecting a guide, or delicate training (she had not), there was none.

Without turning, without breaking his loitering pace, Death in his godly form spoke, *"Where is the voracious girl from years before?"*

Ilys did not answer. She only stared ahead, gripping the reins, her face hidden behind the veil. Death did not press her.

Hours and hours they rode. The landscape bleeding into another. Ilys's thighs chafed with the prolonged effort of riding, but a piece of her welcomed the distraction from her curdling distaste for the God at her side.

Death rode ahead, his mount moving effortlessly over the uneven terrain. His presence warped the air around him; wherever he passed, the grass yellowed, the trees lost their leaves, and the earth itself seemed to recoil from his touch.

Then, without warning, he pulled his steed to a stop.

"We will stop here tonight."

Ilys slowed her horse beside him, following his gaze to the ground below. The land here subsisted lifeless, dry and brittle. She dismounted, unfastening her pack, already moving through the familiar motions of setting up camp. Her heart tugged as she recalled Grim's lessons. Would nothing be hers alone? Was the man who had abandoned her wrapped up in every action, in every word?

Death did not dismount like a man would, nor did he prepare anything for the night. Instead, he slid effortlessly from his horse, a shift of darkness pooling into itself, his form taking shape against the gnarled roots of a leafless tree. He leaned against its trunk, his body neither tense nor relaxed, his limbs draped unnaturally, like a thing that had never known exhaustion but chose to mimic it for her sake. His cloak unfurled around him, the edges unraveling into mist before they could meet the ground.

He was not flesh. He was not bone. A presence stretched between the two, a shadow that did not breathe, did not shift, did not belong here, yet still was.

"Where is Grim?" Death asked.

She scoffed, impressed by the humility of such a question. Was the god not omniscient? Ilys supposed he needed a mortal to enact his will. She took note of the fallibility and contemplated her response.

"He is no longer in your service."

The unnatural god cocked his head.

"Yes, that is plain. Where is he?"

"Why would I tell you such a detail?" She refused to admit her own ignorance. "Should I reveal it so you may cull him?"

"Where is he?"

"I will not tell you," she ground out. How his voice grated, the icy baritone that flooded her ears.

"Why the bite in your voice, Ilys of the Veil? Why meet your god with such wrath?"

Ilys willed her heart to stop pounding, for the blood to stall in her veins. *Why such a bite, Ilys? Why such wrath?* He need not be omniscient to know such an answer. Baron's voice replayed in her head over and over. The image of his earnest, dying eyes cemented in her brain. She would not warrant such a question with a response. Instead she busied herself with the fire. Placing the wood and kindling as such. Replaying Grim's instructions.

Death, displeased, turned towards the scattered wood beside her. He did not gather it as a man would, did not kneel or reach, but with the barest flick of his fingers, the kindling caught flame, small embers glowing in the growing darkness.

"Is it this form? Does it bother you so?"

Just as he had at the Consecration Rites, the shadow unspooled revealing mortal flesh. Swirls of darkness dissipated to reveal the plush lips and the dark, needy eyes she recollected.

"Is this more to your liking?" Death queried.

Ilys eyed the pale line of his collarbone; just below it, she imagined lay a beating, thumping heart. Her gaze locked onto the tunic stretching over his ribs. How easy it might be to thrust her dagger in between. But she did not know what killed a god yet. She dare not risk his wrath, if her life ending did not also result in his own demise.

She willed her breath towards poise, fighting the burning urge to hurt. To hurt. To hurt.

To wound him as he had wounded her.

No, the only way to discover what killed this god would be through the shared confidence of the god himself.

"Much better," she forced out, molding her lips into what she hoped resembled a friendly smile if he could see such beneath the veil.

He lifted an eyebrow, but relented, appeased.

"Will you now divulge where Grim is?" he asked. "I wish no ill will. I merely inquire into the location of the man who served as my travel companion for the last three decades."

"Would I know, I should tell you. He—" She broke off. "He does not wish for me to know."

Death's dark gaze bore into her, inspecting each word. A curious tilt of his head assured her that he found the answer displeasing. *In that we are agreed,* she thought wryly.

Ilys then ate in silence, tearing pieces from the sun-baked bread she had taken from the kitchens that morning. Across from her, Death watched, unmoving.

"This is your first ride with me." His voice broke the stillness, the spaces between his words feeling vast, measured. "I am sure Grim has taught you much. But I do not like to leave room for the unknown."

Ilys swallowed, setting the remains of her meal aside.

Death shifted uncomfortably. Ilys wondered how he found his mortal body. She hoped the experience was disagreeable.

"Upon our ride, there are tasks we must attend to. For some, I will accompany you. Others, I must leave and address myself. But this first ride..." His voice seemed to darken. "I will abide with you."

He leaned back, resting on his elbows, veins pulsing. Ilys eyed the sight of the blood greedily.

"There is a man raising the dead. His magic is outlawed by the Fates—upending the balance of the Veil. His work must end. It cannot continue. We will find him," Death continued. "You will cut his thread, restoring balance."

Ahhh, the order resolved like a note inside Ilys's head. So this was how orders sounded from the god himself. Accustomed to an Ebon Choir attendant dispersing the order, Ilys found herself satisfied to see his cruelty this close. She felt a sneer tease her lips beneath the veil.

She would not be his puppet. But she would play along.

"Ask me questions," he directed.

"I have none."

"There are always questions. Only a fool moves forward with faith in uncertainty," he condescendingly challenged.

She tilted her head, saccharine sharpness edging her words. "How would you like me to end his life?"

Death smiled placatingly. "I am a god, but I may still sense mortal displeasure."

"No displeasure," she assured. "Only questions. At your request." Once more she queried, "How should I end his life?"

"As you see fit. As Grim has trained you."

Her fingers twitched at the name. "You need not say his name."

Death held his tongue, eyes tracing her.

"I will offer a blessing," she continued, voice flat, measured. "Then I will plunge my sword into his heart and watch as his life drains."

"No need for a blessing."

Her gaze snapped to him. "No matter the deeds, all deserve a blessing."

Death shrugged. "The means are your directive."

Ilys hesitated. She had been taught since childhood that the rites were for the gods. The Fates. The Veil. They were sacred, necessary, woven into the fabric of life and death itself. Now, Death looked down his nose at them? He was unworthy of the divinity, haughty in his power, and out of step. He only sought to prove this more and more.

"Rest now," he ordered. "I will snuff the fire when the time comes."

She bristled at the order. "I will sleep when I desire."

"Mortals need rest. You may not value your life," he hummed, his voice smooth, reminiscent of humoring a child. "But our Bargain dictates that I do."

He eyed her delay in obedience. "You will sleep now," he reiterated.

Tense, she obliged, turning onto her side. She slept feet away from him, her body still, her mind restless. Ilys dreamt of nothing. Instead, she lay in the dark, eyes half-lidded, imagining all the ways one might kill a god.

CHAPTER 18

Outside the city square, Ilys had never seen how the Faithful truly lived.

Along the journey, small villages emerged from the autumn-washed landscape, tucked between rolling fields and dense auburn groves. Smoke curled from the chimneys of flat-roofed dwellings, the scent of burning wood and roasting grain thick in the air. Men and women moved through the narrow streets with purpose, carrying baskets of goods, exchanging hushed conversations. Children played in the cobbled paths, their laughter ringing through the crisp air.

This part of the journey, Ilys loved.

Birdsong. The rustling of trees shedding their golden leaves. The sound of life unburdened by duty, by rites, by death.

But, inevitably, they saw her.

A woman, veiled, draped in black atop a white steed. And beside her, Death in all his godlike glory. Today, it seemed, he had decided to ignore her comfort, donning the swirls of darkness and forgoing the striking mortal face.

Parents hurriedly gathered their children, snatching them off the street and pressing them into doorways. Shopkeepers froze mid-sale, hands tightening over coins or bread loaves, fabric bolts suddenly forgotten. A murmur swept through the villagers, not loud, not panicked, reverent in its fear. The Faithful here were not as familiar with the sight as the crowds in the city. In the capital, the Veilwalkers were an accepted yet hated omen—respected and feared, but known. Here, in the scattered villages, they were another entity entirely, spoken of in hushed tones over bedtime warnings and prayers whispered into candlelight.

Ilys dreaded the moment of discovery. Some knelt at the sight of Death, pressing their foreheads to the cold ground. Others simply turned away, disappearing into homes and alleyways like smoke curling through cracks.

And then there were the rare ones, the ones who scowled, who stood their ground, who spat at their feet as they passed.

Death did not react. Neither did she.

"The next village is where we will stop," Death dictated. *"We will find him there."*

Before she could bite her tongue, the question slipped free. "How do you know this?"

Death turned his head, his gaze settling on her. She could not see his face beneath the shifting darkness of his hood, but his posture, the way the air seemed to still around him, told her he was amused.

"Ahhh, now the questions arrive."

Ilys scowled, spurring Spire into a faster pace beside him.

They came to the next village, its outline no different from the ones before. Stone cottages, timbered rooftops, narrow streets. Each village bore the same bones, but this one felt wrong. An eerie quiet lay in the cobblestones, thick as fog. Flies buzzed in dense clusters over forgotten waste, the stench of rot curling through the air. The few villagers who lingered outside moved like shadows, their eyes downcast, their steps hurried.

"Deeper in," Death commanded.

They trotted forward, their horses' hooves echoing against the stones. Beneath the hum of wind and water, Ilys heard life: small, hurried movements behind doors, the occasional dull thump, the scuff of footsteps that vanished before they could be placed.

They turned a corner, following the narrowing path to the end of a lane.

"There," Death nodded.

The air soured around the house, thick and tainted, pressing into Ilys's lungs like an oppressive cloth. She swallowed against it, nausea curling low in her stomach. Her horse whinnied, bowing its head from the sight of the dwelling. Her grip on the reins tightened.

Death dismounted and entered without knocking.

Inside, the home held a modest sitting area. A table sat to the side with untouched plates still set atop it, the contents of a meal long since decayed littering their surfaces. A small wooden shelf sat against the far wall, its few belongings knocked askew and coated in dust. In the center of the room, a chair had been overturned, a half-burned candle spilled onto the floor beside it.

The noise came suddenly—a dull, rhythmic pounding from above, each strike rattling the beams overhead. Ilys's hand instinctively flicked to the hilt at her side. Death's dark form angled upward as though he could see through wood and stone. They climbed the narrow staircase, each step groaning beneath their weight. At the landing, the air thickened. The smell struck her first: iron and rot, cloying, sour.

The landing opened to a small shuttered room. Scrollwork and runes had been etched into the floorboards, curling in unnatural spirals of ink and ash. Their lines seemed to crawl, as though still alive, and in the center lay horror.

Two women were naked and bound, their skin marred with shallow wounds. Cuts designed not to kill, but to mark. To hurt. Their eyes flicked to Ilys as she entered, wide with terror, though no sound left their lips. They trembled like frightened animals.

But the third figure that made her stomach twist. A waxen-skinned body lay slumped before the scrollwork, her chest unmoving, her gray and glassy eyes open, animated though vacant. She was dead, but not gone.

Death moved first. His vast shadow bent low, a gentleness in his inhuman hands.

"*Hush,*" he whispered to the body, coaxing an essence unseen. From her parted lips rose a ribbon of smoke, soft and silver, curling upward into his waiting palm. He closed his fingers around it as though soothing a child, and the gray in her eyes faded to stillness.

"What have you done?" Ilys's voice wavered. "What did you do to her?"

The deity did not look up. "*I have restored her soul to the Veil. Whoever wrought this magic dragged her back from peace and tethered her to the husk of her flesh, forcing her into torment.*"

The words struck like ice. "She is dead?" Ilys pressed her fingers to the woman's throat, desperate, searching for a pulse that would not come.

"I restored her peace," Death bit out, his voice edged with what might have been anger, might have been pity.

Ilys swallowed down her horror, forcing herself toward the living. She dropped to her knees beside the women, hands working the knots that bound them. Their wrists were raw, their bodies shaking under her touch.

"Who has done this?" She tried for an empathetic tone, but the women only cowered, eyes fixed on her with silent dread.

Death's voice broke through the air, low and resonant. "*Whoever wove this has left. I cannot sense their magic here any longer.*"

Ilys kept her focus on the women, ignoring the bile in her throat. "You will be safe now. I will see you to your families. Come—"

They stayed rooted, their wide and unblinking gazes locked on her, as if her voice had never reached their ears. She reached for one of them, desperate to ease the tremors in her shoulders.

"You are free," she promised. "You are safe."

The woman flinched back, dragging the other with her, and both pressed against the wall, shuddering.

Ilys observed this, unease tightening her posture and confusion swirling in her head.

Death's command filled the room like thunder. "*Come, Ilys. No one seeks the aid of a Veilwalker.*"

Her breath caught. She looked at them, at those fearful eyes, the way their bodies shrank from her touch. A hollowness spread through her chest. She straightened, stepping back. Without another word, she turned and followed Death from the room, swallowing her guilt and drilling her duty into her skull once more. A million times.

No one sought the aid of a Veilwalker.

She only brought more Death.

Ilys looked back once, the house shrinking to a smudge against the horizon as they rode. Ahead, Death moved with relentless purpose, tracking the unnatural scent like some otherworldly hound. The land grew harsher as they pressed on; crags rising out of the earth, hills rolling into one another, the road narrowing to a pale ribbon beneath the dimming sky. Death never glanced back, never checked if she followed, fatesbent on his mission.

"Death," she called, her voice cutting against the night air. He did not stir. "Death!" she yelled louder now, a ragged edge in her throat.

Her body ached. Her eyes stung and betrayed her, closing without consent. He had sworn early in their journey that he would guard her mortal needs. Yet now, she faded, her head heavy on Spire's neck. At last, his shadow stirred, breaking from its trance. He turned, taking in her slumping form.

"We will rest at the next village," he assured her.

Under the star-shot night, roofs soon rose ahead. She watched as Death shed his godhood piece by piece, his mortal form appearing, donned for convenience she imagined. He rode into the dark like any other man. She supposed he wished to draw less attention. Yet, with a Veilwalker at his side, there would always be stares. Before they reached the homes, he dismounted in the shadows of the outskirts.

"Take that off," he demanded.

Her hands flew instinctively to her veil. "Absolutely not."

Dread climbed her throat. No. She would not. It was not done.

"You will rest better indoors," he pressed. "They will not serve a Veilwalker. Do you remember those women's eyes upon you?" Ilys flinched at the memory, fingers tightening on the fabric.

"It is against Veil law," she hissed.

"It is inconvenient," he ground out. "I care for no such laws. Take it off." He enunciated each syllable, dark gaze bearing into her.

Her blood boiled. A low growl escaped her as she pulled the veil free and tucked it into her satchel. Fear shot through her with the movement, sharp, electric. Was it fear of breaking the law? Of angering the Fates? Or being seen?

Death flinched at the sight of her wide eyes, her pink lips, her squirming as he took in her personage.

I hate you, she thought to herself. *I hate your eyes upon me.*

He cleared his throat, leading the way towards the inn after stowing the horses in the stable.

Inside, the inn purred, thick with the scent of roasting meat and wood. The fire in the hearth burned low, barely tended, while the air sat stagnant with the quiet lull of a place accustomed to transience. The innkeeper barely looked up as they approached, his attention fixed on the dented mug he looked to polish. A broad man, thick-browed, he wore the expression of someone who had seen too many faces pass through to bother caring about any of them.

"What do you need?" he asked, voice flat, uninterested.

"Two rooms," Death indicated, flashing two long fingers.

The innkeeper snorted, still not bothering to meet their eyes. "I have one."

Death's jaw ticked. "Then one."

The man finally glanced up, taking them in with the same mild disinterest as he might a dull gray sky. "Are you planning to stay together?"

"With but one room, I suppose," Death ground out.

The innkeeper nodded, but his eyes lingered a second too long. "Are you married?"

Death did not react, did not blink. "Will that change the availability of the room?"

The man studied them for a moment longer before shrugging. "I do not house whores." Ilys felt the shift beside her before she heard it, Death's sapped inhale, controlled, measured.

Clipped in the tone, Death took the hint and embellished, "We are married."

The innkeeper gave an absent grunt, already moving to jot a note into the thick leather book on his counter. "Late supper is served here shortly. You don't show, you don't eat." He nodded towards a stairwell. "First door on the left."

Death did not reply, only turned sharply on his heel, moving toward the stairwell with rigid efficiency.

Ilys followed, smirking as they reached the steps. "That was painless."

His gaze flicked toward her, still dark with the remnants of restraint. "Would you rather I had argued? Drawn out the time between you and a pillow?"

She shrugged, pushing the door open to their lodgings. The room unfolded into a plain scene, like most inns in towns like this, with sturdy wooden furniture, a single small window, and a washbasin tucked in the corner. A single bed sat against the far wall.

Ilys dropped her pack onto the floor and immediately sat at the edge of the bed, pulling off her boots. Her feet ached from the long ride, and she rolled her ankles, sighing. She walked to the basin, dipping the cloth provided in the balsam scented water, washing her face. She stared into the mirror at her skin, wiping under eyes and down her throat.

Death stood in the doorway, stalling, before stepping inside, setting down his pack and removing his coat. She caught him watching her. She hadn't meant the act to look sensual, but the water felt so good on her bare skin. So breathable. So free.

"We will leave at first light," he said, coughing. At some point, footsteps sounded outside the door, voices carrying from below.

"Supper?" she asked awkwardly.

Death stood without a word, rolling his shoulders. Ilys followed, and together they descended the narrow stairs, the scent of roasting meat thick in the air.

The inn's dining room materialized quietly, save for the soft strumming of a lyre in the corner, its delicate notes blending with the low murmur of voices from the few other patrons scattered throughout the room. The fire in the hearth crackled occasionally, its warmth a welcome contrast to the chill outside.

Ilys leaned back, fingers tapping idly against the worn wood of the table. The day's ride had been long, and though exhaustion hadn't fully taken her yet, she could feel it dragging at the edges, waiting to settle in once she let her guard down.

The innkeeper arrived without ceremony, setting down two steaming plates of food along with two pints of ale, the liquid dark and thick, foam spilling over the edges. Death pushed his back.

"I'll have water," Death requested, his voice as even as ever.

The innkeeper barely spared him a glance. "You'll drink the ale." Then he walked off.

Ilys smirked, lifting her pint with one hand. She admired a man who denied Death. The smell hit her first: earthy, bitter, and strong. Strong was an understatement. She took a tentative sip, then let out a short breath, the taste commanding.

It was rank. Potent. Likely brewed in a barrel older than she was. And yet, it warmed her instantly, the almost immediate buzz settling in, a low hum in her veins. She welcomed it.

Death, on the other hand, looked disgusted.

She watched, fascinated, as he took the smallest sip, his expression tightening in clear displeasure. He set the pint down as though it had offended him personally.

"Have you never enjoyed a spirit?" Ilys asked, bemused.

Death's gaze flickered toward her, unimpressed. "What need does Death have of spirits?"

She rolled her eyes and turned back to her plate.

The simple meal filled her, stew thick with root vegetables, a hunk of coarse bread, and a sliver of salted and cured meat. Across from her, Death moved with the same precision he always did, methodical even in a task as mundane as eating.

But she noticed things.

His hands, long-fingered and strong, moved more naturally now, absent of the eerie stillness they once held. He gripped the spoon like any man would and tore his bread like someone accustomed to the humdrum hunger. His brow, usually furrowed in thought or indifference, had smoothed as though he had unknowingly relaxed into his mortal form.

And then there were his eyes. Dark as ever, but they lacked the strange, depthless quality they once held. He looked at her rather than through her.

She found herself staring.

Then his gaze flicked up to hers. Her face burned with having been caught, stomach fluttering in embarrassment.

Ilys quickly focused on her drink, tipping back the last of the ale. It remained terrible. She grimaced as the sharp bitterness clung to her tongue, but she felt the warmth crawl up her spine, settling into her limbs. The edges of her thoughts softened, her movements looser, easier. She blinked across the table, watching as Death finished his own pint, more out of necessity than enjoyment, it seemed. He drained it with the expression of someone enduring rather than partaking, and its effects were immediately noticeable. His shoulders, always tense with quiet restraint, had loosened. His usual razor-sharp focus blurred at the edges. The drink had reached him, relaxed him.

Stop staring, Ilys admonished herself.

Instead her tongue, unbound from her usual caution, sought out a question that had been nagging. "What is it like?"

He arched his brow, tone dry. "What?"

"To be a god," she mock-whispered, leaning in. "And then to be mortal."

He stared at the ceiling, contemplating. "Wrong," he said at last. "It feels wrong."

"Why? In what way?" she queried further.

"I can feel my godhood tugging at me. And I can feel my vulnerability."

Her pulse spiked. Baron's face pressed into her memory, eyes everywhere in the room. Heat rose from the drink, filling her chest. "And are you?"

He turned his head toward her, exhaling. "Am I what?"

"Vulnerable?"

His gaze lingered, suspicion knitting into his features. He seemed to sense the eagerness in her, the sharp glint in her eyes.

"Why ask such a question?" His defenses stirred, the faintest edge in his voice.

Her breath caught, but she forced composure, smoothing it with a coy smile. "I am but your servant, Death. Would you have me ignorant of your weaknesses? What a poor protector I should be."

He hummed low in his throat, still studying her, but finally relented, "It is the cost of mortality. In the flesh we feel pleasure, and pain, and we can be drunk." He lifted his cup, swallowing to prove the point. "But it is when we are at our most vulnerable. That weakness always drives us back to our godhood, as the Fates would have it."

"You could fall, just like this?" she pressed, gesturing faintly, praying her eyes did not betray the murderous ache in her heart.

Baron. Baron. His name thundered through her blood.

Death's expression softened, unexpectedly somber. He reached across, curling a strand of her hair around his finger. "I could, yes."

A beat. Then he hummed, and threw his head back in sudden, tipsy, startling laughter.

Struck by the strangeness, she pressed him. "What?"

He smiled, almost fond. "I've just remembered where I know this inn from."

Ilys narrowed her eyes, suspicion tugging at her. *What game did he play now?*

"Has Grim told you of our time in Hirth?"

She shook her head in response.

Death grinned, tilting his cup , watching the dregs swirl. "We passed through here once, years ago. A miserable place. Always wet, always cold. I don't think Grim spoke a single word for three days. We were tracking an immortal. Someone careless, leaving signs of their work like breadcrumbs. It should have been easy." Death paused, amusement flickering in his gaze. "It was not easy."

Ilys waited.

"We opted to blend in. Stopped at this inn." He gestured vaguely to the room around them. "It was packed. A man singing, traders gambling, drunkards loud enough to wake the dead." He let the words settle. "Grim endured." The slight lilt at the end of his sentence told her he had enjoyed saying it.

"One of the men, drunk, bumped into Grim. Spilled ale down his sleeve. Started throwing a fit about Grim being in his way."

Ilys raised a brow, fighting a smile.

"Grim listened," Death continued. "Didn't react. Took the insult, took the spit to the face. Wiped his sleeve off and let the man feel like he'd won." Death tapped a finger against his cup.

Ilys tilted her head. "That's Grim," she noted wryly.

Death smirked."That's what I thought. But the next morning, the entire inn woke to the man screaming because a horse had shit in his bed."

Ilys choked on her ale, a chuckle surprising both of them.

Death swirled the last of his drink before finishing it off. "The moment we stepped outside, Grim started laughing. Lost his mind." He shook his head. "That was when I realized he had done it. He had put it there."

Ilys pressed a hand over her mouth, stifling a laugh. "How?"

"I did not ask." Death's expression fattened into thoughtfulness as he watched her, his dark gaze flickering with earnest mirth.

Ilys traced the rim of her cup, absentmindedly.

"He spoke of you often," Death noted, his dark eyes hazy at the edges, his usual precision dulled by the drink. "He was impressed. Proud."

A flicker of a smile ghosted across her face, but the warmth of it collided with a juvenile ache. The sentiment naturally juxtaposed through the medium of evil that spoke it. That, and Grim's absence nipped at her. She turned her cup between her fingers. Death had plucked at a soft spot of hers. She willed her hatred to rise again.

Baron, she thought. *He killed Baron.*

Death leaned close to Ilys, his warm breath brushing her cheeks.

"I'll tell you what," he whispered. "It's probable this tastes just as that horse shit did." He pushed the cup toward Ilys, knocking food off the table with the movement, a knife clattering to the ground.

The innkeeper gave them a wary glance from across the room.

"Hush," Ilys reprimanded under her breath.

Death smirked, holding up a single finger to her lips. "Hush," he mimicked, grinning as though he had won a great and grand prize.

Ilys swatted his hand away, but her brows furrowed as she watched him, her amusement fading into concern.

"You're drunk," she whispered, half in shock.

He waved a dismissive hand. "Mortals are weak." He gestured vaguely at himself. "Including this one."

She tilted her head, studying him. *Was he slurring?*

"By the unbound," she muttered, unable to stop watching as he derailed in real time, his limbs loosening and lazing.

"I could fall asleep at this table," he confessed.

Ilys sat up straighter. "You should go to bed," she advised warily.

"Yes."

He pushed himself to his feet, only to sway dangerously. She barely caught him before he could crash back down. She braced herself, wrapping an arm around his waist as she hauled him upright. Together, they made their way up the narrow wooden staircase, his weight leaning more heavily into her with every step. By the time they reached the room, he had given up on dignity entirely, letting her half drag him toward the bed.

She deposited him onto the mattress with a huff, brushing her hair out of her face. He flopped onto his back, exhaling deeply, like a man relieved to be at peace with his fate.

Ilys, meanwhile, grabbed her sleeping mat, rolling it out onto the floor. *Indoors is enough of a luxury,* she reasoned.

"For a god, you should be embarrassed right now," she quipped, adjusting the thin blanket she had pilfered from the extra linens.

Death hummed against the pillow. "I should be so many things," he sleepily whispered.

She moved to leave him to whatever strange state of half-consciousness he had found himself in, but before she could fully turn away, his hand shot out, catching her wrist. With surprising strength, or perhaps just desperation, he pulled her down beside him, his arms securing around her like a snare.

"Ilys." His breath blew warm against the hollow of her throat, his voice softer now, slurred but clear. "Please don't kill me yet."

She stilled. Her pulse thrummed against her ribs as she took in his slackness.

How convenient. Her blade sat mere inches away. Death lay indisposed.

She could slit his throat now. Drive the dagger between his ribs. End him while he dozed pliant and human.

She thought of it. Thought and thought, her fingers flexing, muscles taut, the will coiling through her like a strike held back. And still, she hesitated.

Baron's face rose in her mind, his crumpled body, lifeless. Her breath caught, claustrophobia pressing the walls in tight. She would never see him again. She missed him. She could not have him. Grief, raw and gnawing, always there. And it was his fault.

This man.

This god.

His fault.

Tears burned at the corners of her eyes, bitter with hatred.

And then Grim. Grim with his secrets, the pieces of him she would never know. All of it locked inside the creature before her, the god who knew everything of Grim that she did not.

She stared at him long and hard. *Tomorrow,* she promised. *Perhaps tomorrow.*

But tonight... tonight her gaze lingered too long. Her body, heavy with grief and drink, betrayed her resolve. Sleep bled into the edges of her thoughts, until it pulled her under, stealing the decision from her hands entirely.

Chapter 19

Ilys stirred beneath the quilt, sleep hanging on her skin like fog. The room was dim, dawn barely creeping through the small window, painting the wooden walls in soft gray light. She blinked once, adjusting to the quiet, and then she realized she wasn't alone.

Death was pressed hard up against her, one arm slung heavily over her waist, his breath warm against the curve of her neck. His body, solid and unfamiliar in its closeness, caged her in, his grip asleep but firm.

Her mind raced through the events of the night before. The drink. The stumble up the stairs. The way he had pulled her down with him, drunk and unaware of what he was doing.

And now here they were.

She eased herself back, inch by inch, hoping to slip free without stirring him. But the moment she moved, his hand found her again, tightening by instinct.

She froze. For a brief, terrible moment, she thought he was awake. But when she tilted her head, peering at his face, his expression remained pliant, peaceful in a way she had never seen before.

A god, undone.

Her heartbeat pressed hard against her ribs. Then, with calculated precision, she eased herself from his grasp, rolling off the bed and onto her feet. Her body ached from the awkward way she had been lying, but she ignored it. She needed to move, to put space between herself and whatever that had been.

From behind her, Death stirred. She turned just in time to see his eyes open, dark and heavy-lidded with sleep. For a second, he simply stared at her, trying to piece together where he was, what had happened. Then his brows furrowed, and he rolled onto his back, pressing a hand to his face.

"By the Unbound," he groaned, voice hoarse.

Ilys crossed her arms. "Feeling mortal?"

He let out a long exhale, dragging his hand down his face. "It is unpleasant." Then the shuffle of fabric as he stood, the groan of protest from his body barely concealed.

"You're slow this morning," she observed.

"You poisoned me," he countered.

She smirked. "The innkeeper poisoned you."

Death surrendered a reply, only straightening his coat and smoothing the fabric as though willing his appearance to resemble order.

Ilys, watching from where she adjusted the strap of her pack, couldn't help but smirk. "Come," she said, nodding toward the door. "You can lament your poor choices on the road."

Death shot her a look but didn't dignify her with a response.

They descended the stairs, the inn still quiet in the early morning. The scent of wood and faintly stale ale lingered from the night before, mixing with the aroma of breakfast. Ilys strode toward the meager offerings laid out on the table: rough bread, soft cheese, and a thin porridge. Little worth savoring, but warm enough to be welcome. She grabbed a hunk of bread, tearing a piece free as she turned to Death. He had stopped at the bottom of the stairs, composure fixed in place, but the way his jaw tensed was telling.

Ilys lifted a brow, gesturing toward the table with her bread. "You should eat."

Death flicked a glance at the food once, then dismissed it with a quiet shake of his head. "I'll see to the horses."

The morning outside was crisp, the sky painted with thin streaks of pale blue. She inhaled deeply, adjusting her cloak, pulling it closer against the cool air as she made her way toward the stables.

Then she saw him.

Death stood beside the horses, tall and composed, his godhood restored. No longer the man from the night before. No longer the one who had laughed with her over ale and stumbled up the stairs, who had pulled her close as he mumbled drunken confessions.

He was himself again. Dark, seamless, untouched by mortal things. His face smoothed into that careful neutrality she'd learned to dread, the faint stir of shadow curling around him.

Ilys halted, watching him. "I thought we were trying to move discreetly."

Those divine eyes bore into her bare face, carving meaning.

She rolled her eyes, pulling her veil from her bag, donning it once more.

Arsehole, she thought, staring at his back. *Murderer.* Her mind hurled the words like a stone. *I hate you. I hate you. I hate you.* A song of violence thrummed in her skull, a litany reminding her of his trespass, his unworthiness, his disregard for law.

Her distaste only grew as she followed the god. *Next time I will not be so weak,* she vowed. Rage burned through her veins, carrying her forward for hours, until Death finally raised a smoky hand to halt the horses.

Tucked back behind a cluster of trees, smoke curled from the chimney of a lone stead. Without a word, Death turned his horse off the road, angling toward it.

Ilys's pulse fluttered in her throat. Whether born of her own body or conjured from the air around them, she felt the dangerous hum return, wrapping them both.

Death dismounted, leaving his steed untethered. Ilys glanced at Spire, whispering silently, *Stay,* before slipping to the ground and following Death to the door.

The floor groaned beneath their steps, old wood betraying her. Ilys moved as quietly as any mortal could, but no one was as quiet as Death. The cottage was modest, almost neat. A black cloak with gold trim lay draped across the square table in the front room.

But then came the flies. They swarmed the air in thick black ribbons, their hum deafening, curling around the room's true horror.

The closet door had been left ajar.

Bodies. Four of them, piled upon one another, twisted at unnatural angles, their limbs overlapping, tossed carelessly into the small, dark space.

All women.

All disrobed.

Their skin was sallow and pale, their lips cracked open in silent, frozen gasps. Their eyes, hollow and glassed, caught no reflection at all.

Ilys's breath hitched beneath her veil. The scent was overwhelming, thick with rot, sickness, and the unmistakable metallic tang of blood that had been left too long in stagnant air.

Death moved through the home, his presence settling over the room like a judge.

"Upstairs."

She heard it then, the muffled rustling. There was a soft scrape of movement above them, a low mutter, the unmistakable sounds of someone there.

Her stomach lurched, but quietly, Ilys crept behind Death, her steps light, breath shallow, her fingers flexing at her sides. From behind the first door, muffled grunts spilled into the air.

"Not this one," Death directed.

Ilys faltered. *Not this one?* Had he not heard the noises, the muffled cries, the faint scraping? But Death pressed forward, and she followed, her eyes wide.

The next door stood cracked with a thin sliver of candlelight trembling through the gap. Death pushed it open, the hinges groaning in protest.

The space inside was cluttered and small enough to be suffocating. The air reeked of old parchment, spent wax, and coppery, foul smell beneath it. Symbols scarred the stone walls, jagged and desperate, carved as though the writer had been frantic.

At the center knelt a cloaked figure. His face was hidden, his body bowed over a corpse. A woman lay before him, her skin pale as wax; yet, her chest rose. Fell. A sluggish, unnatural rhythm. Her dull, milky eyes flickered as though some trapped thing tried to peer through.

The man stiffened at their intrusion. In an instant he was up, whirling, diving for the window.

Death moved fast. The figure crashed to the ground with a sickening thud but staggered up and fled around the front of the house. Death leapt after him, vanishing into the night.

"Now, Veilwalker," his disembodied voice rang, sharp.

Ilys cursed, following. She hit the ground hard, pain jolting up her legs, leaving her limping as she pushed after him. But already the man had mounted Spire, cloak billowing as the horse carried him into the dark.

"Fuck," shouted Ilys, watching as her mare disappeared. "Fuck!" she screamed.

Death landed on his own steed, extending a hand. "Hurry, Ilys." His hiss curled like smoke.

Her leg screamed with each step. She glared at him, teeth bared.

"There are people inside," she bit out.

"He is our priority."

"If you are so eager to flee, perhaps *aid me*, you arse." She gestured sharply at her gait. Death wheeled his horse closer, his hand still offered. But she ignored it, jaw set. "He is well and gone now. Pause our pursuit, and let us tend to those who remain."

"Veilwalker." The warning cut hard and silvery.

Ilys scowled, a small, dangerous flame kindling in her chest at her own refusal. "I will not pursue him until we have addressed whoever remains inside."

The deity, with his supernatural glower, relented. The air still buzzed with his anger, sharp as static, but he dismounted and followed her inside. Her limp slowed her, and he overtook her easily. Up the narrow stairs, he halted before the door, gesturing for her to enter first, like this were some gathering she had forced him to attend rather than the likely prison of the suffering.

The room was much the same as the last. Three girls bound, their faces pale with terror. This time, Ilys tempered her approach, kneeling, voice soft.

"You are safe now," she promised, working at their knots with careful hands.

Two of the girls shrank back, trembling. But the youngest, no more than fifteen, flung her arms around Ilys's waist, sobbing into her robes.

"Thank you," she whispered. "Thank you."

From the corner, Death's gaze bore into her, cold and unblinking.

Ilys waited until the girls were clothed, then guided them outside. She apologized for not being able to return them herself. When she looked to Death, asking for his mare, she felt only the echo of his haughty laugh in the back of her mind. He gave no answer, turning from her as if she had never spoken.

The girls stumbled down the road, murmuring that their village was near, their hope sparked by Ilys's description of the land.

"You are unfeeling," she spat once they were gone, her words sharp as steel.

Death turned his head, considering her. When he spoke, there was no anger, only certainty.

"I am Death. I feel nothing. I want nothing. I am." He held out a shadowy hand, one that turned to flesh when she grasped it and he helped her astride his mare. *"Thanks to your diversion, you will have to find sleep in my arms. Our pursuit will pause no longer."*

Hatred surged in her chest, a tide she could not quell. *Diversion?* His disregard for mortality, for mercy, was boundless. She dreamt of a thousand ways to kill him—blade through his throat, dagger in his ribs, poison slipped between his lips—until the violent catalog blurred, softened, and sleep stole her against his chest as they rode.

Chapter 20

They traveled the entire next day as the sun was dragging itself across the sky in a laggard, punishing arc. Death pressed forward without pause, relentless, allowing her only the barest mercy to relieve herself before forcing her back into the saddle. Her muscles burned, her spine ached, and still he did not relent.

By dusk, the shadows lengthened, and his temper frayed. The air around him crackled, the edges of his form blurring with agitation.

"*I have lost him*," he cursed, the words a low snarl spat against the wind.

Ilys blinked, heavy-lidded with exhaustion, but his fury sharpened her attention. She almost smiled at it—his failure, his rage.

By the time the village lanterns flickered in the distance, Death slowed his mare. The mortal guise had already settled, dimming the cold brilliance beneath. As they reached the outskirts, his hand suddenly shot ahead. Without warning, he wrenched her backward against him in the saddle and masterfully undid the veil pins before tugging the fabric from her head.

Ilys gasped, instinctively reaching for it, but he didn't so much as glance at her. He crammed the veil into her satchel with brutal efficiency, the gesture cold, final. Then he released her just as roughly, his grip shoving her back into place.

Her scalp prickled in the night air, hair exposed, her face bare. She burned with humiliation, fury sparking in her chest, but he rode on in taut quiet.

When they reached the inn, he dismounted first, not offering her a hand. He tied off his horse, claimed two rooms without a word, and dragged her forward when she faltered, as though she were cargo, not company.

The innkeeper behind the counter scrawled with a ledger open and a stub of charcoal poised in hand. He looked up as Death approached.

"Two rooms," Death said flatly, dropping a stack of coins onto the counter.

The innkeeper wavered for a heartbeat, then slid two keys across the wood. Death scooped them up without acknowledgment, turned, and thrust one into Ilys's palm with a rough shove before striding upstairs.

He did not look back. His door slammed hard enough to rattle the walls, leaving her veilless and seething in the corridor.

Her chamber was small but clean: a narrow bed, washbasin, and single candle singing against the wall. She shut the door hard, dropped her satchel to the floor, and tugged at the ties of her cloak with shaking hands.

She readied herself for bed, movements stiff, mechanical. Boots unlaced. Cloak folded. Dagger laid on the table within easy reach. Each motion failed to cool the heat under her skin.

Because he was right there.

Through the wall's frail boards, his presence seeped—Death, silent and self-satisfied, inhabiting the next room as if the night had left no mark. As though ripping her veil away, parading her bareheaded into the inn, had been his right.

Her hatred seethed, a tide she could not turn back. She hated the way his shadow still clung to her, the way his mortal form seemed to make him more insufferable, not less.

His mortal form, she realized. *His mortal form*.

Her pulse surged. Not tomorrow. Not later tonight. Now.

The dagger was already in reach. She snatched it up, the feel of it grounding her as her breath came quick and sharp. Every excuse she had fed herself before—hesitation, timing, fear—burned away. He was right there, flesh and blood. This was her chance.

She rose from the bed, her bare feet meeting the wooden floor. Her gaze stayed fixed on the door and the sliver of hallway that led to him. She would not wait for the inn to sleep, would not give herself time to falter. She would do it now while her resolve still burned hot and merciless.

Her mind ran through the act in crisp, merciless detail. Slip inside and press the dagger to his throat before he stirred, then one quick slice, and the blood would come. Or, she would drive the blade between his ribs, pinning him to the mattress before his godhood could claw its way back.

She could almost see it already; the shock in his eyes, the stillness that would follow, the vacuity of a god brought low.

Her hand tightened on the hilt. She stepped toward the door.

Now.

The door creaked as she slipped inside. His mortal form lay sprawled on the narrow bed, chest rising in the sluggish rhythm of sleep. The dagger was slick in her grip, her palm greased with sweat.

She crept closer, one breath, then another, until she and the weight of Baron's death hovered over him.

She drove the blade down.

But his hand shot up like lightning, catching her wrist before it could plunge. The dagger wavered, caught between them. He pushed, she pressed, the silent struggle dragging her down onto him, the bedframe groaning.

His dark eyes snapped open, human and startled. She clamped her free hand over his mouth, stifling his sound. He wrenched at her wrist, trying to keep the blade from his chest. She pressed harder, teeth bared, the dagger trembling inches above his heart.

She wanted him *dead*. Every nerve in her body screamed it.

He rolled, twisting, forcing her to the side. The mattress shifted, the wooden frame shrieked. She tightened her hold—trying to stab, slash, anything—but he was stronger, faster, even in flesh. He kept shoving the dagger away from his vital places, his grip bruising her wrist, his knee pinning her thigh.

They muffled their grappling, both desperate to keep the inn oblivious. Her breath rasped through clenched teeth, his jaw set tight. She nearly got him once; the blade grazed his collarbone, shallow but hot. He hissed, clapping a hand over the wound to keep the blood from spilling against the sheets.

"I will kill you," she breathed, venom sharp as steel.

"Ilys," he warned, grounding out, "you need me."

"I will kill you," she promised, voice raised and will ironclad.

He met her eyes, holding her wrist still. And then, softly, laboriously, he said, "When I came for his soul..." His voice was a whisper, low and unrelenting, even as they struggled. "I felt you. I learned all of you. Every last thought of his... was you. Baron worried endlessly for you."

The words gutted her. Her strength faltered, the dagger quivering. Memories clawed at her chest: Baron's smile, Baron's hands, the way he looked at her. Her vision swam, fury and grief tangling until she couldn't breathe.

Death twisted, using her hesitation. He pinned her wrist hard against the mattress, the knife finally wrenched from her hand. It clattered to the floor.

Thrashing beneath him, tears hot in her eyes, she snarled, "You lie."

"I have no need to," he whispered. "What does this solve, Ilys? Killing me? Then who will lead you to the ones who twist the dead? Who will sense the foul magic when it stirs again?" His eyes searched hers, dark and endless. "Would you condemn them, the women you freed, to the same fate? Bound, carved, reanimated, their souls dragged screaming back into flesh? Over and over for a mage's sick pleasure?"

Her chest heaved, the image stabbing her mind. She could see them again, the trembling girls. The gray, vacant eyes of the corpse. Her throat closed, grief splitting her open once more.

"I hate you," she spat, the words torn raw from her.

"I know." His voice softened. "But now you must learn to use me."

For a long moment, she lay beneath him, her heart pounding like a drum of war, fury and sorrow tangled until she could scarcely breathe. His grip was unrelenting, the heady press of his body inescapable. And worse, his words had struck true.

Chapter 21

The night before clung to her skin like a bruise. The dagger slipping, his weight pinning her wrists, Baron's name twisted into a weapon. Neither had spoken of it yet. Now she sat stiff in front of him, his mortal form pressed close at her back, his hands wrapped around her to grip the reins as their monstrous steed devoured the road. Every jolt of the saddle reminded her how easily he had subdued her. How near she had come to ending him. How near she still might be.

Her resolve hardened with every mile. She would follow him until the necromancer was found; After that, she would strike again.

The hills broke open into salt and light, the sea stretched wide and restless below. A town clung to the shoreline, its rooftops black against the white waves. Death slowed the horse so its hooves settled to a halt just above the ridge.

"He is here," he directed. "But cloaked. We must be cautious. I will not have him run again."

Her pulse quickened. "You sense him?"

"Faintly. Something masks him." His voice was tight, distant. "That alone makes him dangerous." He paused, contemplating.

His breath brushed her ear. "I must collect. You will remain here."

Her grip tightened on the pommel. "You mean to leave me? Alone?"

"You will establish yourself," he said, ignoring her protest. "You and your husband were separated. You live near the border, where the skirmishes have begun. Note that he is bound to meet you shortly. I will come and meet you here in seven days."

Her brow furrowed. "Skirmishes?"

Death's gaze swept the horizon, shadow darkening his jaw. "Do you know nothing of the war that wages?"

Her voice rose. "I know some."

"Many have been displaced. It is a fine enough story for a woman traveling alone," he assured her. Death pressed on. "Find work. Root yourself. Endear yourself if you can—though I doubt it."

And then, with no warning, his hand tore the veil from her head, stuffing it into her satchel with a single, brutal motion. Her breath caught, her scalp prickling in the open air.

"You will not wear it here."

She stiffened, fury flooding her cheeks.

"I will return in seven nights."

Before she could bite back a retort, he shifted. The steed shuddered beneath them, its form already unraveling into shadow. He lifted her from the saddle without strain, setting her aside with the care one gives an unwanted coat.

And then he was gone, the horse dissolving into smoke with him astride it, leaving her veilless, alone, and on foot above the seaside town, the silver wash of the sea gleaming far below.

Ilys picked her way down the craggy path with hesitation. How strange, she thought, to have longed so fiercely to be rid of Death, only to find that now, alone in the world, she wished for anyone's company. *Endear herself?* The words mocked her. How was it even done?

A flock of sparrows cut across the sky above, darting through the sea wind like arrows. Her chest ached as she watched them vanish into the horizon. To be so free. The path narrowed, funnelling her toward the bustle of the market. The acrid reek of fish struck first, clinging to the air. She balked, panic tightening her chest, and slipped quickly behind a building. *Just a moment,* she told herself. *Only a moment.*

She rehearsed her story in a whisper, shaping her voice to be warmer and more human—or at least, what she imagined humanity to sound like. Words about her "husband," about separation and loss, rolled stiffly from her tongue. She tried again, softening, gentling, forcing vulnerability into her tone.

"Are you okay?" The voice startled her, rough-edged with a coastal accent. It came just as she thought she had found the perfect note of grief.

She spun, heart in her throat.

A young man stood there, auburn-haired, the rust-red color catching in the light. The sight struck her like a blow as Baron's memory slammed unbidden into her mind. She could not look away. Entranced, undone.

He stepped closer, frowning at the dazed set of her eyes. "Miss, are you okay?"

Ilys blinked, the words of her false story scattering from her lips like startled birds. "I... I am fine," she stammered, though the sound of her own voice irked her; it carried too much of herself, too much truth, and not enough of the careful mask she had rehearsed.

The young man tilted his head, concern softening his expression. His eyes, green shot through with amber, caught the light in a way that made her chest tighten painfully. Baron's eyes had not been the same, not truly, but grief distorted everything. It stitched old wounds onto new faces.

"I just—" she tried again, catching herself, forcing vulnerability into her tone. "My husband. We were separated." The words, practiced only moments before, came easier now.

His expression sharpened, no longer just concerned but intent, as though the words *husband* and *separated* were a call to arms. He stepped closer, lowering his voice.

"Separated how? Here in town? Along the coast?" His gaze flicked past her shoulder, scanning the street as though her husband might stumble into view.

Ilys's throat tightened. "No—near the border."

"The border?" His brows knit, fire sparking behind his green-gold eyes. "Gods. With the fighting there..." He swore under his breath, eyes searching hers again. "Was he taken? Drafted? Hurt?"

Her pulse tripped. The story she had whispered to herself now pressed down on her chest, demanding more shape, more flesh. "We lost one another on the road," she confessed falsely. "There was shouting...smoke. I do not know if he—" She let her voice tremble, let the unfinished thought hang heavy between them.

"Come," he urged, already half-turning as though to lead her. "My uncle is well connected with the guard. He'll send word, and we'll know if your husband's passed through anywhere."

The earnest promise struck deep in Ilys, warming her despite herself. *Was this truly how people treated one another?* Or was it only because she was a woman alone and adrift?

Her gaze studied him, and the illusion faltered. He looked nothing like Baron, not really. Different jaw, different eyes, different voice. She admitted, grudgingly, that his selfless urgency, the way he leapt into action without hesitation, was...attractive.

Arriving at a cramped dockside storefront, the man slid a scrap of parchment and a stub of charcoal toward her.

"Write down his name. His appearance. Anything that will help."

Ilys stalled, the false story snagging in her throat. She had not meant it to carry this far. Her fingers hovered over the parchment, stiff and unwilling. His expectant gaze pressed down on her until she bent to write.

Jorrin. The name came first, sharp as a wound.

She paused, heart hammering, and added a surname her mind seized on in desperation, one she had heard Baron mutter once when cursing a guard captain. *Marrek.* Jorrin Marrek. The letters looked wrong, alien, but the lie was sealed.

The man leaned close, scanning the name, and gave a short, decisive nod. "I'll get this to my uncle. He'll see it reaches the guards."

He looked back at her. "Where are you staying?"

Ilys's stomach knotted. "Nowhere. My husband has all our coin."

His brow furrowed. He studied her a moment longer, wary but not unkind. "Perhaps my sister can house you for the night. I'll ask her."

Relief washed through her, though she bowed her head with feigned humility. Inside, she cursed Death bitterly for not giving her even a single coin to shore up the ruse.

The man folded the parchment into his jacket. "Stay near the market. I'll find you in a bit."

"Wait," she called, and he turned back. "Your name?"

"Owin," he answered. "Yours?"

Ilys hesitated, her mind scraping for another lie, another mask to wear. But she was tired and unpracticed in the art of make-pretend.

"Ilys," she said at last. No one outside the castle would recognize it, she assured herself.

Owin gave a short nod. "Stay near the market. I'll find you soon." And then he was gone, leaving her with the smell of salt and tar thick in the air.

Ilys wandered the market, attempting conversation with vendors. At first they greeted her readily enough, but the moment they realized she carried no coin, their warmth vanished. She felt the shift each time, the polite smile turning brittle, the tone growing curt.

She drifted farther down the road, murmuring to herself that she would return in a bit. Surely Owin would not come back so soon. The market noise faded behind her as the sea opened before her, vast and endless. She had never seen the coast before. Never seen water stretch beyond the horizon, swallowing the sky. On impulse, she stooped to pick up a stone, skipping it across the surface until it vanished. The gesture felt foreign, childlike, but she couldn't help herself. She slipped her boots off and waded in until the cold lapped at her toes. Her thoughts turned to Grim, and she spoke to him in her mind. *It's just like you described,* she noted. *It's perfect.*

The sea spray kissed her face, and she smiled, eyes stinging from the salt. She loved the roar of the waves, how it drowned out everything else. The ocean was a jealous creature, she thought: loud, consuming, demanding her whole attention. *You will feel me. You will hear me. You will know me,* the waves seemed to say, each crash against the rocks a promise. And she let it take her; hair whipped by the wind, skirts dampened by spray, the sea's cold insistence drawing her wholly into the moment.

A palm on her shoulder plucked her back into reality. She turned and found it belonged to Owin.

"You look like a sea witch," he teased with a quick laugh. How long had he been standing there, watching? Her expression must have betrayed the thought, because he added quickly, "Sorry. I did'na mean to startle you."

He stepped up beside her, gazing out at the waves. "My uncle's already sent word. We'll hear soon enough. And, my sister agreed to put you up for a couple nights." He tilted his head, considering. "She's a bit ornery, but she's decent."

Ilys thanked him, startled at how natural the words sounded on her tongue.

"Rare," she observed out loud, "for strangers to extend such kindness."

He only shrugged. "My family's always believed in the greater good. Folks in hardship should look after one another."

"Oh—" He snapped his fingers, remembering. "There's a revel tonight. Food, drink, dancing. You should come."

Her chest tightened. The thought of it—the crush of bodies, the laughter, the stares—made her skin prickle. She already felt stripped bare without her veil; the idea of thrusting herself into a crowded celebration...

"I'm not sure—"

"I know," he cut in gently. "With your husband still missing, it must be hard. But it's free food. A pint of lager. Could help."

She forced a faint smile, though inside she recoiled at the thought of so many eyes fixed on her.

"I'd be honored to attend."

"Grand," Owin said with a grin. His gaze flicked over her muddied hem, the salt-stiff fabric of her dress. "My sister will likely lend you something clean. I can introduce you to the lot before we head over?"

More strangers. More words I don't know how to say. Wonderful.

"That would be lovely," Ilys replied evenly.

The lane wound down toward the cluster of stone cottages, roofs thick with thatch and smoke trailing faintly from a few chimneys. Owin led Ilys to one, its doorway set low beneath the eaves, and rapped his knuckles against the wood, firm but unhurried.

No answer. He knocked again, louder this time.

From within came a muffled curse, "Fucking hell. I'm coming!"

Owin flushed, the tips of his ears turning red. He shifted awkwardly, glancing at Ilys with a sheepish half-smile.

The door swung open to reveal a woman, broad-shouldered, her apron streaked with flour and ash. Stray curls of dark hair clung to her brow, and her sleeves were shoved up past her elbows. Her eyes, sharp and assessing, swept over Ilys from head to toe.

"So," she drawled, one hand braced on the doorframe. "This is the married little thing that's caught my brother's eye." Ilys stiffened, but before she could muster a reply the woman turned on her heel. "Well, don't just stand there gawping. Come in."

She led them into the dim warmth of the cottage, where the air was thick with peat smoke and the yeasty scent of baking bread. A round loaf cooled on the table, steam curling from its cracked crust.

"Don't touch the food," the woman said flatly. "It's for paying customers. Owin tells me you've no coin."

Ilys blanched, heat pricking her face. So much for Owin's talk of hospitality. She hadn't even looked at the bread.

"Kara," Owin cut in quickly, "could you lend her one of your dresses for tonight?" At once, Ilys saw the shift in the woman's posture, her shoulders stiff and jaw tight. Kara's smile was sharp as a knife.

"Do you have any other requests for your sister? Lone mother to three hungry mouths? Perhaps I should fluff her pillows come morning too?" Her tone was all sugar; her eyes were ice.

Owin gestured Ilys toward a chair by the hearth. "Sit," he directed, before following Kara through a side door, promising over his shoulder, "Just a moment."

The words were muffled but heated, like sparks hissing in a banked fire. Then came silence, long enough for Ilys to shift uneasily, before Kara's footsteps stomped deeper into the house and Owin's tread returned.

"Sorry," he said, lowering his voice. "The family had a rough go of it. Kara's...a bit sensitive."

"I don't want to be any trouble," Ilys promised quickly. "Please–"

He cut her off with a small shake of his head. "We lost our brother, and then her husband a couple years back. She can be hard to crack, but she's happy to help. Truly."

Just then Kara's voice rang out from the back. "Bring the waif back. She'll look a proper fool in my gowns with those wee titties of hers. I like mine with room for swinging."

Owin closed his eyes and tipped his head back with a groan, half chuckle, half defeat. "I'm sorry," he offered, exasperated.

Ilys couldn't help a laugh. "Best deliver her these itty things, then." She rose and followed the sound of Kara's voice toward the back room.

The room was cluttered, its corners stacked with baskets of mending, half-finished garments, and a washline strung with drying shirts. Kara stood in the middle of it, arms folded, her sharp gaze pinning Ilys as soon as she entered. She held out a plain dress, roughspun but clean, the color of river clay.

"Try it," Kara said, her voice flat. "If it fits, you'll wear it. If it doesn't, we'll cinch it with rope."

Ilys took the dress carefully, her fingers brushing the coarse fabric. "Thank you."

Kara's eyes narrowed. "Don't thank me. I'm not doing this for you. I'm doing it because my brother's too soft-hearted to turn away strays." Her gaze swept over Ilys, sharp and prying. "You don't look like any wife I've ever seen. Where's your ring?"

"Lost," Ilys answered smoothly, forcing a veracious ring. "I lost it in the skirmish."

Kara gave her a long, skeptical look, then rolled her eyes. "Put the dress on. We're leaving shortly." She stormed from the room, her steps heavy on the floorboards. But Ilys heard her voice, low and cutting, through the door as she joined Owin in the hall.

"She's a fucking liar, Owin. Dunna say I did'na warn you."

Chapter 22

The revel had begun. At first, it was restrained. Voices were low, movements careful. Long wooden tables were set along a stone lane between the cottages, piled with roasted fish, dark loaves of bread, and clay pitchers of ale. Smoke from braziers curled into the salt-wet air, mingling with the scent of seaweed and brine. The houses around them glowed with torchlight, their whitewashed stone walls and thatched roofs stark against the starry sky.

Ilys lingered near the edges, uncertain. She had never seen such a gathering. Neighbors greeting neighbors with claps on the shoulder, laughter easing into the night air. A fiddler sat on a low stoop, plucking a dilatory, lilting tune, his bow sliding gently across the strings.

Then the ale took hold.

The music quickened, the fiddle grew sharp, and the drumbeat deepened. Hands clapped, boots stamped, children wove through the crowd. Someone danced atop a table, skirts flying, drawing cheers from the circle around her. The narrow street rang with voices, laughter, and wild, salt-stained joy.

Ilys stayed back, watching.

"Could you be any more unwelcoming?"

She turned. Owin leaned against a cottage post, a cup dangling loosely in his hand, cheeks already flushed from drink. His grin was boyish, softened at the edges.

"What?" she asked.

"You stand like you're waiting to be judged." He squinted at her, head cocked. "Ramrod straight. Eyes too sharp. Makes folk uneasy."

Her brows drew together. "This is how I stand."

"Aye, and it's eerie," he said, laughing, tipping back his cup. "Like you see everything."

She narrowed her gaze. "Your tongue is loose."

"That's what the ale's for." He bowed his head in mock gravity, then set his drink aside and, without warning, caught her wrist. "Come."

Ilys stiffened. "Where?"

"To dance you."

She frowned. "Dance me?"

"Dance *with* you," he corrected, dismissing his own slip with a wave. "Come, come."

Before she could argue, he tugged her into the crush of revelers. The music surged around them, fiddle shrieking, drum pounding. He spun her into the center, light and loose from drink.

"With the drums," Owin urged, nodding to the beat.

Ilys tried, but her movements were stiff, each step inelegant.

"Not like a nun," he teased, dodging her clumsy foot with a laugh. His hands shifted to her hips, coaxing. "Like this, you see?"

Heat rose to her face, but she followed, letting the drum carry her. Bit by bit, she yielded. Her body softened into the rhythm, her steps matched his. The world blurred into firelight and music.

Owin grinned. "There you go. Good girl."

She shot him a sharp look, but the praise warmed her all the same.

The revel swelled to chaos—torches throwing sparks into the night, ale spilling from lifted cups, feet stomping hard against the stone. Owin twirled her, pulled her close, his touch easy but sure. She realized, to her surprise, she liked the way he touched her—without command, without demand.

Someone clapped Owin on the shoulder as they passed. "Who's the girl?"

"A traveler," Owin answered smoothly.

"Traveler from where?"

Owin gave an exaggerated shrug. "North."

The man barked a laugh and stumbled off, losing interest. Owin only smirked, pulling Ilys back into the circle.

They danced until her head spun and the music seemed endless. Finally, Owin steered her aside, breathless with laughter. He poured more ale into her cup, topping his own, and leaned close to be heard above the noise.

"Are you nervous," he slurred softly, "because it's against the law?"

Ilys blinked. "What?"

"This." He leaned in and pressed a soft, drunken kiss to her lips.

She froze. Her heart lurched. "Why would that be against the law?" she asked, awe-struck, dread prickling beneath her skin. *Did he know she was a Veilwalker?*

"Because you're married." Owin laughed in her ear, breath hot with ale.

Her expression steadied, the panic ebbing. He didn't know, not truly.

He pulled back, wagging a finger at her. "I don't really believe you're married. When Kara asked about your ring, you were strange. All of you is strange."

Before she could answer, his hands molded over her hips, drawing her closer. She had forgotten how much she loved to be touched. She was like a kitten preening for attention, starved for intimacy.

"I think you lied," Owin murmured, a grin tugging at his mouth, "because women don't travel alone."

Her throat worked. "And if you're right?"

His smile turned wicked. "If I'm right, then you should stay with me tonight, instead of my crotchety sister."

He bent and pressed a soft kiss to her collarbone, his laughter rumbling low against her skin. The warmth of Owin's breath lingered against her skin, but then, over his shoulder, she saw it.

Black. An ebony gilded cloak moving where no cloak should be, stark amidst the swirl of color and sweat. Her blood went cold.

Ilys pulled back from Owin sharply, his laughter still spilling against the din of the revel. Her gaze fixed on the figure weaving through the throng, the dark hood dipping just out of sight. She shoved past him, ignoring his startled protest, and pressed into the crush of bodies. Her heart slammed against her ribs. *It couldn't be. Here?*

The cloak slipped through the revelers with uncanny ease, swallowed and revealed again by the crowd's shifting dance. Ilys strained after it, every muscle taut with urgency. Her satchel snagged on the corner of a table. The strap wrenched her shoulder back with a violent tug.

"Damn it—" She yanked at it, fingers scrabbling against the leather. The strap caught on a wooden mug, upending it, ale spilling down her side.

By the time she tore herself free, the figure had ducked behind a man hefting a cask on his shoulder, vanishing deeper into the press of people.

"Ilys!" Owin's voice rang out above the revel. "Ilys, where are you going?"

The sound of her name froze her mid-step. Its timing was a curse.

The black cloak ahead of her turned. For the briefest moment, the crowd parted, and the torchlight struck the man's face.

Lord Veylen.

Ilys's breath caught like a knife in her throat. His Ebon Choir ring was absent, but she would know that cruel, elegant face anywhere.

The press of bodies swallowed him again. She shoved forward, only to collide with Owin.

He caught her arm, laughing. "Ilys, you dropped your satchel."

Her stomach dropped. The satchel lay between them, its contents spilled in the dust.

Owin bent to gather them, still chuckling, until his hand closed on black fabric. He drew it free, the torchlight catching its folds.

Her veil.

The laughter drained from him, eyes widening and confusion clouding to a darker, heavier emotion. "Ilys," he questioned, the name breaking in his throat. "Oh, Ilys..."

She froze, heart slamming, panic and fury crashing together. Behind him, the revel raged on, but all she saw was Veylen's face vanishing into the crowd. Her quarry—her ruin—slipping away.

Owin's voice grew cold, raw with disbelief. He pulled her dagger from the bag, its blade catching the light. He lifted it to her chin, pressing until the point nicked skin.

"Get on your knees, Veilwalker."

The crowd roared with music and drink, blind to the truth unraveling in their midst. Ilys stood caught between two revelations—Veylen at the revel before her, and Owin, the man who had been soft and kind and drunk with laughter, now her captor.

CHAPTER 23

Ilys sat on the cold stone floor with her wrists bound and ankles loosely tied. The rope had rubbed her skin raw, though she barely felt it anymore. A single oil lantern flickered on a crate, throwing long, skeletal shadows across the walls of the abandoned mercantile hall.

It had been a day, maybe longer, since anyone had come for her.

Her mind kept circling back to how she had come to be here. The revel's roar still clung to her ears: fiddles shrieking, boots stamping, drunken voices laughing loud enough to shake the stars. She had been chasing a glimpse of black through the crowd, Veylen's cloak cutting like a blade through the blur of bodies. She remembered her satchel spilling, Owin's laugh as he stooped to gather it, the way his hand stilled when he pulled the black veil free. The way his face changed, disbelief curdling into cold hostility.

Then the dagger at her chin, his voice raw with betrayal. *Get on your knees, Veilwalker.*

The crowd had gone on oblivious—dancing, shouting, drinking—while he dragged her away. To them, he had looked like any drunk man pulling his companion home.

She remembered the side streets slick with mist, the cobblestones glistening under torchlight. His grip on her arm like iron, the press of his blade when she twisted too sharply. Now, here she sat, bound in the dark, the memory gnawing at her.

It had been a day, maybe more. No food, no water, no sign of him. Her wrists ached, the rope coarse and unrelenting, but she had begun to work at it; tiny twists of her hands made the slightest friction where the fibers had begun to fray. It was heavy-footed work, maddening work, but above all, a distraction. Every scrape sent fire through her skin, but she welcomed the pain; it reminded her she was not wholly powerless.

The lock scraped.

Ilys stirred, blinking against the dim flare of lantern light as the door swung inward. Owin stepped inside, closing it behind him with a quiet click. He carried the lantern low, its glow cutting across the floor, painting his face in tired lines. For a long moment, he only looked at her.

"You've been quiet," he said at last, his voice low, rough. "I thought maybe you'd try screaming. Or praying. Anything."

Owin wheezed, his shoulders rising and falling with the effort. "I keep seeing it. That night in the square. The fire. The screaming. Six men dragged into the light." His jaw tightened. "My brother among them. My sister's husband. And you—" His throat bobbed. "You did not hesitate."

Against her will, the memory rose.

The city square, lit red as a furnace. Smoke choking the sky. Six men forced to their knees, the crowd pressing at her back like a living wall. She had lifted her blade with Death's command burning in her ears, every muscle straining against the will that held her. Their eyes still haunted her—pleading, furious, broken. And when the last body had fallen, the mob had surged. She remembered the first fist slamming into her ribs and the stones hurled at her veiled head. Hands clawing, teeth snapping, the roar of hatred threatening to rip her limb from limb. She swallowed hard, blinking the smoke from her eyes even though it was years gone.

"You think I wanted that?" Her voice cracked, harsher than she intended. "You think I long to be the hand of the Bargain I never chose? I nearly killed myself for those deaths. Do you not see? I am bound. A pawn. I carry out the will of a god who delights in cruelty."

Owin stepped closer, lantern light flaring across his face, twisted with grief. "Pawn or not, you held the blade. You looked at my brother and still slit his throat. Might you not have thought twice? Even for a heartbeat?"

Her chest heaved. "And if I had? What would it have changed? Death's hand was on mine. His voice in my skull. I am not free to choose."

His breath hitched, rage twisting with mourning. "You could have spared him a second's thought. That is all I ask." His voice dropped, hoarse. "One second."

Ilys's hands curled against the rope at her wrists. She forced the words out, raw, "I will kill Death. I swear it. I was always planning to. I want to end this Bargain."

Owin's jaw worked, his eyes hard, but suffering wavered at the edges.

"You talk like you're human," he rasped at last, his voice breaking. "But all I see is the King's butcher. No woman. Just a vessel of evil."

Tears stung, burning tracks down her cheeks. "I *am* a woman," she whispered fiercely. "I was a girl, and now I am a woman. I am human. I falter. I fail. Hate me, I understand, but know this: I am not Death."

The lantern swung with his movement, casting long, jagged shadows across the walls. His hand lingered on the doorframe, his shoulders taut. But he did not speak, turning to leave and pulling the door shut, the lock scraping home.

Later, the lantern had burned low, its wick nearly swallowed, the light a frail, stuttering thing on the crate beside her. Ilys's head drooped against the wall, eyes half-lidded, her body aching from stillness, her wrists raw from the rope's constant bite.

The rough drag of the lock pulled her upright.

Her pulse quickened. *Owin*, she thought. He was back again with more venom, more grief to hurl at her. She braced herself, but the man who stepped through the door was not Owin.

Her breath stopped.

Lord Veylen.

He moved with a casual grace, the lantern he carried held high, throwing sharp shadows across his face. The same face she had seen in the revel, hidden beneath a black cloak, cruel and unforgettable. He closed the door behind him, the lock sliding in with a deliberate click.

"Well," he drawled, his voice smooth as oil. "So it's true. I thought perhaps the boy had been mistaken, but no—here you are. The King's little monster."

Ilys's throat tightened. She kept her silence, staring, unwilling to give him the satisfaction of a reply. Veylen stepped farther into the room, the lantern swinging lazily at his side.

"Do you know how easy it is to buy entry here?" He smiled thinly. "A few coins, a promise or two, and even the sanctity of your prison becomes negotiable." He tilted his head, watching her carefully. "For enough coin, we're even allowed to take a turn with you. Did you know that?"

Ilys's stomach knotted, rage rising hot in her chest. She forced herself to meet his gaze, unflinching.

"Yes," he went on, as though savoring the words, "that boy loved his brother. What a beautiful way to honor his legacy, don't you think? Delivering his killer into my hands."

Her voice cracked as she finally spoke. "Why?"

Veylen raised his brows, mock-surprise flickering across his face. "Why?"

Her jaw clenched. "Why the girls?"

For a baleful moment, words eluded him, but then Veylen smiled—a dragging, joyless smile.

"Because I want to," he said simply. His voice lowered, intimate and cruel. "Because I can."

Ilys's hands curled into fists against the rope at her wrists. The fibers scraped her already-raw skin. She felt the faintest give beneath her fingers. She clung to it, small and secret, even as hatred burned in her chest.

"You're vile."

He chuckled. "You'll forgive me if I don't take moral counsel from the Crown's executioner."

Veylen crouched before her, close enough she could smell the faint spice of wine on his breath, the cloying perfume clinging to his cloak. His eyes glinted in the half-light, sharp and merciless.

"You know," he said softly, "I've always admired you. Not for your skill—though you do cut a striking figure—but for your obedience. Your absolute, pitiful obedience. You never flinch. Never question. Not even when you were made to slaughter the innocent."

Ilys bared her teeth.

He lifted a hand, fingers brushing her cheek. She flinched, jerking away as much as the ropes allowed.

"Don't," she hissed.

He laughed, low and amused, tracing the line of her jaw with a featherlight touch before dragging his fingers down to her throat. She struggled, twisting against him, her bound ankles scraping against the stone as she tried to shift away.

"Stop," she snapped, fury rising sharp and hot in her chest.

His hand lingered, pressing lightly against her pulse. "Ah, there it is," he whispered. "The fight. The little flame you've hidden under all that obedience."

Her breath shuddered in her chest. She tried to jerk back, but his weight leaned into her, pinning her against the wall. His thumb pressed beneath her chin, tilting her face upward.

"Look at you," he breathed. "A blade turned inward, cutting yourself long before you cut anyone else."

She twisted violently, slamming her shoulder against his chest. He only laughed, catching her wrists even though they were already bound, holding her tighter.

"Keep fighting, Veilwalker," he encouraged. "It makes no difference. Bound or free, you are mine to play with."

Her teeth clenched, hatred burning her throat raw. "I will kill you."

Veylen's smile widened, predatory, dropping her wrists. "Oh, no. Killing is reserved for my arsenal alone. I'll kill you in a thousand different ways before that day comes. Hurt you. Delight in you. Break you."

Tears pricked her eyes, hot with fury, fear, and revulsion. But beneath it all, her wrists twisted again, scraping and fraying at the rope. Her only weapon left.

The door groaned.

At first, Ilys thought it was another guard, another tormentor bought with coin. The hinges creaked, the lantern flame guttered with the draft, and Lord Veylen turned his head just slightly, irritation flickering across his face.

That moment was all she needed.

Her wrists twisted sharply, harder than before, skin tearing against the frayed rope. The binding gave way with a sudden snap. She lunged, seizing the loose coil and whipping it around Veylen's throat before he could react. His eyes widened in shock as she yanked him down, slamming the back of his skull against the stone wall with all her strength.

The impact rang out sickeningly, reverberating through her bones. His body bucked, his hands clawing at the rope as she held it tight, her knees digging into his chest to pin him.

Her breath came in ragged sobs, each one trembling with rage and panic.

And then—

A shadow leaned against the doorframe, half-hidden in the lantern light. A man, ordinary in form, but his presence twisted the air itself. Calm, composed, utterly out of place. His voice was low, measured, familiar as a dirge.

"Veilwalker," he greeted. "What a strange reunion."

Ilys's head snapped up, hair plastered to her face, tears and sweat mingling. Her chest heaved as she choked Veylen tighter, her knuckles white on the rope.

"Dagger," she panted out, desperation shredding her voice. "Give me your dagger!"

The man stepped into the light, mortal in shape, Death in every shadow at the edges of him. Without hurry, without judgment, he drew a blade from his belt and placed it in her trembling, blood-slick hand.

She nearly dropped it. Her arms were shaking, her grip raw and uneven, but she held the rope fast with one hand, her elbow braced against Veylen's thrashing shoulder.

Veylen gagged, gasping, spit bubbling from his lips. His nails raked bloody lines across her forearms as he fought for breath, but she only pulled tighter, the rope cutting deeper into his flesh. His eyes rolled, whites stark against the lantern glow.

"Do you need help?" Death asked softly, as though offering assistance with a chore.

"No," she rasped.

The hilt trembled in her grip as she found her aim. With a guttural cry, she plunged it into his side, the blade slicing through flesh with a wet sound that turned her stomach. Warmth gushed over her hand, keen and hot, while Veylen convulsed violently beneath her, his body arching as though to throw her off.

She wrenched the blade free and drove it in again. This time higher. His breath hitched, a broken wheeze, blood spilling from his lips. He gargled, choking on it as she twisted the dagger hard. The rope kept him against her, his throat crushed, his body pinned between her fury and the wall. His blood soaked her hands, sprayed across her chest, hot against her throat as it poured. She stabbed again, and again, her breath ragged, her eyes wild.

Finally, his body sagged, spasms weakening into twitches. The dagger slipped in her grip, her hands slick with red. She held the rope tight a moment longer, panting, hyperventilating, her vision tunneling until all she could see was his lifeless face. Then, slowly, she raised her head. Death stood a step away, watching, his mortal face composed. Ilys trembled, every breath a broken gasp, the dagger clutched in her bloody fist.

Death's mortal hand reached down, fast and inexorable. She scowled, but let him pull her up. Her legs nearly gave, and for a heartbeat she leaned into him, her forehead brushing the edge of his shoulder. His body was solid, unnervingly warm in this form.

He felt her shaking, her breath breaking against him, and—awkwardly, as though the motion belonged more to memory than instinct—he rubbed her back. A stilted rhythm at first, then firmer, the feel of his palm drawing her closer.

"Shh," he soothed, the sound rough and uncertain in his throat. "You are safe now. Shhh, shhh."

The words, so alien in his mouth, stirred her. She had been strong for so long, hard and sharp and unbending, but the gentleness—clumsy, halting—unraveled her. For an instant she let herself collapse into it, clutching at his tunic with bloodied fingers.

Her chest heaved. She pulled away sharply, wiping her eyes with the heel of her hand as though she could erase the weakness he had just seen.

Death's gaze lingered. "Come," he said at last, his voice low, threaded with urgency. "Before the rest arrive."

He guided her out the door, his grip firm but not cruel. Ilys barely had time to gather her bearings before a hand seized her arm.

A blade kissed her throat.

Owin. His eyes were red-rimmed and his chest heaved as he held the knife hard enough to nick her skin.

"I'm going to kill you," he rasped.

Death shifted. His form blurred, shadows curling at the edges, his godhood seeping through like fractures in the air. His voice resonated, deeper, ringing with command.

"Release her," he thundered.

But Owin only tightened his grip, the knife pressing deeper, a bead of blood blooming on her throat. His voice cracked, raw with anguish. "Give me back my brother!"

The air split with Death's power, but his voice was grave, stiff. *"You ask for something no one can give. No one should give. Would you wrest your brother from his peace?"*

Owin's face contorted, tears streaming as he pressed the blade harder. His sob shook his words. "He never should have died," he cried out, anguish overtaking him, and in that desperate heartbeat he began to drag the knife across Ilys's throat.

Death moved faster.

His mortal hand gripped the hilt of his own blade and plunged it deep into Owin's chest. The sound was wet, final, the force of it staggering them both. Owin gasped, blood spilling from his lips, the light dimming in his tear-soaked eyes. He dropped at Ilys's feet, the knife falling from his grasp with a metallic ring.

But the cost was immediate.

The shadows that wrapped Death began to tear loose, smoke curling and unraveling from him in wild, violent tendrils. A high, ringing sound pierced the air, vibrating in Ilys's bones, rattling her skull. Her ears throbbed with the pulsing, the unnatural hum swelling like the toll of some unseen bell. Death staggered, his form flickering between god and man, half-shadow and half-flesh. He roared, the sound shaking the air, rattling through the stones beneath them.

"Ilys—" his voice distorted, *"run."*

She stumbled back, shielding her eyes from the storm of smoke. "What is going—"

"I said *run*, Ilys!"

The roar cracked the air itself, sending her reeling. Through the chaos, through the whirling storm of smoke and sound, she caught only a glimpse of him: his face twisted, his godhood ripping at the edges of his mortal skin.

His voice struck again, louder than the din, ringing like a bell through her skull. *"Return to the Sanctum!"*

The words hit her like a blow, leaving no room for argument, no room for thought. The Sanctum. Home. Obedience drilled into her bones.

Ilys stumbled into the night air, the salt of the sea clinging to her tongue. Her eyes darted frantically, searching the dark. *Spire.* She could not return without her. Veylen had taken her; he could have loosed her to the wilds, or worse...

Her pulse spiked. She moved quickly, keeping low and pressing herself into the shadow of buildings. The dress she had worn for the revel was plain enough, but now it was torn and bloodied; every passerby would notice. Any glance might become suspicious. She hugged close to the walls, slipping through alleys, ducking behind fish crates and drying nets. Here, between shuttered shops and dark corners, every sound was sharper; the clatter of boots on cobbles, the shift of doors against salt-wind. She kept to shadow, her breath sharp, each heartbeat a hammer in her throat.

"Spire," she whispered once, a prayer more than a call. She froze, listening. Nothing. Just the tide's hollow drag against the docks.

She forced herself onward, slipping between two leaning sheds where sea-grime coated the stone. Then—there. A faint scrape, the restless shuffle of hooves against cobble. Her head snapped toward it, and she crept closer, crouching low, until at last a pale flank broke through the dark.

Spire.

The mare stood tethered behind a broken cart, reins left to dangle, her coat streaked with salt-dust and grime. Her ears flicked at Ilys's approach, nostrils flaring, but she did not bolt.

Relief hit Ilys so hard her knees weakened. She pressed her palm against Spire's warm neck, burying her face briefly in her mane.

"Good girl," she whispered, her voice ragged. "Quiet now. Quiet."

She checked the alley and found it still empty, no lantern light cutting her way, no footsteps chasing. With shaking fingers, she loosed the reins. Her bloodied dress caught and tore against the splintered wood as she hauled herself up, her palms raw on the rope, but she scrambled into the saddle.

"Go," she hissed. Spire lunged forward, hooves striking sparks, the night peeling open before them. Ilys hunched low, guiding her into the deepest dark, skirting light and sound where she could.

The Sanctum. The command rang in her bones, relentless. *Return to the Sanctum.*

CHAPTER 24

Ilys spoke no word of Lord Veylen.

Not when she returned to the Sanctum, mud and blood stiff in the hem of her plain dress. Not when the King summoned her, his gaze sharp, searching for truths she would not give. She held her tongue.

At first, Lord Veylen's absence drew little notice. The court was accustomed to his disappearances, his secretive errands carried out beyond the palace walls. But when the next summons came, and the herald called his name before the gathered lords, no Veylen stepped forward.

The murmur that followed spread like an ambling fire through the chamber. Within days, the King's herald stood in the courtyard and read aloud the decree: a warrant for Lord Veylen's arrest. He was to be taken alive if possible, slain if not. Treason, it was called. Betrayal of crown and faith alike. Ilys listened from the shadows, her hands folded, her veil hiding her face. Her secret pressed hard against her chest, a truth she could neither speak nor swallow.

She knew the truth; he could never be arrested, never brought in chains before the throne, for she had already driven the dagger into him. And still, she did not speak.

Veylen's death, and the foulness that had clung to his deeds, had left her with incertitude lodged beneath her skin. Doubt. The men who preached from gilded pulpits, who raised their hands as if the Fates themselves spoke through them, they were not divine. They were fallible. Oh, so fallible.

Her eyes lingered on the Ebon Choir with suspicion. Her voice faltered in prayer. Even the rites felt hollow on her tongue. A wariness had rooted itself in her bones, and though she tried to bury it, it grew, unsettling her with every passing day.

It was in this state of unease that she dined with the King.

The chamber was dim but warm, the table set with silver and heavy plates, and the scent of roasted venison and herbs hung fervid in the air. Ilys sat across from him, her veil in place, the cloth pulled low over her mouth. She ate as she always had, lifting morsels delicately, slipping food beneath the folds with practiced precision. Veilwalkers were taught to make even this graceless act seem ritual, dignified.

The King spoke idly at first, praising the preparation of the meal, remarking on the crispness of the greens, the tenderness of the meat. His voice was light, almost kind, as though they dined as father and daughter rather than sovereign and executioner.

Then, as he set down his goblet, his tone shifted. "Death has sent word," he said.

Ilys stilled, her fingers pausing at the edge of her plate.

"He tends to the Fates. The Bargain is intact," the King continued, his voice carrying across the table like judgment dressed in silk. "But he will not return to finish the Veilmarch. He says only that he will send word when he plans to return." The King gave a low, amused laugh, shaking his head slightly as though at some private jest. "Have you unsettled him, my dear? I have never known Death to be unreliable."

Ilys let the words wash over her, but she did not let the event leave her mouth. She did not tell him of Veylen. She did not tell him of the blood in the shadows, of Death's unraveling. She was not sure why the truth lodged in her throat like a stone.

The King prattled on about the wine, about the difficulty of securing venison this late in the season, the color of the figs. She sipped her drink in silence, nodding where politeness was required, the veil concealing her expression.

Then, abruptly, he set down his cup. "With the time you've been given back, I have thought long and hard," he said. "I think you should choose a successor."

Ilys blinked, her voice level though her chest tightened. "A successor? I am able-bodied. I am young. Is there a need?"

The King's lips pulled faintly downward, a frown tugging at his full mouth. His gaze lingered on her, studying her as if he might peel back the veil itself.

"Where is the reverent girl from years past?" he asked.

The King chewed his venison, his teeth working the meat before his face twisted with displeasure. He spat the gristled tissue into his napkin, grimacing.

"The Fates ask it," he said finally. His voice hardened, stripped of warmth. "It will be done." He dabbed his mouth, then rose, adjusting the folds of his heavy robe. His eyes lingered on her one last time, cold and expectant. "Mother Inrith will walk you through the process. See it done by the next moon, Ilys."

He stood, pushing the plate away. "I think we are done, yes?"

She mirrored his stance, smoothing the veil down with collected hands. "Yes, my shepherd."

The next day, when Mother Inrith summoned her, Ilys went without protest.

They sat across from one another at a narrow table, a single candle guttering between them. Inrith's presence filled the chamber, her veil dark as mourning cloth.

"There is a ritual, of course," Mother Inrith directed. The candlelight traced the deep lines of her face. "The Bargain was sealed in blood, and so blood must guide the choice."

"You will drink," Mother Inrith continued, her dark eyes fixed upon her. "As it was in the first days, so it is now. The blood of the first Bargain, passed from Veilwalker to Veilwalker, unbroken until the end of all things."

Her stomach twisted. "And then?"

"You will enter the chamber," Mother Inrith explained, lifting her cup as though in illustration, though she did not drink. "It is a narrow room, bare stone, with a single wall shared with the adjoining hall. On the other side, the faithful will gather. One at a time, they will be led in to stand against that wall while you wait in silence."

Her voice lowered, even, ritualistic. "You will not see them. They will not see you. That is the order of things. You are the hand of the Fates, not the judge of men. You will listen. You will wait. When the Fates stir within you—when the warmth fills your marrow, when your bones know what your mind cannot—you will strike the wall three times." She raised her hand, rapping her knuckles softly on the table. *Thump. Thump. Thump.*

"That is the signal. The attendants will remove that one and bring them to the altar. No sight, no question, no hesitation. You feel. You know. You choose."

Ilys's chest tightened. "And if I feel nothing?"

Mother Inrith's expression did not waver. "You will feel it. All Veilwalkers have. Grim before you. His master before him. The Fates are mysterious, yes, but they are constant in their ways." She leaned back. "It is not yours to decide, child. It is only yours to obey."

When the moon rose to its mark, the Sanctum stirred to ceremony.

And so she stood at the altar, the cup before her, dark as the void between stars. The liquid inside swished, laced with spice, but she knew what it meant to symbolize. The first blood spilled in the Bargain. The first sacrifice. The first Veilwalker who had drunk and been chosen.

It was strange, walking a path so carefully paved and feeling no wonder for where it led. Her fingers brushed the cup; hesitation answered, low and animal in her chest.

The faithful watched from below the altar, submissive in attentiveness. Their faces blurred together into a single faceless entity, encouraging Ilys to shut her eyes.

Let it be done, she prayed. *Let the Fates see. Let them guide my hand.*

The liquid burned against her tongue, rich and too old, carrying centuries within it. It settled into her stomach with warmth that felt more like a stone than any sanctitude. She swallowed, and lowered the cup.

The ceremony had begun.

The chamber unfurled compact and dim. Ilys sat cross-legged on the floor, the cool surface numbing her legs, her hands resting lightly on her knees. Beyond the wall, in the adjoining room, the faithful gathered. She could not see them. She was not meant to.

Mother Inrith's voice echoed in her memory: *When the Fates stir within you, you will know. Rap the wall three times. No sight, no hesitation. Only certainty.*

The first knock came, hollow against the wood.

Ilys held her breath. She waited for a feeling—for warmth in her marrow, for the stirring Mother Inrith had promised—but the emptiness only deepened. Just her pulse clanging in her ear.

A pause. The door opened, then shut again.

The next knock.

Still nothing.

Another. And another.

They came in waves, each presence behind the wall waiting and Ilys sat in the silence, every breath heavier, the oil-thick air stinging her throat.

And so it went for days. Ilys sitting numb on the stone for hours, knocks like a metronome rattling her thoughts as she felt a complete and terrifying nothing. It was a blur of waiting. Waiting and preparing. The rites were whispered to her again and again until they pressed against her skull like a brand. Each night she lay awake, hearing the words over and over: *You will feel it. You will know. You will obey.*

What if I never feel it? the thought whispered. *What if the Fates do not speak? What if I choose wrong?*

Another knock.

She pressed her palms against her knees, forcing herself to still. *Trust in the Fates,* she told herself. *Trust in them.*

Knock.

Nothing.

Knock.

Trust in them.

And then—A thrum. Or perhaps not. Was it real, or just the ache of sitting too long, the pull of her own desperate need to decide?

Her breath hitched and she lifted her hand, hesitated, then rapped against the wall. Once. Twice. Thrice. The sound rang hollow, definitive.

The door opened on the other side and footsteps carried the chosen one away.

Ilys's pulse thundered, doubts gnawing her insides. Had she truly felt the Fates? Or had she convinced herself there was a difference, eager to end the silence, the waiting?

Had she chosen right?

Had she felt it?

She closed her eyes, pressing the words into her own skull like emulsion to a wall.

Trust in the Fates.

Trust in them.

Ilys stepped from the chamber, palms sweaty within her sleeves. Mother Inrith stood waiting, her unshrouded face severe, one hand resting on the shoulder of a small-framed figure.

A child.

Ilys had presumed her successor would be young, but this was too young. The girl could not have seen more than five summers. She was delicate as all children were, her small fists gripped her tunic, her dark curls unruly from nervous fidgeting, and her green eyes canny.

None of Ily's preparations or lessons equipped her for the tightening in her chest at the sight of this child. The girl swallowed, before speaking in a careful, fragile voice.

"My name is Hanna."

Mother Inrith frowned and squeezed her hand.

"That is not your name. Not any longer. You belong to the Veil. The Fates themselves will rename you." She gestured toward Ilys. "Come. We'll settle the rites."

A priestess guided Hanna to kneel before the dais, and Ilys knelt beside her, struck by the vast difference in their size. The awe festered. This was to be her successor?

"Ilys." Mother Inrith's voice cut sharp. "Begin the claiming rite."

"Through shadow and silence..." Ilys paused, looking to the girl. *Had she not been taught what to say? Was Ilys meant to guide her?*

Hanna blinked, lips parting in confusion. Ilys lowered her voice, gentler. "Say it with me, little one. Through shadow and silence."

"Sh—shadow and silence," Hanna whispered, stumbling but eager to please.

Ilys squeezed her hand. "I claim you."

"I... claim you." Her chest tightened. She pressed on, though the words felt cruel on her tongue.

"Through blood and burden, I keep you." The child frowned, struggling. Ilys slowed her speech, breaking the vow into pieces.

"Through blood... and burden."

"Through blood... and bur-den."

"I keep you."

"I keep you."

Their voices barely held together, Hanna's uncertain, Ilys's quaking beneath the veil.

At last, Ilys guided her through the final binding.

"Through fate and beyond..."

"Through... fate and beyond..."

"We walk as one."

"We walk as... one."

When the last words faded, the priestess pressed the heavy book between their joined hands, her tone low and reverent.

"And the Veil bears witness," declared Mother Inrith. "Now, take her hand. Read from the pages and press upon her a new name, one of the Veil."

Ilys's heart pounded. Her thoughts betrayed her, circling the question she had long ago buried: *What had my name been?* It prickled at the back of her mind, unreachable. *I am not Ilys,* she thought, *not truly.* The child's hand tightened in hers.

Ilys turned the pages with her free hand. Names spilled before her eyes. None belonged to this child. None fit. *Why me?* she thought. *Should it not be the King's right to name her?*

But when she looked again at the girl, she saw only Hanna. A name as rooted as the child herself. A name that could not be erased.

"Hanna," Ilys announced, voice firming.

Mother Inrith's head tilted, her mouth a thin line. "That name does not belong to the Veil, Ilys." She lingered on Ilys's name like a lash, her voice a harsh whisper.

"Hanna," Ilys repeated, louder, surer. "The Fates whispered it to me themselves."

The girl squealed with delight. "I am Hanna!" She pressed close to the veiled figure without fear.

Mother Inrith snapped the book shut. "Hanna, then." She turned to the priestesses. "Tend to the girl." As she swept past Ilys, her skirts brushed the floor, her voice low and warning near the veil. "Careful, little Veilwalker."

Chapter 25

Twenty-fourth year in the life of Ilys of the Veil

Death did not return.

Two winters had passed, and still, he remained absent.

But the work continued. Hanna's small hand trembled around the hilt of the knife, her wide eyes stayed fixed on the rabbit's blood seeping into the greedy earth. Morrigan paced nearby, hackles raised, tail stiff with agitation. He had been like this ever since Hanna came into their keeping, territorial to the point of menace. The great black dog circled them now, a low whine in his throat.

Ilys knelt beside her, stabilizing Hanna's hand until the trembling stilled. "You did well," she affirmed.

It struck her then how quickly the years had passed since the naming, how fully Hanna had lodged herself into her heart. Two years, and the girl had become a constant at her side, her laughter bright as bells, her trust immediate and unguarded. Ilys loved her, fiercely and tenderly. She clung to the feeling and fought it all the same. Love had never been durable in her experience.

Hanna swallowed, still staring at the rabbit. "What now?" she whispered.

"Now," Ilys directed, "we give it to the Veil."

Hanna's fingers tightened around the knife. "Will you say it with me?"

Ilys shifted so they knelt side by side. "Thy thread is cut."

Hanna's breath caught before she whispered, "Thy thread is cut."

"Thy name is lost."

"Thy name... is lost."

"The Veil shall hold."

"The Veil shall hold."

Finally, Ilys breathed the last word, soft as the wind, "Vasha." The child shuddered as Ilys gently pried the knife from her grip. "Come."

The girl stood, smaller than ever beside her. After a heartbeat, her hand slipped into Ilys's free one. Morrigan fell into step on Hanna's other side, walking so close his flank brushed her tunic, guarding her from both directions.

As they neared the gates of the Sanctum, the low rattle of wheels reached Ilys first, followed by the whicker of a single horse. A small carriage waited at the threshold, modest but well-kept, its canvas cover dusted with the red of the road. A servant held the reins loosely, standing aside as Rowenna descended the step.

Flushed from travel, curls escaping their braid, Rowenna gathered her skirts in one hand to keep them from the mud. With the other, she steadied a boy not much younger than Hanna; a boy who seemed determined to fling himself back toward the road, all kicking heels and wild energy. Rowenna caught him against her hip with practiced ease, her breath leaving her in a huff that turned into a laugh.

"No." Ilys uttered the word under her breath, eyes narrowing as she took in Rowenna.

"What?" Rowenna asked, blowing a stray strand of hair from her face as she wrangled young Beck, who squirmed in her grasp with all the strength of a child determined to escape.

"You're pregnant." Ilys nodded, resolutely. "He plopped another in you!"

Rowenna stilled, then cast a wry glance up at Ilys, her expression caught between amusement and exasperation. *A child stands betwixt us*, her eyes seemed to say, as though Ilys had forgotten the very real, very restless boy in her arms and the young Veilwalker beside her.

Ilys leaned closer, voice low. "Your bosom is *unnaturally* large. The whole Sanctum knows by now."

Rowenna snorted softly, shaking her head, but she didn't deny it. She settled Beck against her hip with a sigh, patting his back as though to calm both him and herself. He had grown. Two covenant years had passed since Rowenna had first placed him in Ilys's arms. He no longer lived as the fragile bundle he had been; sturdy now, full of mischief, his tawny curls wild and his cheeks still round with the remnants of infancy.

Ilys felt Hanna shift against her, peering from beneath the edge of her veil. She kept one small hand curled in the fabric of Ilys's sleeve.

"This is Beck," Ilys said at last, nodding toward the boy.

Hanna only gawked, mute behind the soft ebony of her veil. Beck squirmed harder at the sight of her, curious, reaching with grubby fingers as though determined to snatch the veil itself.

"Beck," Rowenna chided gently, catching his wrist before he could grab it. "Manners." The boy grinned, utterly unrepentant.

Ilys crouched beside Hanna, her voice even. "You may sit, if you like. He is loud, but harmless."

After a long hesitation, Hanna's grip loosened on Ilys's sleeve. She let Ilys guide her down to the grass, where she sat stiffly, hands folded in her lap. Beck plopped down beside her with a thud, immediately offering her a stick as though it were the finest treasure in the kingdom. Hanna blinked at it. Then, because she was polite to madmen, she took it.

Rowenna crouched nearby, her tone warm and coaxing. "He shares his best sticks only with the most important guests."

"Just like his father," Ilys quipped, voice full with innuendo while patting Rowenna's belly. Rowenna swatted at her hand, laughing. The pair watched the children play, carving lines into the dirt.

"There now," Rowenna said maternally, amusement glinting in her eye. "Two fine map-makers. Where will this road take them, do you think?"

"Somewhere far from us," Ilys pouted, melancholy nipping at her mind.

Rowenna's sharp eyes lingered on Ilys, reading her too well. "What is it?"

Ilys swallowed, her throat tight. "I am terrified," she admitted, "of what will happen when push comes to shove. When they see how I look at her—how the love pours out of me. We are not to have attachments."

Rowenna's expression softened. "She is your successor. It is natural to spend time with her. To tend to her."

"I hope they see it that way," Ilys said. Her voice felt like it might splinter. "There is a war I wage with myself every day, to love her or to push her away. I know not which will bring her closer to happiness and safety."

Rowenna hummed, gazing at Hanna where she sat beside Beck. The girl had begun to tap the stick lightly against the ground, the rhythm of it coaxing Beck into fits of giggles.

"You are already giving her what she needs," Rowenna said at last. Then, after a pause, "I see Grim in you, clear as day." The words landed like an arrow loosed straight through Ilys's center.

They lingered long after, the conversation winding as the light thinned to gold, then to violet. Beck eventually grew drowsy, nodding against Rowenna's shoulder, and even Hanna's stick tapping slowed to a soft, absent rhythm. "How did you know I needed you so dearly?" Ilys asked at last, her voice somber in the growing dusk.

Rowenna smiled and pressed a kiss to each of Ilys's cheeks. "Your last letter was painfully dull. I thought I'd save you from yourself."

Ilys let out a breath of a laugh. "Then I promise to send nothing but dry, dowdy content from here on out."

Rowenna's answering grin arrived leisurely and sure. "I'll visit again in the spring, Veilwalker. I promise."

Rowenna lifted Beck into the carriage, the boy already half-asleep against her shoulder, the rattle of wheels fading down the road. Dusk settled fully by the time Ilys and Hanna turned back toward the Sanctum.

"Will you sit with me tonight?" Hanna queried.

Ilys glanced down at her, noting the way her fingers curled tight in her sleeve, braced for refusal. Hanna, over the course of months, had begun to learn all the ways in which the world withdrew.

"Of course," she reassured.

Relief softened Hanna's face and Morrigan huffed beside them, pressing his massive head briefly against her small hand, urging her forward.

At the Sanctum gates, priestesses reached out their hands for the child. Ilys spared the lot a bare glance. "I will take her," she directed, her tone brooking no argument.

The women faltered, but stepped aside. Ilys rested her hand on Hanna's narrow shoulder and guided her through the shadowed halls, torches guttering in their sconces, Morrigan padding after them. In the sleeping quarters, Hanna curled onto the cot, hands tucked beneath her chin, small enough to vanish beneath the blanket.

Ilys brushed her hair back, her voice low and maternal. "Would you like a story?"

Hanna nodded eagerly.

So Ilys began one, begging the words from Grim's book into her mind. A boy traveling alone, speaking to the stars. Hanna hushed Ilys.

"Not one of those," she whined. Ilys's ego bristled.

Hanna untucked herself from the bed, throwing her legs to the ground. She padded over to the table across from her bed, unearthing Ilys's sketchbook from the pile of paper. She delivered the sketchbook with an earnest invitation.

"One of these," she requested.

Ilys observed the cool hoarding of breath in her chest. Her mind sought for an appropriate denial, but scoured without reward. These were not stories. They were nightmares. They were sins. They were dreams unsung.

Swallowing thickly, Ilys picked up the bound leather. Fumbling hesitation wreaked havoc on her grasp. *Turn the page*, she urged. *Make the darling girl happy. Meet her needs, make her smile.*

Morrigan. Grim. Baron. It depicted Ilys's last drawing before the day she had lost it all.

"Who is that?" Hanna pointed, smudging the lines of Grim's veiled face. The charcoal streaked the girl's hand. Ilys wiped it gently, tenderly transferring the charcoal to her own palm.

"Careful," Ilys noted. "The drawings like to bite." Hanna eyed the medium suspiciously, now clearly avoiding contact with the dark art.

"His name is Grim," Ilys explained.

"Who is he?" Ilys should have known a name is not enough. We deem the silly monikers so important, yet Grim was not a standalone adjective. It could not capture his gruff adoration. His careful self-hatred. His scattered love.

"You know Otris?" Ilys mentioned the cook's son, seeking to illustrate the role in the words she could find. Hanna nodded in response. "And you know Ostris's father? The lumbering man always toting him about?" Hanna affirmed through her dainty headshake.

"Grim was much like that to me as I grew. He touted me and taught me right from wrong. Much of what I teach you."

"He was your father?" Asked Hanna.

"Not quite, no," Ilys corrected. Gods, she longed for the words. Predecessor? Should that be the title she names Grim? The title felt hollow and sparse. No title could not convey the adolescent mourning his name evoked for Ilys. The way she wobbled and the world shook before her, unfamiliar in her place in the face of his absence.

Ilys pictured the waves she'd witnessed at the coast. She imagined them churning, swallowing the grief and the confusion. Taking it back out to sea. She gathered her composure, allowing the waves to toil and do the work she could not.

"I will tell you a story of the whole," Ilys unfolded, her smile soft as balm. "Perhaps it will answer where my words fail." She began, voice laced with veneration, "There once was a girl, and the world stole her name. She was given to a storm of a man: old, gruff, and called Grim. He taught her to wield a blade and to stare so fiercely into the darkness that even the shadows would blink first. But though the girl grew fierce, her heart grew soft. Each day she ran to the birds and begged them to take her with them, to teach her how to fly.

"'*You must stay,*' they told her. '*You are not made to be like us.*' She begged again and again, but still they could not see the bird inside her."

As it is with all young children, sleep crept in and quietly stole Hanna away. Ilys thought it a rather plain place for the story to end, but supposed the girl satisfied enough to dream. Ilys snuck from the room, pinching the small candle flame til it bled darkness.

Stumbling back to her chamber, she fought to ignore the bird in her own heart.

CHAPTER 26

It had been two years since her first Veilmarch, the one she could not see through to its end. Since she had slain Lord Veylen. Since Death had crossed the line, choosing to protect her instead of merely collect, and then vanished into smoke.

Ilys could not describe the sensation, but she knew that though two years had passed, she would not be granted a third. Death would come for her this Veilmarch. She knew it in her blood.

One evening, while dining with the King, veal and carrots were set before them. Hanna had not yet been invited to join their table. The King remarked, almost wistfully, that he already mourned the solitude he and Ilys still shared, soon to be lost to the presence of the child.

Ilys smiled placatingly, but inside her head she scorned him. *Then why did you ask me to name a successor?* she thought. But she chided herself, knowing the King's place as a servant to Death just as she knew her own.

The King scraped his knife against the stoneware plate, pushing the veal from side to side before speaking. "I asked you to this dinner because we've had word. Death will arrive in a day's time."

Ilys offered a silent thanks to her veil, masking the dread that coiled in her gut behind a diplomat's composure. She did not want him back.

The King, always more attuned to the intangible than even Death himself, seemed to catch the shift in her spirit. "I wish it were not so," he said softly, setting his palm flat against the table, the gesture almost a reach, almost a comfort.

"I think it is important that while you are away, Hanna sees to her first execution."

Ilys choked on the mead she'd just drawn into her mouth. "What?"

"It's time she became more intimate with what is asked of her."

"She is seven," Ilys said flatly.

The King cocked his head, consuming Ilys's presence with a barbed curiosity. "You were only nine," he pointedly offered.

"It is—" Ilys coughed. "Too young. Entirely too young."

He quirked an eyebrow, a discontented tug teasing the corners of his lips. "Where is the reverent girl I raised? Have you so quickly forgotten your role, your divine nature?"

The words rattled around in her head. Her vision blinked between the dining table and visions of Hanna. Sweet, tiny Hanna, looking to Ilys with blood on her hands.

"I uphold my duty, my Shepherd. I only ask that we wait longer for the girl to mature."

"She is no girl," he snapped, sudden and surprising. "She is a Veilwalker." He closed his eyes, visibly cooling and fighting for resolve. "You are not yourself, Ilys. I worry that you were forced to the helm too early. Too soon."

Grim's departure flashed through her mind.

The King settled deeper into his chair, lounging comfortably in himself. "I believe some direction may help. Some additional oversight to aid you. Such a burden to shoulder alone, at your age."

"My Shepherd, I apologize. I did not mean—"

"Veilwalker," he cut her off. "A member of my Ebon Choir will attend you and the girl from here on out. No need to harangue further. Clearly youth has blurred your purpose."

He stood, leaving the table. More and more, she found their conversations ending as such: a king's demand followed by a tantrum. She had forgotten herself in the meeting, and now both Hanna and Ilys would pay for it.

Ilys' gaze bored into the top of Hanna's head as the girl flipped through the sketchbook that evening. They were seated on the low couch in Ilys's chambers, the fire burning low in the hearth, shadows playing across the stone walls. The faint scratch of the pages susurrated throughout the quarters—Hanna's favorite sound, it now seemed.

It had become a habit of hers, this plucking of the leather book from Ilys's desk and opening it without question or permission. With Grim, Baron, and Rowenna gone, no one treated Ilys with such casual familiarity. Her heart leapt every time the child did, even if the medium Hanna clung to was painful.

Hanna stopped at one sketch and pointed to it. "You said he is in the guard, but I never see him."

Oh, Hanna. The girl materialized with an affinity for questions that tortured. How strange, silly, and utterly horrid to Ilys that Hanna had never met the hulking man. How precious Baron would have found her. How entertaining he would have been, performing for not one, but two girls utterly enthralled with him. Ilys's eyes burned at the thought.

"He's gone now," Ilys admitted nimbly, her voice throttled and watery. "He lives in the Veil."

Hanna, attuned to the shift in Ilys's diction, turned to her veiled predecessor. She slid her veil off and crawled into Ilys's lap, ducking under the larger veil as though it were a tent. Her small palms pressed against Ilys's cheeks, wiping the tears there.

"I'm sorry that happened," Hanna offered, lilting and tender.

Ilys broke further, sobs wracking her body. *She was sorry? This darling child was sorry?* A ridiculous notion. And yet the words lifted Ilys. No one had ever offered her such a sentiment before.

Yes, she thought bitterly, *how sorry we all should all be.*

A short rap at the door culled the tears. Ilys cupped Hanna's face, tucking the child's small features into her palm as she slipped the veil back from its makeshift duty as shelter. The fabric fell between them once more, a wall re-raised.

"Coming," Ilys called, her voice level. The Ebon Choir attendant assigned to the Veilwalkers had already begun flitting on the outskirts of their existence. Gabriel, the man was called, seemed fatesbent on never leaving them to peace. All in one day's work.

"Goodnight, my pet," she bid, brushing a last touch across Hanna's hair before stepping away.

"Goodnight, Ilys," the girl called back. "I love you," Hanna mumbled into her pillow.

Those fickle words lodged like iron nails in Ilys's palms.

She slipped from the room without sparing Gabriel a glance. His towering frame loomed to her right, but she felt his needy presence without sight.

"Fates bless you, Gabriel," she said, the words wry as she swept down the hallway.

"Veilwalker," he replied, but did not follow.

Ilys's mouth tightened. Of course—the King had set the Ebon Choir attendant to watch Hanna, not her. The knowledge sat sour in her chest. Gabriel meant no harm, she knew, but the thought of anyone hovering so near the child without her close by scraped against every instinct she had. She'd be gone within a day. Then who would guard Hanna?

Her mind turned to Elspeth. They were not intimates, but Ilys trusted her enough and she admired the quiet, maternal way the woman tended to Hanna. Ilys would speak with her before she left and make certain she understood to stay close to the girl. Keep her safe.

Ilys stepped back into her chamber, the door shutting softly behind her.

She would have to impress Hanna's safety upon Gabriel as well. The Ebon Choir might answer to the King, but the King answered to Death. And soon, Death would answer to Ilys. It would be a simple thing to corner Gabriel and remind him just how thin the barrier to the veil could grow, making it clear which side he would find himself on if harm ever touched the girl. The thought coaxed a loitering, dangerous smile to her lips as she drew the veil from her face, the fabric pooling like shadow in her hands. There was a kind of lawlessness and pride in loving something small. A fierce, unyielding urge to protect it, one that bred a defiant contempt for every gray and measured action.

"And what has made you so pleased?" The voice, cool and unhurried, came from behind her.

She turned to find Death, mortal and lanky, lounging on her bed. She flipped to face him, face bare and heated.

"What are you doing here?" she barked.

He only smiled, coy, and pressed a finger to his lips. *Hush,* his gesture seemed to say. He crossed one leg lazily over the other, burrowing deeper into her sheets as though staking a claim.

"I arrived early," he said with a shrug. "I thought I'd absorb the sights." His gaze slid deliberately to the sheer nightdress draped over the chair—the one she had nearly stripped to put on.

Ilys unsheathed her dagger and stalked toward him. He did not wear his usual heavy robe, but a black tunic that hung loose against his frame, baring a long pale stretch of throat and a sliver of chest. He did not flinch at the flash of steel, only smiled wider.

"Angry Veilwalker," he observed, as though naming a caricature.

She pressed the blade's tip beneath his chin, forcing his head back. "What are you doing here?" she hissed.

He leaned into the knife until blood beaded, red against white. "I am here to see you."

"To retrieve me?" Her head tilted, voice sharp. "The gate has served well enough every other time. Why my chambers?"

"To talk, Ilys." His voice dropped soft. His long fingers closed gently around her wrist, easing the dagger aside. "Good girl," he said when she let him.

She relented, not out of mercy but because confusion and curiosity stayed her hand. Killing him could wait. Stepping back, she drew a breath, willing the spice-scent of him to leave her senses. It had been two years since she'd stood this close. She lowered herself onto the chair draped with her nightdress, posture deceptively languid.

"By all means, let us natter," she said, edged with saccharine elaboration.

He rose from the bed, gesturing lazily toward her sleeping quarters. "I meant to catch you off guard," he admitted. "I imagined you'd try to kill me quickly on this journey, without the compromise we made the last time we met."

Ilys glowered at his very correct assumption. He smiled wilder at her lack of denial, nodding and moving on.

"I have a new proposition. One I believe suits us both well."

Ilys quirked an eyebrow, working very hard to decode every behavior. Death knelt before her just inches away and Ilys wriggled, sure she could feel his breath through her skirts.

"Yes?" she urged him to elaborate.

"I propose that you should not—" he paused—"kill me." His gaze bore into her, devouring every bread crumb she left that may hint at her emotions. "And in exchange, I will make it such that you will not be forced to take any lives this march."

Ilys bit her lip, contemplating the dark god's seemingly sincere gaze. Grim had instructed her in hand-to-hand combat, in human anatomy, and blood-thick ritual. But never had he explained best practice when negotiating with a god.

"And this deal would remain in perpetuity?" she questioned.

"Only this march," he corrected.

She huffed. "That is not tempting. I will be a murderer once more come another winter."

His expression sharpened; a reckoning flickered behind his eyes, like embers under ash. "There will come a time," he said quietly, "with the new Death, when you will take once more. The Fates will demand it. But with me, in this last climb, you will not kill. You will collect. You will abide with me. You will walk the Veilmarch at my side, and your blade will stay clean until the end."

"I will only accept it should it extend," she dictated. "For as long as I do not kill you, I will not be forced to take a life on any march."

"I cannot make that deal, Veilwalker," he ground out.

"Why?" she bit back, nails digging into her palms carving half moons in the skin.

"Because this is my last."

Ilys laughed, a dry and disoriented sound. "Death does not retire."

He rose with care, brushing invisible dust from his dark trousers, a pointless, human motion. "Ilys," he said, voice low and unguarded. "I am ending."

"Ending?" The word scraped out of her throat.

"Dying, Ilys."

"And if I kill you first?"

"If you strike," he said, voice stripped of its old theatrics, "you do more than kill a god. You pull on threads the Fates have knotted for centuries. Men will die uncounted because their ends have been misread. Children will choke on breaths that were meant to last. The Veil is not a rope you can cut and re-tie to suit your hurt. It is the pattern of all leaving. Break it now and nothing will leave as it should." He swallowed. "You would become not avenger but chaos. Not Veilwalker but an aberration the world will not forgive. Let the Fates take me when they are ready."

Her lips curled, glutted in their disdain. "You're lying."

"I am bound," he said, urgency roughening his voice. "When I saved you—when I killed that boy—" His hands lifted, clumsy, as though grasping for words too large to shape. For the first time, Ilys saw not omnipotence but a god fumbling. "The Fates do not leave us unchecked. Every god is tethered, weighed, balanced. The Veil itself holds those bindings tight. You think I take lives at whim, but each one is numbered, each one permitted. Saving you broke that rhythm."

Ilys blinked, then barked a laugh, bitter and disbelieving. "And yet you take so many lives you cannot possibly be called to take." She circled him, blade tracing idle patterns in the air. "You expect me to believe that the Fates keep ledgers, when you sweep the board clean whenever it suits you?"

"I do not suit myself." His voice rose, low and harsh. "I carry their design. You see slaughter; I see a pattern. That is why my power is thinning. That is why this march is my last." He paused, his throat working. "I am not lying to you. I have already paid the price of stepping outside my bounds—your breath still in your lungs is proof."

"Then prove it," she said, voice low, daring. "Make another bargain. Not words. The old way."

His gaze climbed to hers, shadows flickering through it—defiance, surrender, an impulse hungrier in between. A crooked smile ghosted his lips. "You want blood."

"I want binding," she corrected, stepping closer, close enough to feel the heat radiating from his mortal skin. "Blood is only the cord. Swear you will not call for my blade this march. Swear I will not be ordered to kill in your name."

He only looked at her, gaze tracing her features with a strange, covetous intensity. Then, with willful grace, he scored his palm with the dagger. Blood welled, rich and luxurient. "And what will you give me in return?" he queried.

"I will not strike you down before your march is ended," she vowed, as she cut her own flesh, and then pressed her palm hard against his.

The wounds met with a hiss of warmth, their mingled blood slick between their skin. The Veil stirred at the contact, a low thrum that made the stone beneath them feel alive.

"Speak," she demanded, though her breath hitched with the command.

He leaned in, his lips grazing the shape of her ear as he spoke, "I, Death, in this last Veilmarch, bind myself to you. I shall not call for death by your hand. You will walk at my side, while I alone collect. Until I am ended, this bond will hold."

Her grip tightened, refusing to give him space, nails biting into the back of his hand. "And if you break it?"

"If either of us does," he said after a beat, voice low, "the Veil will collapse." Their blood cooled between their palms, tacky and dark.

"At dawn," he dictated, "you walk with me, not against me."

"I may not kill you, but I am not walking *with* you," she bit out.

The dying God only tutted, strolling toward the door with that infuriating ease. Even now she glimpsed how his waning divinity made him reckless. How Death's own mortality riled some boyish irreverence to the surface, teasing and human in ways that set her teeth on edge.

"Ilys," he said lightly, glancing back over his shoulder. "It almost sounds as though you don't like me."

She waltzed close, voice honey-sweet against his mouth. "I'll laugh when the light leaves your eyes." Then she shut the door in his face.

Part III

The Book of the Veil – Part III

"Sealed in the first days, spoken in the last, unbroken until the end of all things."

VII. The Veilmarch (Hiram 3:1-12)

1. And it was spoken that the Veilwalker is bound by three duties: to sever, to serve, and to walk the path unseen.

2. And of these, one is sacred above all, whispered only in the dark places where no witness lingers. It is not written in stone, nor spoken in the halls of the faithful. It is not fit for the ears of kings or the hands of priests.

3. For the Veilmarch belongs to the Veilwalker alone.

CHAPTER 27

Death is dying.

Death is dying.

Death is dying.

Ilys instinctively placed items in her bag, preparing for the journey. Lift an item. *Death*. Tuck an item. *Is*. Lift an Item. *Dying*.

The words punctuated each movement, every breath. How ironic. How cyclical. How gratifying. After his announcement, the rest of the conversation blurred in Ilys's memory. She had agreed; for Death's last march, she would not seek to end his life, as long as she would not be asked to end any others.

But she wished she had asked more questions. *How did a god die? What came after? Who would fill the role?*

She snapped the bag shut, urging composure to follow. There would be an entire journey's worth of questions. She had to think of Hanna. Of Morrigan. She must prepare everything and everyone for her departure. Gone were the days of slipping away, without warning.

She smoothed the fabric of her veil, then slipped the satchel over her shoulder. How strange, that her entire life could be reduced to what fit inside this single bag. The thought made her skin prickle, as though she were wearing a garment too tight. Squaring her shoulders, she crossed the corridors toward the courtyard where Elspeth would already be waiting with Hanna. At this hour, they would usually begin training. Today, it became the place they would say goodbye.

The moment Hanna caught sight of Ilys, she wriggled free of Elspeth's grasp and ran to her.

"Elsie says you're leaving," she said, her voice small and wounded.

Ilys could almost see the quiver of her lower lip beneath the veil. She had meant to tell Hanna the night before, but the melancholy stirred by thoughts of Baron had drawn her mind elsewhere.

Ilys rested a hand on the small Veilwalker's head. "We spoke about this possibility, remember? I promise it won't be long."

"We've never been apart!" Hanna cried, clutching at her sleeve. Ilys nearly laughed at the protest. They *had* been apart—Hanna had lived the first five years of her life without her—but the girl clung to her now as though Ilys were the only world she had ever known.

Ilys knelt, her veil brushing against Hanna's, her voice dropping to a conspiratorial hush. "I have to go, little one, but I'll be back soon. You'll wish I had stayed away longer, just so you wouldn't have to endure my silly exercises."

Hanna flung her arms around Ilys's leg, pinning the dark fabric to her calf and thigh. Morrigan had crept close without a sound and now pressed his head against Ilys's other leg, as though anchoring her in place. For a moment they were a small, fragile family huddled together on the cobblestones beneath a flat, gray sky.

Beyond the gates, Death's silhouette waited. He wore no godhood today. Only the shape of a man whose mortal eyes fixed on them, quiet and somber. Ilys forced herself to ignore him.

She slipped the sketchbook from her satchel and pressed it into Hanna's arms. "For when you miss me." Then, glancing at Elspeth, who lingered a few paces behind, she added, "I'm sure Elspeth has plenty of stories about Grim she'd be happy to share."

Hanna clutched the book to her chest and squeezed tighter with her free arm, as though sheer will might keep Ilys from leaving. Lost in the moment, Ilys barely registered Mother Inrith's approach until the woman's hand closed over Hanna's arm, prying her free. The Mother's voice cut through the courtyard, sharp and brittle with age.

"Let us not confuse duty with emotion. Say farewell to the Veilwalker, Hanna."

Obedient as ever, Hanna allowed herself to be led away. Ilys fought the instinct to intervene, shoving the discomfort down, layer by layer, until it settled like a stone in her chest. Weakness could not be shown, not today. Gabriel's ascension to his new role proof enough of that. She closed her eyes, inhaled once, and turned toward the gates. Hanna's muffled whimpers followed her, but she pretended not to hear.

Ilys led Spire from the stables to stand beside Death's waiting mare, her hand gliding down her pale mane in a calming motion meant as much for herself as for the horse.

"To be so missed," Death remarked.

Ilys glared at him through the veil. "Do not speak to me of her." She swung onto Spire's back and tilted her head, urging him to mount and ride.

The air beyond the Sanctum swelled with the icy morning frost, stinging Ilys's cheeks. Only when the walls had faded into the mist behind them did she let herself breathe more freely. Death rode at her side, unusually quiet, his mortal frame outlined starkly against the gray horizon. He seemed smaller like this.

"What shall I call you now?"

He shrugged. "I am still Death."

"No," she challenged, tilting her head. "Death intimidates. Death is eternal. You are a silly, pithy mortal now."

A short laugh escaped him. "How good of you to remind me." He thought on it, his hands loose around the reins. "I do not know that a name is worthwhile for the time I have left. Names are for natural creatures. I no longer know what I am."

"I have questions," she noted. He did not respond, but looked at her from the side of his eyes thoughtful, urging the queries from her mouth.

"When will you die?"

"Endeavor to not sound so eager, Ilys." His voice petted the s, exaggerating the silkiness of her name.

"When?" she repeated, haughty and bored. Inside she clamored for answers.

"I know not the exact moment, but I will not live to see another Veilmarch. This is all I've been told."

"How will you die?" she badgered, already moving on. It was macabre, the detached way she spoke of his death, and she reveled in it.

Death leaned back, his face half in shadow, and for once he did not wear a smile. "You know of the Veyth, don't you?"

Ilys frowned, surprised. "The threads? Of course. Every child of the Sanctum learns them. The Fates weave the Veyth and cut them when it is time for a soul to pass."

"Good," he said softly, as though she had passed some test. "Then you know there is not one thread for each person, but one thread for all. A single skein, endless, looping back on itself. When a mortal dies, their knot is severed and their portion of the thread feeds the weave again."

She swallowed, uneasy. "And you?"

He turned his palm up, staring at it as though he expected to see it fray. "Gods are not cut. We are unraveled. Slowly. Strand by strand." His voice dropped lower, almost conspiratorial. "My Veyth is already loosening. You've seen it. I am less than I was. A fiber is taken from me, spinning it toward the one who will replace me. One day there will be nothing left to pull. The world cannot bear two of me. So it thins me out until I am gone, and my successor is whole."

Her fingers twitched at her side, aching for her dagger, yet finding no one to stab.

"And you simply let this happen?"

His mouth curved, wry and tired. "What else is there to do, little Veilwalker? To resist the Veyth is to snarl the whole weave. Better to be unraveled cleanly than to tangle the world."

"So noble from the mouth of a creature of cruelty."

"Cruel? What have I done that is so cruel?"

"You take those that displease you. Simply because you can."

"I listen to the fates, Ilys. There is no abstract emotion driving my decisions. The one time I faltered, the one time I acted outside of my domain, was the day I saved you. And look what it has cost me."

"What do you mean?" she pried.

He spared her a drill glance, his mare trotting ahead.

The rain came down gradually at first, a drizzle that misted against their faces as they rode. But by the time the sun had sunk behind the curtain of storm clouds, the heavens opened in earnest, spilling sheets of cold, unrelenting water over the land. The dirt path beneath them softened into a slick mess of mud, their horses slogging through it with heavy, labored steps.

Ilys was miserable.

Her clothes clung to her. Her veil, drenched and useless, stuck to her face, water running in thin rivulets down her neck, collecting in the folds of her cloak. She curled deeper into herself, hunching her shoulders against the downpour, but it did little good. Ahead of her, Death rode just as silently, his dark figure barely visible through the veil of rain. Just as wet, just as cold, he did not complain and it irritated her beyond comprehension. A crack of thunder rumbled overhead, rolling through the sky like distant war drums.

Then his voice carried through the storm."We will stop here," he called.

She could barely make out his form as he veered off the road toward a small, weather-beaten inn nestled against the trees. The building sat dark and low to the ground, its slanted roof dripping from the storm, the narrow windows teasing light.

Too cold to argue, she heeded.

By the time she reached the inn, her hands were numb, her legs sore from gripping Spire's slick coat. Death had already dismounted, his mortal form shadowed beneath the rain, his hair plastered against his forehead. He turned as she swung down from the saddle, barely composing herself before his hands were on her, firm but careful, guiding as her feet hit the ground. She shivered violently, the cold settling deep in her bones. Without a word, he pulled his cloak from his own shoulders, the heavy, sodden fabric hanging dark with rain, and wrapped it around her.

She scowled, gripping the edges, water pooling at her fingertips."You think you are helping," she nit-picked, her voice rough with discomfort, "but your cloak might as well be a body of water itself." She shrugged off his touch, shaking out the drenched fabric, annoyed at the gesture, annoyed at him, annoyed at all of it.

He sighed but did not comment, instead moving toward the inn's entrance, pushing open the heavy wooden door. A gust of warmth spilled out, greeting the pair. The keeper barely looked up from behind the counter, only nodding once Death set down the coins.

One room. Once more.

Ilys did not fight it. She wanted dry clothes, a place to sit, a place to be warm.

Their plain room boasted two narrow beds pushed to opposite sides of the space and a wooden table with an old, faded game board carved into its surface between them. She peeled off her veil, wringing it out as best she could before dropping onto the edge of one of the beds, her muscles aching from the long ride.

Death only shrugged off his coat, ran a hand through his wet hair, and sat on the opposite bed, shaking out his own dampened sleeves.

Outside, the rain pounded against the roof, the wind howling against the wooden walls. Ilys knelt beside the fire, hands outstretched, begging the warmth to take hold. The heat licked at her palms, at her forearms, but it did not sink into her bones the way she needed. Cold still clung to her skin, settled deep in the spaces between her ribs, wrapped around her like a second, wretched skin. She had fought it long enough, stubborn against the discomfort, but she saw no use in it now.

The dress had to go.

The heavy muslin clung to her, soaked through, smothering like a burial shroud. Leeching the heat from her body faster than the fire could return it, she cringed at the unbearable sensation. Her fingers located the ties at her back, stiff from the rain, and she forced them apart, rising stiffly to move behind the folding screen in the corner.

Peeling the dress away was its own battle, the wet fabric reluctant to part from her, sticking to her arms, her waist, dragging against her thighs. She found the relief immediate, though unfamiliar. Standing there, left only in her thin chemise and slip, she felt exposed. She inhaled before stepping back out into the warm glow of the fire. With the wet dress discarded, her body moved lighter, free of its suffocating hold. She knelt once more, the heat finally starting to reach her skin, spreading through her limbs.

Then, the sound of fabric shifting.

A rustle, a shuffle, the teasing shedding of soaked outer layers.

She did not turn to look.

"I asked that they bring sup to us," he relayed, his voice even, unbothered as he wrestled his clothing from his body.

She nodded, eyes fixed on the fire, her mind willing itself to stay there, to settle on the flicker of flames, the crackle of wood, the way the heat pressed against her cheeks.

But she was aware of him in a way she had never been before. The small sounds. The soft exhale of breath as he worked his wet sleeves off his arms. The low sigh as he rolled the stiffness from his shoulders. The quiet friction of cloth against skin.

The room shrunk too small, the firelight too dim, the air too leaden with the remnants of the storm.

She swallowed, willing her body to stay still, willing her mind to remain blank. She needed a good fuck, was all, she assured herself.

When sup arrived, they ate sprawled on the floor near the fire, both too stubborn to relinquish the warmth even if it meant dining in the least dignified manner possible. The room had dried around them, the once-damp wooden walls now glowing with firelight, the scent of charred wood mixing with the heavy aroma of stew and buttered bread. Their clothes, hung over the backs of chairs, steamed in the heat, their boots left near the hearth to dry.

Death, still clothed in a loose linen shirt, his sleeves rolled up to the elbows, tilted his head as he chewed. His dark hair, curled at the edges from the rain, a few errant strands falling into his eyes. He made no effort to push them away.

"It's quite good," he admitted through a mouthful, gesturing vaguely at the plate in his lap.

"The best of food in our travels," Ilys agreed, tearing off another piece of bread and dipping it into the stalwart stew. The savory broth clung to her fingers as she brought it to her lips.

Ilys leaned her head against the wall, letting the heat soak into her bones, relishing the simple pleasure of feeling dry. Across from her, Death set his empty plate aside, watching her with an inarticulate expression.

"Shall we play a game?" He nodded toward the small wooden table, with a board set out between the two narrow beds.

She hesitated, glancing over only to find Fox and Geese.

Her heart pulled. Grim's face flashed in her mind, the memory of long evenings spent on cold castle floors, his grumbling every time she bested him. The thought brought endless comfort.

"Let's," she encouraged, standing and moving toward the bed. She perched on the edge, pulling the game board toward her, her fingers brushing the carved surface with reverent homage.

Death sat opposite her, settling onto the other bed with the same lazy grace he always carried. He stretched out, leaning one elbow against the mattress, his fingers tapping idly against his knee as he studied the board.

"Have you played this?" she asked, watching him carefully.

He made a low, thoughtful noise, staring down at the small, worn game pieces. "The exact gameplay evades me," he admitted.

Ilys smirked, adjusting the board, feeling the old habit settle over her. She walked him through the rules: one fox, seventeen geese. The fox's goal is to outmaneuver the geese, capturing them by leaping over them. The geese, slower but greater in number, must trap the fox in a corner.

She placed the pieces with practiced ease, rolling her shoulders before glancing up.

"Are you about to flounce me?" Death asked, narrowing his gaze as he picked up the fox piece between his long fingers, rolling it absently.

She watched his hands, the way his fingers moved, deft and careful, unhurried. Mortal hands now lined with a body's adjustment to time. They were warm hands, she knew, though she had never given herself the space to think of them as such before.

"I am but an amateur," she confessed, her voice sweet and demure, but the glint in her eyes betrayed her.

He arched a brow, unimpressed. "You lie terribly."

She laughed, arranging her geese into formation. "I am a seasoned player."

And seasoned she was. She made quick work of him, maneuvering her geese with merciless precision, cornering his fox in only a handful of moves.

His scowl deepened, fingers drumming against the edge of the board as he studied his loss. "Again," he ground out.

She smiled, resetting the pieces, watching the way his brow furrowed, the way his teeth needled his lips in stern concentration. This time, he played more relaxed, his movements more calculated. His fox grew more elusive, slipping from her traps, learning her rhythm. She almost considered the possibility that he might win.

Almost.

But in the end, she still cornered him, forcing his fox into a cage of its own making. Ilys clapped her hands gleefully.

"Are you a sore winner?" he questioned, brow arched in disappointment.

She leaned in, her voice a whisper against the warm air between them. "I am an ecstatic, jubilant winner," she corrected. "There is nothing sore about it."

His eyes flickered over her face, dark and searching, memorizing her. He reset the board, nodding his head for her to take her turn.

They played again. This time, he fought harder, his strategy shifting, adapting. The game stretched long into the evening, their breaths the only sound aside from the occasional crackle of the fire. His fox lunged, his pieces moved with renewed cleverness, and for the first time, she felt the onset of nerves.

Still, in the end, she surrounded him. His loss was inevitable, no matter how well he had played.

"You poor thing," she cooed, reaching out to lightly pat his hand. "Was that all you had?"

His fingers twitched beneath hers, and she felt the warmth of his skin, solid and real beneath her touch.

"In every story Grim offered, he never once told me you were so... " Death paused, searching for a word.

"Smart? Strategic? Glorious?" she offered, grinning.

"Fiendish," he corrected smoothly. "Conniving. Evasive."

They were close now. Too close.

She hadn't noticed how their movements had drawn them in, how the verbal sparring had tethered them in space, breath mixing in the small sliver of air between them. She could feel the heat of him, the way his presence filled the room, pressing against her like a declaration unspoken.

She swallowed, returning her gaze to the board, pretending nothing had shifted. But his gaze lingered.

"One more," he requested, his voice softer now.

She faltered, then smiled, resetting the board.

She beat him again. But this time, he did not seem put out by the loss. Instead, a new light manifested in his expression, quiet and contemplative, like a man who had opened a book he had not expected to enjoy, only to find himself unable to put it down. That look stayed with her long after the fire dimmed. She lay in the quiet of her bed on one side of the small chamber, staring at the darkened ceiling, the memory of it abiding in the warmth of her chest.

CHAPTER 28

Ilys woke to the muted hush of early morning. The fire had long since burned down to smoldering coals. Death had already risen, the bed across from hers made up neatly, as though he had never slept there at all. She found her veil, left to dry over the back of a chair, stiff from the night's rain, and the garments she had left hanging still cool to the touch. She stretched, rolling the stiffness from her shoulders, then glanced at the small game table between their beds.

The board had disappeared.

She frowned, rubbing the sleep from her eyes, then turned toward the door, where Death stood adjusting the straps of his pack, punctilious in movement.

"Have you truly been so offended by the game that you've tossed it into the fire?" she asked, tilting her head, her voice rough with sleep.

He barely glanced at her. "I have taken it."

"Death," she chided, pulling her cloak around her shoulders as she stood, "you cannot take that game."

"I am a dying man," he said simply, fastening his coat. "And I like it. I should have it."

She opened her mouth to argue, but he cut her off with a dismissive wave. "Hush. I paid the old woman for it."

Ilys scowled, moving to gather her things. He had been up for hours already, she could tell, the room stripped of any sign of their brief stay. She felt rushed again, the way she always did when he forged ahead—ground giving way, tugging her from stillness before she found her footing.

They stepped out into the cold morning, the sky a dull slate gray, brimming with the promise of more rain. A fog clung to the trees beyond the inn, wrapping around the malnourished trees, stretching papery over the distant road.

She followed him to the horses, tightened Spire's reins, and secured her bags. Death moved with quiet efficiency beside his own steed, his fingers working the straps with ease, the black leather of his gloves worn from years of use. His dark coat hung open at the throat, his mortal skin pale against the high collar of his tunic. Dark hair curled at his temples. Ilys wondered herself capable of capturing that curl, the indolent, endearing spiral that it was.

"Tell me," Death said finally, "When do you know to press in?"

She turned in the saddle. "Press in?"

"In the game," he clarified. "The geese. When do you know to move forward?"

"As if I would reveal my secrets to my nemesis," she said, tilting her chin.

He scoffed, "We are not nemeses."

"No?"

"No."

The word sat between them, heavier than it should have been.

"What do you miss most when you are dragged out here alongside me?" he queried thoughtfully.

She considered the question, the corners of her mouth twitching. "Mor," she admitted. "I never sleep as well without him."

He furrowed his brows. "How long has Mor been your lover?"

A startled laugh tore from her lips before she could stop it, the sound sharp against the cold air. She should be angry that he asked after her love life. After all, she knew what Death had in store for those loved by Veilwalkers.

"Mor is Morrigan," she corrected, shaking her head. "My hound."

He leaned back, stretching his neck until it cracked, a faint grin tugging at his mouth. "Ah." His gaze flickered toward her then. "Do you have a name for your steed as well?

She tilted her head, watching him. "Of course. She is Spire. Do you?"

"As a god, I... " he vacillated.

"What?" she pressed.

He seemed to struggle for words, his expression darkening. "There are not many ways to describe it."

She frowned, waiting.

"I did not feel, as a god," he said finally. "I knew duty. I knew purpose. But I did not feel emotions as you know them." He reached out absentmindedly, fingers brushing over the mare's neck. "Now, as a mortal, I look at this creature and I think, by the Unbound, how long have you traveled with me? No other being has accompanied me longer, and I find myself grateful." He continued, his voice quieter now, "As a god, I was not cognizant of such things. This horse is... otherworldly, in its own way. I do not know that it acknowledges anything beyond its duty."

"It does." Ilys assured him.

"How do you know?"

"Even otherworldly creatures are not safe from your arsehole-ness. She surely feels and knows more than duty."

"Clever." He nodded, a smile teasing his lips, but just as soon as the amusement arrived it ran. He held a hand up, stopping the pair.

"What?" she asked, her body already tensing. "What is wrong?"

His gaze locked on the rising smoke. "Souls calling for collection," he said carefully. "They are calling from battle. It is a war field. Gopin rests on the border of Annon and Tyl," he noted, eyes scanning the horizon. "Two nations at odds. Tyl does not hold the patience for Annon's demands, and Annon has grown fat on their threats."

Ilys followed his gaze, watching as the shape of Gopin took form. A river cut through the land just beyond it, the border itself marked by no true wall, just a quiet, ever-shifting line between one people and another.

"Do they actively fight?" she asked.

"There is not much life left," he admitted.

She turned to look at him then, at the way his jaw set, the flicker of memory old and weary in his gaze.

"You still feel your purpose like this? Can you still collect?" she gestured to his mortal form, to the fragile flesh and bone he was now bound to.

"It is dimmer," he explained gruffly, "but there."

She did not know if that comforted her or unsettled her more.

"You need not come if you do not wish to," he offered. "I will find you a safe place nearby."

She let out a sharp breath. "You are mortal," she snapped.

He blinked at her, confusion flickering across his face. "Yes?"

"You are not Death," she wryly dictated. "You are an unnamed mortal, very capable of dying."

He sighed, already sensing her direction of thought. "It is not my time to die, Veilwalker."

"It is not," she agreed, voice cold. "Because I won't let it be. I will accompany you." She kicked Spire forward, riding ahead of him. "You need a successor before you can end your poisonous reign here."

Death exhaled, long and dilatory, before nudging his own nameless steed forward. "My savior," he mockingly praised under his breath.

Ilys ignored the unease curling in her stomach, ignored the way the air seemed to mock the closer they drew to the rising smoke.

A slaughter awaited them.

They moved through the fog on foot, their horses tied beneath a grove of leafless trees. Ilys kept low, boots soundless on the gritty earth, her cloak drawn close. Beside her, Death walked with care, no longer weightless. The trees broke and the field stretched before them like a wound.

Bodies lay twisted in the churned mud, caught in the stillness that came after battle. Smoke clung to the ground in heavy coils, rising from a broken pyre that had long since gone cold. Ash drifted like snow through the air. The stink of blood and rot lay rampant across the soil.

And in the distance, movement.

Six figures moved among the dead, clad in the stained remnants of Tyl's verdant colors. No banners. No order. One kicked over a corpse and cut free a belt. Another dragged a sword behind him, letting it scrape just to hear the sound. One bent to lift a body by the hair, turned the face up to the light, then shoved a blade through the throat.

They were not looters. Not quite. Not soldiers, either. They were men who had remained because no one had told them to go.

Ilys crouched behind a low rise and pulled Death down with her. "N ow," she whispered. "Shift. Do it now."

Death's gaze swept the field. She saw him pause, saw the moment he felt the souls still residing, faint as smoke caught in the wind.

"I feel them," he said.

"Then take them," she urged. "Before we're seen."

He closed his eyes. Drew in a breath. The air bent around them. His outline blurring as it once did at the height of his divinity.

Then it passed. His shoulders slumping and the magic slipping from him like a breath.

"I cannot," he confessed.

Ilys gripped his sleeve. "Try again."

"I did."

She looked toward the field. Too late.

One of the men had turned. "There's movement on the rise," he called, voice dull.

The others looked up.

Another said, "Armed?" Boots shifted in the mud.

"Run," Ilys whispered.

But Death didn't move. He stood, hands empty and latent.

"Once more," he growled, but the effort met only silence.

The short one called up to them, "Who do you belong to?" His voice reached the pair unhurried, curious, and confident.

Death raised his chin. "We belong to none. We are here to do the Veil's work."

The men paused, amused.

"You speak like a man of Annon," observed the first, stepping forward. He stood short and broad-shouldered, armor cobbled from rusted scraps. Soot streaked his face, and his beady, vulture-like eyes darted over her.

"You wear no seal," the man said. "No lord's colors." His gaze shifted to Ilys. "She looks like a priest's dog."

"You've no cause here," Ilys said. Her voice didn't rise. "Turn back." The insolence of it rattled her. *Had they no fear of a God? Of the Fates?* Yet when Ilys looked at Death, her gaze caught on the vulnerable pulse beating in the strong coils of his neck.

Another spoke behind him, "Anyone left breathing is fair game."

A third added, "You'll break just the same."

They moved as one, wordless.

Death reached for Ilys, but she pulled away, drawing her blade.

"You'll find I do not break," she raised.

They came fast, four of them. One hung back, watching, still picking through the corpses. The first lunged at Death.

Ilys stepped between, steel meeting steel in a jolt that rang through her bones. Her sword caught his, deflected just enough. She twisted, slammed her hilt into his jaw. He reeled, and she ducked the return blow, but her feet slipped in the mud. She caught herself. Just barely.

Another came in from the side.

She turned into him, grabbed his wrist, drove her knee into his stomach. He grunted, doubled over. She buried her blade in his ribs. He folded around it, breath catching in a wet rattle.

She pulled free, and a leaden weight struck her back hard.

She hit the ground flat, ribs jarred. A man crashed atop her, a knife in hand, driving it down toward her throat. The blade inched closer. She couldn't move her legs. Couldn't breathe.

She jerked her head sideways, then snapped it up, smashing it into his nose. He grunted, faltered.

She twisted, got her arm free, elbowed his throat. He rolled off, coughing. She scrambled to her knees, mud in her teeth, vision blurring.

Another came.

He surged forward, all muscle and armor. She threw up her sword just in time; the hit stung to the bone. He caught her collar and slammed her into the tree. Her head cracked, ribs howling.

"You're just a girl," he dumbly offered.

She spat blood into his face and stabbed up under his jaw. The blade lodged deep, her arm trembling with the force of it. He twitched. Dropped.

Behind her, another sound. She turned.

One of them had reached Death, knocked him to the ground. Death raised a hand, but the man kicked it away.

Ilys charged. She tackled him low, driving them both into the mud. They rolled. She came out on top, straddling him, sword in both hands.

She didn't speak. She drove the blade into his chest.

Once.

Twice.

A third time.

Only then did he stop moving. The field fell quiet. Only the wind remained.

Ilys stood, covered in blood and mud. Her hair stuck to her face, her breath ragged. Her sword sagged in her hand.

Death sat slumped nearby, his coat torn, blood running from a cut at his brow. One glove gone. His eyes met hers, hollow with shame.

"You," he began, voice hoarse, "you should not have done that."

She turned to him, furious. "And you," she accused, voice low, "should be a god."

He looked away. The field did not answer. The dead did not rise.

She wiped her blade on the grass, then walked to him and held out her hand.

He took it, her grip iron.

Without a word, Ilys mounted Spire, though her ribs protested with each breath and her left arm throbbed from shoulder to wrist. Blood caked her fingers where she hadn't noticed a cut, and her cloak was heavy with it, both hers and others. She didn't bother wiping her face. She'd take the discarded, muddied veil and hide. Hide from the bodies. Hide from Death. Hide from herself.

They did not speak as they crested to where the trees gave way again, and the forest spilled them into a second field, wider and infinitely worse. The battlefield opened before them like a hollowed body, gutted and laid bare.

Ilys rode ahead, her fingers white-knuckled around Spire's reins, the bones in her side shifting with every jolt. Her breath came shallow, each inhale scraping the inside of her chest. Crows had already descended, their black wings flickering like scattered ink across the field, tearing into whatever flesh had been left unclaimed, starved and greedy.

The mud had been churned into foul sludge with the rain that had fallen and the blood that had spilled. It sucked at the hooves of her steed, clinging to Spire's legs as they moved forward. Men lay where they had fallen, their armor dented, their bodies twisted in unnatural angles. Some still clutched their weapons, fingers locked around hilts. Others had been stripped, their bodies left bare and crumpled, uniforms stolen by the desperate or the victorious.

A man lay on his back, his throat cut so deeply that his head had nearly separated from his body, the gash yawning dark against his pale flesh. His uniform soaked through with blood, the crest of Tyl barely visible beneath the gore. A soldier of Annon knelt beside him, his body slumped forward, dying in prayer, a spearhead still buried in his side.

She passed another body, a boy—too young, her mind supplied distantly—whose helm had fallen from his head to reveal hair matted with blood. His eyes were open, glassy, fixed on the sky that no longer cared for him. His ribs had been caved in, his breastplate crushed beneath a fallen horse that had died on top of him, its legs twisted, its mouth still stretched open in a frozen scream. Ilys pet Spire, instinctually, reassuring, and begging the horse not to see. Death revealed its full spectacle, all the malice and gore laid bare.

Ilys did not stop. She did not look away.

Another body, another ruin. A woman lay bound, her throat cut clean from ear to ear, blood dried black against her tunic. She hadn't died in battle; this was no act of war, just a slower kind of violence. A cruelty left behind after the fighting had stopped.

Ilys's stomach twisted, but she swallowed it down.

The battlefield stretched on, a mass grave in the making. More bodies. Some alone, some tangled together, limbs entwined; even in death they clung to one another. Some were headless, their skulls taken as trophies while their bodies were left faceless in the mud. Some had been left to rot where they fell, others dragged into piles and set aflame. Smoke still curled from the embers, the charred remnants barely distinguishable as human.

She guided Spire around a heap of corpses, stacked like logs, ribs bending beneath the crush. Some still wore their expressions of terror, mouths frozen in screams, eyes bulging from sockets that had begun to sink.

Rain leached the color from their uniforms, reduced their banners to rags, and scoured their flesh to what remained: blood, sinew, bone.

Death followed behind her, silent. He did not speak. He did not command nor call her to hurry. He let her see.

She could feel him watching. She rode on.

Ahead, more crows had gathered, their black wings glistening in the dull light, their beaks slick with the remnants of the feast they had been granted. One tore at the flesh of a fallen man, pulling away a strip of skin, the sound wet, viscous. Another hopped between the ribs of an exposed chest cavity, pecking at whatever soft parts remained.

She turned to Death, her voice sharp. "Where shall you collect?"

He sat atop his horse, still wrapped in his mortal body, his dark coat speckled with mud, his hair wind-tossed, his face a study in control.

His gaze swept the field before him. "It will come."

Ilys swung down from Spire and her boots sank into the clinging mud. The battlefield smelled of blood, earth, iron, and rot. She threaded through the bodies without looking too long at any one of them.

Then she heard him.

Not all the bodies were still.

Further ahead, a man still lived, choking on wet breath. Small mews of pain guided the pair to him. He clutched at his stomach, intestines spilling through his fingers, dark and glistening, steam rising faintly from them in the cold. He blinked at her as she passed, lips trembling, as if forming words took more effort than dying. Each breath gurgled, blood rising in his chest. He lifted a shaking hand toward her, fingers spread in a plea.

"Please," he rasped. He would not last long.

Ilys knelt beside him, unsheathing her blade and from behind her, Death shifted in his saddle. "Ilys."

She ignored him.

The man's eyes fluttered, unfocused, struggling to keep hold of the moment. His fingers twitched.

She gripped the hilt tighter. Her hand ached from where she'd slammed it into a man's jaw less than an hour ago. She inhaled.

"Vasha," she whispered, driving the blade home.

It ended in a breath. Relief left him first, then everything else. Blood welled up around the blade as she withdrew it, staining the mud beneath him.

"That is not your decision to make." Death spoke low, edged with warning.

The air around them changed. Ilys turned her head just in time to see him change.

The mortal weight of him faded, his frame stretching, sharpening, settling into a shape not meant for this world. His coat billowed, his features refining into a cold and distant perfection. The space around him warped, the air bending to accommodate what could no longer be called a man.

He kept his eyes on the battlefield, on the bodies, on the souls rising loose from them. Death moved with a reverence that Ilys had never quite understood, a quiet, practiced efficiency that spoke of repetition, done not once or twice but a thousand times over. His steps were mesmeric, as though he could have walked this battlefield blind and still known exactly where to go. He approached each body with the same quiet solemnity, pausing only for a breath before moving on. A transition from life to death, from presence to absence.

Ilys watched, her fingers brushing idly at the air where the souls had passed, her hand following the invisible path of what lingered for only a moment before vanishing.

A soldier lay sprawled across the mud, his face slack, his eyes dull, a deep wound carved through his side. His body reposed, yet Death stopped beside him, tilting his head, listening. Then, he raised a hand, fingers barely moving, and a tide of energy rolled through. The soldier's body sagged, energy releasing from it, rising in a way that barely caught the light before fading entirely.

Death bowed his head, murmuring words Ilys could not hear.

Then, he moved to the next.

Death knelt beside a woman, her fingers curled in the fabric of her ruined tunic and a streak of dried blood trailing from the corner of her mouth. He lifted his hand just enough to stir, to loosen. Though her lungs no longer worked, the woman sighed, her body slackening as her soul slipped free, disappearing into the air like breath on a cold morning.

His lips moved again in a whisper too soft for Ilys to catch.

Again and again, he repeated this ritual, the same careful movements, the same hushed words. They moved through the twisted bodies of Annon and Tyl alike, through the remnants of a war that had left a gaping wound in its wake.

A dying man groaned softly, his chest rising and falling in shallow, uneven breaths. Ilys paused, watching as Death knelt beside him, lowering his head, listening. The man's lips barely moved, the faintest ghost of speech escaping before his body shuddered and went still.

Death raised his hand, calling on his power. The shift in the air came like a sigh. *Finally*, it seemed to say. *Finally.*

Ilys closed her eyes briefly, pressing her fingers to her brow. The last soul slipped free, and the battlefield settled once more.

Death straightened, his dark coat grazing the bloodied earth, his gaze lifting beyond the ruin before him. He inhaled deeply and as he did, the field itself seemed to pull inward. Every body, every lifeless form, what remained within them gave way on a final exhale, a quiet surrender. Vitality drained from flesh, pouring like unseen threads into his embrace, drawn back into whatever lay beyond the Veil.

The bodies, now emptied, seemed somehow less than before, their presence dulled, their fingerprint upon the world diminishing with the last of what had tethered them here.

Death stood at the center of it all, his form unmoved

"Is it done?" she asked, her voice softer than she had intended.

He glanced at her, his dark eyes smooth as still water: reflective, yet withholding.

"Let us leave," he ordered.

Neither looked back.

Chapter 29

The closer they came to Marrai, the city neighboring Gopin, the more people they passed. Families, merchants, and travelers all grabbed what they could and moved with the urgency of those who had seen a power they could not fight.

She turned to Death, expecting some kind of reaction. But the god beside her did not acknowledge the exodus around them. Not in the way she did. He did not look at the frightened expressions, the hurried steps. He appeared angry—furious, even—in a manner so human it surprised her.

Annon soldiers already filled the streets of Marrai, their armor glinting as they moved between barricades and vantage points. The air carried the metallic bite of readying for more battle.

The distant sound of hooves breaking sounded through the square, escalating the urgency camped amongst the crowd. A low, rolling thunder of approaching riders. War horns rang out, their eerie, hollow wail carrying across the town, coming from both sides of the river. Ilys's limbs shuddered at the sound. Death's expression darkened further.

He turned sharply, veering down an alleyway, peering out at the approaching mass of soldiers cresting the hills on either side. The banners of Tyl snapped in the wind, and even from a distance, the gleam of steel caught the dull, overcast light.

He cursed under his breath, staring out at the oncoming tide of men and their war. Looking all around for any exit, charcoal eyes glazed with unease.

Ilys guided Spire closer, her pulse thrumming in her ears. "What now?" she hissed.

"We leave," he said simply.

She shot him a glare. "Through that?" She gestured toward the mass of soldiers closing in. They had entered Marrai planning to stay the night, but now the city found itself surrounded, Annon's forces bracing for the clash.

He turned to her then, his expression void, his eyes dark as the river before a storm. "Would you rather stay and be crushed beneath it?"

Ilys didn't answer. Instead, she sheathed her sword, dismounted, stepped past him, and guided Spire toward the cover of the stable ahead, running through the alley as her heart hammered against her ribs. Death followed without a word, but she felt his menace. He disapproved.

Outside, men screamed. Hooves pounded against the packed earth. Steel clashed, and the wet, sickening sound of a blade meeting flesh followed.

Ilys pressed herself against the wooden wall, Death beside her, his body contouring her own. Juxtaposing the quiet of the stable and the banal scent of hay, war raged just beyond the walls.

The building shook as impact rattled the wooden beams, dust falling from the rafters, settling onto her shoulders. She clenched her fists, willing herself to breathe evenly, even as the battle pressed closer.

At some point, Death shifted beside her, tilting his head, listening beyond the immediate chaos.

"This will not end quickly," he ground out.

Ilys exhaled through her nose, fingers flexing at her sides. "No."

He turned toward her fully then, his presence weighty in the dim light, reiterating, "We should have left."

"We would not have made it through them," she argued, angry and tired and soaked in blood.

Death hushed her, leading the horses deeper into the stable, tucking them into the farthest stalls, hidden from sight.

At some point, exhaustion overtook the tension. Ilys sat first, resting her back against the wooden wall, tilting her head. Her limbs ached. Her body complained from too many days in the saddle. She had been trained to endure, but battle, even when outside the fray, bore differently.

Death sat beside her eventually, lowering himself with the kind of unhurried grace that made her want to strike him. Solid. Untouched.

For a long while, neither of them spoke.

Outside, the hours stretched. The sharp cries of wounded men carried through the walls, along with the wet clang of swords, the ugly thunder of retreat and charge. The sound crawled under her skin. Her stays felt too tight, her lungs caged. Each metallic clash outside pressed harder against her ribs until she could no longer get air. Her eyes locked on the bloodstains drying on her skirts and her hands. The veil scratched across her cheek, unbearable. She ripped it away, sucking in shallow, frantic breaths.

"Ilys?" Death questioned, wary and alert.

She surged to her feet. The stall shrank too small. The walls were closing in. Sweat slicked her skin. The stink of rot, the copper of blood, the distant cries of dying men; it all pressed down until she could taste bile. Her fingers tore at her bodice, yanking until the seams gave way. The black fabric fell from her shoulders, and the unfettered air allayed her testy, bare skin. Silent tears streaked her face as she kicked at her skirts, clawing at the hem.

Away. Away. Get it off. Get all of it off!

"Ilys," he hissed, eyes ripe with worry.

She collapsed against the ground, the hay scratching at her exposed back and the thin chemise. Her chest heaved as if she had been running.

And then a man's body slammed her down, knife flashing, ribs shrieking as she held him off. Another came, faster, stronger. The words *you're just a girl* rang in her skull before she shoved her blade up under his jaw.

The other memory struck next, sharper than the first.

The man in the mud, intestines spilling through his fingers. Steam rising from him in the cold. His hand reached toward her, lips forming *please.* She'd knelt, unsheathed her blade. Death had said her name, but she had ignored him.

Vasha, she had said, and pressed the blade down.

Back in the stall, her body convulsed with a dry sob. She clawed at the dirt, desperate to scrape herself clean, to peel the memory out of her own skin.

"Why?" she pleaded, hoarse and childlike. "Why is this what I was made for?"

At the sight of her tear-streaked face, Death crawled to her, grabbing at her hand. She latched on, clinging without thought, drowning and finding the only solid thing left. The impulse rattled him; he leaned away in surprise, but she only held tighter, grounding herself against his palm.

"Breathe," he said, low but insistent. "Breathe, Ilys."

Her breath hitched harder, ragged and shallow. He bent close, their foreheads nearly touching. "Count with me. My breaths—match them." His voice demanded so tender, but stern.

She tried, her chest stuttering in time with him.

"I know you're already counting mine," he teased darkly, mouth curving against her temple. His eyes caught hers, unblinking, pulling her into the rhythm.

One inhale. One exhale.

Again. And again.

His thumb traced pacifying lines against her arm, his heartbeat languorous beneath her ear, a metronome anchoring her to him. "There," he affirmed, gaze still locked on hers. "Stay with me. Just keep counting."

He gathered her against him and she folded into his resolute hold. Her cheek pressed to his chest; his heartbeat carried on, infallible. The sobs came again, wet and helpless as they shuddered through her whole frame.

He held her with one arm wrapped around her waist, the other splayed across her shoulders, his thumb sweeping charged lines against her arm. He rocked her gently, unhurried and rhythmic.

His mouth found her forehead and lingered, pinning her to the present. The sounds of war continued, but their bodies betrayed them. Breath by breath, eye to eye, merciful sleep finally crept in.

Ilys woke to the quiet.

Not the peaceful stillness of dawn, nor the fleeting hush before the world stirred awake. But a quiet that teased an absence of life. The horses shifted in their stalls, restless but subdued, as though they, too, sensed what waited beyond the walls.

Death sat beside her, his head tilted, dark eyes distant. Then, without looking at her, he stood, and drew the cloak back over his own shoulders.

She pushed herself upright, brushing straw from her sleeves, watching him instead of speaking.

Death strode to the stable doors, pressing a gloved hand against the aged wood. He listened, then pulled it open enough to peer out.

Ilys waited. Her fingers curled into her palms.

After a moment, he turned back and extended his hand.

She hesitated only for a breath before taking it, letting him guide her into the morning. But she found herself instead guided into a nightmare.

The streets ran red.

Not in the way of battle, where blood flew wild in the clash of steel on steel. This blood pooled. It stained. It dried stratified and dark across dirt and stone.

Bodies littered the roads, contorted where they had fallen, left where they had been struck down. Men in armor, yes, but others too: women clutching at their children, elders with their hands still raised in surrender, merchants in blood-soaked tunics.

Homes had been ripped apart, their doors torn from their hinges, their belongings scattered like careless afterthoughts. A broken chair lay upturned in the street, a wheel from a cart splintered into pieces beside it.

She stepped over the body of a man, his throat torn open, his fingers still curled around the hilt of a rusted dagger. Further ahead, she saw a woman sprawled in the dust, her long hair tangled in a pool of congealed blood. A deep gash split her back, but the way her arm reached toward the doorway made Ilys stop.

She reached for something—or someone.

Ilys followed the angle of her hand. A small form lay just inside the house. A child. Ilys's breath hitched.

She moved before she could stop herself, stepping over the threshold into the ruined home. A young girl—no older than Hanna—lay twisted on the ground, her small hands clenched, her face locked between fear and pain. Ilys sank beside her, her breath rasping in her own ears. Fingers that held in battle, quivered now as she brushed a tangle of dark curls from the child's face.

She had Hanna's curls.

She had Hanna's age.

Ilys swallowed the bile rising in her throat. She pressed her fingers to the girl's bloodstained eyelids, closing them with careful precision. Her lips parted, a whisper slipping through, unbidden.

"Monsters." Her own voice barely sounded like hers, kneeling in the ruin of this home, in the ruin of this child.

A gust of wind howled through the broken streets. Across the river, beyond the town, Tyl's land stretched vast and untouched; its rolling hills and rich fields stood unbothered, unburned, and undisturbed by the horror left in their wake.

She stared at the wide expanse, at the wealth of it.

"I hope their country burns," she whispered. A prayer. A vow.

Ilys remained crouched beside the girl, her hands resting on the child's small, bloodied form. The wind ghosted through the streets, carrying with it the echoes of violence long since passed. She didn't move, not while the horror curled like a noose around her ribs.

Behind her, Death stepped forward, his boots silent against the blood-stained earth. He did not kneel, did not reach out, did not attempt to pull her from the moment.

"You call these men monsters," he said, his voice cool and even while watching the wreckage, the ruin. "And I will not disagree." His gaze shifted, scanning the desolation before them. "But who reared their violence? Who raised their horses? Who called for their swords to be burnished?"

Ilys stiffened, her fingers curling where they rested against the child's cold skin. She thought of the lessons drilled into her since childhood; the people of Tyl were the savages across the river, the lawless men who took what they wished and held no honor nor mercy.

But Death spoke not of men, but of nations. And Annon, for all its righteousness, for all its prayers and sacred oaths, was not innocent.

She clenched her jaw, swallowing against the rising bile in her throat.

Death's voice lowered, almost to himself. "Some men honor no gods. Obey no Fates. They carve into the world thick with desire," he lectured, "and we are left with the deficit."

The wind pressed dust into her skin, but the tears streaking her unveiled face sliced through it, leaving pale trails against her cheeks. She did not wipe them away.

"Come," Death said simply.

She thought he would take her out of the town, lead them away from this ruin, but instead, he turned back toward the stables. They moved silently, careful to avoid the bodies, stepping over shattered belongings and bloodied footprints. The town still smelled of rot and smoke, and the air held the heaviness of what had been lost.

The world outside had screamed itself raw, but the stable remained, untouched by the carnage outside. The horses stood restless in their stalls, their quiet offered near reprieve. The world made sense here—among creatures who did not lie, who feared without hatred and hungered without sin. She thought of Morrigan then—the familiar weight of him pressed against her leg, his breath a soft percussion against the soil. She missed that rhythm, that quiet exchange between beings who required merely presence. No words, no worship. Only trust, given and kept. Horses did not raze villages to prove dominion. They did not invent cruelty and call it order. They fled when danger came. They fought when cornered. They lived within the truth of their own need.

"Stay," Death ordered.

Ilys sat heavily against the wooden wall and pressed the heels of her palms against her eyes. The flies still buzzed in her ears. The sight of the child's small, twisted form burned into the back of her mind.

She heard Death move, his footsteps measured as he left her there. She did not know how long he had gone. Minutes. Hours. Time felt frayed, slipping through her hands, indistinct.

By the time he returned, the light had shifted, the afternoon stretching toward dusk. He pulled her to her feet without a word and guided her out of the stables past the dying embers of a town that had already been lost.

Her breath caught at the sight he had escorted her towards.

The bodies were gathered, lined side by side in careful rows. Civilians. The men, the women, the children, placed as if in sleep, their hands folded over their chests, fresh-cut flowers bunched between their fingers.

Death stood beside her. "Give them the rites," he said. "I must collect. Give them your rites. Ease your mind."

She knew the words by heart—the blessings carved into her tongue before she could even name her own soul. They rose now, unbidden, pressing at her throat: the ritual phrases, the promises of peace, the command to release and return. She had spoken them a hundred times. Had drawn the line between life and death with a seasoned hand. Had believed that mercy could be measured by obedience.

But as she looked upon them—their broken bodies, their faces emptied of everything but fear—the words curdled. They did not fit here. They belonged to marble halls and polished altars, to the sanctified performance of loss. Not to this. Not to those who had been cornered, stripped, slaughtered without choice or dignity.

Kneeling beside the first body, Ilys placed a hand over the still chest, her voice barely more than breath. The words were old, older than the rites she had been forced to learn, intoned in passing by Grim, a story half-forgotten until now.

"Where the fire dims, you will rest.
Where the water stills, you will wait.
Where the stars gather, you will be known."

She pressed her fingers lightly against the cold brow, closing her eyes ."Vasha."

She moved to the next, repeating the words until they hummed in the earth, sang in the streams, and sang in the wind.

The air shimmered and curled around Death, reaching and unfurling.

And then, they came.

The light caught their edges, pale and flickering, as they moved toward him like wisps of breath on cold air. They did not resist. Death raised a hand, gloved fingers barely tilting, and the souls—drawn to him—responded, moving in graceful currents as though carried by a tide unseen. Not violent. Not unkind.

The Veil awaited them, and they went willingly.

A shepherd leading his flock to the place beyond knowing.

One by one, the spirits faded, their forms dissolving into the hush of twilight. No cries. No struggle. Just a fading, a release.

The last soul slipped from sight, the air settling once more as the Veil closed behind them like a door gently drawn shut.

She looked to Death, breath ragged and wet, and saw him as he was made to be.

Chapter 30

"We are bound to receive attention now," Death said.

Ilys knew he spoke of her chemise, but she could not and would not don her bloodied dress. Death's robes did a fine job of covering her. Except now, astride Spire, she looked down and it occurred to her that her nipples peeked through the sheer white of her chemise.

"More so than when I am veiled in all my divine regalia?" she questioned, quirking an eyebrow. His gaze caught on her pink buds clinging stubbornly to the cotton, lingering just long enough to make her stomach clench with heat.

"Yes, I presume so," he affirmed, forcing his gaze forward.

She cursed the sudden, treacherous warmth pooling low in her belly. Did his mortal form notice such things? The thought made her burn hotter, and yet—gods help her—it was almost welcome. It cut through the guilt and self-disgust coiled tight in her chest. Her thoughts spiraled, turning sharp and self-deprecating, until Death's voice cut through them.

"Ilys?" His tone sharply asked, snapping her back to herself. "Did you hear what I said?"

She blinked, dazed. "What?"

"There's lodging up ahead. We'll stop and get a warm meal, yes?"

"That sounds fine."

He studied her, worry etched across his brow, then turned away without pressing further.

Before the last two years, Ilys had never stepped foot outside the Sanctum, and now the exchange of coin for a night's lodging barely made her pause. She leaned against the wall, waiting while Death made arrangements. Her fingers combed through her hair, cringing at the stiff, crusted texture.

When he finished, she slipped up beside him and addressed the woman behind the desk. "Is there a river or stream nearby where I might bathe?"

The woman glanced at her with a faintly puzzled expression. "You wouldn't want to, dear."

Ilys frowned, but the woman turned back to her ledger.

"Waste, Ilys," Death explained near her ear, his voice low and wry. "The rivers here are filled with it."

The woman looked up again, satisfied with her work. "There's a bathhouse next door. I'll take you there once we've gotten your rooms settled." Ilys had never heard the term, but her body betrayed her begging and cowing at the word bath. It cared not what form it came in.

The woman guided them up the stairs, to their room. Ilys realized she had not heard the discussion of their actual arrangements. It was a room with two beds once more.

"Sharing?" Ilys queried.

The woman smiled at the disdain in Ilys' voice, quietly leaving the pair.

"There are two beds," he defended.

"Was there only one room available?" she pressed. He cowed.

He faltered, caught. "I—" He searched for the right words. "After all we've seen, you would prefer we stay apart?"

"Is someone frightened?" she teased, though the last few days tugged at her as well.

"New as I am to mortal feelings, I have no name for it," he admitted quietly. "But I should like you near." He seemed to hear the intimacy in his own words and added quickly, "In case of another attack."

"So I may save you again?" she needled.

His demeanor immediately changed, face falling. "I am sorry, Ilys. I promised you a clean slate this march." His pity rankled her.

"You did not ask me to end those men," she said, looking away as she began to tidy her meager belongings.

"Yes, but—" he started.

"I'm going to bathe." She cut him off and left him standing there, words caught in his throat.

Steam clung to the air as she sank into the bath. The heat burned her skin, but Ilys welcomed it. She ducked her head under once, holding herself beneath until her ears filled with the hush of the water. No crowd, no screaming, no Death's pitying voice. Only the muted pound of her heart and the smothered ache in her chest. She surfaced with a gasp, hair plastered to her cheeks, and for a brief respite she felt lighter.

So she did it again.

This time she stayed longer. The water folded around her, drowning sound and shape alike. Her lungs protested, pain blooming sharp and hot, but she didn't move. She wanted that quiet to swallow her whole. Her chest convulsed, her body begging her to breathe, but still, she stayed.

A hand seized her by the shoulder, yanking her violently to the surface.

She coughed and choked, water streaming down her face, her chest heaving as she clutched the stone edge for balance.

"What are you doing?" Death demanded, voice sharper than she'd ever heard it, ragged and near-panicked. His sleeves were soaked, water dripping from his fingers where they gripped her, his own body half-submerged alongside her.

Small and raw, like a child caught in the act, she confessed, "I wanted quiet, just for a moment."

Death's face darkened. "Do you think me invincible, Ilys? That I could wrench you back from the Veil itself? Do not play so carelessly with your life."

Her mouth curled. "It is my wretched existence. I will play with it however I choose."

His jaw tightened. "Would you spit in the face of what I have sacrificed? Of what I have lost?"

"What are you talking about?" she snapped, anger flaring.

"Why do you think the Fates stripped me of my godhood?" His voice rose, sharp and cutting. "Have you truly no clue?"

She stared at him, blank and mute.

"I am but a collector," he said, voice suddenly low, dangerous. "But you—" The tendons of his palm flexed. "You forced my hand."

Her mind reeled, dragging her back to that night: Lord Veylen's blood, the cell, Owin's broken body, Death standing over her, saving her.

"This is because—" she started.

"Yes." His mouth twisted. "Well done, Ilys. After nearly a century, you've managed to kill a god in one stroke."

"I did not ask you to kill Owin," she said, forcing the words through her throat.

"You did not last a day on your own!" he shouted, voice cracking. "Would you have preferred I left you there? Let them finish what they started?"

"Yes."

"Ilys—"

"Yes." Her voice rankled. This was not Ilys the Veilwalker speaking, not the obedient sanctum-born servant; this was Ilys the bird, untethered and broken. "I wish you would have."

Ilys no longer yearned to kill this Death. She knew not when that changed, only that it had. She found no satisfaction in imagining his end. No joy in the thought of his undoing. What she felt instead was older, darker. The anger toward him that had once kept her alive, that malicious flame, now curled around *her* own heart. It burned, cutting her open from the inside.

"No," Death said, shaking his head as though he could will her into compliance. "You will live, you foolish creature."

"I will not."

His hand shot out, gripping her chin, forcing her to meet his gaze. "You will, Ilys."

She seized his forearm, her own words coming like a strike. "I. Will. Not."

Her breath came fast and shallow. Only then did she notice how close they were, how close he had come to drag her from the water. His breath cooled her wet cheeks. His white shirt clung to him, soaked through, outlining every sharp line of him.

Her body was a storm, betraying her, and she welcomed it. The fire drowned out the gray, drowned out the dread. Finally—finally—she felt something.

She bit him, sharp and quick, her teeth sinking into the meaty heel of his hand. His eyes went wide, the shock giving way to desire hotter, darker. She dragged his thumb to her mouth, licking the droplets of water from it, tasting salt and skin. His gaze locked onto the motion, pupils blown wide, lust sparking there like struck flint.

"Ilys." His voice warned, but the admonition frayed at the edges.

She bit down on his thumb again, slower this time, and he groaned. Grabbing his wrist, she guided his hand down, pressing it against the swan-like curve of her throat, making him hold her there. His breath hitched.

Lower still, she pressed his palm against the swell of her breast, molding his hand until his fingers curled around her. He squeezed, unthinking, and she felt him lean closer, his forehead nearly brushing hers.

She could feel him, hard against her stomach, the heat of him grounding her as much as it set her alight.

The contact must have shocked him as he pulled back.

"Gods, Ilys." He reclaimed his hand and pressed his palms to his eyes hard. "Come. I will not stay, but I will not leave you here alone."

She swallowed the small embarrassment. "Leave. I'll be fine." She pulled away, pushing back into the waters and concealing her naked body once more.

"I will wrench you from the waters and carry you if I have to," he promised.

In answer, she ducked beneath the surface again, a willful act of defiance. Death waded toward her, jaw tight, refusing to play her game.

"Now," he ordered, voice low and sharp.

Ilys broke the surface with a roll of her eyes and swept past him, striding for the edge of the pool. Every step felt like a provocation.

More than ever, she wished she did not have to sleep just across the room from this dying god.

CHAPTER 31

Blowing out the lantern, Ilys watched the room fall dark. She laid awake, hyper aware of him on the other side of the room. The energy between them taut as a bowstring until morning broke.

When the light finally crept in, she found a blue dress draped over the chair. New and plain, but finely made. The innkeeper must have brought it at his request. She found she liked the color against her skin, so unused to seeing herself in anything but ceremonial charcoal.

He had not spoken of it nor looked at her as she dressed. A silent offering. A peace he did not know how to speak aloud. Ilys offered him a silent nod as she mounted Spire, not knowing how to voice thanks for a gift given so quietly.

"How much further until the entrance?" she asked, her voice low.

"We will not reach the Veilmarch for days," he replied without looking at her, his eyes drawn instead to the glow ahead.

Music carried on the night air as they rode into the next town, the square alive with fiddles, clapping, and the smell of fire and ale. The space illuminated, lit by lanterns strung from corner to corner while garlands of greenery mixed with preserved blood-red dahlias hung from the roofs.

It reminded her of her first march, of the night she had met Owin. The night he had smiled like a savior before finding her out and taking her prisoner. Her first dance and her first true betrayal.

She felt Death's eyes on her now, heavy and unblinking. Needy.

"How can they celebrate," she asked, "when three towns away there is slaughter?"

He swung down from his mare in one fluid motion. "Right," he said shortly, then turned back to her. "Get down."

"There's light still, we could make more distance—"

"No." The single word snapped like a whip. He seized Spire's reins. "We stop here."

"What are you doing?" she demanded, pulse quickening.

"Rewriting a memory."

She stared at him, heat licking her skin at his gaze. Then, she swung a leg over the saddle and let herself drop to the earth, wandering over through the warm bodies chattering, laughing, and singing. Morbidly fascinated by the cool contrast to what she had witnessed other warm bodies commit just a day before, she inhaled every detail.

Children held hands in a lazy circle, turning the wheel of their form. High pitched giggles floated towards her and it pinched her tired heart. She missed Hanna.

Enthralled with the scene, she crept towards the table filled with clay cups frothing with amber liquid. She sniffed the drink suspiciously and, not finding it too unkind to her nose, lifted it to drink deeply. Wheat and honey slid down her throat, loosening her spirit.

The music shifted to a brighter, faster sound. A couple broke into the center of the circle, spinning and stamping in perfect time. Another pair followed, and another, until the space grew crowded with cheers and clapping.

Then the crowd parted. Ilys stood alone at the edge of the square, the only one not yet called to the center. A daring smile ghosted across her face as she stepped forward.

The fiddler caught sight of her and changed his tune to match her pace, quick, untamed. She began to turn, hesitant at first, then faster, her skirts snapping around her legs. The crowd whooped. Ilys clapped to the beat, spinning until the air burned in her chest.

When she caught sight of him at the edge of the light, she stopped, hair falling wild about her face, breath ragged. Death watched her, still as stone. A laugh slipped from her, sharp and strange in her own ears. She turned again, this time toward him, daring him to move, to stop her, to do anything but watch. And he did watch—hungrily—as though she had been meant for this moment all along.

Before she could think better of it, a laughing woman grabbed Ilys's hands and spun her into the circle. They whirled together, skirts and hair flying, the crowd clapping in time. The music quickened, wild and bright, pulling Ilys along until she perched breathless.

Then a man stepped forward, catching her by the waist and sweeping her off her feet. For a dizzying instant she flew, suspended in the hot air of the square, before he set her back down with care, one of his hands firm on her waist and the other clasping her palm. He guided her through the dance, prancing her from one end of the circle to the other, each turn sharp, each step sure. The crowd whooped and stomped along, delighted by the spectacle. Ilys giggled; an unguarded, surprised sound that startled her even as it left her mouth.

Death still watched, offering a small smile that softened the hard lines of his face until he looked almost lovely. The music built, rising higher and higher until it ended in a screeching, triumphant note. The man twirled her once more, then released her, bowing with exaggerated flourish before jogging off to join his friends.

Ilys stood in the center of the square, flushed and laughing, her chest heaving. And Death remained, still at the edge of the crowd, still watching her. The revel was her stage, and he her only audience.

Death cut through the revelers with long, unhurried strides, his gaze never leaving hers. When he reached her, he leaned close enough that she could feel the ghost of his breath.

"Come," he said, low, meant for her alone. "You must feel starved."

He took her wrist and steered her through the crowd. The dancers parted easily for him, some still laughing, some still watching her as though they expected the dance to continue. The square's edge opened into a table spread with more clay cups of cider, steamed cacao, dark loaves, sugared pastries, and puddings glossy under the lantern light.

Ilys ignored the drinks, still too breathless to think of anything warm. Her hand closed around one of the puddings, cool and heavy, and she scooped a bite past her lips. The taste was a revelation. The sweet balanced with bitter in a soft-as-cream texture, while the grit of chocolate caught at her teeth. A satisfied moan escaped her, unguarded and soft and she forgot herself. When she glanced up, Death watched her with a look that warmed and unsettled her all at once.

"What?" she asked, her tone too sharp, defensive against the way her chest fluttered.

"Nothing." His mouth curved, laggard and amused. "I can tell it suits you."

He reached forward without asking, his thumb grazing her chin. When he drew back, a smear of chocolate glistened against the pad of his thumb. He didn't wipe it away. Instead, holding her gaze, he brought his thumb to his mouth and sucked it clean, leisurely savoring.

Heat flared up her throat, her pulse stumbling, reminded of their encounter in the bathhouse.

"Saving some for later?" His voice dropped lower now, almost mocking, as though daring her to answer.

Ilys could think of no banter. She dropped the spoon back into the empty cup and turned away, but not before she caught the ghost of a smile tugging at his mouth, dark and satisfied, as though he had just won a game she hadn't realized they were playing.

When she tore her eyes from Death, her gaze snagged on a scene near the edge of the revel. A young woman, barely more than a girl, with dark braids coiled tight against her head and a garland of faded flowers slipping down one side. Her dress once dyed a cheerful yellow, now molded to her form, muddied, spattered with dirt where she had been pushed against the pole. Her cheeks were already flushed from dancing, but fear had turned the color sharp and blotchy.

The man who gripped her loomed broad through the shoulders, his belly pressing against the seams of a stained jerkin. Blond hair clung to his scalp in greasy knots, his beard catching the lantern light like wire spun from filth. He had her trapped with one hand fisted in her bodice, tugging at the laces hard enough to bruise. She tried to twist away, still polite even in her refusal, murmuring words meant to soothe. But when she shoved him and snapped, his response was a ringing slap that cracked across her face.

Ilys froze, pulse hammering. She looked around, expecting someone, anyone, to intervene. But the fiddles still shrieked, the dancers still laughed, and no one seemed to see. Or perhaps they had chosen not to. Perhaps the struggle of a woman would always be too quiet.

She shoved her empty pudding cup into Death's hands and strode toward the pair, boots cutting sharp against the stones.

"Hey!" she shouted over the music, her voice slicing through the air. A few nearby revelers glanced her way, but no one moved.

"Hey!" she called again, louder this time, when the man still ignored her. He had the girl's chin in a bruising grip, forcing her to look at him.

Ilys seized him by the hair and yanked him backward. He swore and spun on her, breath hot with drink, bloodshot eyes narrowing.

"What the fuck do you think you're doing?" he bellowed, spit flying.

She squared her shoulders the way Baron had taught her and drove her fist into his face. His head snapped back, blood spraying from his crooked nose.

"Get the fuck off her," she snarled, planting herself between him and the girl.

The girl scrambled back, wide-eyed, her hand pressed to her reddening cheek. She wavered for only a moment before bolting into the crowd, vanishing like a startled bird.

The man reeled, blinking against the blood and fury in front of him.

"Stay out of this, bitch." His voice seeped out as a wet slur, his beard shining where it caught the lantern light. He lunged again, reaching past her.

"What, am I not to your liking?" Ilys purred, her voice a blade's edge. And then she hit him again.

He stumbled this time, clutching his face, swearing.

"Leave her alone," she hissed, "or have some fun with me instead."

The man roared and came at her, this time swinging. Ilys ducked, felt his fist graze her temple, and slammed her knee up into his gut. He doubled over, wheezing, but lashed out blindly, catching her shoulder hard enough to spin her. She snarled and tackled him, the two of them going down hard on the stone.

They rolled, clawing, kicking, grappling like feral dogs. His fist caught her cheek. Her elbow cracked against his ribs. Her braid came loose, hair tangling across her face. The crowd had gone deathly still around them, music forgotten. Then the glint of metal flashed between them.

Ilys felt the bite of the knife before she saw it. Hot pain lanced her shoulder, sharp and sudden, and for one stunned second she only stared.

"Fuck," she spat, staggering back, one hand pressed to the wound. Blood seeped hot through her fingers, staining her palm.

The man grinned through the blood on his own face, smug and cruel. "Should've stayed out of it."

Her vision went red. She drove her foot into his jaw, once, twice, again until his head cracked against the stones. He swore and tried to rise, dragging the knife with him. Death caught up before she could lunge again.

He dropped to one knee at her side, pressing a hand hard against the wound, his eyes blown wide with fear.

Then he stood.

The man had barely gotten to his knees when Death's hand fisted in his collar, hauling him upright like he weighed nothing. Death's face looked carved from fury, the shadows around him seeming to deepen. He slammed the man back against the post so hard the lantern shuddered above them, then drove his fist into the man's jaw with a crack that shocked the square.

"Stay the fuck down," Death growled, low and lethal. The man slumped, half-conscious, spitting blood into the dirt.

Death let him fall like discarded meat, then dropped back to Ilys, his hands already moving to staunch the bleeding. His voice came tight, urgent. "Hold still."

Ilys hissed, clutching at his wrist to keep him there. "I had him."

His jaw worked, but he didn't argue, just pressed harder against the wound, his body between her and the rest of the square, as though daring anyone else to try. Without a word, he swept her up into his arms.

She stiffened on instinct, but her body betrayed her, melting against him.

He carried her toward the horses, his grip steady, his breath even, but his eyes, his eyes were dark, clouded, and afraid.

Chapter 32

At the horses, he swung her carefully into the saddle. The motion tore at her side and she hissed through her teeth, clamping a hand to the wound.

"Hold on," he said shortly, mounting behind her. His arm bracketed her ribs as he dug his heels into Spire's flanks. They rode hard out of town, past the lantern light and into the empty road, his mare following behind. The fields on either side blurred in the dark. Each hoofbeat sent another jolt through her body. Each jolt felt like a white-hot blade twisting deeper.

"How far?" she asked finally, her voice tight, her breath coming sharp. He didn't answer right away, only pressed her closer to him, keeping her upright.

Rain began to fall, a thin, cold drizzle that soon soaked through her dress and plastered her hair to her face.

At last, he swore under his breath. "We will not make it to the next town," he bit out, reining Spire toward a side road. "I must tend to you now."

She gritted her teeth. "We could have stopped there."

"Yes," he said darkly, "I'm sure they would love tending to the woman who just attempted to murder one of their own."

She twisted her head toward him, fury sparking even through the pain. "How am I in the wrong?"

"You are not," he said simply, voice grim. "But nonetheless, we must stop."

He guided Spire off the road, into the shadow of an abandoned chapel half-hidden by trees. They found the roof caved in, the bell long gone, the stone steps slick with moss. He dismounted and lifted her down carefully, his cloak already soaked through. Inside, the altar still stood, and just enough shelter existed to keep the fire he struck alive. The flames crackled, casting jagged shadows up the chapel's crumbling walls. Rain slipped through the holes in the roof, pattering against the stone floor.

Ilys sat propped against the altar, one boot discarded, the other half-untied. Death sat across from her, his cloak open and streaked with mud, one knee drawn up, his hands dangling loose. He hadn't stopped watching her since they'd arrived.

"You breathe like the pain's setting in," he said finally, voice quiet.

"It's been in." Her tone was flat.

He nodded once. "You should let me see it."

"Why? So you can scold the wound?"

The corner of his mouth tugged. "No. I have salve and bandages."

She glanced at him, the faintest turn of her head. "And hands that shake when you reach for your power. Tell me, do they steady when you dress wounds?"

He didn't flinch. "You could find out."

Her jaw flexed. Then, without a word, she peeled down her bodice and bared the wound.

Death rose and crossed to her, quiet as the wind through the ruined rafters. He knelt, dipped two fingers into the tin of salve, and worked it gently over the worst of the cut. His touch bore a careful reverence.

She hissed softly when it bit at the raw edges.

"I warned you," he noted.

"You didn't."

"I meant to."

He held his tongue while cleaning the rest of the blood from her side, rinsing the cloth in the rainwater basin. When he finished, he didn't step back immediately. His shadow still stretched over her.

"What was the point of that?" he asked, referring to the violent encounter.

Ilys's eyes flicked toward the fire. "I am tired of violence. Of cruelty. I wanted him to taste it just as potent."

"Through more violence?" He queried, measured, but a hidden steel beneath it.

"Do you see some alternative?" Her head snapped toward him. "Was there a magic spell I forgot? A ritual in which everyone will drop their weapons and cease hurting one another?"

His jaw worked, but a response cheated him.

"I once thought the point of life was to seek happiness," she went on. Her voice arrived quieter now, yet sharper for it. "But now I see it only intends to make us strong. And I should only like to be a happy, pithy thing."

"You can be."

"I cannot. They will not allow it. Even if I was not made what I was, you wait around every corner. You chase us up every stairway. If it is not sickness, it is murder. If it is not murder, it is war. Is there nowhere safe from you?" Her voice cracked. "Is there nowhere far enough away from the hurt of it all?"

"I think you are right," he said after a moment, the admission pained. "But in this new state, I have seen the latter as well."

She turned her head toward him, wary. "What do you mean?"

"Happiness."

Her brow furrowed. "And where, pray tell, has Death found happiness?"

"I see it in you when you speak of Rowenna. I saw it in you when you were dancing. I see it in you when you press your face close to the wind, breathing it in. You soak up the world. If that is not happiness, then I am a stranger to it."

His eyes were on her now, intent and unblinking.

Her skin prickled under his gaze. "Yes, a stranger then." She tipped her chin up, refusing to let him have his point. "And may you remain one."

Only the crackle of the fire and the drip of rain seeped through the roof. He stayed, kneeling before her, the heat of him close enough to feel. And then, without asking, he sat back against the altar beside her. When he opened his cloak, she stared at him, uncertain.

"Just rest," he said quietly. "A moment." She hesitated, but the fight, the wound, and his quiet steadiness pressed down on her until she leaned in, until her cheek found his chest.

He tensed, breath halting, but didn't move away. Instead, after a long beat, his arm slid around her shoulders, anchoring her there. His heartbeat thundered under her ear. It startled her, how quick and strong and alive it sounded.

"You're afraid," she said at last, her voice soft and dry.

He didn't answer.

Her chin tipped up just enough for her to see the edge of his jaw. "Why is your heart racing, Death? Is it the storm? The gash in my shoulder? The end you face?" Still nothing, only the subtle stiffening beneath her cheek.

Then, very softly, Ilys queried, "Or is it me?"

He let out a breath, nearly a laugh, though it sounded more like surrender. His hand smoothed over her arm as if to quiet her.

"You're feeling things now," she whispered, eyes falling shut. "Isn't that strange?"

His heart only thudded faster. And still, he didn't let go.

The morning crept in lazy and grey, pressing against the stones of the chapel. Rain tickled softly through the broken roof, pooling in the cracks of the floor. Smoke lingered faintly, more memory than warmth now.

Ilys stirred. Her body ached. The bruises had set deeper with sleep. The gash throbbed in a dull rhythm with her heartbeat. She blinked blearily at the rafters above, then turned her head. Death sat a few paces away, back against the altar, methodically slicing a bit of bread with his knife. His cloak sat folded beside him and his posture was precise, persistent.

She struggled to push up, biting back a hiss as her shoulder pulled.

"You should eat something," he dictated.

She reached for the bread without thanks. Chewed, finding it dry and stale, catching in her throat. She swallowed anyway.

"I think the bruising is worse," she said.

"You'll need it cleaned once more," he said. "I have water."

"Are you offering or just narrating?"

His mouth twitched. "Both."

He stood, crossing to the basin without hurry. He rinsed the cloth. She watched him, watched the set of his shoulders, the quiet focus of his hands. How envious she was of that cloth. Of that water. Anything that might be touched by those long, lanky hands that was not her skin.

He knelt beside her and began undoing the bandage. His touch careful and reserved.

She tilted her head. "You're quiet this morning."

"So are you." He returned, pressing the cool cloth to her shoulder with deft movements. He refused to linger or be indulgent.

"You're... different," she said finally.

"It's morning," he said simply. "Mornings are different."

"Is that so?"

He finished the knot and stood. She watched him adjust the straps on his pack, standing carefully, testing her ribs.

"So. Rither Hollow," she named their next destination.

He nodded. "If we leave within the hour, we'll reach the edge before dark."

"And if we don't?"

"There's a chance we'll be sleeping in the open."

She reached to the sky, stretching her pained muscles. "Sounds familiar."

She caught him looking at her then, just a flicker, just a breath, but found it all the same. When he realized she'd noticed, he looked away. The sound of laces tightening, of water pouring into flasks, of boots scraping stone. All practical.

But as she slung her bag over her uninjured shoulder, she said, without looking at him, "You didn't sleep much either?"

"No."

"Because of the storm?"

He paused and adjusted his coat. "Something like that."

She gave a short nod. Let it rest.

But as they stepped into the cold morning light, she walked just a little nearer to his side than she needed to. Not quite touching.

And he let her.

They rode from the chapel on a narrow and wet path, the soil soft beneath the horses' hooves. The rain had lessened to a fine drizzle, beading on their cloaks and soaking into the earth. They didn't speak for some time. Ilys watched the way Death rode, one hand loose on the reins, the other resting against the saddle horn. He didn't fidget. He never fidgeted. He moved with careful economy, as if the body he wore were on loan and might break beneath the wrong gesture.

The rain caught in his lashes. A dark curl teased his eyebrow. *Unfair*, she thought, shifting in the saddle. *To look like that and not know it.*

When they reached a bend in the trail that overlooked a low field scattered with bare trees, Death slowed his horse and looked over. "We'll stop here for a rest."

Ilys dismounted stiffly, wincing as her boots hit the ground. Her body sang with complaint, each muscle sore, each joint tight. She stretched her arms overhead, hissing softly when her shoulder pulled.

"Don't overdo it," Death said without looking at her, already tying his horse to a low-hanging branch.

"I can't very well ride hunched like a crone all day," she argued, wiggling her fingers out toward the misty horizon.

"You'd frighten fewer people."

"I frighten enough."

A flicker of a smile.

She stepped off the trail a little, behind a bramble of shrubs, and took care of what needed doing, quickly and quietly. When she returned, Death had spread his cloak on a dry patch of grass and knelt beside the packs, preparing the salve again. His sleeves were rolled up to his forearms, and the muscles there flexed with each small movement of his hands.

Ilys slowed, watching him.

The light cast the scene in a silky silver. She watched the careful way he opened the tin, the thoughtful way he stirred it with the tips of his fingers. Even that, especially that, was tender. His hands, broad and strong, moved with medicinal calculation. She imagined them on her again and had to look away before her face gave her away.

"Come here," he said, not looking up.

She did, and sat down beside him on the cloak. He pulled her bodice down gently at the collar and inspected the wound with a furrowed brow. His fingers brushed her collarbone in the process, just a passing touch, clinical.

It lit her nerves like fire.

The salve cooled where it touched, but she found skin warm. Ilys felt it all, every light brush, every moment he steadied her with one hand on her arm or the small of her back, but when his thumb pressed gently along the edge of the bruising, she gasped.

"Sorry," she offered without thinking. What did she have to be sorry for?

His voice came even, calm. "Don't be."

He finished the binding quickly, with the same measured efficiency as always, but she could feel the effort it took for him to keep it neutral, distant. His hands lingered a moment too long at the knot.

When she shifted, his fingers slid away.

She watched him pack the salve back into the satchel, sleeves still rolled, wrists dusted with dried herbs. His forearms flexed as he cinched the strap tight, and her eyes followed the line of movement before she caught herself.

"So now that you're," she paused, searching for the right word, "mortal… and eating, and drinking, and feeling things… Tell me all that you love about food."

Death blinked at her, clearly caught off guard.

She smiled faintly. "Favorites. Least favorites. What makes you want to steal a second bite, what makes you think the world is broken."

He spoke fondly, "I like warm bread. The kind with a crust you can tear. Soft inside. With butter, if it's salted."

She nodded, satisfied.

"And honey," he added, almost sheepishly. "Not stirred into anything. Just as it is."

"On a spoon?" she asked.

He looked at her. "Or fingers."

Her brows lifted, amused.

He went on, voice quiet. "Stew that has been left to sit too long on the fire. When it thickens. And the meat falls apart. Roots cooked until they lose their bitterness. And blackberries. The kind you find half-fermented on the vine."

She watched him now, not smiling exactly, but expression soft. "What do you hate?" she asked.

"Vinegar," he said instantly. "It covers too much. Salt, when it's careless. Burned garlic. And eggs. Above all, eggs." Death paused and looked at her, mirth warming his glance. "And you?"

She tilted her head thoughtfully. "Roasted pear. When it's soft but not falling apart. With a bit of cream. And, cheese. Good cheese. Sharp, hard. The kind you have to slice thin."

He nodded once, approving, imagining it himself.

"I like tart things," she continued. "Cherries, green plums. And pepper, if it burns just a little. I've no taste for polite flavors."

"What do you hate?"

She squinted toward the horizon. "Boiled cabbage. Lukewarm broth. Bread that crumbles before you bite it."

He looked over, brow faintly raised. "Not fond of softness?"

She shook her head. "Not fond of disappointment. If it looks hearty, it should be. If it smells rich, it shouldn't taste like water."

She plucked a blade of grass, rolled it between her fingers.

"I didn't expect you to have so many opinions," she said after a moment.

"Why?"

"I assumed you'd eat like a monk, just enough to survive."

"I did. Until I had reason not to."

She met his eyes. "And now?"

A beat passed."Now I want more."

The words hung in the air between them, suspended.

Death rose to check the horses. Ilys watched the fluid, confident way he moved—no wasted motion. His hand smoothed over the neck of his mare, and she leaned into him, trusting. He whispered under his breath, words she couldn't hear, and the gentleness in it tugged low in her chest.

She watched the way his cloak stretched across his shoulders and the faint triangle of skin exposed at his throat where his shirt hung open. He caught a strand of mane between his fingers and tucked it behind the mare's ear with such absent care that it made her chest tighten.

He was still learning this body. Still learning himself.

And she was learning to want him.

CHAPTER 33

The thought clung to her as they rode on, the night cool and sharp around them. The road stretched dark and empty, lantern light from the last village long gone. Each time Spire's gait shifted beneath them, she felt the solid wall of Death's chest at her back, his hand near the reins. She found it maddening how much she noticed him now.

After a while she spoke, pulling at anything to distract herself. "Tell me, then," she said, voice light, needling, "what it was *really* like, being a god?"

"I'll tell you but in exchange you—"

"Surely you're not proposing another bargain," Ilys cut in with a scoff.

"No. Merely a conversational trade."

"A trade is a bargain," she argued.

"Fates, Ilys. Let me speak." He chuckled, the sound low against her ear. She went still at the command, surprising herself with how quickly she obeyed, how easily her body fell into his rhythm without the usual bristle toward the god.

"A question for a question," he said more softly. "You ask about godhood, and in return you'll answer me about what it's like to be mortal."

She shifted to get comfortable and, in the process, wriggled back against his chest. Heat rose up her neck, blooming beneath her skin as she became acutely aware of the line of his body against hers.

"Deal," she said quickly, almost a plea. *Talk,* she begged inwardly, *so I don't have to think about how close we are.*

He cleared his throat, searching for language that would fit.

"Being a god," he said, "is like standing beneath a frozen lake. I could see the world above me—light, color, movement—but I couldn't break through to it. Everything I touched was distant, dulled by the ice between us. I heard the living in their joy and grief, the pulse of their small, beautiful lives, but never as more than echoes." He paused, his thumb absently brushing the reins. "The threads passed through me. I could feel them hum—birth, death, all of it—but they never belonged to me. I was the still point in the pattern, not part of it."

His breath came out bleary. "It was quiet. Too quiet. The kind that eats at you. And sometimes, from somewhere deep in that silence, something mortal would stir. A small voice, calling out from the dark beneath the water. It wanted warmth. It wanted to touch. It wanted to *live.*" He looked down at her then, his tone softening. "And I ignored it for a very long time."

Ilys shivered at the image but forced a more detached tone, hoping to steady herself. "Sounds... dreadful."

His laughter traveled down her body. "Yes," he agreed. "Yes, it was."

He drew in a thoughtful breath, the sound humming against her spine. "Now then, my turn. What to ask, what to ask..." he murmured, teasing. "If you could bottle up any memory," he decided, "what would it be?"

Ilys blinked, caught off guard. She sifted through the catalogue of her life and was surprised, almost embarrassed, by how many moments came to mind. For all the blood and ruin, she had lived a lovely life. Her childhood had been full of play and sunlight. She'd been insulated by affection, surrounded by those who loved her. She'd known warmth, laughter, even good sex and a soft bed at the end of it.

But to choose only one?

It struck her, suddenly and cruelly, that her four favorite people—Rowenna, Baron, Grim, and Hanna—had never shared a single moment all together. She mourned the absence of that impossible memory.

How strange, she thought, that our capacity for love and loss grows in equal measure.

While she loved her people, one memory circled and circled inside her head. The feeling of lightness. The sun on her face. Nature, its cast of creatures, and symphony of life.

"When I was a small girl," she said softly, "I crafted myself wings and ran through the grasses behind the Sanctum. I felt so free. So full of possibilities. So utterly myself—unencumbered, unobserved. And I knew that when I finished playing, I could lumber over to Grim or Baron and be doused in love and safety. I had a sureness then," she breathed, "of a beautiful life to come. I would bottle that up, drink it every day with every meal, and I would be a happy woman."

He only reached for her hand, his fingers brushing over hers before closing gently around them. His thumb traced idle circles against her skin, the calloused pad rough to the touch. When he finally gave her hand a small squeeze, she looked down, startled by the tenderness of it.

"What?" she asked at last, trying for levity, her voice low. "No insult? You won't make fun of me?"

"I know not how to elicit mockery out of such envy," he said at last.

Ilys bristled uncomfortably in the face of such earnestness. "My second answer," she said dryly, "would be a truly *fantastic* bout of fucking."

Death barked a laugh, startled and delighted. "Gods, Ilys. You cannot say such things."

She arched a brow. "Is Death so unfamiliar with carnal pleasure?"

"Death is unfamiliar," he replied, a wry pause. "His mortal form, however, is its most diligent student."

Her eyes widened, and a wicked smile curved her lips. "Tsk, tsk," she chided.

"Your religion," he started. "They choose a name for you, yes?"

Ilys hummed her assent.

"What was your name before?"

She groaned softly. "I ask such *fun* questions, you arse. Must you always be so serious?"

"I should like to know," he said simply.

She exhaled, exasperated. "As would I. If I ever had a name, it's gone from me."

His silence settled between the pair. She had come to admire it, to realize it was not detachment but a contemplative, staid sort of listening and thinking.

"Ilys is yours now," he said after a moment. "In whole."

"What do you mean?" she asked.

"They stole your name, but you birthed a great life entirely your own out of the remnants."

She tried to glance back at him, but her wound pulled, and she hissed softly. "You speak so strangely."

"You've made art from the poison."

"Are you drunk?" she laughed.

"Not at all," he said, and she could hear the faint smile in it.

She shook her head. "My turn, then. Do you have a name?"

"Cynan," he confessed. "My mother named me for a great leader of our people."

She mouthed the syllables, testing. "Cynan," she repeated, then again, slower, like tasting it. "I think it suits you."

"More than Death."

"Perhaps even more than Death. Tell me about your people," she urged. He had a mortal name, most likely a storied mortal history. A million questions plucked at her tongue, but she chided her mind.

"It is my turn," he argued.

"Do not be so uptight for once. Talk with me. Tell me of your people."

"Now you, too, have chosen a depressing subject," he poked.

"Teach me how to say something in your people's tongue then. You're always saying strange things under your breath."

He hummed, considering. "Most of what I remember are curses."

"Perfect," she said brightly.

He laughed. "You would choose profanity as your first lesson."

"I'm nothing if not practical."

"Fine." He leaned in slightly, his breath warm against her ear. "*Cachu hwch.*"

She frowned, trying to shape it. "Kah-hoo... hook?"

He snorted. "Not even close."

"Well, what does it mean?"

"Pig's mess. Or," he added thoughtfully, "utter disaster. It applies to most of your decisions."

Ilys barked out a laugh. "Pigs mess? That is hardly profanity."

"It loses something in translation," he claimed, chuckling, but soon after his tone grew serious. "Rither's Hollow is just ahead."

Ilys tilted her head slightly, catching the faint glimmer of lamplight in the distance. "And there we stop?"

"Yes." His tone allowed no debate. "You need rest."

The road widened into a narrow main street, flanked by shuttered shops and houses with thatched roofs. Here and there, candles still burned behind windows, and a single inn sat squarely at the center, its sign swinging gently in the night breeze. Death swung down from the saddle first, then offered her a hand. Inside, the inn smelled of smoke and cider. The few remaining patrons barely glanced up as Death approached the counter. He peered back at Ilys, emotive and warm, before speaking, his hand flexing and his voice strained.

"We should like separate rooms, if you have them."

The innkeeper gave him a long look, then snorted. "If I have them." He took the offered coin and tucked it into his apron. "End of the hall."

Death nodded once and turned, already moving toward the stairs. Their rooms stood opposite each other, identical in their plainness. Sturdy wooden furniture, a single narrow window, a basin tucked into the corner. Death's door stood jar when she stepped into her own space, dropping her pack onto the bed. She sat, fingers tracing the edge of the mattress.

Dinner offered no surprises—stale bread, watered ale, the din of strangers pretending at comfort. The same rough-hewn table, the same dimly lit room. The same malty ale, dark as ink, set down with the same disinterest this time by the innkeeper's wife. What set this apart was their nearness now—the road behind them, the silences they'd learned to share, the words both chose to swallow.

Death took a provocative sip of his drink, setting the mug down with measured ease. Ilys watched him carefully, expecting the same grimace of disgust he had worn the last time she watched him drink, but it never came.

"You can hold your drink now," she noted.

He glanced at her, unimpressed. "I am adjusting."

She took a sip herself, immediately regretting it. "That's unfortunate."

He huffed a quiet laugh. "It is a skill like any other."

She rolled the mug between her hands, studying him. "You teased that you were mortal once."

"Yes," he confirmed. "Once."

She sat back, considering this. "And then you became what you are."

He nodded. Gods, she found him infuriating. She urged him to elaborate without her cues. He must have known her curiosity coiled greedily on her tongue.

"How?"

Death's gaze flickered toward the fire. "I was chosen."

"That's not an answer."

"And yet, it is the only one I will give."

She scowled. "That's cruel."

"You have called me worse."

She scoffed but could not argue. He simply lifted his cup again, watching her with quiet amusement.

"You were mortal," she repeated, almost to herself.

"I was."

"And now you are dying."

"I am."

She stared down at the table, pressing her fingertips into the wood. "Then who will drag me to Veilmarch?"

His eyes darkened, shadows flickered in the firelight, catching in the deep creases of his gaze, making him look almost unfamiliar, almost someone else entirely. "That, Veilwalker, remains to be seen." He shook off whatever had settled in his expression, turning back to his drink, the liquor loosening his tongue. "Tell me, then, what will keep you busy when you return to the Sanctum?"

Ilys turned the cup between her fingers, watching the amber liquid lap against the rim. "I will tame Mor further," she noted.

His gaze urged her on, expectant. She sighed, thinking of what awaited her in the coming months.

"I will write Rowenna often." His face opened, pleading for more. She tapped a nail against the wooden table, exhaling sharply.

"And I will draw," she shrugged, "everything in sight."

See, she thought. This is what a good conversationalist looks like.

His brows lifted , curiosity flickering in his expression. "You draw?"

She shot him a warning look. "Do not tease me."

"I do not," he defended, hands lifting in mock surrender. "I am curious. I have not seen you draw."

"I do," she vacillated. "Quite well."

His lips curled faintly. "Really?"

She nodded, a blush creeping up her neck. She reached for her drink again, the warmth of the ale dulling the edge of her discomfort.

"Draw me," he demanded suddenly.

She scoffed. "No."

"Come on then," he urged, shifting forward in his seat. "There will not be another time. Do it. Draw me. I should like my mortal form remembered somehow." His smirk turned roguish. "I have seen your scripture. They draw me quite ominously. Someone should remember the good grace of this face."

She laughed, a rare, genuine thing. "Get us another round of drinks, and perhaps Ilys two pints down will consider it."

He shot to his feet before she'd finished, a rare spark of eagerness driving him as he crossed the room to the barkeep. She watched him, the way his mortal form moved, the way his shoulders bunched as he leaned over the counter, the effortless grace that remained despite the flesh and bone.

When he returned with their pints, she sighed, setting her cup down. "I did not expect such willingness." Standing, casting one last glance around the room before nodding toward the stairs. "Come. Let's take them to the room. I shan't draw you with all the ruffians about."

He grinned, smug and pleased, falling into step beside her as they made their way up the narrow staircase. The wooden steps creaked and the lanterns lining the hall burned low, casting long shadows along the walls.

He set the drinks down on the small table by the window and leaned against the frame, watching her as she rummaged through her pack, pulling free a small book and a stick of charcoal.

Ilys sat on the edge of the bed, thumbing through the pages until she found a clean one.

"Sit," she commanded.

Death did as she asked, lowering himself into the chair across from her. He draped one arm lazily over the back, watching her with quiet amusement.

"Will I look handsome?" he roguishly queried.

"That remains to be seen," she echoed dryly, pressing the charcoal to the page.

Her gaze drifted to him again and again, to the light tangled in his dark curls, to the warmth his mortal skin seemed to hold. Even diminished, he unsettled her with how easily beauty clung to him. Even more so, perhaps. Ilys sat cross-legged on the bed, her charcoal-stained fingers smudging faint streaks of black across her knee as she wiped them absentmindedly. Death leaned closer, the edges of his form bathed in flickering gold of the fire, his mortal warmth a stark contrast to the cold nights they had spent in the open air.

She focused on the lines of his face, the sharp cut of his cheekbones, the tired weight beneath his eyes. A god wearing a man's flesh. A man wearing a god's past. He let her work, his gaze drifting out the window, fingers idly tapping against the table.

"The Veilmarch," she started, watching as his attention sharpened. "Did you walk Baron?"

His brows knitted. "I do not–"

She held up her hand, shaking her head. "Sorry. You have not met him. You would not know." Her voice softened as she turned back to her drawing.

Then she stopped, studying his face before speaking again. "He was a hulking man. Beard. He knew Grim well. Loved us both well."

Death regarded her in silence, gaze turning contemplative. "I do not remember." His voice slipped quiet with reluctance. "I am sorry, Ilys. I carry so much with me, even in this mortal form, but so many parts are blurred, unattached. I do not know."

She nodded, exhaling softly, returning to the piece.

"What were you like as a mortal?" she asked after a pause, taking a break to drink her ale. "Before," she added.

He pursed his lips and shook his head, refusing to answer.

She tilted her head, studying him as he watched the fire, avoiding her gaze.

With the final strokes, she turned the drawing toward him. "Do you like it?"

He took the parchment in his hands, his fingers brushing against the edge as though he might unravel from the charcoal itself.

"It is well done, " he complimented, his voice thoughtful. Then he looked at her, dark eyes softening. "Ilys," he chided gently, "you have kept this a secret."

She smirked, stretching her right arm behind her. "If the unknown parts of my being are secrets, then there are a million hidden truths between us."

"I should like to know them all." His voice dropped, soft and rough at once, and he leaned close, so close she caught the faint sting of ale on his breath, the heat of his skin bridging the space between them.

She moved to finish her drink, shaking off the feeling. "A game?" she offered.

He leaned back on his hands, eyes narrowing playfully. "I am not in the mood to lose."

"Then don't." She shrugged, the barest hint of flirtation curling in her voice.

They set up Fox and Geese on the floor, their knees nearly brushing as they placed the pieces. The wood grain bit against her fingertips

"I will get us more ale before we begin,"he announced, pushing himself up, a little less steady on his feet than before.

Ilys smirked, watching him disappear through the door. He returned moments later, cups in hand, spilling a generous amount of ale as he maneuvered back into the room. She burst into laughter, tipping her head back as he swore under his breath. They laughed, leaning into the warmth of their shared drunkenness, the ease of familiarity pressing against them like a well-worn cloak.

They played, the pieces clicking against the board, each move measured yet playful. Ilys baited him into traps, and he fought against them, determined, furrowing his brows as he strategized.

"Correct me if I'm wrong but it looks like you are in quite a *cachu hwch.*" she said, mangling the words beyond recognition.

Death burst into laughter, accidentally knocking a piece from the board. "So horribly wrong," he managed between laughs. "And you play *dishonorably,*" he accused, watching as she trapped his last escape with smug precision.

She smiled sweetly. "You knew that before we started."

The fire burned low in the hearth and the inn had quieted, the murmurs of late-night drinkers thinning until only the occasional clatter of a dish or the muffled laughter of some unseen patron filled the space. Their cups sat nearly empty, the last traces of foamy ale clinging to the rims.

Death's gaze flickered over her, tarrying. Then, with a resigned sigh, he moved his last piece into her trap.

"You are a menace," he teased, setting his cup down.

She propped her elbow on a knee, resting her chin on her hand, the corners of her lips curving. "I have been told."

Ilys traced absent circles against a knot in the wood board, eyes half-lidded as she sighed deeply.

Death's brow furrowed and he asked a question as if it had been weighing on him for some time. "You speak of Baron, but rarely of Grim."

His question struck the leaden force that had sat heavy on her chest for years. She swallowed, whistling a quiet breath through her teeth, trying to force the ache out with it. Tears pricked the edges of her vision, unbidden and unwelcome.

"You do not hear from him?" Death asked.

"He was tired," she noted. "I could tell. I could see it." She stared at the fire, watching the flames twist and writhe. "The way he carried himself, the pause in his duties. He was done with the killing." She ran a finger over the rim of her cup, voice barely above a whisper. "And I imagine he could not forgive me after what I have done."

Death's gaze sharpened. "What have you done, Ilys? That he did not ask of you himself?"

She turned her eyes to him, wet and brimming with quiet devastation. "I killed Baron."

The words were spoken without hesitation, without embellishment, and yet they rang through the space between them like a knell. The fire cracked, a single ember flaring before turning to ash.

"It was my duty," she continued, voice flat. "The Fates demanded it. And there are a million other explanations that justify it." She banished a bitter breath. "But love does not care for details." Her hands curled into fists, nails biting into the flesh of her palms.

"I killed the man Grim loved. A man I loved." Her voice wavered, breaking on the edges. "He will never want to lay eyes upon me again. And I understand that."

Tears slipped down her cheeks, and she let them, setting her cup down as she steadied her breath, pulling herself together piece by piece.

Softly, she asked, "Are you scared to die?"

He hummed, rolling his cup between his fingers, his eyes distant. "I have walked so many souls into the hands of the Fates. There is a part of me that knows what waits." He tilted his head, considering. "But there is a mortal part, one that did not exist before, that very much wants to live." He gestured vaguely around them, to the warmth of the fire, to the clatter of dishes in the other room, to her presence beside him. "And to keep feeling this."

Ilys watched him, a strange tenderness taking root in her chest. The drink lent her courage, or maybe the pull that had always lived between them finally demanded to be answered. She shifted, moving onto her knees, crawling closer until she sat just before him. The space between their bodies narrowed and she reached out, pressing her palm against his chest, against the exquisite thrum of his heart.

"This?" she whispered.

His breath hitched, his gaze flicking to where her hand lay. His lips parted, his expression wanton. He nodded, serene, as if her touch had tethered him to this earthly plain.

She hummed, her thumb brushing absently against the fabric of his tunic, feeling the warmth of his skin beneath. Her eyes roamed his face, memorizing him in the dim firelight, the sharp lines of his cheekbones, the faint crease between his brows, the way his lips parted as though to speak.

She bent toward him until her lips found the small rise above his brow. When she pulled away, his eyes were on her, charcoal and searching.

"Ilys," he breathed, his voice quieter than she had ever heard it. Unsure.

She did not pull away.

"Tell me to leave, and I shall," she vowed.

Her breath met his skin, hazy and warm, the air between them pulled to a trembling thread. Beneath her palms, he held himself rigid, caught in that fragile pause between want and refusal.

She pressed her lips to the pulse at his neck, feeling the tantalizing thrum of life beneath her mouth. The warmth of his skin, the scent of him, earth and smoke and a fragrance uniquely his, curled around her senses.

Her fingers ghosted along the edges of his jaw, the roughness of stubble catching against her touch.

He had always been untouchable, unknowable, a thing that drifted between worlds without belonging fully to either. Here, now, he lived in full—breath warm against the air, body caught between being and restraint.

"But I will tell you," she whispered against his skin, her lips barely brushing the words into him, "that I am lonely." Her hand slipped down, pressing lightly against his chest. His heart hammered beneath her palm. "And I should like to stay."

His hands came to rest against her waist, fingers curling as though testing her. He breathed with care, but she could feel the conflict in the way his fingers flexed, in the way his body refused to yield even as it longed to.

The hesitation stretched, ponderous and uncertain.

Then, tentative as the turning of the tide, his lips brushed against her temple, soft, uncertain, reverent. His grip on her waist tightened, and he released a tortured exhale.

"Then stay," he begged, voice rough and resigned.

The words settled between them. She felt them in the space where their bodies did not quite touch, in the way his hands tightened against her waist as though grounding himself, as though coming to terms with the thing they were about to undo between them.

Ilys drew in a breath and pressed closer, her fingers following the line of his collarbone, dipping into the hollow of his throat. His skin radiated heat, startling in its warmth. His mortal form burned, a stark contrast to the cool, distant presence she had known for years. He had always been a shadow. Now, he was real. A man. A dying god clinging to his last breaths of life, to the pulse of the ephemeral.

He let her explore him like that, let her trace the sharp lines of his jaw, let her fingertips memorize the shape of him.

At her side, the charcoal stick she'd been sketching with earlier still lay forgotten on the table. Without thinking, she reached for it, pressing the dark edge to his shoulder, to the rise of his collarbone. He stilled, but did not stop her. The charcoal moved in reverent lines, mapping him where her fingers had been: his ribs, the hollow of his throat, the taut skin where torso met leg. Each stroke blurred against his skin, black dust marking the proof of his mortal form.

Then, like gravity pulled him forward, he moved.

His lips found her temple again, hesitant. Then her cheek, softer still, his breath ghosting against her skin. An unraveling, careful and measured, as though he savored a sweet he had long denied himself.

She turned into him, catching his mouth before he could second-guess himself, before he could think to stop.

It was a quiet kiss, their lips meeting. Not rushed, not desperate, but older than either of them could name. His fingers flexed at her waist before sliding up the curve of her spine, pulling her closer as though she might disappear if he let her go.

Ilys hummed against him, a sound of satisfaction, of confirmation. She had imagined this, that it would feel like to kiss him, to strip away his godhood, to find the man beneath. But this felt different. This was real.

He groaned low in his throat, a sound caught between amusement and need, roughened by the effort to stay composed. His hands splayed wider across her back, fingers pressing firm, tracing the fabric of her dress as though committing it to memory.

She pulled back just enough to study his face. His pupils were blown wide, dark swallowing his irises. Ilys traced her fingers through his hair, letting the curls slip through her grasp, watching as he closed his eyes at the sensation. He was learning himself, learning this form, and she relished the power in that knowledge, that she could teach him something new.

Her hands moved lower, palms pressing against his chest, feeling the drum of his heart, the breath expanding in his ribs. He had a body that responded, a body that wanted.

"I should like to know all of you," she confessed, her lips ghosting over him once more, an offering, an invitation.

His fingers dug into her waist, his breath catching. "Then stay," he repeated, this time sure and greedy.

The air between them pulsed, thick with want, sacred and trembling. And when she kissed him again, deeper this time, slower still, not to stake a claim but to bear witness, to worship. Her mouth moved and savored each second as though it might be the last. Death's hands slid up her back, certain in their purpose. They curved over her shoulder blades, thumbs brushing beneath the straps of her gown. He drew back just enough to look at her, to ask permission with the question in his eyes, though no words left his mouth.

She answered without speaking, lifting her arms , inviting him to pull the fabric from her shoulders.

He moved like a tide, inevitable, unhurried, undeniable. His fingers trailed along the bare lines of her shoulders, following the slip of her gown as it fell from her collarbone. His hands trembled faintly as they cupped her sides with reverence, like a priest handling relics too holy to touch. And then, his palm passed over her breast.

She stilled beneath his hand, breath faltering as her nipple peaked against the callused pad of his thumb. It sent a shock through her like lightning in water. Her body arched toward him, unthinking, a silent plea. He felt it, the shiver that ran through her, the way her breath caught, and he stilled, absorbing it like a man newly fluent in sensation.

He looked at her with awe in his eyes, not quite believing she had been given to him, even for a moment. Her fingers slid beneath his shirt, brushing over the planes of his stomach, the ridges of his ribs. Lean muscle met her touch, heat radiating from him, divinity still humming just beneath the surface of his mortal skin. She pushed the fabric up, baring him inch by inch, and he let her. Her palms skimmed his chest, mapping the muscles there, pausing over the thunderous beat of his heart.

She looked up into his face again, saw how undone he was by the sight of her bare before him. His hand moved again, this time bolder, fingers brushing the curve of her breast, thumb teasing her nipple in a supple, exploratory circle. She gasped, her hips shifting instinctively, brushing against the heat that had begun to pulse between them.

He groaned then, low and helpless, forehead dropping to hers. "Is this what it is to want?" he whispered, voice rough with wonder.

"Yes," she whispered, teeth catching on her lower lip as she leaned into his hand, needing more. "And worse. And better."

His other hand found her hip, pulling her forward, settling her against the rigid line of his desire. Her breath hitched, pleasure rising, curling through her spine. She wanted—gods, she wanted—to lose herself in this, to be unmade and remade by his hands.

His mouth found her throat, and his lips brushed over the hollow beneath her jaw, the slope of her shoulder, the quick flutter of her pulse. Patience lived in every motion, his hands careful, searching, as though he could memorize her body by touch alone. She could feel him trembling now, not with hesitation, but restraint. His chest rose and fell with the effort of holding himself together, of not simply devouring her. His body wavered, then lowered, until he knelt before her, akin to a worshiper.

Her gaze dropped to where her hand rested against his chest. Faint smudges of charcoal marked his skin where she'd traced him before, streaked now by sweat and her own fingerprints. It felt wrong to wipe them away.

His palms moved down the length of her thighs, rough and warm. He caught her calves, thumbs brushing the backs of her knees, then traced to her ankles, anchoring himself in the shape of her. His hands returned, gliding up again over the curves of her—his touch both pious and searching, molding to every line. He cupped the backs of her legs, thumbs working into the knots of tension he found, drawing them loose in quiet, circling strokes.

She watched him, breath caught, heart in her throat. His head bowed, dark curls falling forward as he pressed a kiss to the inside of one knee, then the other. Steadfast and attentive. Her skin prickled in his wake.

He worked higher, his mouth trailing a series of unhurried kisses up the insides of her thighs. Every inch lavished, each kiss a vow. Her legs trembled beneath him. Her breath caught again and again as he mapped her with a devotion bordering on torment.

When he reached the place where her thighs met, his hands curled around them, thumbs circling the tender skin there. He didn't rush. He didn't claim. He learned. He memorized.

His thumbs swept to the apex of her, rapacious and indolent. She gasped, her hips jolting forward before she could stop them, knees giving just. His hands steadied her, a grounding pressure on her thighs as his thumbs circled again, feeling her. Savoring her.

Her hands found his shoulders, gripping tight as she bit her lip to hold in the sound rising in her throat. But he looked up at her, eyes gleaming with venal candor.

Give me that sound, his eyes conveyed. *Give me that sweet noise and I will make the trade worthwhile.*

"You're shaking," he observed, the barest trace of a smile at the corner of his mouth, though his voice roughened with want. He pressed another kiss, higher now, his breath feathering against her most sensitive skin. One hand remained, clutching her thigh, the other brushing along the outside of her hip, anchoring her, worshiping her. His mouth followed his hand, tasting, until she thought she might fly apart from the sweetness of it. He pressed a palm to her stomach, forcing her to lean back against the bed.

She had never been touched like this. Not just for pleasure, not just for possession, but a touch to show she was seen. Tended to. Known.

And when he looked up again, lips parted, face flushed with the sheer act of devotion, she sank her fingers into his hair, grasping it in surprised ecstasy. She closed her eyes, and for the first time in her life, allowed herself to be held. And with relentless strokes of his tongue against her, she rode a wave of sensation so unfamiliar, so addictive, that she knew even in the midst, as her vision swam, that the feeling had only begun.

Chapter 34

She woke to the room she did not know, to a body she did not trust, to the shape of him asleep beside her.

For a heartbeat she lay very still, listening. The inn creaked in the ribs. Someone coughed down the corridor. A cart rattled outside, iron wheel hitting a loose stone. Death lay on his side, one arm slack between them, his hair pushed off his brow yet absurdly tidied in sleep. The fire tampered down to a red seam and the scent of last night still clung to the air, warm and human and undeniable.

Her stomach turned.

No. The word came without sound. It rose like sickness.

She slid out from the sheet and stood. The room blurred. She found her dress by touch and dragged it over herself, fingers clumsy at the laces. Her shoulder throbbed where the bandage tugged. She did not put her boots on right away; she did not want the sound. She wanted the door. She wanted air.

The stair complained under her weight, startling the low hush of embers and swept sawdust. The innkeeper's wife glanced up from a bucket, eyes quick, then down again, mercy in the look of a woman who had seen too much to ask. Outside, the morning shone a paper gray. Mist hung from the eaves. The street had not yet woken to its own noise. She sat on the inn steps to pull on her boots and had to stop halfway, bracing her forearm against her knee, fighting the urge to retch.

What have you done?

She forced the laces tight, stood too fast, steadied on the doorframe, then walked. Anywhere. Away from the inn with its clean, lemoned sheets and the imprint of his body on a mattress that now knew her shape.

A boy swept a doorway with more zeal than success. A woman tipped wash water into the gutter and nodded once at Ilys without curiosity. Smoke bled from a handful of chimneys, urging the day ahead.. Her feet took her toward the small square. A shrine leaned there, half-collapsed, its stone saint weathered to a softened face. Someone had tucked a sprig of rosemary into a crack. She stood in front of it and tried to have a thought that was not a feeling.

I cannot do this.

Last night unspooled in hard flashes. She shut it out with both hands as if the mind were a door.

The nausea rose again, bright and daft. She swallowed it. She crossed the square to the pump and worked the handle until water came in a clean rush. She cupped her palms and threw it into her face. The shock refused to steady. She drank from her hands anyway, chin dripping, breath juddering like a lame wheel.

He is dying. The thought came uninvited and sat down with its arms folded. *He is dying and you just taught yourself the shape of his mouth.*

A dog trotted past with a crust in its teeth. Somewhere a smith struck iron. She walked again, out of the square and along a lane where back gardens surrendered winter cabbages and tired rosemary to the fog. Her shoulder began to ache in earnest. The gash pulsed in time with her steps. *Good,* she thought, small and vicious. *Feel that. Remember what you are for.*

You are for the Veil. You are for the blade. You are not for this.

A memory she had not asked for rose clean: his hands grasping and his mouth pulling, lavishing—

She stopped with her palm flat to a garden wall, breath loud in her head. The sickness curdled into grief, and she refused that, too.

If Grim could see you. If Baron—

She shut her teeth on his name. The taste of it hurt.

A cart approached behind her. "You'll want to step off the lane," the driver said without malice. She obeyed, found the ditch edge, waited for it to pass. The man lifted two fingers in thanks. She watched the wheel go by and thought, wildly, of time. How it moved whether she wanted it or not. How last night already belonged to it.

Her hands shook and she tucked them into her sleeves and kept walking until the town thinned. Past the last thatch, the road shouldered up into low fields and a hedgerow tatty with last year's nests. Fog clung to the grass in scraps. She stood there, on the edge of leaving, and tried to measure it: how far she could go before he woke. How far she would have to go before she did not turn back.

The answer was not far at all.

"That bad?" His voice low, even, and too certain slipped through the mist.

Her gut twisted. She turned, and of course he was there, his dark eyes fixed on her. They weren't hard or cold as she might have preferred, but thoughtful, warm, almost amused—as though her storm were just another weather he had expected all along. She hated the way her pulse jumped under his regard, how her body leaned toward him even as her mind snarled to pull away.

Ilys groaned, head tipping back.

He spared her the trouble of answering, only nodded toward the inn. "Breakfast?"

She huffed, brushed past him, and walked ahead, willing herself not to feel the gravity of his presence at her back.

The inn smelled of smoke and onions, of wool steaming near the hearth. The benches were already crowded with traders and farmers, but the innkeeper's wife found them space at a corner table. She set down two bowls with a dull thud: watery broth, cabbage gone limp, and a wedge of bread that fell apart the moment Ilys touched it.

Her appetite died on sight.

Death looked from her plate to her face, one brow lifting. "Do you have anything else?" he asked the innkeeper's wife. His tone polite but firm

The woman frowned. "This is breakfast."

"She does not care for—"

"Do not finish that sentence." Ilys's voice cut sharper than she meant, but the heat in her chest only swelled when he glanced back at her, unruffled.

"You do not like that," he said simply.

Her spoon clattered against the bowl. "And how would you know?"

His gaze held hers, exasperating in its dogged nature. "Because you told me."

"That was a conversation," she snapped, voice rising despite the nearby ears. "Not an invitation to memorize my every whim like a nursemaid."

The bench scraped as she leaned forward, glaring. Her stomach knotted, not from the broth, but from the quiet certainty in his eyes.

"I did it without thinking," he said at last. His tone lost its edge, almost conciliatory. "I'm sorry. Dine away." He made a small, dismissive wave toward her bowl, as though that settled it.

They ate in brittle silence, each scrape of her spoon against the bowl loud as a strike. Her anger festered with every bite, swelling like a wound she could not bind.

"How is your shoulder?" he asked finally, pleasantly, as though the night before had given him the right.

Her spoon clattered against the table, resolve snapping. "We are not lovers!" she shouted, too loud, too raw

Conversations faltered. A few heads turned.

Ilys's chest heaved, every breath ragged with the effort of holding herself together.

Death didn't rise to meet her fury. He didn't argue. He didn't even blink. Instead, he reached across the table with that same calm precision that infuriated her and pulled both their bowls toward him, stacking them placidly. Then he stood, lifting the dishes in one hand.

"Let's take this to our room," he said evenly, but his eyes were molten with meaning.

Her heart stuttered. "Our—"

"Now," he cut in, low, leaving no room for her protest.

The nearby patrons quickly returned to their own meals pretending all events regular and normal. Ilys pushed back from the bench, her legs shaky, heat coiling beneath her skin. She followed him, furious with herself for obeying, furious with the rush of want tangled with dread in her blood.

They climbed the stairs and the din of the common room faded behind them. The boards creaked under their weight. Death's hand curled tighter around the bowls as he led her down the narrow corridor. He didn't look back, but she could feel his awareness on her as surely as if he had.

She followed, breathing hard, every step an argument she hadn't yet spoken. Her pulse thrummed in her throat like a bird trying to beat its way out of a snare.

He reached her door, nudged it open with his shoulder, and stepped inside, setting the bowls on the little table by the window.

Ilys lingered in the doorway, fists curled at her sides, her breath uneven. She hated that he could still look at her like that, with a mere stare, communicating that she was wholly known.

"Well?" she demanded, voice hoarse.

He closed the door with one lazy push. The latch caught.

"I think it's best you start, Ilys. What was that?"

The words broke out of her raw and bright, as much to herself as to him. She felt like she was building her own case, sentencing herself in real time.

"I cannot do this," she said, her voice cracking. "I only want to be with you because I dislike myself so much I cannot imagine any relationship more fitting." She wanted to wound, so she did. Her eyes found his and she spat the final blade.

"I hate you."

"I do not think that is true," he said, calm as a tide.

"I tried to kill you. You hate me." She took two steps and struck her fists against his chest, sharp and human. "We are enemies."

He caught her wrists, firm but not cruel, fingers closing until her bones remembered they were bones. "No," he said, a denial that did not blink. "I love you."

She stared at him, stunned into anger. "How can you say that?" She gestured at the two of them. "This is fucked."

"This," he gritted, pulling her closer even as he held her wrists wide, "is the only thing I have glimpsed that is the farthest thing from that. You are scared, and I understand. I am a blip in your long life." His breath shook once, then steadied. "I do not have the privilege of being afraid of this. I am dying."

Her chin tipped up, defiant. "And you think I'm afraid?"

His eyes caught hers. "Yes. You are terrified. You chase the fire and call it choice. You throw yourself into storms so no one else can cast you there first. You would rather drown on your own terms than admit you want saving. And while this body weakens and my hold on the world thins, I watch you and I learn the shape of purpose. I love you." He pounded emotion into every syllable.

Her mouth twisted, the words tumbling sharp and fast. "You are a lonely, fading god. You are desperate and you are friendless. You do not know what love is."

"You seek to maim, and that is fine by me, Ilys." His mouth curved, not in humor, in truth. "I love you. It is selfish. It is macabre. It is ironic, but I do. And yes, I have been lonely. We are both lonely, and we understand each other in a way no one else could. All of that is true. So is this: I love how age hardens you and softens you in the same breath. I love your appetite for whimsy and your refusal to stomach injustice. I love your laugh when you forget to guard it and your smile when you choose to be merciful with it. I love you, Ilys."

"Stop," she begged, voice breaking.

"I will not," he said, and he laughed once, rough, almost tender.

"I hate you," she promised, but the words shook.

"I know," he answered, as if he were telling her a bedtime fact, full of understanding and no surprise.

She kissed him like a strike. He met her like a wall. The room jolted with the impact of their bodies, the back of her thighs hitting the bedframe, the cup on the table skittering to the floor. Her wrists were still pinned in his hands until she yanked free and caught his collar instead. He pressed her into the post and she arched into the pressure, not to flee it, to feed it.

"I hate you," she whispered into his mouth.

"I love you," he breathed back, and the words did not soften anything. They made it worse, which made it better.

She shoved him and he let it move him a step, then came back in, taking her mouth again. Teeth, then heat, then hunger all over again. He turned her and she turned with him, a knot that did not wish to be undone. Fingers found laces with more force than skill. Cloth rasped skin. His palm spread over the bandage at her shoulder and he paused, a single heartbeat of gentleness. She hissed the word against his ear—a yes that left no doubt, only invitation.

When he thrust into her, her breath caught hard, ragged, her body opening around the force of him. And in that wild, desperate rhythm she could not control, a memory pierced her—the echo of his voice from another night. *Breathe, Ilys. Count with me.*

"Look at me," he said as they panted into one another's mouth.

She clung to him fighting the pull to shatter, nails biting his back, every motion pulling her deeper into the truth she swore she didn't want, but that grew harder to deny.

"I hate you," she gasped again, though her body betrayed her, meeting him with abandon, slick with denial as he gripped her up against the frame, his fingers working between them with knowing precision. She cursed him silently—his arrogance, his practiced skill, the ease with which he drew her apart—but still her body bowed to it, helpless. She came first, fast and humiliating.

He watched her unravel, protests falling from her lips as her face flushed with pleasure, and he followed soon after, breath ragged, hands digging into her waist, anchoring himself to the moment.

When he stilled inside her, she wanted to shove him away, to reassert the distance she'd carved with every word. But instead, he eased her down, kneeling before them both. His hands were tender now, smoothing the disarray he had helped create. And she found herself frozen, helpless to that tenderness.

"Ilys," he said quietly.

She didn't answer. She couldn't. Her throat felt too tight, her body still trembling from what they'd done. But he caught her gaze anyway. His eyes were dark and unbearably gentle.

"Make another bargain with me." He reached for her hand, gingerly enough that she could have pulled away, but she didn't. When his lips brushed her knuckles, the gesture so careful, so unlike the chaos of moments before, that it felt like being touched by a promise she hadn't agreed to yet.

Her breath caught. "What?" she managed, the word breaking halfway out of her.

"Let us have this," he said. "This sliver of happiness. I will die soon, and you may pick apart every piece of it that unsettles you after. But may we have it now?" His thumb swept once over the back of her hand. "May I try to make you happy, again and again, in the little time left to me?"

She stared at him, her heart pounding so hard it made her ribs ache. Part of her wanted to laugh because it sounded so easy when he said it. Another part wanted to claw her way out of his grasp, run until her lungs burned.

"You think that's what I need?" she whispered finally.

"No." His eyes softened even more. "It's what I want."

Her lips parted, but no sound came. The room smelled of salt and skin, the bedclothes rumpled under her fingers. She thought of the night before, of every place she'd let him touch, of every place she'd wanted him to. She thought of how the sound of his heartbeat had steadied her even as she cursed him.

"You'll die," she said, almost accusing.

"I will." His voice steadied itself, but his hand held on harder, the restraint in him breaking at the edges.

Her breath shuddered out of her. She closed her eyes, then opened them again, meeting his stare. "One sliver," she affirmed, the words trembling out of her. "No more."

He smiled, not a triumphant thing, but a quiet, aching one, and pressed his forehead to hers. "One sliver," he echoed.

"This is *cachu hwch,*" she said wryly, sighing deeply.

Death only caught her mouth with his, smiling faintly. "Hopeless," he whispered, and kissed her again.

CHAPTER 35

Ilys woke to Death leaning over her.

"Wake," he urged softly. "I am a dying man."

Her eyes fluttered open, bleary with sleep.

"I think *I* have died," she groaned.

He pressed a needy kiss to the swell of her breast. "That's in poor taste," he observed, the dryness undoing any real reprimand.

He sat back on his heels, inspecting the bandage at her shoulder. The wound had begun to knit, yet his frown lingered—thoughtful, near worried. As he studied her, his fingers moved in slow, absent circles over her breast, his gaze intense enough to make her squirm.

"What?" she asked, smoothing a hand over her face. It struck her suddenly how long she had gone without her veil; how strange, to find she no longer missed it—that life without it had begun to feel like its own kind of normal.

"I am familiar with the intricacies of the soul," he said, voice quiet. "But I fear there is not enough time to acquaint myself with the mysteries of this body." He bent and pressed his lips to her swollen bud, then glanced up. He stood already dressed, sleeves rolled, his cloak folded neatly over the chair as if he'd been waiting there for some time.

"I encourage you to do so. Right now," she said with a laugh. "Time is of the essence."

His answering growl rumbled low as he laid his face against her stomach, his cheek warm on her skin. "If only."

He straightened, drinking her in with a hunger that felt almost reverent. "I must commit a grievous sin," he confessed at last.

Her brows rose. "What?"

"I must dress you now."

She laughed, breathless, as he knelt and pulled her chemise carefully over her head, mindful of her injury. His hands moved with rare gentleness as he drew the fabric down and laced her dress, tugging each tie into place with practiced precision.

He hoisted her onto Spire's back with more care than she liked to admit she needed, adjusting her hands on the reins until he was satisfied.

"Where do we head?" she asked, her voice still rough from sleep.

"Dacw is our last stop," he said, stepping to his own steed's side.

Ilys tilted her head finding the name unfamiliar. "That's new."

His mouth curved, subtle, but there. "I will enjoy showing it to you." Light stirred his expression as he swung into his saddle. "It's where I was born."

Before she could ask what he meant, he nudged his horse forward.

"Come, Veilwalker," he called over his shoulder, his voice laced with challenge.

Ilys scoffed, narrowing her eyes. He had done it on purpose, dropped the word like bait and left her dangling, questions sharp in her throat.

Such a tease.

She pressed her heels into Spire's sides, setting her mount into motion, the chase shaking the last remnants of sleep from her bones.

The city of Dacw stretched before them. Death guided his horse through the winding streets, his posture composed, his gaze flicking over each corner and corridor with the casual awareness of a man who had seen it all before. He did not seem surprised by the changes, only watchful, mentally mapping the places that had remained untouched and those that had been reshaped by time.

Ilys followed closely, letting her eyes roam the foreign streets, bustling markets, and the rising scent of the sea carried inland on the breeze. The air carried a deeper warmth than the south ambrosial with the scent of citrus and spice. Market stalls overflowed with unfamiliar fruits, their rinds waxy and their flesh bright as jewels. Fabrics in rich, vibrant hues hung from shop eaves, catching the last of the afternoon light, their gold-threaded edges gleaming.

"You look as though you're seeing ghosts," she observed.

"I have walked these streets since childhood. I am not surprised by the change, but I notice it all the same." His spoke with a prudent calm, but his gaze lingered on a once-familiar doorway, now bricked over. "This was once a tailor's shop." He gestured to a bakery, its shutters flung open to the scent of fresh bread. "And this was the home of a man who bred horses. A cruel man, by my recollection."

They rode deeper into the heart of Dacw, past carved stone archways and quiet courtyards draped in climbing ivy. Children wove between the market stalls, shouting in a dialect she did not recognize. Death slowed his horse near the edge of a bridge, its stone darkened with age.

Ilys watched him carefully, his gaze fixed on the water as though it might return the pieces of his past. She did not press him, though curiosity burned on her tongue. They walked the streets on foot now, moving at a leisurely pace, Death guiding her past rows of clay-roofed homes and narrow alleys lined with fruit trees. He spoke little, only to point out places of note: the temple steps where he once loitered, the baker's stall that had always smelled of honey, the worn path toward the cliffs where the city met the sea. He was not nostalgic, nor sentimental. But he acknowledged these places, greeting an old acquaintance whose presence no longer stirred his heart, but whose company he could not ignore.

Ilys studied him as he moved through the streets. His fingers brushed along a weathered door frame, and his gaze lingered on a carving in the stone worn down by the years. He carried himself differently, in a way she had never seen before. Whether it was the grace of returning home or the quiet surrender of a man outlived by his own past, she couldn't say.

Death walked beside her, tall and silent, the hood of his cloak pushed back. His hand hovered near hers as they moved, never quite reaching for it, but brushing often enough that she knew it was not by chance.

They moved through a shaded alley where stone steps wound up between stacked homes. He paused, his hand brushing the low wall beside them.

"My brother and I used to slide down these on baking trays."

She turned toward him, surprised and laughing.

"We had stolen them."

His fingers ghosted along the stone as they continued walking. She stopped near a low wall tangled in ivy and leaned against it, the breeze lifting her hair. He moved in close, standing just before her. His hand came up without thinking, fingers sweeping her hair behind her ear again, knuckles grazing her jaw.

"You're warmer here," she said softly.

He didn't answer right away. His gaze rested on her mouth.

"I wasn't always Death," he said.

Her throat tightened. "Often the gloom sticks to you. You are so much lovelier in this little town."

He stepped into her space fully, pressing her gently back against the wall. One hand came to rest at her waist. The other braced against the stone by her head.

His voice dropped, low and close. "I can be so very lovely."

Then he kissed her. Not careful. Not timid. He kissed her like he remembered it. Like he'd done it before in another life and meant to do it again. His hand slid to the small of her back, pulling her to him. Her fingers caught the front of his cloak, anchoring herself. The stone at her back held its chill, but his warmth pressed through it—through her—until she felt only the shape of him, the absence of all else.

He broke the kiss only to rest his forehead against hers, breathing her in and her hands moved beneath his shirt, splaying across his chest.

He drew her into the shadow of an alcove, tucking them out of sight like a secret. There, with his mouth on hers again, he melted, silent and open, tasting the air between them like it belonged to him.

The sky deepened into dusk, and they made their way to the outskirts of the city, where the land sloped toward the cliffs. The wind carried the scent of salt and earth, and the sea stretched before them, vast and endless. Ilys stood at the edge, the cliffside beneath her boots crumbling, wind tangling in her hair. Death stood beside her.

"You said you wanted to show me this place." She asked, "Did it give you what you wanted?"

With his gaze fixed on the horizon he answered. "No."

She turned to him. "And what did you want?"

He looked at her then, mournful. "To belong to it again." A wry smile touched his lips, almost self-mocking.

Without thinking, she reached for his hand, lacing her fingers through his. He did not pull away.

The water lapped gently at the sides of the tub, steam curling in the air between them. Ilys sat across from Death, one knee bent, her foot propped against his shoulder, toes just brushing the curve of his neck. Her movement looked effortless, but intention lived in every inch of it. A silent trust unfolding as she gave herself to him, one breath at a time.

Her posture remained regal, even as the bath's heat melted the tension from her spine. She watched him, head tilted , studying the way his broad shoulders curved against the rim of the tub, his inky hair curling at the ends.

His hands moved with care, lathering a soft cloth with scented soap and running it along the length of her leg, from the arch of her foot down the curve of her calf. Her chest ached at the sight.

"We are friends, yes?" she asked, her voice soft but certain.

Death laughed, leaning back , mimicking her proper posture with exaggerated seriousness. "I suppose we are."

She watched him a moment longer, then, after a beat, "Tell me how you became a god."

His gaze drifted toward the ceiling before returning to hers, eyes clouded, peering through the veil of time itself. "It is not a nice story."

"And yet a girl raised to kill is lovely," she countered, stretching her arms along the rim of the tub, her fingers idly tracing the worn wooden edge.

He huffed a quiet laugh, but it did not reach his eyes. "There was a war. Annon was not yet a country. It would not be for some time. I was leading men, taking back land that had once been ours. Land we needed to survive, to feed, to hold against those who sought to strip it from us. There were men above me, men who called the attacks, who made the decisions. I was their hands, their blade. I executed. I led men to their deaths for reasons I did not fully understand."

She watched the way his fingers swirled the water idly, the way his jaw tightened before he forced himself to relax.

"I was not well for a time," he continued. "Worn thin by war, weakened in body and mind. I had fought, killed, bled for something larger than myself, and yet I felt... lost. It was then she came to me."

"Who?"

"A woman. In mortal form. A visitor with an offer. Though, in truth, it had already been accepted for me long before breath was given to the

Fates." He shrugged, a half-smile flickering and dying before it could mean anything. "The middle part is fuzzy."

"Being a god?" she prompted.

He nodded. "It leaves me more and more every day."

Ilys regarded him carefully, her gaze trailing over the way the candlelight flickered against the sharp angles of his face and how the hollows of his collarbones gleamed with beads of water.

"Have you named a successor?"

Death stilled, his fingers swirling the water once more, slower this time, thoughtful. One hand remained at her ankle, where it rested lightly on his shoulder. His thumb swept gentle arcs just above the bone.

"I think you would make an excellent Death," he said, voice low and sure, like he wasn't trying to convince her, only telling the truth.

Ilys scoffed, narrowing her eyes as she scooped a handful of warm water and flicked it at his face. Droplets scattered in the candlelight like tiny stars, landing soft and shining across his skin.

"Absolutely not."

He blinked through the splash, unbothered, a smile beginning to play at his lips.

She shifted, her leg brushing against his chest, the movement casual, but intimate.

And then, quietly, without drama, he dipped his head and pressed a kiss to her ankle. Her breath caught. Another kiss, a little higher, his lips brushing the delicate curve of her shin. Then another. A trail of warmth in his wake.

She splashed him harder this time, laughing through the heat rising in her throat. "Do not distract me."

Death sputtered, shaking the water from his hair as a rare, unguarded laugh slipped free. But it faded as quickly as it had come. He leaned back against the tub, his fingers trailing idly through the water.

"There is a successor." He pared his voice down to its edge. "I understand the woman better now. It is not a choice I make. Rather, it happens. It is taken care of."

Ilys stilled, watching him, searching his face for an answer he did not give her. His gaze lost in the flickering glow of the dimly lit room. She wanted to pry, to dig into the cryptic way he spoke, to make him say the things he always left buried beneath half-answers. But the way his mouth pressed into a thin line, the way his fingers moved slower through the water, told her to leave it be.

Instead, she shifted, pushing off the edges of the tub, sliding toward him. The water rippled, sloshing against the worn wooden frame as she came to settle in his lap, her knees bracketing his hips. Her fingers found the charcoal curls at the nape of his neck, twisting idly as she tilted her head.

His hands hovered, hesitant, uncertain, before settling at the curve of her waist, his fingers pressing against slick skin. She leaned in, pressing her lips to his shoulder. Her teeth grazed the skin before biting down, not enough to bruise, but enough to mark in a sharp, quiet claim.

"Vicious thing," he remarked against the shell of her ear, his voice dipping low, dark amusement curling at the edges.

Ilys only hummed, pressing another bite lower, her lips trailing lazily along his shoulder.

Chapter 36

Morning light pooled through the frost-laced windows, casting the room in soft gold. Dust floated lazily in the air, hanging on the stillness, the quiet warmth of waking. Ilys rolled over, stretching like a cat, her limbs sliding over the sheets until she found him. Her palm rested against his stomach, fingers brushing absently over the faint ridges of muscle there, her breath warm against his skin. She pressed her face against his back, her eyelashes feathering against the sharp planes of his shoulder blades.

He stirred, breath hitching, as warmth creeped up his throat and across his cheeks.

She could feel the way he tensed, how awareness crept into his form before he settled into it, into her. She let her hand drift upward to skim the path between his ribs, following the line of his sternum. A reticent invitation.

He turned beneath her touch, without hesitation, without words, until they faced each other, the sheets shifting gently around them.

She leaned against him while he traced absent circles over her collarbones like he had nowhere else to be.

"We will live in a castle on the coast and have seven children, all named Morrigan," he narrated. "Rowenna and her children will join us, and they will run away from the fat old sod."

She huffed a quiet laugh against his skin. "I've heard he's quite nice, actually."

"Unfortunate," he said, with mock disappointment. Then, more assuredly, "We will live long lives drinking awful mead and eating wonderful meals. You will draw, and I will..." he broke off.

"Find something to do?" she finished for him. She smiled at the game he'd cobbled.

"Yes," he admitted. "I will find a pastime worthy of our life."

"We will be happy and together," Death continued, extending the dream, painting the future in broad invisible strokes.

Ilys drew out a breath, caught somewhere between a smile and a frown. She lifted a hand, pressing a finger gently to his lips.

"I stuck a sword between a man's ribs when I was twelve," she whispered. "Ended the life of a man akin to a father. I do not dwell in fairytales, Death. I do not deal in nothings."

He studied her, dark eyes unwavering. "*I* say we dwell in fairytales," he countered. "Let us play in nothings. I have seen too much, near a millennium."

"Not in this form," she corrected.

"Not in this form," he agreed.

Her fingers trailed down his torso greedily. His skin was warm beneath her touch, so solid now, no longer shifting between existence and void.

"Not like this," she whispered.

"Not like this," he echoed, his thumb brushing over her lips, pensive, earnest.

"This is what we will do," she declared, resolved and confident.

Death watched her, bemused, before mirroring her form, sitting upright. "And what is that?"

"Say these words," she instructed.

She spoke the vows of Annon, ancient words meant to bind lives together before the Veil, before the Fates.

"*Before the Veil, I name you.*

Before the Fates, I claim you.

Through shadow and breath, I bind you.

Through death and beyond, I keep you."

Line by line, he repeated them, his voice softer, lacking ritual but cradling devotion. When the last word left his lips, she nodded in approval.

"Now," she said, plucking a piece of linen that had come loose from the sheets, "with this ring, you will be my husband."

She reached for his hand, prepared to tie the fabric in place.

But his fingers twitched. His gaze shifted.

"Ilys," he protested, uncertainty threading through his tone.

She ignored him, working to secure the linen around his wrist. He pulled his hand away, gently at first.

"No, Ilys," he said, firmer now. "No."

She stilled, watching him, wounded. He reached for her, his hands cradling her face, his touch careful. "We play, yes. But the truth is this, you have devoted a life to this. Forgone choice. Forgone happiness. I will die."

Her lips parted, a protest forming, but he did not let her speak.

"I will die soon," he continued, quiet but unwavering. He tilted his head, pressing the truth into her heart with his words. "And when I am gone, you should marry. Live. Find happiness."

She shook her head, reaching for his hand again. "You will be my husband."

"I will not, Ilys. I will die."

She didn't care. Tears pricked her eyes, but fierce resolve badgered her on. She wrestled him for his hands, determined, stubborn. The struggle tumbled into playfulness, light despite the words exchanged. She tried again and again to fit the makeshift band around his wrist, laughing as he fought her off, dodging, resisting. He caught her wrists, then lost his hold, their limbs tangling, their bodies pressing close in a struggle neither of them seemed eager to win or lose.

He stilled. His lips brushed against hers, soft, careful. His hands smoothed over the canvas of her back, drawing her closer.

The fight forgotten.

The vows left to the wind.

Death shifted beside her, rolling onto his elbow, his fingers brushing a loose strand of hair from her face. The room was steeped in the cold blue light of late afternoon, the weak winter sun filtering through the frost-laced window. The fire had burned low, embers barely pulsing beneath the ash, and the chill in the air curled around them, threading through the linen sheets.

"Ilys," he breathed.

She groaned, curling closer, her body tucking instinctively into the warmth of his chest.

"Ilys," he said again, softer this time, though the insistence remained.

She shifted, inhaling deeply, her breath warm against his throat. "No," she protested, voice pummeled with sleep.

His lips ghosted against her temple, a sigh against her skin. "We have to go."

The words settled over her, heavy and unrelenting. She blinked herself awake, eyes finding his, still hazy with the remnants of sleep.

"Veilmarch," he relayed, the syllables threading into the space between them, a quiet pulse in the air. "It pulls."

She studied him, the way his fingers flexed against her hip, his body already coiled with the tension of inevitability. Her stomach curled at the thought, at the quiet way he endured his fading godhood, the way the burden pressed into his very being. She nodded, bracing herself against the cold as she shifted upright, rubbing her hands over her face. The blankets slipped from her shoulders, pooling at her waist before dipping lower, revealing the pale stretch of her thighs and the curve of her calves, bare against the crisp air.

Death, still lounging beside her, let his gaze wander over the exposed skin, his fingers following in its wake.

His palm slid over her knee, warmth cutting through the chill. The rough pad of his thumb traced circles higher along her thigh, a rhythm meant to cool them both.

A sudden brightness lit his tone, impatience edging the excitement. "Then we return to this, yes?" His lips found the inside of her leg, plush and wanton. She hummed, her fingers threading through the dark waves of his hair. "I promise." He lingered, pressing another kiss against her skin, before abandoning the warmth of her leg, resigning himself to what waited beyond the door.

Winter howled outside, rattling the shutters, reminding them of the world that did not wait.

Chapter 37

The March

They rode hard through the bitter wind, its teeth gnashing at their faces, skeletal shadows of trees clawing long across the snow-laden path. Ilys's legs ached, her wound throbbed with each stride of her horse, and her face stung with icy spray. The pain, the weariness, all of it fell away when she saw it.

The Divide.

The land broke clean in two. A wall of green forest stretched before them, sun-drenched and impossible, the trunks of ancient trees standing sentinel in the crisp light. Where frost ended, spring began. No thaw, no mud, no gray slush; the line between the boundary was sharp, as though winter itself had been carved away by an unseen hand. A wound in the world.

Spire balked, ears flattening, hooves striking the frozen ground. Death's mount snorted as well, stamping the earth, eyes rolling white. Neither animal wished to cross.

"Step down, Ilys," he instructed, dismounting with fluid ease as he led her into the sun-drenched greenery.

Ilys slid from the saddle, boots crunching in snow. At the threshold she paused, breath clouding in the cold, eyes fixed on that unnatural shimmer where one season bled into another. Then she stepped forward.

The moment her boot crossed, winter fell away. Warmth enveloped her, moss breathing beneath her feet, golden shafts of light dripping through high boughs. The forest closed around them, and the pulse of the Veil whispered at the edges of her skin. It did not feel like entering another place, but another body. Living. Watching. Leaves rustled though no wind stirred. Bark shivered beneath her fingertips when she brushed it. More than once, she swore she heard her name whispered low, breathed through the weave of branches.

And then, like a mirage taking form, the portal loomed.

An impossible monolith, neither stone nor glass, shifting at the edges like the veil of a dream. The light within it flickered, unsteady, like an untrustworthy reflection. As they approached, she lifted her hand, fingers grazing the bark. The wood was warm beneath her touch, thrumming.

The doorway to the Veil.

Death turned to her, holding out a length of black silk, folding it carefully over his palm before reaching for her hand.

"I will take the mantle of my godhood," he said quietly. "It is required for this."

Ilys swallowed, watching as he looped the silk around her wrist and knotted it with careful precision. His fingers moved deftly, securing the fabric with an ease that suggested long practice. Then, without hesitation, he bound his own wrist and pulled the silk taut, knotting it over and over again until the black threads coiled against his skin like vines.

"These are the bindings of our bargain," he instructed. "You cannot release them. The Veil will cull you. It will take what is not secured."

She flexed her fingers, feeling the silk bite against her pulse. "That is ominous."

"But true." He raised a brow, finishing the last knot. "So heed me, Ilys."

She turned back to the doorway, the surface shifting like dark water

The silk jerked suddenly as he yanked it close. She stumbled forward, colliding against his chest, breath catching as the warmth of him crowded her senses. His hand steadied her, firm at her back.

He bent his head, lips brushing against the line of her jaw, words breathed into her skin. "Do not loosen it. No matter what. Promise me."

Her pulse thrummed wildly beneath the binding. "I promise."

He exhaled raggedly then drew the length of silk taut between them, bound his own wrist, and pressed the knot until it cut against his flesh.

And together they stepped into the Veil.

The Veil did not open—it swallowed.

Air folded around them, the tether pulsing at her wrist once, twice, before settling into a rhythm not her own. The limitless scene caressing her skin as if stepping into the hollow chest of a creature vast and alive.

At first there was forest. Trees arched high overhead, their trunks smooth as bone, their branches carpeted with black leaves that whispered as she passed. Not in wind—there was no wind here—but in voices, faint and sibilant, echoing her name. She clenched her jaw, refusing to glance too long at the shifting bark, but she swore the knots in the wood bent into the shape of eyes.

Flowers carpeted the moss, but as her boots brushed against them, they folded closed, retreating from her touch. The scent landed sharp—too sharp—like herbs crushed between impatient fingers. Her pulse drummed louder, and the silk at her wrist answered, tightening. She looked up to find Death's back just ahead, but when she blinked, he was impossibly far, a shadow dissolving between the trees. The tether stretched and lengthened, threads trembling.

Then the forest ended.

A plain opened wide, its earth dark and oiled slick. Each step sank fractionally, the ground shuddering faintly beneath her boots. She froze, breath shallow. The soil pulsed, a second heartbeat beneath her feet. She bent, palm grazing the ground, and nearly cried out when the drumming leapt up her arm. The Veil throbbed with its own life, tethered to hers.

A bell tolled.

The sound reverberated across the plain, not distant but close, like it had been struck beneath her ribs. Each chime rattled through her bones, rolling outward, urging her forward. She obeyed without thinking, each step landing in rhythm with the next peal.

How long she walked, she could not say. Minutes bled into hours, then into a blur beyond measure. Her legs did not ache, yet her thoughts frayed, thinning at the edges. Memories slipped loose—Hanna's face, the Sanctum's corridors, even Baron's laugh—all dissolving, smoking like parchment in fire. She clenched her fists, trying to drag them back, but the more she grasped, the more they unraveled.

Ahead, Death's form flickered again. Close. Then far. Then impossibly small against the horizon. The tether slackened suddenly, nearly falling away from her wrist. Panic slashed through her. She yanked it tight, stumbling forward until it pinched her pulse once more.

Death. Her mind cried his name. *Death.*

The figure turned, only half his profile catching the glow. She gasped, breath ragged, willing him to pause. *Slow. Wait for me.*

His answer coiled through the binding, low and resonant, vibrating against her skin. *Then keep pace, Ilys.*

Ass, she pushed through the bond.

A ripple of warmth traveled up the tether, subtle but undeniable. She felt the god chuckle, the bond deep, amused, indulgent. It disarmed her, left her raw. How much of the mortal man she was falling in love with still lived inside this godhood? Or had they always been one and the same?

They reached a river. Not water, but liquid light, shallow and slow-moving, silver as Rowenna's wedding veil. The tether dragged through it like ink, leaving dark streaks that swirled and vanished beneath the current. She waded in, gasping at the sudden cold that burned her skin. A laugh echoed from beneath the surface, low and familiar. Baron's. She bent sharply, searching the glow for a glimpse of him, but the river swallowed the sound, carrying it away.

Her breath faltered. She staggered, and for one terrifying moment she thought the silk had slipped again.

But then Death tugged, steady and sure, pulling her out.

She lifted her gaze to him, his godly form flickering in the starlit glow, and she let herself soften. To see not only the immortal weight he bore, but the man beneath it. And in his pull she felt the rarest of things: the ache of being cared for. Guided. Led. Safe.

On the far bank, the air lightened, and she found herself in a field that stretched into endless night. The sky sprawled black velvet, the stars hanging low and impossibly close, bright enough to burn. They shifted as she walked, constellations bending, tilting, reshaping in her periphery. The longer she looked, the less they resembled stars at all.

Ilys's throat tightened. She felt she could cry. She had brushed against this closeness before: running wild through summer fields, breathless with the sting of grass against her shins, standing before the waves, their endless rhythm rising to swallow her smallness whole. In those fleeting instants, she had thought she understood the vast and unknowable.

But here, beneath this sky, she came nearer still. Her heart ached with it, brimming, spilling over. Looking into the blaze of false stars, she felt as though she were touching the fabric of human life itself threaded through with sorrow and joy, pain and wonder, woven into eternity.

The bell tolled again. Louder. Sharper. And the people came.

Not at once, but in fragments. They slipped in and out of her vision like reflections on rippled glass, until more gathered, stepping from every curve of hill and hollow of glade. They were not wisps. Not shadows. Whole. As they had been in life. Some wore fine garments, the embroidery at their hems catching the starlight. Others walked barefoot, their hands still dirt-stained, as though they had just left their work. A man passed, smiling softly, a book tucked beneath his arm. A woman carried a bundle of herbs, plucking leaves absentmindedly between her fingers. A child knelt in the flowers, hands outstretched, catching a tiny bug unseen between his palms. Garments catching starlight. Rings dropping from hands as mist. Belongings falling useless to the ground.

The line stretched on, moving with quiet purpose toward a horizon she could not yet see.

It was endless. River and plain and forest emptied themselves into this single procession, every figure drawn by the same inexorable pull. Their steps rose and fell together, soft as rain, yet the sound thundered in her chest. The tether at her wrist vibrated with it, each footfall a pulse through her blood, through the earth, through the stars themselves.

They followed him. Not like subjects trailing a king, nor mourners behind a bier, but as though he were the tide and they the sea itself: pouring forward, unresisting, inevitable. The Veil bowed to him, opened for him, its rhythm keeping time with his stride.

Ilys stood at the edge of it, breath ragged, overwhelmed by the immensity of what she witnessed. This was no solemn duty. No sacred ritual. This was the world's climax, the truest truth hidden beneath every scripture and lie: all life flowing into his hands, all threads drawn to their end.

Ilys's gaze swept the procession, dazzled and undone by its immensity—until a sharp sense pierced through the perfume of crushed grass and cold starlight.

A scent.

Leather darkened with rain. Tobacco smoke clinging to wool. A note of iron, faint as memory. Her lungs seized. She knew that smell as surely as her own skin.

Baron.

Her head snapped toward the line, eyes raking desperately across the endless procession until she saw him. Broad shoulders. The familiar slope of his jaw. And his hair, auburn still, though muted now with strands of copper fire catching the strange starlight. He walked with the same unhurried stride she remembered, boots leaving no mark upon the grass, gaze fixed on the horizon where Death led them.

"Baron." The name tore out of her, ragged, wild.

The tether yanked taut as she surged forward, silk burning her wrist. She shoved through the silent figures, vision tunneling. "Baron!" she cried again, louder, desperate, running now, heart pounding against her ribs.

This time, he faltered.

The turning felt like revelation. His eyes, when they found her, shone with the far glow of constellations. The procession dissolved around them. There was only him.

He stepped toward her, out of the rhythm, out of the tide, breaking the procession's perfect order. With each pace, the scent of him grew stronger, the memory of his warmth, his low laugh, the press of his hand at her back.

"Ilys."

Her name on his lips nearly undid her. She stumbled forward, clutching at him, tears spilling hot down her cheeks. His hands—familiar, callused, real—rose to cup her face. The tether at her wrist thrummed in protest, vibrating and recognizing the trespass.

She pressed her forehead to his, breath trembling, half joy, half ruin.

Baron swayed against her, disoriented, his gaze flicking back to the endless line of souls as though seeing it for the first time. His voice faltered. "I was just—"

"What?" Ilys gasped. Her grip tightened. "What is it?"

Confusion darkened his eyes. "I don't remember... coming here."

Her stomach dropped. He didn't remember dying. Heat surged sickening through her chest, all she had done pressing in hard and merciless. All the words she had never thought she'd have to say tangled in her throat.

"Baron," she forced out, voice cracking. "You are in the Veil."

He blinked at her, then laughed softly, rubbing a hand across his face. "Yes, I know, my girl. Of course I know." His smile flickered, crooked, achingly familiar. "I was just with Grim."

Her breath caught. "Baron," she rasped, desperate now. "You are dead. I killed you."

At that, he stilled. His gaze cut into hers, searching, steady, strangely gentle. "Ilys," he said quietly, firmly, punctuating every word. "I know." He brushed her tears with his thumb, shaking his head faintly. "My sweet girl. Don't cry."

The guilt she had carried like armor shattered. It poured out of her in sobs as he pulled her close, his voice a balm against her ear. "Come," Baron urged softly. "Shhh. Enough. Let us find Grim."

Her body stiffened. She pulled back, staring up at him, confusion cutting through her grief. "Why do you keep saying that?" Her voice cracked, sharp with fear. "Baron—we're in the Veil. He's not coming."

He stopped then, truly looking at her, his gaze pouring into the girl he had raised, heavy with a tenderness she had almost forgotten.

His lips parted, the question falling like a stone. "Do you not know?"

And as she followed the tilt of his head, the world behind him rippled. Reality mottled and reformed until out of the glow, just behind Baron's shoulder, she saw him.

Grim.

Chapter 38

The Last Year in the Life of Grim of the Veil

People mistook Grim's gruffness for a lack of feeling. They could not have been more wrong. He was well-read, quietly poetic, and possessed a capacity for love so vast it frightened him—truly terrified him. He loved Baron. He loved Ilys. He even loved their crooked, bloodstained life. So when they had wrestled him to the ground, knees digging into his back, the grit of the stone floor biting into his cheek—it surprised the King, this range of emotion. Grim's chest heaved, but no air seemed to reach him. His hands throbbed where the splintered wood had cut them.

Baron.

He twisted against the guards, teeth bared, until their force crushed the fight out of him. The chamber was too still now, except for the wet sound of steel parting flesh. His vision blurred. He felt the moment break inside him like a bone splintering. The sound of Ilys's voice, so young and obedient, struck him harder than any blow. She was becoming exactly what he had made her to be.

When they dragged him down into the bowels of the keep, he did not resist. The cell was narrow, chilled, and the door shut with a finality that echoed in his ribs. He sat with his back against the wall, his veil twisted in his hands. He did not pray. He had no words left for the Veil. He only had Baron's hazel eyes, staring through him, and the image of Ilys with blood on her hands.

It should have been him on his knees.

Weeks passed before the King finally came.

Grim had almost forgotten what light looked like. His cell smelled of iron and mildew, his hair hung in his face, his veil lay in tatters at his side. The chains around his wrists had rubbed the skin raw, but he hardly noticed anymore. He had begged the guards for death every day when they passed by. None had answered him.

When the door opened on a grind, he thought they had come to grant him that wish.

Instead, the King stood framed in the doorway, haloed by torchlight, with his hands clasped loosely behind his back. His robe trailed the floor like a living shadow.

"I knew you were perhaps not my most loyal Veilwalker," the King said softly, almost musing, "but I did not expect you to be the most stupid."

Grim lifted his head, his lips cracked and bleeding from disuse. "This is not stupidity," he spat, voice low, feral. "This is a man who has peeled back every lie. Every falsehood you'd beg the world to believe is scripture."

The King tilted his head, regarding him with mild amusement. "And what do you think is a lie?" he asked, glancing sidelong at the guards flanking him as though sharing a private joke.

"All of it." Grim bared his teeth in a sneering smile. "Outside of Death. Outside of the Veil itself. All the pieces that give you power."

The King's mouth curved in mock sympathy. "I know you were made for cutting, Grim. But I had hoped you were not so simple of mind."

"You would question the deity who told me this himself? You would question Death?"

The King's expression sharpened, the indulgent curve of his lips curling into cruelty.

"You lie."

Grim surged forward, the chain clattering. "Death tires of your crooked Bargain," he snarled through the bars. "He'll find a way to be rid of you soon enough."

"The Bargain is good for everyone," the King cooed, almost pitying. "He would be a fool to break it."

"It serves you and you alone, you immortal bastard. You promise them bounty. You promise them protection. Yet what does that Bargain really say?" Grim spat. "Death will not come for you at your natural end. You cut the blameless down, escape age and discomfort, and expect no end to such an imbalance?"

The King laughed, a low, delighted sound. "Death cannot harm me, Grim. And you remain here, under my lock and key, eating my food, sleeping on my stones. Who should cull me, then? You?" He paused, then smiled like a wolf. "No, perhaps not you. Perhaps Ilys?"

Grim's stomach twisted.

"My darling girl," the King said, as though savoring the words. "Do you think she has it in her? She just killed your lover and still you think her capable of rebellion?"

Grim's face went slack, a mask of iron.

"Not Ilys," he ground out. Though not for the reasons the King believed he understood. "One day," Grim promised, voice dark and quiet, "you will find yourself on the end of the sword."

"Likewise, my friend." The King leaned in close, fingers curling around the bars. "You should hope Ilys does not find her successor too quickly." His eyes glinted, cruel with mirth. "Once we have that little failsafe, you'll meet your god again soon enough." He lingered there just long enough for Grim to feel the threat settle into his bones before he turned and swept away, leaving only the stink of torch smoke and the rattle of Grim's breathing.

Grim sagged back against the wall, tasting blood on his tongue.

Let me die, he thought. *Let me go. Let me follow Baron.*

The months bled together and Grim had stopped marking the days—there were too many scratches on the wall already—and had begun to think perhaps they had simply forgotten him here.

Then one morning, the hinges shrieked and light spilled in. The King ducked into view, his expression gleeful, a boy with a secret he could not wait to share.

"You are a granddad, Grim," he said brightly, as though announcing the birth of a child. "Ilys claimed her successor just this morning."

The words hit like a hammer. Grim's throat constricted.

The King tutted, amused. "You don't seem proud."

At a gesture, the guards unlocked the cell door. The clink of keys and rattle of chains sounded louder than the King's voice. The door swung wide. The King stepped inside like a man entering a garden.

"You know," he said conversationally, drawing a slim blade from his belt and stroking a thumb along its edge, "sometimes I get a little envious of you lot." He crouched down until they were eye level, the blade glinting in the torchlight. "There really is no thrill like that of inflicting pain."

Grim could not move, though every muscle in his body trembled with the urge to lunge.

"It's time to cleanse you, Grim." The King's tone softened, almost reverent. "It's time you met the Veil."

CHAPTER 39

He stood behind Baron, haloed in the trembling light of the Veil.

For a breath, her mind refused to name him. Then recognition struck, brutal and immediate.

"Grim?"

A million moments fluttered before her eyes, overlapping like leaves caught in a storm. Grim adjusting her grip on a knife, his voice, fatherly and patient. Grim reading by candlelight, the book balanced in one hand, the other tapping absently against his knee. Grim's rare, gruff laugh, hidden behind a shake of his head. His arm around her shoulders after a long day. Baron and Grim together, leaning close over a game board, speaking in low tones, their laughter filling the space between them. A hundred—a thousand—mundane reflections, fragments of a life long lost, standing before her now in the form of this man.

No. Not man. Soul.

Grim was in the Veil.

He turned toward her slowly, eyes softening. "You've grown," he said, voice rough as gravel worn smooth.

Her knees weakened. She surged forward, hands trembling as she reached for him. "You left me."

Grim flinched. "That's what they told you."

Her voice trembled. "They said you couldn't look at me after Baron. That you couldn't bear it."

Grim's expression twisted—pain, guilt, something older than both. "No, Ilys. I never left you." Grim shook his head slowly. "I could have borne anything but losing you. He knew that."

Her pulse roared in her ears. "Then where were you?"

"The night Baron fell," he started soberly, "they dragged me below the keep. Said the Veil demanded a reckoning. But it wasn't the Veil." His gaze drifted, as if he were watching it happen again. "He said I was collateral. I was to be kept until you were to take your successor."

Ilys stared at him, throat burning. "You were there all that time?"

Her vision blurred, fury and disbelief crashing together in her chest, strangling the air from her lungs. All these years, she had hated him. She had resented his absence. She had mourned him in the ways one mourns the living: convinced that he had chosen to leave her behind. But he hadn't. He had been there. Trapped. Alone. While she—

"Only then, only after the next blade was chosen, would he 'cleanse' me." His voice grew brittle on the word. "And he did."

The Veil seemed to darken, its pulse shivering through the air like breath drawn through teeth. A stunned silence fell. Ilys's heart pounded in her ears.

"Why would he—" Her words fractured, choking out between gasps. "The King killed you?"

Grim's arms wound around her, pulling her close with his strong, iron-willed grip. He didn't speak. He just held her. Let her sob into his shoulder, let her fists curl into the fabric at his chest, let her mourn what had been stolen from them. She wept. For the years lost. For the nights she spent cursing his name. For the prayers she whispered to the Fates, begging to forget him. She wept for the boy she had never known, for the man who had raised her, for the Veilwalker who had been used and discarded like a spare blade waiting to be drawn.

She sobbed, and Grim, steadfast, unmovable Grim, held her like he had never let go.

"Look at me, Ilys," he commanded, shaking her from the sobs that wracked her body. She squeezed her eyes shut, trying to block out everything, the unraveling of the world she thought she knew. But Grim wasn't letting go.

Grim's grip tightened on her shoulders, grounding her. "Look at me, Ilys." His voice called again, cutting through her sobs, stark and adamant. She squeezed her eyes shut, fighting the nausea rising inside her. Grim shook her once, sharply. "Eyes open."

She obeyed, meeting his gaze.

"Why did he do this?" He repeated her question to her. "Because the Bargain was never for Death. It was for the King."

Her stomach lurched. "What do you mean?"

"Death needed a servant, one to walk beside him when the world began twisting its own threads. Men had started weaving magic into the skein, pulling at fate to live longer, to cheat the end. The Veilwalker was born from that need, to keep the balance, to cut away what refused to die. That part was true, yes."

He paused, gaze flicking toward Death, who stood silent and vast. "But when the King saw what Death required, he saw a way to turn it. The first Bargain he struck was not to save the kingdom—it was to save himself. Death would not come for the King at his natural end. The Veilwalker's march each autumn, the rituals, the consecrations, they were meant to feed the illusion that it was all for balance. But every step you took, every soul you claimed, was a tithe of power keeping him untouched by Death."

Her pulse quickened, dread rising. "But The Book... "

"*The Book of the Veil* is a lie," Grim said plainly. "It speaks of protection, order, and sacred duty. But the King made it to serve his own ends. It is a crafted illusion." His voice hardened. "He reshaped reality. Death is cast as a villain, feared and hated. But Death demands no blind obedience. No terror. Only balance. The King twists it, using their deaths as lessons. Fear is his greatest tool. Faith is his strongest weapon."

Ilys trembled, memories rising sharply of sitting cross-legged as a child, The Book heavy and reassuring on her lap. Stories of duty and safety and purpose wrapped her in warmth, made her believe she was chosen, protected. Her breathing quickened, nausea intensifying. Those comforting truths she held so tightly were but a fragile fiction, easily shattered by Grim's cool veracity.

Ilys pressed a shaking hand to her mouth, overwhelmed.

She felt sick.

"It's a lie," she whispered, her voice cracking like ice thawing.

Grim's expression did not change, an unsettling calm against the storm raging within her. "It always has been."

Baron pulled her close, "We all believed it, Ilys. All of it, until it was too late."

"So all of it—all of it was to keep him alive?"

"Yes," Grim said. "And to make certain no one could undo it."

Baron broke it first. "You cannot go back there. Not after this."

"I can't leave," Ilys whispered. "Not when he's still on that throne."

Baron reached for her hand, his voice gentle, pleading. "You can. You must. You are the last thing he cannot claim. If you stay, he'll hollow you out until there's nothing left to fight with."

Grim said nothing, but the look in his eyes told her he agreed.

Ilys's breath trembled. "There's a girl," she said suddenly. "At the Sanctum. Her name is Hanna."

Baron's brow furrowed. "Hanna?"

"My successor." The word broke her. Ilys turned sharply, staggering as dizziness swept through her. Her vision blurred, shadows creeping into the corners of her eyes. Her breath came raggedly, painfully, each inhalation scraping against the hollow pit that had opened in her chest. A tremor spread through her fingertips, unsteady hands clutching at anything solid, trying desperately to anchor herself as reality fractured around her.

"What have I done?" she whispered, voice raw, pleading, desperate for answers she feared would never come. She looked up, eyes wild, wide, wet with confusion and anguish. "Why?" she demanded, her voice edged with disbelief and despair.

Baron caught her before she fell. "Easy," he murmured, one hand steady at the back of her neck. "Easy, love."

"Listen to me, Ilys," he said, voice low, deliberate, each word a tether. "What's done can be undone. But not by blood, not by rage. Take her. Take the girl and go."

"You want me to run while he still sits on his throne?" she demanded, voice raw. "You want me to pretend none of it happened? That you—Baron, that *you*—"

Baron caught her hands, steady but gentle, his expression soft with sorrow. "I want you to live," he said quietly. "For once in your life, Ilys, live for something other than him."

She shook her head, gasping for breath, tears streaking her cheeks. "He killed you. He chained Grim. He made me—" Her voice faltered, breaking on the memory. "He made me everything he wanted."

Baron gave a faint, rueful smile. "Then stop being what he wants."

Before she could speak, the Veil pulsed, the sound of a heartbeat that wasn't hers. Death stepped forward, the air tightening, his godhood weighing down the light.

Ilys spun, her fury snapping loose. "No," she snarled, stepping between them. "No, no, no—you will not take them!"

Death's gaze was unreadable, still as carved obsidian. "It is not my will, Ilys. You know this."

"You knew!" she screamed, shoving against his chest. The hum of his being vibrated through her palms, a living current that made her bones ache. "You knew all of it, and you let me believe! You let me think I was chosen, that it meant something sacred. You let me kill for him. For a lie. You—" her voice broke, trembling— "you lied to me."

Her fists struck his chest again and again, useless against eternity. She cursed him, cried his name with venom, until her strength crumbled into sobs. And still, Death did not stop her.

Behind her, arms gathered her in. Grim. "Ilys."

The sound of his voice steadied her, fragile as it was. She turned, eyes red and wet.

Grim cradled her face in his hands. "He is not at fault for this," he said gently. "When I learned the truth, I bound him to silence. I thought it was mercy." His gaze wavered. "I was wrong."

"You made me a murderer," she choked.

"I was blind in my complacency," he confessed.

Her breath caught painfully, her fingers gripping his wrists.

Grim swallowed, his tone trembling. "You were always mine, Ilys. Not as a weapon. Not as a creed. Mine to protect. My brave one. My clever one." His voice cracked. "My dear one."

He pressed his lips to her forehead. She felt a tear, his, fall against her skin. "My stubborn girl. My fierce girl."

Ilys looked between them, trembling. "You can't both leave me."

Baron smiled. "We're not leaving you," he said. "We're peeking around the corner. You'll catch up one day far from now, when you're good and ready."

"I don't even know where to go," Ilys whispered.

His broad grin deepened as he stooped to press a kiss to her forehead. "Do what you've never been allowed to: choose. Find a place to sleep, then a reason to wake. That's where you start. It's no trouble at all."

Ilys's breath hitched, breaking sharply, tears falling pursy and fast, soaking into his coat, pooling over his heart. Her breath hitched, her body shaking. She could feel it now, the Veil drawing them back, the light dimming at their edges.

"Please don't—" she whispered.

All the sudden she was nine years old once more, staring at a doorway that sought to thieve everyone she loved.

Baron leaned into her ear. "Say the blessing," he ushered. "Nice and slow. One could fall asleep."

Ilys froze. The words caught somewhere between her ribs. Her lips parted, but nothing came at first, only a shuddering breath, the ache of knowing what came next.

Baron's thumb brushed her hand. "Go on," he said softly. "You know it."

She swallowed hard, eyes shining. Then, barely above a whisper:

"Where the fire dims, you will rest."

Grim's hand found hers and squeezed three times, the old signal of comfort. She nearly wept at the tenderness of it.

"Where the water stills, you will wait."

Their voices met, the old blessing that belonged to them alone—unsanctioned, unspoken in any temple, a prayer for partings and quiet nights.

"Where the stars gather," they said together, "you will be known."

Through her tears, she watched helplessly as they stepped into shadow, dissolving like smoke into darkness, leaving only emptiness in their wake.

CHAPTER 40

Ilys could not hear the wind. She could not feel the cold bite of winter on her skin nor her own body as Death pulled her from the Veil's threshold. Her limbs felt distant, untethered, like they belonged to someone else. She did not move, did not speak, did not breathe.

Grim was gone.

Her lungs seized. Air refused her. The ringing built until it swallowed everything—the Veil's hum, the wind's cry, the voice still reaching for her.

Hollow grief hollowed deeper.

The journey back through the sacred glade passed in a blur. She did not recall Death leading her away, nor the way his hands tightened around her arms, steadying her when she swayed. The moss and grass that once pulsed beneath her feet were only earth now, dull and lifeless. The trees no longer whispered as they passed.

She did not hear Death shift back into his mortal form. She did not register the way his jaw tightened, nor notice when his shoulders curled inward from his own burden pressing heavily upon him.

Only when he stopped did she realize they had left the forest.

The green ended abruptly, severed by winter's reach. Spire and Death's black mare stood where they had left them, their breath curling into the cold air. The sight of them felt impossibly distant, a scene in a life that no longer belonged to her.

A hand closed around her wrist. "Ilys."

She did not react.

"Ilys," he said again, more forceful now, his grip tightening, shaking her once.

The numbness swallowed her whole.

Death exhaled sharply, his fingers flexing against her arm before he released her. Without a word, he lifted her onto his horse. One hand stayed at her waist, not just to keep her upright, but to trace circles over her ribs, coaxing her breath back into rhythm. Her pulse fluttered weakly beneath his palm, a faint reminder that she still lived, even as her mind drifted far from the present.

Then he looped Spire's reins to his own and mounted behind her, spurring the ride.

She barely noticed the motion, the sway of the horse beneath her, the rhythmic thudding of hooves against frostbitten earth. Time moved without her. The road stretched on in endless miles, the sky above melting into a dull gray, shifting from afternoon into evening.

Somewhere along the way, her body slumped against him. She barely registered the warmth of him, the quiet rise and fall of his chest, the grip of his hands at her waist. The inn appeared like a mirage, the glow of its lanterns flickering in the distance. She did not stir when he pulled the horses to a stop, nor when he slid from the saddle and caught her in his arms.

The innkeeper did not question them. Perhaps it was the look on Death's face, or the glassy, hollow emptiness in Ilys's eyes. He offered the room in silence, unwilling to disturb the ruin they carried in with them.

She did not notice when Death lowered her onto the bed, nor when he pulled off her gloves, setting them beside her. He hesitated, then reached for her boots, loosening the laces with careful, deliberate hands.

Still, she did not move.

Death sat beside her for a long moment, his gaze heavy and indecipherable as he rubbed a hand down his face.

"You will rest," he ordered though she gave no indication she had heard him.

Without another word, he stood and stepped away.

Ilys woke curled into herself, her body wound so tightly that every joint ached; her fingers were pressing into her arms as though she could keep herself from unraveling. Her breath came shallow, uneven. Her pulse was a frantic, fluttering thing beneath her ribs.

The room was dim, the candle on the table having long since burned down to a stub, its wax pooled in a stagnant drip. No light crept in from the night outside. The air smelled of old wood and damp fabric, the faintest traces of the stew and ale from the evening before floating in the quiet corners.

She did not know how long she laid there, staring at the wall, her mind replaying every second, every breath, every moment from the Veil.

Grim's hands, warm against her cheeks.

His voice, fond despite the truth, unraveled before her.

The way his gaze softened as he spoke her name.

The way he had held her, kissed her tears away, whispered promises he could not keep.

The way he had walked through the doorway.

Gone.

Her breath caught in her throat, ripping through her chest and spreading like ice in her veins. She squeezed her eyes shut, willing it away, willing all of it away, but it only settled deeper, sinking into her marrow.

The creak of a floorboard snapped her eyes open.

Death stood in the doorway.

The sight of him made her stomach twist violently, nausea curling up her throat. He was mortal again. His godhood had been shed in the return journey, leaving behind only the man. The liar. The one who had known.

"Get out." Her voice came hoarse, raw from sleep and grief, but the venom in it was unmistakable.

Death's brows furrowed. "Ilys."

"Get out." She pushed herself upright, arms trembling under her own body, but she did not falter. Her blood burned with a fury that scraped against her ribs like jagged bone. "You lied to me," she hissed, breath sharp and uneven. "You knew. You knew and you let me..." Her voice fractured, but she swallowed the wretched sound rising in her throat.

Death took a careful step forward, scrutinizing her every tendon, every breath. "Ilys, please."

"GET OUT."

She launched the nearest object at him, a tin cup left on the nightstand. It hit the doorframe with a sharp clang, missing him by inches.

"GET OUT, GET OUT, GET OUT!" Her screams rang through the room, through the walls, sharp and unrelenting. She reached for whatever was near: a pillow, the candlestick, a book, anything to throw, anything to drive him away.

"I was bound by blood, Ilys!" he shouted. It was so rare to hear him raise his voice, it rattled her. "I was bound. He sought to protect you through my silence. So you did not have to feel what he felt. Act as he did."

"You should have found a way," she ground out.

"This will not solve anything."

She wrenched against his hold, desperate to escape, desperate to strike again. "You think you are judgment," she spat, her voice hoarse with grief, with fury. "You are nothing more than a stupid dog, heeding commands without question, without thought. You cannot audit your instincts, cannot challenge what has been whispered into your ear since the dawn of time."

She shook, her body trembling. Her breath came in ragged gasps, her vision blurred.

"I implore you," she whispered, raw and aching, "beg you, to have a conscience. I know you can feel love. I know you can feel empathy. You foolish, foolish man. Help me kill him."

"When you kill him," he said finally, voice low, even, "what do you think will happen? A new government will rise? Fair and loving? The world will be just? That is a fantasy, Veilwalker."

Her breath hitched. She wrenched at his hold again, but he did not yield.

"Live your life," he said. "Do not waste it in this way."

The sob tore from her, sudden, violent. "I want to die."

His grip faltered. Just enough. Moisture shimmered along his lashes as he bent to her.

"*Anwyl Vyth. Anwyl Veth.*" The language of gods spilled from him: soft, aching, and urging. Ilys flung the litany from her mind.

"My whole life," she whispered, shaking, "I have murdered. I did not blink. I did not hesitate. I killed innocents in the name of an evil man who has lied and stolen and hungered for centuries. And I called it duty."

"What does it matter," he asked, "if it is the Fates or a mortal man? You killed, yes. But it was not your will either way."

"I killed them," she sobbed.

He only held her, rooted, unmoving, as she slumped forward against him, the fight leaving her in one exhale.

His arms curled around her, cradling her against his chest. His breath paced laggard and measured against her temple, his body solid beneath her shaking form.

"Sleep," he directed. "Sleep, and we will talk in the morning."

Ilys woke to stale dried tears on her pillow, her face tight and swollen. Her throat ached, raw from sobs she barely remembered, from words torn out of her in desperation. Her body felt different, lighter in some ways, emptied in others. She did not feel grief, not now. Not in the quiet hush of the morning.

She felt focused.

Ilys dressed swiftly, then paused once at the doorway, her gaze on Death's quiet form. A gentle pang stirred within her chest, unexpected yet familiar. She turned away sharply, letting the feeling pass like a shadow slipping beneath her feet.

Outside, the inn's yard was cloaked in fog, pale tendrils clinging stubbornly to the chilled earth. She saddled her horse quickly, movements automatic, a comforting ritual in uncertain times. Her mount shifted beneath her with familiar patience, sensing the urgency in her tightened grip on the reins. With one last glance back toward the darkened windows of the inn, she set her jaw and nudged the horse forward.

Towards the Sanctum.

Chapter 41

The halls of the Sanctum were quiet in the dead of night, the cold stone beneath Ilys's boots swallowing the sound of her steps. Hanna curled in her arms, half-asleep, her small fingers knotted in the folds of Ilys's cloak.

She moved fast, stepping over Gabriel's body. She'd considered spinning a cover story to talk her way past him, but the risk was too great. She couldn't chance Hanna being taken away. So Gabriel had gone down—and he wouldn't be getting up again.

The child's weight barely registered. *She will not be me.* That thought drove her forward.

The Sanctum's corridors winded like veins, its walls old and aching with prayers long since faded. Ilys knew its turns, its passages, the ways the stone whispered in the night. But she had not accounted for Mother Inrith. The old priestess drifted down the hall ahead, waiting. Her white eyes, clouded and sightless, fixed somewhere beyond Ilys as she stopped. Ilys halted, every muscle tensing, readying for reprimand, for demand, for the doctrine to slam down upon her. Hanna stirred, pressing her face against Ilys's chest.

Mother Inrith's face rearranged itself, mouth curling upward by rote.

"The day has come?" she questioned, tilting her head in thought, her voice soft as parchment turned by a gentle hand.

Ilys's grip on Hanna tightened. "Mother?"

Mother Inrith swayed, her gaze unfixed, looking through her rather than at her.

"Mother," Ilys pressed, "what do you mean?"

The Mother laughed. “Obedient, but never devoted. You were always a broken bell, dissonant and barren.”

Ilys gritted her teeth, tucking Hanna closer. “Do not speak of devotion. I gave my life for his lies.”

“You were devoted to praise, never the faith,” Inrith condescended. Escape tugged at Ilys, but her pride rankled at the dismissing of her sacrifice.

“I was wholly devoted,” she pushed back, tears stinging her eyes. “I gave everything for my faith, stupid and green as I was. How dare you?”

“No,” the Mother denied primly. “But I see you are quite committed to your retelling.”

“Have you no shield to the lies I speak of?”

“You call them lies, I call it meaning. I call it sustenance for a sickly existence.”

“Your mind is gone,” Ilys spit, tired of the flowery, meaningless words.

“What else would I believe in, girl?” The Mother’s laughter deepened, brittle and knowing. “What is life without meaning?”

Ilys clutched the girl tighter, anger breaking through the confusion.

“I killed to give your life meaning? What excuse is that? What sense is that?”

Mother Inrith lifted a finger to her lips, barring words. “Tick tock, Veilwalker.”

The priestess reached toward her, as though to touch her cheek, but her hand only brushed the air. Then, with a soft hum and that same dreadful calm, she turned and pattered away.

Ilys stood frozen, watching the old woman disappear into the shadows of the corridor. She ran faster, carrying Hanna down the final stretch, slipping through the heavy doors of the Sanctum and into the night.

The cold met her immediately, biting and sharp as she crossed the courtyard in long, quiet strides. The stables waiting ahead, the scent of hay and wood curling through the air. Spire whinnied softly as she entered, her white coat gleaming faintly in the moonlight filtering through the rafters. Ilys worked quickly, securing the girl to her front, wrapping her snug in bulky wool, tucking her safely against her chest.

Hanna stirred again, blinking up at her, confused, but Ilys hushed her gently, pressing a hand to her hair. "Hold tight, little one."

With practiced ease, she mounted Spire, her body fitting into the familiar rhythm of the saddle.

She did not look back. Not at the Sanctum. Not at the place where she had spent a lifetime kneeling, killing, believing.

She rode. The girl nestled closer, trusting, unknowing of the choice being made for her.

Ilys did not pray. She did not whisper to the Fates. She only rode, guiding Spire toward the one place she knew Hanna would be safe. To Rowenna.

Rowenna's husband quietly gathered Beck, bundling him in warm layers before guiding them toward the village. With a quiet sort of grace, he left the women to their solitude, sensing their need for privacy. Ilys settled Hanna into the bed Rowenna had offered, smoothing stray strands of hair from her face and murmuring for her to sleep.

Once the small girl had begun her dainty snores, Ilys returned to the front room and painted the whole of it for Rowenna. The truth of the Bargain. The King's cruelty. Grim in the Veil.

Rowenna met her gaze quietly, carefully gauging the depth of her friend's resolve. Tears pricked Rowenna's eyes, glittering gently.

"I am so sorry, Ilys," she whispered softly, rubbing a comforting hand over Ilys's. Taking her hand into her own, Rowenna pressed a tender kiss against it, her tears softly brushing against Ilys's knuckles. "What will you do?"

Ilys's eyes flashed with sudden, fierce resolve. She spoke evenly, a stark contrast to the chaos within. "I will kill him."

Rowenna, pulled away her hand, shaking her head. "Absolutely not."

"After all I've told you, you would still be loyal to Annon?"

"Of course I am not loyal. He is a monster, Ilys," she argued. "But you will not kill him. You would invite Death yourself."

"Rowe, how many have I killed over the years?" she pressed.

"I—" Rowenna started.

"Exactly, you do not know. Because I have killed that many. Yet still you doubt my abilities?"

"If what you say is true, if he is older than the kingdom itself, then he will not be like all those men and women before," she pushed back. "I worry, Ilys."

Ilys cupped a hand to her friend's cheek. "Do not worry."

"Grim never wanted this for you," Rowenna reminded her softly, sorrow heavy in her tone.

"Grim is gone," Ilys replied fiercely, her voice tight with grief and rage. "This isn't for Grim. This is for me, for the tattered soul I've been left with. I will strangle him with what remains."

Ilys reached out, gripping Rowenna's hand urgently. "I need you to do something for me. Take her to Tyl. Be with Leif's family," Ilys urged softly but firmly. "*If* I fail, the King will come for you and your family next. You must leave this place, Rowenna."

"See—*if*." Rowenna pressed, illustrating her point. Ilys chuckled at the attitude that had yet to leave her friend, now a seasoned mother.

"On the very slim occasion that I should fall. You will take her, yes?" She stared at Rowenna. "Say yes, Rowe."

Rowenna drew a breath, troubled. "There are men in Tyl just as cruel, just as corrupt."

Ilys sighed heavily, weariness shadowing her face. "I am exhausted by talk of balance and cycles. I know that hate will always breed more hate. Another ruler, another tyrant, another monster will rise as quickly as we strike one down." Her voice quieted, threaded with raw honesty. "I no longer seek to balance scales I cannot hold. I only wish to return a fragment of what I've taken in the name of that endless cycle."

Rowenna pulled Ilys to her chest, holding her tight. "I will do it. I will do it."

The door creaked open, spilling cold air into the room. Leif stepped in first, his broad frame filling the doorway, the boy tumbling past him like a pair of loose arrows.

"Beck!" Ilys barely had time to brace before he collided with her, small arms wrapping around her waist. She bent to meet him, clutching him close, breathing in his familiar, earthy scent.

"You're back," Beck said breathlessly.

"I am," Ilys said softly, smoothing his hair, "but only for a moment."

Rowenna rose, her face pale but set. "Wake her," she urged quietly, tilting her head toward the bed where Hanna slept, her breathing evening. "She would want to know this is the last time."

Ilys's gaze lingered on Hanna, her chest aching at the thought. Then she shook her head.

"It is not the last time," she said, her voice firm, as though willing it to be true. "And I wouldn't dare wake such a lovely dream." She padded over to the little Veilwalker, pressing a soft kiss to Hanna's brow, her lips lingering there. When she straightened, she pressed a finger to her lips, bidding Rowenna to cease arguing.

Then, with a hand trembling just enough to betray her, Ilys brushed the hair back from Hanna's face.

"My stubborn girl," she whispered, her voice both fierce and breaking. "My fierce girl. How proud you've made me."

Ilys turned to Rowenna, drawing her close despite the swell of her belly, giggling at the space between them.

"I cannot wait to meet her," she said, gaze fixed on the curve of Rowenna's stomach.

"Her?" Rowenna arched a brow. "Confident."

Ilys kissed each of her cheeks, breathing in the lavender scent of her oldest friend, her first great love. She leaned close, lips brushing Rowenna's ear. "I laid with Death," she whispered, a spark of mischief in her tone.

Rowenna smacked Ilys's uninjured shoulder, eyes wide. "You did not."

Ilys bit her lip and nodded, and the two of them collapsed into laughter, helpless and breathless. Rowenna gulped air like it might fill the hollow where sorrow threatened to creep in.

"I love you," she said, voice soft but certain.

"I love you," Ilys returned, her eyes wet as she tilted her face toward the ceiling, hiding her fear.

When she turned to Leif, her voice had steadied. "Leif, come here, you old bastard." She wrapped her arms around him, holding tight. "I will haunt you if you do wrong by her."

He laughed awkwardly, patting her back, not realizing this was Ilys's tell—her quiet way of saying goodbye.

Despite her promises, despite her hopes, she did not plan to return.

CHAPTER 42

With Hanna safe, everything that followed came easier. Ilys felt lighter, bolder with every step. She slipped back into the Sanctum under the cover of night, her heart beating in time with her resolve. When she turned the corner toward Hanna's chamber she froze. There, slumped against the door, was Morrigan.

His small body curled protectively against the threshold, his fur darkened with dust, his nose pressed to the seam beneath the door as if guarding what lay within. One ear twitched when he heard her, and his tail thumped weakly against the floor.

Ilys's breath broke in her throat.

She sank to her knees, her hand trembling as it reached for him. "Oh," she whispered, her voice cracking. "Oh, my love... I forgot you."

The words burned as soon as they left her mouth. Morrigan licked her wrist, whining softly, the sound sharp enough to splinter her. She gathered him close, burying her face against the rough warmth of his coat.

"I'm so sorry," she murmured, her voice shaking. "I didn't mean to leave you here. You shouldn't be here. You shouldn't be anywhere near this place."

He only looked up at her, eyes bright with the kind of loyalty that had always undone her.

"You have to go," she whispered urgently. "Go find her. Go find Hanna. She'll keep you safe."

He tilted his head, but if anything settled deeper into her embrace.

Still, he would not move.

When she stood, he followed, tail low, steps soft beside hers. She walked him down the silent corridor, through the servants' hall, all the way to the side gate that opened onto the outer court. The wind slipped in through the iron grate, cold and biting.

She knelt again and took his face in her hands. "Please," she whispered. "Go. Find her. Stay alive."

He whined softly, the sound small and human in its sorrow.

Ilys forced herself to step back, tears in her eyes. "Dammit, Morrigan. Go."

He stayed.

She smiled through her tears, reached down, and kissed his muzzle—a trembling, lingering press of lips to fur. "Goodbye, love."

Before she could change her mind, she stepped back and pulled the gate closed between them. The latch fell with a hollow click.

He barked once, startled, and pawed at the bars, whining low in his throat.

Ilys pressed her forehead to the cold iron. "Go," she whispered. "Please."

He didn't. He stood there watching her, tail still, ears low, until the shadows swallowed him whole. She stayed until she couldn't bear it, until the ache in her chest turned to steel. Then she turned back toward the Sanctum.

In the laundress's room, the hidden heart of the castle's labor, she chose an ornamental dress, just as she had planned the night before. Every detail she had walked through a million times over in her mind. And yet, for foolish, sentimental reasons, she halted at her chamber door and peered inside one last time. Twenty-two years of her life were pressed into this single space, walls lacquered with memory. When she surveyed the whole of it, she found she was not alone.

Death's eyes, dark and infinite, met hers.

"Ilys," he breathed, a plea buried beneath the gentleness of her name. He sat on the edge of her bed, pale and brittle, as though the night itself might shatter him. The difference a single day had made left her throat tight.

"What has happened?" she whispered, sinking to her knees before him, one hand rising instinctively to his cheek finding his skin ice cold.

"Does dying not suit me?" His mouth curved in a thin smile, but it faltered when she did not return it. "Life drains from me every second," he admitted quietly. "Faster now since we completed the March. My successor will come soon."

His hand closed around hers, thumb tracing over her knuckles before he pulled their joined hands to his lap. His voice dropped, urgent now.

"Ilys," he said, almost a prayer. "You should not do this."

"Don't," she urged. Her fingers grazed his jaw softly, tracing lines she knew as intimately as her own. "I have to do this."

Death's jaw tightened, anguish flickering briefly across his carefully composed features. "I cannot protect you from this."

Ilys reached gently toward his face, her fingers grazing his cheek in tender acknowledgment. "I never asked you to."

His eyes opened again, vulnerable and searching hers desperately. "Please. You cannot balance the scales with an eye for an eye," Death pleaded.

Ilys cupped his face, thumbs gently sweeping over his cheekbones. "I would have to kill him a hundred times over," she noted, her voice heavy with pain. "But once will have to do."

"Ilys—"

She hushed him with the flat of her hand. "Listen. I need you to do two things for me, love."

He watched her, wary and aching. "Name them."

"First," she said, eyes urgent, "take Morrigan to Rowenna's. He's right outside the gate and someone needs to spoil him. Promise me you'll see him there."

A sad smile broke across his face. He reached up and brushed her thumb with his knuckle. "Done," he said simply. "I'll get him to Rowenna."

"And the second," she noted while reaching for his face, fingers ghosting over the sharp line of his jaw, "dress me one last time." she requested, picking the dress up from its place on the ground.

"Will you not share your plan first?" he queried. "Not even with an old friend?"

She smiled against his lips. "So you may stop me?" she hummed. "I think not."

"Yes," he agreed, "let me dress you."

Ilys loosened the ties of the blue gown he had given her so many nights ago, letting it slip from her shoulders and puddle at her feet. She stood in just her chemise, pale and unguarded. He smiled at the shape of her body, like it was his loveliest, oldest acquaintance. Even now, she flushed under his gaze.

He rose to his feet, taking the new dress from her hands. His movements were leisured as if each gesture were part of a rite. He gathered her hair over one shoulder before sliding the fabric down her arms, careful not to let it drag against the ground.

"Arms," he directed, and she obeyed, slipping them through the sleeves. He smoothed the bodice into place with long, careful hands, tugging the ties at her back until the garment hugged her frame. He touched her with precision, impersonal in intent, but his knuckles lingered, tracing her spine.

When the final ribbon was tied, he turned her toward him, his hands resting lightly on her shoulders. He simply looked at her, the quiet stretching between them like a thread pulled taut.

"It suits you," he said at last, his voice low. Oh, the way he looked at her, such sorrow in his eyes. "*Anwyl Veth.*" He closed them, but still she could feel their quiet pleading.

"Out with it," Ilys ordered. "Tell me what it means." It was almost comforting, seeing him slip back into his odious, otherworldly ways, cloaked in secret words.

He laughed quietly at her sharpness, lowering his mouth to the fine blue veins at her wrist, grazing them with his teeth.

"It means—" he began, and she shivered at the brush of his tongue as he followed the curve of her hand.

"Beloved—"

Each syllable was punctuated.

"Do—"

A hedonistic touch.

"Not—"

Languid and cutting all at once.

"Go."

"You've said that to me before," she noted, wishing she could stay beneath his touch.

He hummed against her skin, a soft note of affirmation. "You're always trying to go. Always trying to die."

"I happen to like the man in charge of such things," she countered.

"This is no joke, Ilys." His hands came up to grasp her wrists, holding them in place, unwilling to let go just yet. "You *will* die."

"I am a Veilwalker." Her voice did not waver, a smile ghosting across her lips. "I have loved Death well, and I do not fear him."

She pressed a feather-light kiss to each of his eyelids. Then, to the curve of his cheekbones, to the edge of his earlobes, the fine knuckles of his hands, she traced the places she would not have the chance to again.

Finally, her lips found his gently, in a heartbreaking tenderness, a last precious memory. She drew away, breath shaking.

"Goodbye, husband," she said softly, her voice full of quiet love and infinite sorrow.

Then she turned, moving swiftly away, leaving him standing helpless.

Only after she was gone, vanished into shadow, did he notice the thin band of linen carefully tied around his finger.

Through death and beyond, I keep you.

CHAPTER 43

The cold mask clung against her skin.

Ilys fastened the silk ties at the back of her head, adjusting the fit until it sat perfectly in place. It was a foolish thing, ornate, gilded, and shaped in the likeness of a bird. The beak curved downward, elegant but severe.

A ridiculous tradition.

On the Eve of the Bargain, the nobility masked themselves in reverence. The reasoning was simple, or so the priests had always said: on this night, when the King reaffirmed his covenant with the Veil, the dead could see the faces of the living more clearly. And the unnatural, those who had escaped fate's grasp, could recognize those who had sent them to their deaths.

So, they masked themselves. They concealed their faces, dispelling recognition, believing that a simple covering could shield them from vengeance.

Superstition. Theater.

The dead did not linger here.

But Ilys still wore the mask. Not for tradition. Not for the sanctity of the celebration.

For anonymity.

The Eve of the Bargain was a spectacle, a night of reverence wrapped in indulgence. A night where the court bathed in wine and excess while pretending at holiness. She had never been invited before—Veilwalkers did not belong at the King's joyous table—but she had always known the traditions. She had always known where the nobility would be.

And she had always known how to enter unseen.

The tunnels beneath the Sanctum were older than the castle itself. Dug long before stone was laid, before the first King had ever set foot in Annon. They ran deep, winding beneath the palace like veins, a hidden web of passages few still remembered.

Grim had taught her.

Ilys walked them now, her footsteps soundless against the drenched stone, the candle in her hand flickering against the low ceiling. At the tunnel's end, a ladder led up to the undercroft of the castle, a forgotten corridor leading directly to the western wing, where the grand ballroom awaited.

She extinguished the candle. Climbing swiftly, she emerged into the dim corridor, the scent of incense and aged stone filling her lungs. The murmur of distant voices reached her ears in the form of laughter, conversation, the hum of revelry.

She slipped from the shadows, masked and unseen, following the sound.

The ballroom was a sea of gold and crimson, the flickering glow of candelabras casting long shadows across marble floors. The scent of spiced wine and burning myrrh curled through the air, mingling with the warmth of too many bodies pressed close in whispered conversation.

Every guest was masked. Plumes of peacock feathers, velvet and satin, and porcelain molded into delicate visages of saints and spirits covered the crowd. Some faces were painted into sharp, inhuman grins, others blank and expressionless, eyes obscured behind dark lenses. The anonymity was suffocating and freeing all at once.

She passed through the throng, unseen and unnoticed.

Wine flowed into gilded goblets while laughter danced between the notes of a hidden string quartet. The whole room gleamed—luminous, shimmering with excess.

The King had not arrived yet.

He would come when the revelry had reached its peak, when the room was flushed with wine and indulgence, when the nobles were at their most pliant. He would stand before them, recite his hollow prayers, reaffirm his holy duty.

And they would cheer, would raise their cups, would bow their masked heads and thank him for his sacrifice.

Ilys's hands curled into fists beneath the folds of her silk skirts.

She moved deeper into the ballroom, closer to the head of the hall.

A woman passed her, perfume clinging to the folds of her gown, her laughter muffled behind a silver fox mask. A man in deep navy silk bowed low to another, his mask adorned with golden filigree. Everywhere, faces blurred into a faceless sea, identities discarded for the sake of spectacle.

It was strange, to move so freely. To be here, unrecognized, unburdened by her title. She could be anyone.

A hand extended before her, a man's gloved fingers hovering in invitation.

"May I have this dance?"

She turned, lifting her gaze to the figure before her. The fox's golden grin hid his expression, its curve subtle, knowing. Black silk framed his height, every line of him marked by the ease of one who leads without asking.

She inclined her head, placing her hand in his.

The music shifted, the steps beginning, and he drew her in.

"You are light on your feet," he complimented as they fell into step.

She offered a coy tilt of her head, voice measured. "You are too kind."

He spun her once, bringing her close, his breath warm against her temple. "I have been watching you."

She did not falter. "How fortunate for me."

The room spun around them, the gilded columns of the ballroom blurring as they turned, the faces of the masked dancers indistinct. But she saw what she needed.

The King had arrived.

A tall figure in white and gold, his mask shaped like a sunburst, the rays sharp and gleaming. He moved through the crowd, surrounded by his men, his presence commanding, effortless.

"The King," Fox observed against her ear, his tone laced with admiration. "You must be honored to be in his presence this night."

She turned her face, the edge of her lips curving beneath her mask. "More than you know."

The dance continued, a gentle push and pull, bodies gliding and parting, the revel a sea of color and movement. The King had begun to greet his guests, pausing here and there to exchange words, nodding graciously, lifting goblets in recognition.

Ilys let her partner lead, let him twirl her, let the music fold over them like a tide. But her eyes never left the King's presence. Every movement of the sovereign awoke a fresh anxiety in her limbs. When he stood, his guards following, that same anxiety drove her to abandon the dance prematurely.

She was irrational. The entirety of her plan derailed before her eyes. She was eager for his blood. Childlike in her mission.

Ilys moved like a shadow, weaving between clusters of revelers, masked faces flickering past her peripheral as she followed the King's retreat.

He walked calmly, too calmly, his hands folded behind his back, his golden robes trailing over the marble floors. His guards flanked him, their black-clad forms cutting through the revel like wolves through a flock, clearing a path through the confusion.

Ilys quickened her steps, her heart hammering against her ribs. He could not leave. Not yet.

A hand caught her wrist.

She moved on instinct, twisting, wrenching free, pivoting into a strike. Her elbow connected with the masked man's throat—one of the guards. He stumbled back, choking, reaching for his blade.

More followed. She had been seen.

Ilys did not hesitate. She lunged, sweeping a blade from the folds of her gown, the silver glinting once before it found the nearest throat. A gurgle, a gasp, warmth spilling over her fingers, darkening the fine fabric of her gloves.

The next guard came fast, sword swinging. She ducked low, feeling the whistle of the blade part the air above her. She drove her dagger upward, catching the space between his ribs, twisting. His breath left him in a ragged exhale, and she let him drop, already turning to face the next.

Steel clashed.

She caught the edge of a saber against her dagger, the force of the blow vibrating up her arms. The guard loomed stronger, taller, but she moved faster. Dropping her weight, she drove a kick into his knee, sending him stumbling. His balance broke for half a breath—just enough. Her blade struck deep, tore free, and another enemy closed in.

A fist cracked against her jaw, white bursting behind her eyes. She reeled, tasting blood, her body lurching sideways.

A hand wrenched into her hair, dragging her back. Another caught her wrist, twisting her blade from her grasp.

No.

She struggled, wild and feral.

A blow to her ribs, the breath driven from her lungs. She kicked out, connected with a shin, and heard a grunt of pain. A shift in her grip, dagger slipping into her palm from the slit in her dress.

She plunged it blindly, feeling it sink deep.

A strangled cry. The grip on her hair loosened. She twisted free, gasping, stumbling.

There were too many.

Another guard caught her from behind, pinning her arms. She thrashed, teeth bared, her head snapping back against his face. A crunch. A curse. She slipped free, dropping into a crouch, reaching for another blade.

And then—a voice she knew.

"Ilys."

The King.

CHAPTER 44

The King did not rush toward her. He did not call for his guards to finish what they had started. He was a man who had never once felt the need to hurry. After all, time stretched before him like the vast, undrinkable ocean.

Ilys stood, her breath still coming fast, her body thrumming with the ache of the fight, of the fists that had bruised her ribs, the grip that had wrenched her hair back. Blood—hers, theirs—dampened the front of her gown, but she did not move, did not reach for another blade. Not yet.

The guards parted at his approach, bowing their heads, though none dared turn their backs on her. She still threatened, even with empty hands.

The King stopped a few paces before her, head angled just so, the torchlight glinting along the gold of his mask. He lifted a hand and unfastened it, revealing the face beneath.

The years had been kind to him. The softening lines of age had settled into a quiet regality, patience tempered by understanding. He studied her with a faint smile, not unkind, but appraising, curious.

With an almost amused tilt of his head, he said,"Are you finished, my dear?"

Ilys did not answer.

"You made quite the mess," he continued, glancing at the guards, some still groaning in pain, clutching wounds that would likely fester by morning if left unattended. "I am not surprised, of course. That is your nature, is it not? A blade in the dark, a hand with no mind of its own, only purpose."

Ilys clenched her jaw, forcing her breath riveted. "I know what I am," she said.

The King smiled wider. "Do you? Then tell me, Veilwalker, what will you be, now that you have no master? No leash?"

"I will be the end of you," she promised, recalcitrant and hostile.

He chuckled softly. "Oh, Ilys." His voice poured over, paternal, almost pitying. "I have given you purpose. I have made you holy. Without me, what will you have?"

"A life," she whispered.

He sighed. "No, my dear. You will have regret."

The King lifted one elegant hand, signaling silently to the guards behind him. They moved swiftly, cautiously, encircling her without hesitation this time, the tension of her threat still hanging heavy in the air.

"Bind her," the King commanded softly, watching impassively as they closed in.

Ilys did not resist, not now. Her body had spent itself in violence already; to fight further would achieve nothing. They seized her wrists roughly, shackles clamping down tightly, metal biting into her already bruised flesh. Her vision swam momentarily, but she forced herself upright, shoulders squared even as chains were locked around her ankles, shortening her stride to a humiliating shuffle.

"Take her to where Grim was held," he continued, his tone dismissive yet edged with quiet cruelty, as though aiming to break her resolve. "Let her contemplate her choices. Perhaps solitude will teach her what loyalty did not."

She held his gaze, unblinking, until the guards forced her to turn away, pushing her roughly toward the narrow staircase that wound downward, away from the regal corridors and gilded light of the palace.

The air grew colder, stale, as she descended, torches fewer and farther apart until only shadows remained. The dungeons lay beneath layers of stone, ancient walls dense enough to swallow all sound, to bury screams until they turned silent and forgotten.

A cell door creaked open, iron grating against iron, a hollow sound that resonated deep within her bones. They shoved her inside without ceremony, the chains rattling heavily as she stumbled, catching herself against a rough stone wall. The door slammed shut, reverberating with brutal finality, the lock sliding into place like a blade driven home.

She stood still, allowing herself to feel the full weight of her imprisonment, the dark pressing in, oppressive and bloody-minded. Gingerly she knelt down, pressing her hands into the dirt, fingers digging into the grit and grime of the cell floor. She reached outward, palms flat against the cold stone walls, searching desperately for anything that might remain of him.

"Grim," she whispered softly, her voice barely audible. She closed her eyes, breathing deeply, seeking the echo of his strength, the residue of his defiance.

The door groaned open.

Ilys didn't move. She remained on the floor of her cell, her back to the door, hands loosely clasped in her lap. The chains around her ankles dragged as she shifted, enough to signal that she was alert. She refused to look.

"I thought you might be more forthcoming after some rest." The King's voice was measured, composed, with just enough warmth to suggest civility.

Ilys nestled deeper into the freedom she carved out in her consciousness. Silence had teeth, and she had learned to wield them.

He stepped inside."I don't like the dungeons. Too bleak. But they have their uses." A pause. "Where is the girl?"

Still, she didn't answer, fixing her gaze on the far wall, studying a crack in the stone.

The King sighed, low and theatrical. "Come now. Where is Hanna?"

That name.

Ilys turned her head, just enough for him to see her profile.

"Did it ever bother you?" she asked, her voice hoarse from disuse. "That even after all your titles, your sermons, your scriptures...your life hinges on a terrified child?"

The King's smile did not falter, but it tightened. Just a hair.

"She is more than a child. She is a symbol. A legacy. She is mine."

Ilys rose to meet him, the pull of the chains whispering against the floor. "No," she protested. "That's the one thing she never was."

His eyes narrowed."I offered you sanctity," he said, voice harder now. "Purpose. I made you divine, Ilys. And this is how you repay me? By hiding the girl? By dragging your broken body through my halls like a martyr who never earned the cross?"

Ilys took a step toward the bars, her smile faint but sharp. "You never made me divine. You made me useful."

The mask cracked.

He stepped closer, close enough that she could see the tremor in his hands, the thread of rage held barely in check.

"You do not get to bait me," he said, voice low, dangerous. "You think yourself clever. Brave. But you have never known true suffering, Ilys. You've danced at its edges, yes. But I can drag you into the center of it."

She leaned in, her breath ghosting the space between the bars.

"Then do it," she whispered. "Break me, if that's all you know how to do. But if you were half the prophet you pretend to be, you wouldn't need to ask me where she is."

The King stared at her, fury boiling just beneath the skin of his composure. Then, quietly, he reached through the bars and placed a single hand against her throat, not tight, not yet, but threatening in its ease.

"I built a kingdom from ash and obedience," he proudly detailed. "Do you think I will hesitate to build a tomb beside it?"

She did not flinch."Then dig."

He released her abruptly, her touch burning. He stepped back, spine straight, expression cold once more.

"Enjoy the silence, Ilys," he said, already turning away. "In time, even your defiance will wither."

The door slammed shut behind him and the lock slid home with the finality of a grave.

Chapter 45

The boots returned with purpose.

Four sets this time. Their rhythm echoed down the corridor, accompanied by the metallic rattle of chains and the low hiss of coals being stirred to life.

Ilys remained where she was, kneeling now, not by force, but because she had chosen not to stand. Her hands rested in her lap. Her head bowed, the long curtain of her dark hair veiling part of her face.

The door opened without haste. The King stepped through, his silhouette backlit by torchlight. He wore his ceremonial robe, black and heavy, embroidered with the silver threads of the Veil's sigil. A priest's raiment, not a ruler's.

Behind him came the guards, silent and grim, bearing the brazier and its tools. Hooks. Chains. Irons carved into sacred shapes.

Ilys did not look up.

"I bring doctrine," the King said, his voice calm, almost soft. "And correction."

No answer.

He stepped towards her, eyeing the torchlight that caught the edge of her face, the blood drying at the temple from yesterday, the bruises blooming like ink beneath the skin.

He knelt beside her, robes pooling.

"I thought perhaps you had time to reflect," he confessed. "You once loved scripture. You carried *The Book of the Veil* with reverence. I remember your hands shaking when I first allowed you to read from it aloud."

Still, she said nothing.

The King turned toward the brazier. He selected a brand, thin and curved, shaped like the Eye of the Veil. He held it over the coals. The metal began to glow.

"You were my finest creation, Ilys. The sharpest blade I ever honed." His voice lowered. "But you are not blameless in this ruin."

The iron hissed in the flame.

He turned and approached her again.

"I offer you mercy," he said. "Pain, yes, but mercy too. A chance to return. A chance to serve again. I can make you holy."

No reaction.

Her gaze remained lowered, eyes half-lidded, her hair hanging like a shadow across her cheek. She looked like stone.

He pressed the brand to her shoulder.

The sound it made was an obscene, a wet hiss, the sear of scorched flesh. The pain surged like fire into her chest, her spine.

She did not scream.

He watched her face closely. Sweat clung to the roots of her dark hair. Blood at the corner of her lip where it had cracked open. But no sound. No plea. No prayer.

Another brand, this time to the forearm.

Still, no response.

A guard shifted uncomfortably behind him.

The King stepped back. His hands were trembling. He dropped the brand into the brazier with a clatter and turned toward her again, teeth bared in grimace.

"You believe your silence is power. That it shields her. That it protects you."

She stared at the wall past him. A thread of blood rolled down her wrist and pooled at her knee.

He struck her. The sound split the cell, shrill as breaking glass. Her head turned with the force, dark hair spilling forward to hide her face.

She blinked once, eyes wet but unyielding.

He crouched again, voice now a growl wrapped in scripture. "And the soul shall break as the body burns, and the silence shall scream louder than the mouth ever dared."

Still she said nothing.

He reached for her throat, gripping gently with threats, not force.

"I can break every piece of you," he whispered. "And I will. You will beg before the end."

Ilys turned her face, eyes meeting his for the first time that day. Not with hatred, not with fear, just quiet, bone-deep refusal.

He dropped his hand just as though it sullied him to touch her and stood quickly, spine stiff with restraint.

"Leave her," he said to the guards, already turning. "Let her stew in her silence."

The door closed. The lock turned.

She remained kneeling in the dark, the air compact with ash and the scent of burned flesh. Her hair stuck to her cheeks, and her limbs trembled now, weak from blood loss and pain. But she stayed upright.

Silent.

Still.

Unbroken.

The Great Hall reeked of sanctity and smoke. Incense burned in black iron bowls at every corner, thickening the air with myrrh and bloodroot. The Eye of the Veil peered, painted on the stone floor in lamb's blood, still tacky underfoot. Banners hung like funeral drapes. The nobles gathered in muted silks, their jewels dulled by ash. The priests were already chanting.

And at the center stood the altar, no longer symbolic.

It had been re-fashioned. Shackles at the base. Grooves in the stone to catch the runoff.

The doors opened.

Ilys was dragged in, half-conscious, her body limp, her feet trailing streaks of blood behind her. Her shift struggled, a little more than rags now, soaked through in places, torn in others. Flesh showed beneath: burned, cut, swollen. Her shoulder displayed a ruin of blistered skin, the brand raised like a second mouth.

Two guards hoisted her onto the altar, strapping her arms to the iron hooks. Her head lolled. Hair clung to her face in clumps, dark with sweat and gore.

The King entered behind her, robed in black and silver, his hands bare. His crown had changed, now a circlet of twisted nails, rusted and sharp. In one hand, he held *The Book of the Veil*. In the other, a broad serrated blade, forged for this ritual alone and stained from use.

He stood above her.

"Before us lies the hollow shell of a once-holy thing," he declared, his voice smooth and theatrical, echoing beneath the high vaults. "A Veilwalker who drank from poisoned wells. Who opened her body to shadow. Who held hands with the Unbound. I alone can fix her."

He stepped closer and touched her face with two fingers, lifting her chin. Blood had dried beneath her nose. One eye labored to open, swollen half-shut.

"This is not cruelty," he promised. "This is love made sharp."

He began to read.

"And the flesh shall be carved from the wayward,
Until only the sanctified remains.
Let not her blood defile the ground,
But consecrate it in suffering."

He raised the knife.

The first cut went deep, across the belly, horizontal and unflinching. Not enough to kill. Just enough to make her scream.

She did.

Not a loud scream, but a choked, raw sob that echoed like a prayer swallowed wrong. Her back arched against the restraints. Blood poured from the wound, spilling down her sides, staining the altar dark.

The priests began to chant louder.

The King kept reading.

"They who forget the Veil shall wear its teeth.
Let the blade remind her spine of scripture."

He turned the blade sideways and drove it into her thigh.

Bone grated. Her body spasmed.

Another cry tore loose, less human now, more like a wounded animal. Her hands clenched against the shackles, nails tearing as she pulled. He sliced again, across the ribs this time, opening skin with practiced ease. Blood soaked the altar. It dripped onto the symbol drawn below her, turning the Eye red.

The King's voice did not waver.

"This is the baptism of pain.
This is the gospel of the blade.
This is how we purge the beloved."

He dropped the knife.

Another priest brought forward a set of hooked irons, still glowing faintly from the brazier.

He didn't hesitate.

He drove one into her shoulder, just beneath the collarbone, dragging it down as if rending parchment. Flesh curled away. Muscle twitched. Blood sprayed, hot and bright.

Ilys screamed again, but only once. Then she went silent. Her eyes open, staring.

She remained. Breathing. Watching. And somehow... still defying.

The King leaned close to her ear, voice low. "I can carve until your bones are clean," he whispered into her skin as he took the final tool, a holy brand shaped like the Veil's tear. And he pressed it over a fresh wound, where skin and flesh were already open.

She bucked. Her throat arched to howl, but no sound came. Her mouth opened, blood on her teeth. Then she stilled.

Not unconscious. Just beyond. A breath passed. Then another.

The King turned to the assembly, arms wide, robe soaked at the hem with blood.

"She has been cleansed. Witness her repentance!"

No one moved.

Even the priests faltered in their chant. They had not seen repentance. They had seen something else entirely.

And though her body hung broken on the altar, and blood still dripped steadily from her wounds, Ilys did not weep. Her lips had parted. A single wordless shape had formed there, curled like defiance on her tongue. And it was not Vasha. Not forgiveness. Not surrender.

"*Liar.*"

She mouthed it over and over, the word slipping through her teeth. She would say it despite every flesh wound. She would say it til her heart stopped. She would give the word life until her very last breath. It was important, she knew. Even now, the false worship of this man exhausted her more than any mutilation. Any laceration.

The King raised his hands one final time. "Let her be carried to the Sanctum. Let her wounds fester in darkness, and let the Veil decide what remains."

Two guards stepped forward.

They unshackled her wrists, lowly, almost reverently. One reached for her arm as she slumped sideways, catching her beneath the shoulders. The other tucked a coarse shroud over her bare chest. Her blood soaked it instantly. She made no sound.

They didn't rush. She looked barely alive.

One of the guards whispered, "Careful. If we tear her open again, she'll bleed out."

And they didn't notice when she slipped her hand into the robe of the priest who had held the brazier.

Didn't feel the small, bone-handled knife vanish into her fingers.

Didn't see the flicker of focus behind her half-lidded eyes.

They lifted her carefully. Carried her like a sacred deity, or a body absent. Blood dripped from her fingertips, trailing behind like a second signature.

Then, she moved.

It was not strength. It was not speed. It was pure will.

She twisted midair, elbow slamming into the temple of the younger guard. He staggered, crying out. She hit the ground hard, her body folding around the pain, but she rolled, already rising.

The crowd gasped.

The King had just turned away when he heard the scuffle. He pivoted in time to see her, broken and bare-footed, dragging herself upright, blood slicking her chest and thighs, hair stuck to her face like black sinew.

And the knife. Small. Filthy. Glinting in her grip.

She looked at him and ran.

It wasn't fast. Her body was torn. She limped, lurched, almost crawling at first; but she moved, driven by something not even the Veil could name. A scream rose from the priests. Guards shouted.

The King backed away, stunned. "Stop her, stop her!"

But she was too close. No one reached her in time.

She tackled him at the base of the dais, the knife already coming down.

The first stab landed in his shoulder. He shrieked.

The second hit his collarbone, splitting skin and cartilage.

The third, buried in the soft place beneath his rib, and stayed there.

He scrabbled at her, howling. "You ungrateful—" he spat, trying to shove her off, blood bubbling from his mouth.

But she kept going.

Her face was blank. Her hand was soaked to the wrist.

She carved.

Again.

And again.

And again.

She wasn't aiming for the heart. Not really.

She was erasing him, shaving away his shape, his mark, the place he had taken in the world. She opened his chest like a seam, drove the blade through the Eye brand on his sternum, tore symbols from his skin the way he'd tried to carve them into her.

"You will leave nothing behind," she whispered.

She kept stabbing. Her hands slick. Her arms trembling. The knife caught on ribs, slipped, and found new purchase.

She drove the dagger into his chest.

For Grim. For Baron. For Hanna.

For every life stolen in the name of his greed. His desires.

He gargled now. Convulsing. Dying.

She didn't stop until his body fell still.

Didn't stop until her hand could no longer close around the hilt.

Didn't stop until the mark he had made of her was answered.

And then, only then, she collapsed atop his corpse, breath coming in short, rasping gasps. Her body shook. Blood soaked her, pooled beneath her, coated her mouth where she had bitten through her own lip.

But her eyes stayed open.

The priests were still frozen. The guards uncertain. No one moved.

Ilys, the broken Veilwalker, had made her offering.

Not to the Veil.

Not to the King.

To herself.

And in that moment, she became holy in a way he had never been.

She smiled. A quiet satisfaction settled in her chest as she crouched, his form crumpled on the floor beneath her, flimsy and undone. She closed her eyes, inhaling deeply, pressing a prayer to the Fates as her lips formed the final word.

"Vasha."

Then came the sound of air splitting.

A sharp, distant whoosh, followed by the sickening bite of metal into flesh. Pain bloomed across her body before she could comprehend it, piercing, splitting, everywhere at once.

Her breath caught as she staggered, confusion flashing through her mind even as she already understood.

She looked down.

Arrows.

A dozen, maybe more, protruding from her chest, her side, her stomach. The world blurred, tilting strangely at the edges, her limbs suddenly heavy, distant.

"Oh," she murmured faintly.

Her dagger slipped from her fingers, clattering against the stone floor, its weight no longer hers to carry.

Chapter 46

Time unraveled.

Her body slumped beside his, riddled with arrows, broken open.

But pain?

Pain was gone.

There was only light.

Cool and dim, like moonlight through frost-glazed glass. Silence held her in gentle arms, vast and clean. Not emptiness. Not absence.

But peace.

She hovered just above herself. Above the blood. Above the ruined hall and its stunned congregation. She could see her limbs splayed, red pooling beneath her, her eyes closed now, soft, not vacant. A final exhale still clung to her lips.

She did not feel it leave.

It felt instead like being carried. Like the first time she was small and half-asleep, and Grim had lifted her from the hearth and taken her to bed. That quiet shift. That wordless trust.

She drifted.

And the world around her blurred into mist and memory.

A maternal sound rustled. Faint. Familiar.

Wind through tall grass.

When the haze cleared, she stood, barefoot, at the edge of a field.

Golden meadows stretched out in all directions, bending under a breeze that did not touch her skin. Wildflowers bloomed in soft colors, violet and white and warm blood-red. The sky arched wide above, pale and radiant, without sun or stars. And ahead of her rose the veil itself, shimmering and vast, a living curtain of light and shadow stitched with flecks of starlight.

She lifted her arms without thinking. The wind moved with her. Beneath her, the field rolled like waves. The air curled around her ribs the way it once had when she was small and free and brave.

The same girl.

She looked toward the veil.

And there, a figure waited.

The mantle draped loose around his shoulders, the cloth at his wrists lifting in the soft wind. His hands were bare now, no blade, no weight, no duty. Only the faint shimmer of a linen band still circled one finger.

He looked up as she approached and her breath caught. The shape of his smile undid her.

"I waited for you," he called, voice like the sweetest shade.

She ran to him.

Not stumbling. Not staggering. The grass parted for her, and the sky bloomed open.

He opened his arms and she crashed into them, into him, with the force of everything she had carried. She buried her face in his chest. His arms came around her at once, light and certain, trembling with the relief of a belonging long-lost made real again.

He smelled the same. Felt the same.

Callused hands, warm and sure, curled into her spine.

"Ilys," he breathed into her hair. "Wife."

She pulled back just far enough to see him. Her hands rose to cradle his face, prayerful and reverent, tracing the shape of him like memory made flesh. Her thumbs brushed beneath his eyes. She touched his mouth with two fingers, re-learning.

She leaned in and pressed her lips to his forehead, his cheek, the tip of his nose, his mouth. The kisses were not shy, not desperate. They were homecoming.

She rested her brow against his, their foreheads bowed together, as though in prayer.

"Ilys." He whispered against her mouth. "Ilys."

Her name in his mouth was a benediction.

Behind them, the veil shimmered, a live and luminous boundary waiting to be crossed. It pulsed like breath. Like welcome. Like recognition.

She took his hand.

In the end, she found being unbound not to be damnation, but akin to deliverance: duty dying and belonging at last to herself.

And so, entwined, they slipped into the silver hush beyond the Veil.

Part IV

Where the fire dims, you will rest.
Where the water stills, you will wait.
Where the stars gather, you will be known.
The night will name you without speaking.
It will call you by what you have done,
what you have lost,
and above all,
what you still dare to hope for.
And you will stand
finally
beneath the holy light
and feel yourself belong
to something vaster, lovelier than pain.

Epilogue

The Sanctum breathed a different silence now.

No chanting. No guards. No fire. Just dust and ivy climbing through the cracks in the stone.

Hanna sat cross-legged on the floor of the old room, her room once, but Ilys's first. The walls were bare now, the veil hooks long rusted. A shaft of late afternoon light filtered through the broken shutters, falling in golden strips across her lap.

Morrigan lay beside her, chin resting on his paws. His coat had gone gray at the muzzle, the years softening him into gentleness. He had followed her here without being called, padding silently through the corridor as if guided by instinct alone.

When the wind shifted, he lifted his head, ears pricking. He gave a soft, restless whine, then turned toward the door, scraping a paw against the stone—the same sound he used to make when Ilys went out of sight and he wanted her back.

The sketchbook lay open in Hanna's hands.

She turned the pages one by one, the thin paper whispering against her fingertips. Faces looked back at her, not perfectly drawn, but alive with motion. Beck and Baron. Grim with his mouth set in warning and love. Rowenna, half-smiling. A rabbit. A sword.

And Ilys, a self-portrait, over and over.

Sometimes veiled.

Sometimes not.

Sometimes flying.

Hanna touched one drawing, the smallest one, barely a thumbnail in the margin. Just a girl on a stone slab with sticks strapped to her back. Her arms raised. Her mouth opened, laughing.

She hadn't remembered this one.

Outside, the wind shifted through the trees. The light flickered. Hanna closed the book and held it to her chest.

She whispered the word that had been whispered to her so many times, in the dark, in the light, in the quiet space between nightmares and waking, "Vasha."

Not a blade's parting prayer. Not a king's command.

She had never learned it that way.

She hadn't needed to.

Vasha was what Ilys said every night before she turned down the lamp, before she kissed her forehead. It was the word Ilys used when she cupped Hanna's face with both hands and called her brave. It was what she whispered in awe, once, when Hanna had sung aloud in the garden, clumsy and off-key. It was what she said, smiling through tears, when Hanna gave her a flower she'd pressed between pages.

It was never an ending.

It was love.

It was thanks.

It was a promise to come back.

And now, sitting here where it all began, Hanna said it again, not because she had to. Not because anyone asked her to. But because it was hers, now.

"Vasha," she said.

And it meant: I remember her. I carry her. I choose her still.

And somewhere far from the Sanctum, far past the veil, the wind lifted like laughter.

ACKNOWLEDGEMENTS

Thank you to my friends and family who supported me throughout this long, laborious journey. To my mother and father, thank you for believing in my dreams, lofty and flimsy as they may be. To my siblings, I adore you. Thank you for always caring for your oft-irrational older sister. To my loving in-laws, thank you for welcoming me as your own and supporting this embarrassing and vulnerable endeavor. It has meant the world to me.

Jazzy, how lucky am I to have a creative caretaker and dear friend in you? *Veilmarch* is nothing without the care you have given it. To Cass, my editor extraordinaire, thank you for your encouraging phone calls, your fine-tooth comb, and above all, your steadfast support.

Finally, thank you to my darling husband and our three pets, who might as well have been born of the both of us. Luke, you were created with me in mind. No one is more supportive, more doting, or believes in me more. I love you.

www.ingramcontent.com/pod-product-compliance
Lightning Source LLC
Chambersburg PA
CBHW011306310726
49023CB00071B/1179/J

* 9 7 9 8 9 9 9 9 7 1 4 0 1 *